STEPHEN KING
NIGHT SHIFT

Stephen King is the author of more than fifty books, all of them worldwide bestsellers. Among his most recent are *Full Dark, No Stars; Under the Dome; Just After Sunset; Duma Key; Lisey's Story; Cell;* and the last three novels in the Dark Tower saga: *Wolves of the Calla, Song of Susannah,* and *The Dark Tower.* His acclaimed nonfiction book *On Writing* is also a bestseller. In 2003, he was awarded the National Book Foundation Medal for Distinguished Contribution to American Letters, and in 2007 he received the Grand Master Award from the Mystery Writers of America. He lives in Maine with his wife, novelist Tabitha King.

www.stephenking.com

NIGHT SHIFT

STEPHEN KING

NIGHT SHIFT

Anchor Books
A Division of Random House, Inc.
New York

FIRST ANCHOR BOOKS MASS-MARKET EDITION, JULY 2011

Copyright © 1976, 1977, 1978 by Stephen King

All rights reserved. Published in the United States by Anchor Books, a division of Random House, Inc., New York, and in Canada by Random House of Canada Limited, Toronto. Originally published in hardcover in the United States by Doubleday, a division of Random House, Inc., New York, in 1978.

Anchor Books and colophon are registered trademarks of Random House, Inc.

This is a work of fiction. Names, characters, places, and incidents either are the product of the author's imagination or are used fictitiously. Any resemblance to actual persons, living or dead, events, or locales is entirely coincidental.

Owing to limitations of space, permissions acknowledgments may be found on page 506.

The Library of Congress has cataloged the Doubleday edition as follows:
King, Stephen, 1947–
Night Shift.
1. Horror tales, American. I. Title.
PZ4.K5227Ni [PS3561.I483]
813'.5'4 77-75146

Anchor ISBN: 978-0-307-74364-0

Book design by R. Bull

www.anchorbooks.com

Printed in the United States of America
21

CONTENTS

INTRODUCTION

I am often given the big smiling handshake at parties (which I avoid attending whenever possible) by someone who then, with an air of gleeful conspiracy, will say, "You know, I've always wanted to write."

I used to try to be polite.

These days I reply with the same jubilant excitement: "You know, I've always wanted to be a brain surgeon."

They look puzzled. It doesn't matter. There are a lot of puzzled people wandering around lately.

If you want to write, you write.

The only way to learn to write is by writing. And that would not be a useful approach to brain surgery.

Stephen King always wanted to write and he writes.

So he wrote *Carrie* and *'Salem's Lot* and *The Shining,* and the good short stories you can read in this book, and a stupendous number of other stories and books and fragments and poems and essays and other unclassifiable things, most of them too wretched to ever publish.

Because that is the way it is done.

Because there is no other way to do it. Not one other way.

Compulsive diligence is almost enough. But not quite. You have to have a taste for words. Gluttony. You have to want to roll in them. You have to read millions of them written by other people.

You read everything with grinding envy or a weary contempt.

You save the most contempt for the people who conceal ineptitude with long words, Germanic sentence structure, obtrusive symbols, and no sense of story, pace, or character.

Then you have to start knowing yourself so well that you begin to know other people. A piece of us is in every person we can ever meet.

Okay, then. Stupendous diligence, plus word-love, plus empathy, and out of that can come, painfully, some objectivity.

Never total objectivity.

At this frangible moment in time I am typing these words on my blue machine, seven lines down from the top of my page two of this introduction, knowing clearly the flavor and meaning I am hunting for, but not at all certain I am getting it.

Having been around twice as long as Stephen King, I have a little more objectivity about my work than he has about his.

It comes so painfully and so slowly.

You send books out into the world and it is very hard to shuck them out of the spirit. They are tangled children, trying to make their way in spite of the handicaps you have imposed on them. I would give a pretty to get them all back home and take one last good swing at every one of them. Page by page. Digging and cleaning, brushing and furbishing. Tidying up.

Stephen King is a far, far better writer at thirty than I was at thirty, or at forty.

I am entitled to hate him a little bit for this.

And I think I know of a dozen demons hiding in the bushes where his path leads, and even if I had a way to warn him, it would do no good. He whips them or they whip him.

It is exactly that simple.

Are we all together so far?

Diligence, word-lust, empathy equal growing objectivity and then what?

Story. Story. Dammit, story!

Story is something happening to someone you have been led to care about. It can happen in any dimension—physical, mental, spiritual—and in combinations of those dimensions.

Without author intrusion.

Author intrusion is: "My God, Mama, look how *nice* I'm writing!"

Another kind of intrusion is a grotesquerie. Here is one of my favorites, culled from a Big Best Seller of yesteryear: "His eyes slid down the front of her dress."

Author intrusion is a phrase so inept the reader suddenly realizes he is reading, and he backs out of the story. He is shocked back out of the story.

Another author intrusion is the mini-lecture embedded in the story. This is one of my most grievous failings.

An image can be neatly done, be unexpected, and not break the spell. In a story in this book called "Trucks," Stephen King is writing about a tense scene of waiting in a truck stop, describing the people: "He was a salesman and he kept his display bag close to him, like a pet dog that had gone to sleep."

I find that neat.

In another story he demonstrates his good ear, the ring of exactness and truth he can give dialogue. A man and his wife are on a long trip. They are traveling a back road. She says: "Yes, Burt. I know we're in Nebraska, Burt. But where the hell *are* we?" He says: "You've got the road atlas. Look it up. Or can't you read?"

Nice. It looks so simple. Just like brain surgery. The knife has an edge. You hold it so. And cut.

Now at risk of being an iconoclast I will say that I do not give a diddly-whoop what Stephen King chooses as an area in which to write. The fact that he presently enjoys writing in the field of spooks and spells and slitherings in the cellar is to me the least important and useful fact about the man anyone can relate.

There are a lot of slitherings in here, and there is a maddened pressing machine that haunts me, as it will you, and there are enough persuasively evil children to fill Disney World on any Sunday in February, but the main thing is story.

One is led to care.

Note this. Two of the most difficult areas to write in are humor and the occult. In clumsy hands the humor turns to dirge and the occult turns funny.

But once you know how, you can write in any area.

Stephen King is not going to restrict himself to his present field of intense interest.

One of the most resonant and affecting stories in this book is "The Last Rung on the Ladder." A gem. Nary a rustle nor breath of other worlds in it.

Final word.

He does not write to please you. He writes to please himself. I write to please myself. When that happens, you will like the work too. These stories pleased Stephen King and they pleased me.

By strange coincidence on the day I write this, Stephen King's novel *The Shining* and my novel *Condominium* are both on the Best Seller List. We are not in competition for your attention with each other. We are in competition, I suppose, with the inept and pretentious and sensational books published by household names who have never really bothered to learn their craft.

Insofar as story is concerned, and pleasure is concerned, there are not enough Stephen Kings to go around.

If you have read this whole thing, I hope you have plenty of time. You could have been reading the stories.

JOHN D. MacDONALD

FOREWORD

Let's talk, you and I. Let's talk about fear.

The house is empty as I write this; a cold February rain is falling outside. It's night. Sometimes when the wind blows the way it's blowing now, we lose the power. But for now it's on, and so let's talk very honestly about fear. Let's talk very rationally about moving to the rim of madness . . . and perhaps over the edge.

My name is Stephen King. I am a grown man with a wife and three children. I love them, and I believe that the feeling is reciprocated. My job is writing, and it's a job I like very much. The stories—*Carrie, 'Salem's Lot,* and *The Shining*—have been successful enough to allow me to write full-time, which is an agreeable thing to be able to do. At this point in my life I seem to be reasonably healthy. In the last year I have been able to reduce my cigarette habit from the unfiltered brand I had smoked since I was eighteen to a low nicotine and tar brand, and I still hope to be able to quit completely. My family and I live in a pleasant house beside a relatively unpolluted lake in Maine; last fall I awoke one morning and saw a deer standing on the back lawn by the picnic table. We have a good life.

Still . . . let's talk about fear. We won't raise our voices and we won't scream; we'll talk rationally, you and I. We'll talk about the way the good fabric of things sometimes has a way of unraveling with shocking suddenness.

At night, when I go to bed I still am at pains to be sure that my legs are under the blankets after the lights go out. I'm not a child anymore but . . . I don't like to sleep with one leg sticking out. Because if a cool hand ever reached out from under the bed and grasped my ankle, I might scream. Yes, I might scream to wake the dead. That sort of thing doesn't happen, of course, and we all know that. In the stories that follow you will encounter all manner of night creatures; vampires, demon lovers, a thing that lives in the closet, all sorts of other terrors. None of them are real. The thing under my bed waiting to grab my ankle isn't real. I know that, and I also know that if I'm careful to keep my foot under the covers, it will never be able to grab my ankle.

———

Sometimes I speak before groups of people who are interested in writing or in literature, and before the question-and-answer period is over, someone always rises and asks this question: Why do you choose to write about such gruesome subjects?

I usually answer this with another question: *Why do you assume that I have a choice?*

Writing is a catch-as-catch-can sort of occupation. All of us seem to come equipped with filters on the floors of our minds, and all the filters have differing sizes and meshes. What catches in my filter may run right through yours. What catches in yours may pass through mine, no sweat. All of us seem to have a built-in obligation to sift through the sludge that gets caught in our respective mind-filters, and what we find there usually develops into some sort of sideline. The accountant may also be a photographer. The astronomer may collect coins. The schoolteacher may do gravestone rubbings in charcoal. The sludge caught in the mind's filter, the stuff that refuses to go through, frequently becomes each person's private obsession. In civilized society we have an unspoken agreement to call our obsessions "hobbies."

Sometimes the hobby can become a full-time job. The accountant may discover that he can make enough money to support his family taking pictures; the schoolteacher may become enough of an expert on grave rubbings to go on the lecture circuit. And there are some professions which begin as hobbies and remain hobbies even after the practitioner is able to earn his living by pursuing his hobby; but because "hobby" is such a bumpy, common-sounding little word, we also have an unspoken agreement that we will call our professional hobbies "the arts."

Painting. Sculpture. Composing. Singing. Acting.

The playing of a musical instrument. Writing. Enough books have been written on these seven subjects alone to sink a fleet of luxury liners. And the only thing we seem to be able to agree upon about them is this: that those who practice these arts honestly would continue to practice them even if they were not paid for their efforts; even if their efforts were criticized or even reviled; even on pain of imprisonment or death. To me, that seems to be a pretty fair definition of obsessional behavior. It applies to the plain hobbies as well as the fancy ones we call "the arts"; gun collectors sport bumper stickers reading YOU WILL TAKE MY GUN ONLY WHEN YOU PRY MY COLD DEAD FINGERS FROM IT, and in the suburbs of Boston, housewives who discovered political activism during the busing furor often sported similar stickers reading YOU'LL TAKE ME TO PRISON BEFORE YOU TAKE MY CHILDREN OUT OF THE NEIGHBORHOOD on the back bumpers of their station wagons. Similarly, if coin collecting were outlawed tomorrow, the astronomer very likely wouldn't turn in his steel pennies and buffalo nickels; he'd wrap them carefully in plastic, sink them to the bottom of his toilet tank, and gloat over them after midnight.

We seem to be wandering away from the subject of fear, but we really haven't wandered very far. The sludge that catches in the mesh of my drain is often the stuff of fear. My obsession is with the macabre. I didn't write any of the stories which follow for money, although some of them were sold to magazines before they appeared here and I never once returned a check uncashed. I may be obsessional but I'm not *crazy*. Yet I repeat: I didn't write them for money; I wrote them because it occurred to me to write them. I have a marketable obsession. There are madmen and madwomen in padded cells the world over who are not so lucky.

I am not a great artist, but I have always felt impelled to write. So each day I sift the sludge anew, going through the cast-off bits and pieces of observation, of memory, of speculation, trying to make something out of the stuff that didn't go through the filter and down the drain into the subconscious.

Louis L'Amour, the Western writer, and I might both stand at the edge of a small pond in Colorado, and we both might have an idea at exactly the same time. We might both feel the urge to sit down and try to work it out in words. His story might be about water rights in a dry season, my story would more likely be about some dreadful, hulking thing rising out of the still waters to carry off sheep . . . and horses . . . and finally people. Louis L'Amour's "obsession" centers on the history of the American West; I tend more toward things that slither by starlight. He writes Westerns; I write fearsomes. We're both a little bit nuts.

The arts are obsessional, and obsession is dangerous. It's like a knife in the mind. In some cases— Dylan Thomas comes to mind, and Ross Lockridge and Hart Crane and Sylvia Plath—the knife can turn savagely upon the person wielding it. Art is a localized illness, usually benign—creative people tend to live a long time—sometimes terribly malignant. You use the knife carefully, because you know it doesn't care who it cuts. And if you are wise you sift the sludge carefully . . . because some of that stuff may not be dead.

———

After the *why do you write that stuff* question has been disposed of, the companion question comes up: *Why do people read that stuff? What makes it sell?* This question carries a hidden assumption with it, and the assumption is that the story about fear, the story about horror, is an unhealthy taste. People who write me often begin by saying, "I suppose you will think I'm strange, but I really liked *'Salem's Lot*," or "Probably I'm morbid, but I enjoyed every page of *The Shining* . . ."

I think the key to this may lie in a line of movie criticism from *Newsweek* magazine. The review was of a horror film, not a very good one, and it went something like this: ". . . a wonderful movie for people who like to slow down and look at car accidents." It's a good snappy line, but when you stop and think about it, it applies to all horror films and stories. *The Night of the Living Dead,* with its gruesome scenes of human cannibalism and matricide, was certainly a film for people who like to slow down and look at car accidents; and how about that little girl puking pea soup all over the priest in *The Exorcist*? Bram Stoker's *Dracula,* often a basis of comparison for the modern horror story (as it should be; it is the first with unabashedly psycho-Freudian overtones), features a maniac named Renfield who gobbles flies, spiders, and finally a bird. He regurgitates the bird, having eaten it feathers and all. The novel also features the impalement—the ritual penetration, one could say—of a young and lovely female vampire and the murder of a baby and the baby's mother.

The great literature of the supernatural often contains the same "let's slow down and look at the accident" syndrome: Beowulf slaughtering Grendel's mother; the narrator of "The Tell-Tale Heart" dismembering his cataract-stricken benefactor and putting the pieces under the floorboards; the Hobbit Sam's grim battle with Shelob the spider in the final book of Tolkien's Rings trilogy.

There will be some who will object strenuously to this line of thought, saying that Henry James is not showing us a car accident in *The Turn of the Screw;* they will claim that Nathaniel Hawthorne's stories of the macabre, such as "Young Goodman Brown" and "The Minister's Black Veil," are also rather more tasteful than *Dracula*. It's a nonsensical idea. They are still showing us the car accident; the bodies have been removed but we can still see the twisted wreckage and observe the blood on the upholstery. In some ways the delicacy, the lack of melodrama, the low and studied tone of rationality that pervades a story like "The Minister's Black Veil" is even more terrible than Lovecraft's batrachian monstrosities or the auto-da-fé of Poe's "The Pit and the Pendulum."

The fact is—and most of us know this in our hearts—that very few of us can forgo an uneasy peek at the wreckage bracketed by police cars and road flares on the turnpike at night. Senior citizens pick up the paper in the morning and immediately turn to the obituary column so they can see who they outlived. All of us are uneasily transfixed for a moment when we hear that a Dan Blocker has died, a Freddie Prinze, a Janis Joplin. We feel terror mixed with an odd sort of glee when we hear Paul Harvey on the radio telling us that a woman walked into a propeller blade during a rain squall at a small country airport or that a man in a giant industrial blender was vaporized immediately when a co-worker stumbled against the controls. No need to belabor the obvious; life is full of horrors small and large, but because the small ones are the ones we can comprehend, they are the ones that smack home with all the force of mortality.

Our interest in these pocket horrors is undeniable, but so is our own revulsion. The two of them mix uneasily, and the by-product of the mix seems to be guilt . . . a guilt which seems not much different from the guilt that used to accompany sexual awakening.

It is not my business to tell you not to feel guilty, any more than it is my business to justify my novels or the short stories which follow. But an interesting parallel between sex and fear can be observed. As we become capable of having sexual relationships, our interest in those relationships awakens; the interest, unless perverted somehow, tends naturally toward copulation and the continuance of the species. As we become aware of our own unavoidable termination, we become aware of the fear-emotion. And I think that, as copulation tends toward self-preservation, all fear tends toward a comprehension of the final ending.

There is an old fable about seven blind men who grabbed seven different parts of an elephant. One of them thought he had a snake, one of them thought he had a giant palm leaf, one of them thought he was touching a stone pillar. When they got together, they decided they had an elephant.

Fear is the emotion that makes us blind. How many things are we afraid of? We're afraid to turn off the lights when our hands are wet. We're afraid to stick a knife into the toaster to get the stuck English muffin without unplugging it first. We're afraid of what the doctor may tell us when the physical exam is over; when the airplane suddenly takes a great unearthly lurch in midair. We're afraid that the oil may run out, that the good air will run out, the good water, the good life. When the daughter promised to be in by eleven and it's now quarter past twelve and sleet is spatting against the window like dry sand, we sit and pretend to watch Johnny Carson and look occasionally at the mute telephone and we feel the emotion that makes us blind, the emotion that makes a stealthy ruin of the thinking process.

The infant is a fearless creature only until the first time the mother isn't there to pop the nipple into his mouth when he cries. The toddler quickly discovers the blunt and painful truths of the slamming door, the hot burner, the fever that goes with the croup or the measles. Children learn fear quickly; they pick it up off the mother or father's face when the parent comes into the bathroom and sees them with the bottle of pills or the safety razor.

Fear makes us blind, and we touch each fear with all the avid curiosity of self-interest, trying to make a whole out of a hundred parts, like the blind men with their elephant.

We sense the shape. Children grasp it easily, forget it, and relearn it as adults. The shape is there, and most of us come to realize what it is sooner or later: it is the shape of a body under a sheet. All our fears add up to one great fear, all our fears are part of that great fear— an arm, a leg, a finger, an ear. We're afraid of the body under the sheet. It's our body. And the great appeal of horror fiction through the ages is that it serves as a rehearsal for our own deaths.

The field has never been highly regarded; for a long time the only friends that Poe and Lovecraft had were the French, who have somehow come to an arrangement with both sex and death, an arrangement that Poe and Lovecraft's fellow Americans certainly had no patience with. The Americans were busy building railroads, and Poe and Lovecraft died broke. Tolkien's Middle-Earth fantasy went kicking around for twenty years before it became an aboveground success, and Kurt Vonnegut, whose books so often deal with the death-rehearsal idea, has faced a steady wind of criticism, much of it mounting to hysterical pitch.

It may be because the horror writer always brings bad news: you're going to die, he says; he's telling you to never mind Oral Roberts and his "something *good* is going to happen to *you*," because something *bad* is also going to happen to *you,* and it may be cancer and it may be a stroke, and it may be a car accident, but it's going to happen. And he takes your hand and he enfolds it in his own, and he takes you into the room and he puts your hands on the shape under the sheet . . . and tells you to touch it here . . . here . . . and *here* . . .

Of course, the subjects of death and fear are not the horror writer's exclusive province. Plenty of so-called "mainstream" writers have dealt with these themes, and in a variety of different ways—from Fyodor Dostoyevsky's *Crime and Punishment* to Edward Albee's *Who's Afraid of Virginia Woolf?* to Ross MacDonald's Lew Archer stories. Fear has always been big. Death has always been big. They are two of the human constants. But only the writer of horror and the supernatural gives the reader such an opportunity for total identification and catharsis. Those working in the genre with even the faintest understanding of what they are doing know that the entire field of horror and the supernatural is a kind of filter screen between the conscious and the subconscious; horror fiction is like a central subway station in the human psyche between the blue line of what we can safely internalize and the red line of what we need to get rid of in some way or another.

When you read horror, you don't really believe what you read. You don't believe in vampires, werewolves, trucks that suddenly start up and drive themselves. The horrors that we all do believe in are of the sort that Dostoyevsky and Albee and MacDonald write about: hate, alienation, growing lovelessly old, tottering out into a hostile world on the unsteady legs of adolescence. We are, in our real everyday worlds, often like the masks of Comedy and Tragedy, grinning on the outside, grimacing on the inside. There's a central switching point somewhere inside, a transformer, maybe, where the wires leading from those two masks connect. And that is the place where the horror story so often hits home.

The horror-story writer is not so different from the Welsh sin-eater, who was supposed to take upon himself the sins of the dear departed by partaking of the dear departed's food. The tale of monstrosity and terror is a basket loosely packed with phobias; when the writer passes by, you take one of his imaginary horrors out of the basket and put one of your real ones in—at least for a time.

Back in the 1950s there was a tremendous surge of giant bug movies—*Them!*, *The Beginning of the End*, *The Deadly Mantis*, and so on. Almost without fail, as the movie progressed, we found out that these gigantic, ugly mutants were the results of A-bomb tests in New Mexico or on deserted Pacific atolls (and in the more recent *Horror of Party Beach*, which might have been subtitled *Beach Blanket Armageddon;* the culprit was nuclear-reactor waste). Taken together, the big-bug movies form an undeniable pattern, an uneasy gestalt of a whole country's terror of the new age that the Manhattan Project had rung in. Later in the fifties there was a cycle of "teen-age" horror movies, beginning with *I*

Was a Teen-Age Werewolf and culminating with such epics as *Teen-Agers from Outer Space* and *The Blob,* in which a beardless Steve McQueen battled a sort of Jell-O mutant with the help of his teen-aged friends. In an age when every weekly magazine contained at least one article on the rising tide of juvenile delinquency, the teen-ager fright films expressed a whole country's uneasiness with the youth revolution even then brewing; when you saw Michael Landon turn into a werewolf in a high-school letter jacket, a connection happened between the fantasy on the screen and your own floating anxieties about the nerd in the hot rod that your daughter was dating. To the teen-agers themselves (I was one of them and speak from experience), the monsters spawned in the leased American-International studios gave them a chance to see someone even uglier than they felt themselves to be; what were a few pimples compared to the shambling *thing* that used to be a high-school kid in *I Was a Teen-Age Frankenstein*? This same cycle also expressed the teen-agers' own feeling that they were being unfairly put upon and put down by their elders, that their parents just "did not understand." The movies are formulaic (as so much of horror fiction is, written or filmed), and what the formula expresses most clearly is a whole generation's paranoia—a paranoia no doubt caused in part by all the articles their parents were reading. In the films, some terrible, warty horror is menacing Elmville. The kids know, because the flying saucer landed near lovers' lane. In the first reel, the warty horror kills an old man in a pickup truck (the old man was unfailingly played by Elisha Cook, Jr.). In the next three reels, the kids try to convince their elders that the warty horror is indeed slinking around. "Get outta here before I lock you all up for violating the curfew!" Elmville's police chief growls just before the monster slithers down Main Street, laying waste in all directions. In the end it is the quick-thinking kids who put an end to the warty horror, and then go off to the local hangout to suck up chocolate malteds and jitterbug to some forgettable tune as the end credits run.

That's three separate opportunities for catharsis in one cycle of movies—not bad for a bunch of low-budget epics that were usually done in under ten days. It didn't happen because the writers and producers and directors of those films wanted it to happen; it happened because the horror tale lives most naturally at that connection point between the conscious and the subconscious, the place where both image and allegory occurs most naturally and with the most devastating effect. There is a direct line of evolution between *I Was a Teen-Age Werewolf* and Stanley Kubrick's *A Clockwork Orange* and between *Teen-Age Monster* and Brian De Palma's film *Carrie*.

Great horror fiction is almost always allegorical; sometimes the allegory is intended, as in *Animal Farm* and *1984,* and sometimes it just happens—J. R. R. Tolkien swore up and down that the Dark Lord of Mordor was not Hitler in fantasy dress, but the theses and term papers to just that effect go on and on . . . maybe because, as Bob Dylan says, when you got a lot of knives and forks, you gotta cut something.

The works of Edward Albee, of Steinbeck, Camus, Faulkner—they deal with fear and death, sometimes with horror, but usually these mainstream writers deal with it in a more normal, real-life way. Their work is set in the frame of a rational world; they are stories that "could happen." They are on that subway line that runs through the external world. There are other writers— James Joyce, Faulkner again, poets such as T. S. Eliot and Sylvia Plath and Anne Sexton—whose work is set in the land of the symbolic unconsciousness. They are on the subway line running into the internal landscape. But the horror writer is almost always at the terminal joining the two, at least if he is on the mark. When he is at his best we often have that weird sensation of being not quite asleep or awake, when time stretches and skews, when we can hear voices but cannot make out the words or the intent, when the dream seems real and the reality dreamlike.

That is a strange and wonderful terminal. Hill House is there, in that place where the trains run both ways, with its doors that swing sensibly shut; the woman in the room with the yellow wallpaper is there, crawling along the floor with her head pressed against that faint grease mark; the barrow-wights that menaced Frodo and Sam are there; and Pickman's model; the wendigo; Norman Bates and his terrible mother. No waking or dreaming in this terminal, but only the voice of the writer, low and rational, talking about the way the good fabric of things sometimes has a way of unraveling with shocking suddenness. He's telling you that you want to see the car accident, and yes, he's right—you do. There's a dead voice on the phone . . . something behind the walls of the old house that sounds bigger than a rat . . . movement at the foot of the cellar stairs. He wants you to see all of those things, and more; he wants you to put your hands on the shape under the sheet. And you want to put your hands there. Yes.

———

These are some of the things I feel that the horror story does, but I am firmly convinced that it must do one more thing, this above all others: It must tell a tale that holds the reader or the listener spellbound for a little while, lost in a world that never was, never could be. It must be like the wedding guest that stoppeth one of three. All my life as a writer I have been committed to the idea that in fiction the story value holds dominance over every other facet of the writer's craft; characterization, theme, mood, none of those things is anything if the story is dull. And if the story does hold you, all else can be forgiven. My favorite line to that effect came from the pen of Edgar Rice Burroughs, no one's candidate for Great World Writer, but a man who understood story values completely. On page one of *The Land That Time Forgot,* the narrator finds a manuscript in a bottle; the rest of the novel is the presentation of that manuscript. The narrator says, "Read one page, and I will be forgotten." It's a pledge that Burroughs makes good on—many writers with talents greater than his have not.

————

In fine, gentle reader, here is a truth that makes the strongest writer gnash his teeth: with the exception of three small groups of people, no one reads a writer's preface. The exceptions are: one, the writer's close family (usually his wife and his mother); two, the writer's accredited representative (and the editorial people and assorted munchkins), whose chief interest is to find out if anyone has been libeled in the course of the writer's wanderings; and three, those people who have had a hand in helping the writer on his way. These are the people who want to know whether or not the writer's head has gotten so big that he has managed to forget that he didn't do it by himself.

Other readers are apt to feel, with perfect justification, that the author's preface is a gross imposition, a multi-page commercial for himself, even more offensive than the cigarette ads that have proliferated in the center section of the paperback books. Most readers come to see the show, not to watch the stage manager take bows in front of the footlights. Again, with perfect justification.

I'm leaving now. The show is going to start soon. We're going to go into that room and touch the shape under the sheet. But before I leave, I want to take just two or three more minutes of your time to thank some people from each of the three groups above—and from a fourth. Bear with me as I say a few thank-yous:

———

To my wife, Tabitha, my best and most trenchant critic. When she feels the work is good, she says so; when she feels I've put my foot in it, she sets me on my ass as kindly and lovingly as possible. To my kids, Naomi, Joe, and Owen, who have been very understanding about their father's peculiar doings in the downstairs room. And to my mother, who died in 1973, and to whom this book is dedicated. Her encouragement was steady and unwavering, she always seemed able to find forty or fifty cents for the obligatory stamped, self-addressed return envelope, and no one—including myself—was more pleased than she when I "broke through."

In that second group, particular thanks are due my editor, William G. Thompson of Doubleday & Company, who has worked with me patiently, who has suffered my daily phone calls with constant good cheer, and who showed kindness to a young writer with no credentials some years ago, and who has stuck with that writer since then.

In the third group are the people who first bought my work: Mr. Robert A. W. Lowndes, who purchased the first two stories I ever sold; Mr. Douglas Allen and

Mr. Nye Willden of the Dugent Publishing Corporation, who bought so many of the ones that followed for *Cavalier* and *Gent,* back in the scuffling days when the checks sometimes came just in time to avoid what the power companies euphemistically call "an interruption in service"; to Elaine Geiger and Herbert Schnall and Carolyn Stromberg of the New American Library; to Gerard Van der Leun of *Penthouse* and Harris Deinstfrey of *Cosmopolitan.* Thanks to all of you.

There's one final group that I'd like to thank, and that is each and every reader who ever unlimbered his or her wallet to buy something that I wrote. In a great many ways, this is your book because it sure never would have happened without you. So thanks.

Where I am, it's still dark and raining. We've got a fine night for it. There's something I want to show you, something I want you to touch. It's in a room not far from here—in fact, it's almost as close as the next page.

Shall we go?

Bridgton, Maine
February 27, 1977

NIGHT SHIFT

JERUSALEM'S LOT

Oct. 2, 1850.

DEAR BONES,

How good it was to step into the cold, draughty hall here at Chapelwaite, every bone in an ache from that abominable coach, in need of instant relief from my distended bladder—and to see a letter addressed in your own inimitable scrawl propped on the obscene little cherry-wood table beside the door! Be assured that I set to deciphering it as soon as the needs of the body were attended to (in a coldly ornate downstairs bathroom where I could see my breath rising before my eyes).

I'm glad to hear that you are recovered from the *miasma* that has so long set in your lungs, although I assure you that I do sympathize with the moral dilemma the cure has affected you with. An ailing abolitionist healed by the sunny climes of slave-struck Florida! Still and all, Bones, I ask you as a friend who has also walked in the valley of the shadow, *to take all care of yourself* and venture not back to Massachusetts until your body gives you leave. Your fine mind and incisive pen cannot serve us if you are clay, and if the Southern zone is a healing one, is there not poetic justice in that?

Yes, the house is quite as fine as I had been led to believe by my cousin's executors, but rather more sinister. It sits atop a huge and jutting point of land perhaps three miles north of Falmouth and nine miles north of Portland. Behind it are some four acres of grounds, gone back to the wild in the most formidable manner imaginable—junipers, scrub vines, bushes, and various forms of creeper climb wildly over the picturesque stone walls that separate the estate from the town domain. Awful imitations of Greek statuary peer blindly through the wrack from atop various hillocks—they seem, in most cases, about to lunge at the passer-by. My cousin Stephen's tastes seem to have run the gamut from the unacceptable to the downright horrific. There is an odd little summer house which has been nearly buried in scarlet sumac and a grotesque sundial in the midst of what must once have been a garden. It adds the final lunatic touch.

But the view from the parlour more than excuses this; I command a dizzying view of the rocks at the foot of Chapelwaite Head and the Atlantic itself. A huge, bellied bay window looks out on this, and a huge, toad-like secretary stands beside it. It will do nicely for the start of that novel which I have talked of so long [and no doubt tiresomely].

To-day has been gray with occasional splatters of rain. As I look out all seems to be a study in slate—

the rocks, old and worn as Time itself, the sky, and of course the sea, which crashes against the granite fangs below with a sound which is not precisely sound but vibration—I can feel the waves with my feet even as I write. The sensation is not a wholly unpleasant one.

I know you disapprove my solitary habits, dear Bones, but I assure you that I am fine and happy. Calvin is with me, as practical, silent, and as dependable as ever, and by midweek I am sure that between the two of us we shall have straightened our affairs and made arrangement for necessary deliveries from town—and a company of cleaning women to begin blowing the dust from this place!

I will close—there are so many things as yet to be seen, rooms to explore, and doubtless a thousand pieces of execrable furniture to be viewed by these tender eyes. Once again, my thanks for the touch of familiar brought by your letter, and for your continuing regard.

Give my love to your wife, as you both have mine.

CHARLES.

Oct. 6, 1850.

DEAR BONES,

Such a place this is!

It continues to amaze me—as do the reactions of the townfolk in the closest village to my occupancy. That is a queer little place with the picturesque name of Preacher's Corners. It was there that Calvin contracted for the weekly provisions. The other errand, that of securing a sufficient supply of cordwood for the winter, was like-

wise taken care of. But Cal returned with gloomy coun-
tenance, and when I asked him what the trouble was, he
replied grimly enough:

"They think you mad, Mr. Boone!"

I laughed and said that perhaps they had heard of the
brain fever I suffered after my Sarah died—certainly I
spoke madly enough at that time, as you could attest.

But Cal protested that no-one knew anything of me
except through my cousin Stephen, who contracted for
the same services as I have now made provision for.
"What was said, sir, was that anyone who would live in
Chapelwaite must be either a lunatic or run the risk of
becoming one."

This left me utterly perplexed, as you may imagine,
and I asked who had given him this amazing communi-
cation. He told me that he had been referred to a sullen
and rather besotted pulp-logger named Thompson, who
owns four hundred acres of pine, birch, and spruce, and
who logs it with the help of his five sons, for sale to the
mills in Portland and to householders in the immediate
area.

When Cal, all unknowing of his queer prejudice, gave
him the location to which the wood was to be brought,
this Thompson stared at him with his mouth ajaw and
said that he would send his sons with the wood, in the
good light of the day, and by the sea road.

Calvin, apparently misreading my bemusement for
distress, hastened to say that the man reeked of cheap
whiskey and that he had then lapsed into some kind of
nonsense about a deserted village and cousin Stephen's

relations—and worms! Calvin finished his business with one of Thompson's boys, who, I take it, was rather surly and none too sober or freshly-scented himself. I take it there has been some of this reaction in Preacher's Corners itself, at the general store where Cal spoke with the shop-keeper, although this was more of the gossipy, behind-the-hand type.

None of this has bothered me much; we know how rustics dearly love to enrich their lives with the smell of scandal and myth, and I suppose poor Stephen and his side of the family are fair game. As I told Cal, a man who has fallen to his death almost from his own front porch is more than likely to stir talk.

The house itself is a constant amazement. Twenty-three rooms, Bones! The wainscotting which panels the upper floors and the portrait gallery is mildewed but still stout. While I stood in my late cousin's upstairs bedroom I could hear the rats scuttering behind it, and big ones they must be, from the sound they make—almost like people walking there. I should hate to encounter one in the dark; or even in the light, for that matter. Still, I have noted neither holes nor droppings. Odd.

The upper gallery is lined with bad portraits in frames which must be worth a fortune. Some bear a resemblance to Stephen as I remember him. I believe I have correctly identified my Uncle Henry Boone and his wife Judith; the others are unfamiliar. I suppose one of them may be my own notorious grandfather, Robert. But Stephen's side of the family is all but unknown to me, for which I am heartily sorry. The same good humour that shone in Stephen's letters to Sarah and me, the same light of high intellect, shines in these portraits, bad as they are. For what foolish reasons families fall out! A rifled *escritoire,* hard words between brothers now dead three generations, and blameless descendants are needlessly estranged. I cannot help reflecting upon how fortunate it was that you and John Petty succeeded in contacting Stephen when it seemed I might follow my Sarah through the Gates—and upon how unfortunate it was that chance should have robbed us of a face-to-face meeting. How I would have loved to hear him defend the ancestral statuary and furnishings!

But do not let me denigrate the place to an extreme. Stephen's taste was not my own, true, but beneath the veneer of his additions there are pieces [a number of them shrouded by dust-covers in the upper chambers] which are true masterworks. There are beds, tables, and heavy, dark scrollings done in teak and mahogany, and many of the bedrooms and receiving chambers, the upper study and small parlour, hold a somber charm. The floors are rich pine that glow with an inner and secret light. There is dignity here; dignity and the weight of years. I cannot yet say I like it, but I do respect it. I am eager to watch it change as we revolve through the changes of this northern clime.

Lord, I run on! Write soon, Bones. Tell me what progress you make, and what news you hear from Petty and the rest. And please do not make the mistake of trying to persuade any new Southern acquaintances as to your views *too forcibly*—I understand that not all are content to answer merely with their mouths, as is our long-winded *friend,* Mr. Calhoun.

Yr. affectionate friend,
CHARLES.

Oct. 16, 1850.

DEAR RICHARD,

Hello, and how are you? I have thought about you often since I have taken up residence here at Chapelwaite, and had half-expected to hear from you—and now I receive a letter from Bones telling me that I'd forgotten to leave my address at the club! Rest assured that I would have written eventually anyway, as it sometimes seems that my true and loyal friends are all I have left in the world that is sure and completely normal. And, Lord, how spread we've become! You in Boston, writing faithfully for *The Liberator* [to which I have also sent my address, incidentally], Hanson in England on another of his confounded *jaunts,* and poor old Bones in the very *lions' lair,* recovering his lungs.

It goes as well as can be expected here, Dick, and be assured I will render you a full account when I am not quite as pressed by certain events which are extant here—I think your legal mind may be quite intrigued by certain happenings at Chapelwaite and in the area about it.

But in the meantime I have a favour to ask, if you will entertain it. Do you remember the historian you introduced me to at Mr. Clary's fund-raising dinner for the cause? I believe his name was Bigelow. At any rate, he mentioned that he made a hobby of collecting odd bits of historical lore which pertained to the very area in which I am now living. My favour, then, is this: Would you contact him and ask him what facts, bits of folklore, or *general rumour*—if any—he may be conversant with about a small, deserted village called JERUSALEM'S LOT, near a township called Preacher's Corners, on the Royal River? The stream itself is a tributary of the Androscoggin, and flows into that river approximately eleven miles above that river's emptying place near Chapelwaite. It would gratify me intensely, and, more important, may be a matter of some moment.

In looking over this letter I feel I have been a bit short with you, Dick, for which I am heartily sorry. But be assured I will explain myself shortly, and until that time I send my warmest regards to your wife, two fine sons, and, of course, to yourself.

> Yr. affectionate friend,
> CHARLES.

> Oct. 16, 1850.

DEAR BONES,

I have a tale to tell you which seems a little strange [and even disquieting] to both Cal and me—see what you think. If nothing else, it may serve to amuse you while you battle the mosquitoes!

Two days after I mailed my last to you, a group of four young ladies arrived from the Corners under the supervision of an elderly lady of intimidatingly-competent visage named Mrs. Cloris, to set the place in order and to remove some of the dust that had been causing me to sneeze seemingly at every other step. They all seemed a little nervous as they went about their chores; indeed, one flighty miss uttered a small screech when I entered the upstairs parlour as she dusted.

I asked Mrs. Cloris about this [she was dusting the downstairs hall with grim determination that would have quite amazed you, her hair done up in an old faded bandanna], and she turned to me and said with an air of determination: "They don't like the house, and I don't like the house, sir, because it has always been a *bad* house."

My jaw dropped at this unexpected bit, and she went on in a kindlier tone: "I do not mean to say that Stephen Boone was not a fine man, for he was; I cleaned for him every second Thursday all the time he was here, as I cleaned for his father, Mr. Randolph Boone, until he and his wife disappeared in eighteen and sixteen. Mr. Stephen was a good and kindly man, and so you seem, sir (if you will pardon my bluntness; I know no other way to speak), but the house is *bad* and it always *has been,* and no Boone has ever been happy here since your grandfather Robert and his brother Philip fell out over stolen [and here she paused, almost guiltily] items in seventeen and eighty-nine."

Such memories these folks have, Bones!

Mrs. Cloris continued: "The house was built in unhappiness, has been lived in with unhappiness, there has been blood spilt on its floors [as you may or may not know, Bones, my Uncle Randolph was involved in an accident on the cellar stairs which took the life of his daughter Marcella; he then took his own life in a fit of remorse. The incident is related in one of Stephen's letters to me, on the sad occasion of his dead sister's birthday], there has been disappearance and accident.

"I have worked here, Mr. Boone, and I am neither blind nor deaf. I've heard awful sounds in the walls, sir, awful sounds—thumpings and crashings and once a strange wailing that was half-laughter. It fair made my blood curdle. It's a dark place, sir." And there she halted, perhaps afraid she had spoken too much.

As for myself, I hardly knew whether to be offended or amused, curious or merely matter-of-fact. I'm afraid that amusement won the day. "And what do you suspect, Mrs. Cloris? Ghosts rattling chains?"

But she only looked at me oddly. "Ghosts there may be. But it's not ghosts in the walls. It's not ghosts that wail and blubber like the damned and crash and blunder away in the darkness. It's—"

"Come, Mrs. Cloris," I prompted her. "You've come this far. Now can you finish what you've begun?"

The strangest expression of terror, pique, and—I would swear to it—religious awe passed over her face. "Some die not," she whispered. "Some live in the twilight shadows Between to serve—Him!"

And that was the end. For some minutes I continued to tax her, but she grew only more obstinate and would say no more. At last I desisted, fearing she might gather herself up and quit the premises.

This is the end of one episode, but a second occurred

the following evening. Calvin had laid a fire downstairs and I was sitting in the living-room, drowsing over a copy of *The Intelligencer* and listening to the sound of wind-driven rain on the large bay window. I felt comfortable as only one can on such a night, when all is miserable outside and all is warmth and comfort inside; but a moment later Cal appeared at the door, looking excited and a bit nervous.

"Are you awake, sir?" he asked.

"Barely," I said. "What is it?"

"I've found something upstairs I think you should see," he responded, with the same air of suppressed excitement.

I got up and followed him. As we climbed the wide stairs, Calvin said: "I was reading a book in the upstairs study—a rather strange one—when I heard a noise in the wall."

"Rats," I said. "Is that all?"

He paused on the landing, looking at me solemnly. The lamp he held cast weird, lurking shadows on the dark draperies and on the half-seen portraits that seemed now to leer rather than smile. Outside the wind rose to a brief scream and then subsided grudgingly.

"Not rats," Cal said. "There was a kind of blundering, thudding sound from behind the book-cases, and then a horrible gurgling—horrible, sir. And scratching, as if something were struggling to get out . . . to get at me!"

You can imagine my amazement, Bones. Calvin is not the type to give way to hysterical flights of imagination. It began to seem that there was a mystery here after all—and perhaps an ugly one indeed.

"What then?" I asked him. We had resumed down the hall, and I could see the light from the study spilling forth onto the floor of the gallery. I viewed it with some trepidation; the night seemed no longer comfortable.

"The scratching noise stopped. After a moment the thudding, shuffling sounds began again, this time moving away from me. It paused once, and I swear I heard a strange, almost inaudible laugh! I went to the book-case and began to push and pull, thinking there might be a partition, or a secret door."

"You found one?"

Cal paused at the door to the study. "No—but I found this!"

We stepped in and I saw a square black hole in the left case. The books at that point were nothing but dummies, and what Cal had found was a small hiding place. I flashed my lamp within it and saw nothing but a thick fall of dust, dust which must have been decades old.

"There was only this," Cal said quietly, and handed me a yellowed foolscap. The thing was a map, drawn in spider-thin strokes of black ink—the map of a town or village. There were perhaps seven buildings, and one, clearly marked with a steeple, bore this legend beneath it: *The Worm That Doth Corrupt*.

In the upper left corner, to what would have been the northwest of this little village, an arrow pointed. Inscribed beneath it: *Chapelwaite*.

Calvin said: "In town, sir, someone rather superstitiously mentioned a deserted village called Jerusalem's Lot. It's a place they steer clear of."

"But this?" I asked, fingering the odd legend below the steeple.

"I don't know."

A memory of Mrs. Cloris, adamant yet fearful, passed through my mind. "The Worm . . ." I muttered.

"Do you know something, Mr. Boone?"

"Perhaps . . . it might be amusing to have a look for this town tomorrow, do you think, Cal?"

He nodded, eyes lighting. We spent almost an hour after this looking for some breach in the wall behind the cubby-hole Cal had found, but with no success. Nor was there a recurrence of the noises Cal had described.

We retired with no further adventure that night.

On the following morning Calvin and I set out on our ramble through the woods. The rain of the night before had ceased, but the sky was somber and lowering. I could see Cal looking at me with some doubtfulness and I hastened to reassure him that should I tire, or the journey prove too far, I would not hesitate to call a halt to the affair. We had equipped ourselves with a picnic lunch, a fine Buckwhite compass, and, of course, the odd and ancient map of Jerusalem's Lot.

It was a strange and brooding day; not a bird seemed to sing nor an animal to move as we made our way through the great and gloomy stands of pine to the south and east. The only sounds were those of our own feet and the steady pound of the Atlantic against the headlands. The smell of the sea, almost preternaturally heavy, was our constant companion.

We had gone no more than two miles when we struck an overgrown road of what I believe were once called the "corduroy" variety; this tended in our general direction and we struck off along it, making brisk time. We spoke little. The day, with its still and ominous quality, weighed heavily on our spirits.

At about eleven o'clock we heard the sound of rushing water. The remnant of road took a hard turn to the left, and on the other side of a boiling, slaty little stream, like an apparition, was Jerusalem's Lot!

The stream was perhaps eight feet across, spanned by a moss-grown footbridge. On the far side, Bones, stood the most perfect little village you might imagine, understandably weathered, but amazingly preserved. Several houses, done in that austere yet commanding form for which the Puritans were justly famous, stood clustered near the steeply-sheared bank. Further beyond, along a weed-grown thoroughfare, stood three or four of what might have been primitive business establishments, and beyond that, the spire of the church marked on the map, rising up to the gray sky and looking grim beyond description with its peeled paint and tarnished, leaning cross.

"The town is well named," Cal said softly beside me.

We crossed to the town and began to poke through it—and this is where my story grows slightly amazing, Bones, so prepare yourself!

The air seemed leaden as we walked among the buildings; weighted, if you will. The edifices were in a state of decay—shutters torn off, roofs crumbled under the weight of heavy snows gone by, windows dusty and leering. Shadows from odd corners and warped angles seemed to sit in sinister pools.

We entered an old and rotting tavern first—somehow it did not seem right that we should invade any of those houses to which people had retired when they wished privacy. An old and weather-scrubbed sign above the splintered door announced that this had been the BOAR'S HEAD INN AND TAVERN. The door creaked hellishly on its one remaining hinge, and we stepped into the shadowed interior. The smell of rot and mould was vaporous and nearly overpowering. And beneath it seemed to lie an even deeper smell, a slimy and pestiferous smell, a smell of ages and the decay of ages. Such a stench as might issue from corrupt coffins or violated tombs. I held my handkerchief to my nose and Cal did likewise. We surveyed the place.

"My God, sir—" Cal said faintly.

"It's never been touched," I finished for him.

As indeed it had not. Tables and chairs stood about like ghostly guardians of the watch, dusty, warped by the extreme changes in temperature which the New England climate is known for, but otherwise perfect—as if they had waited through the silent, echoing decades for those long gone to enter once more, to call for a pint or a dram, to deal cards and light clay pipes. A small square mirror hung beside the rules of the tavern, *unbroken.* Do you see the significance, Bones? Small boys are noted for exploration and vandalism; there is not a "haunted" house which stands with windows intact, no matter how fearsome the eldritch inhabitants are rumoured to be; not a shadowy graveyard without at least one tombstone upended by young pranksters. Certainly there must be a score of young pranksters in Preacher's Corners, not two miles from Jerusalem's Lot. Yet the inn-keeper's glass [which must have cost him a nice sum] was intact—as were the other fragile items we found in our pokings. The only damage in Jerusalem's Lot has been done by impersonal Nature. The implication is obvious: Jerusalem's Lot is a shunned town. But why? I have a notion, but before I even dare hint at it, I must proceed to the unsettling conclusion of our visit.

We went up to the sleeping quarters and found beds made up, pewter water-pitchers neatly placed beside them. The kitchen was likewise untouched by anything save the dust of the years and that horrible, sunken stench of decay. The tavern alone would be an antiquarian's paradise; the wondrously queer kitchen stove alone would fetch a pretty price at Boston auction.

"What do you think, Cal?" I asked when we had emerged again into the uncertain daylight.

"I think it's bad business, Mr. Boone," he replied in his doleful way, "and that we must see more to know more."

We gave the other shops scant notice—there was a hostelry with mouldering leather goods still hung on rusted flatnails, a chandler's, a warehouse with oak and pine still stacked within, a smithy.

We entered two houses as we made our way toward the church at the center of the village. Both were perfectly in the Puritan mode, full of items a collector would give his arm for, both deserted and full of the same rotten scent.

Nothing seemed to live or move in all of this but ourselves. We saw no insects, no birds, not even a cobweb fashioned in a window corner. Only dust.

At last we reached the church. It reared above us, grim, uninviting, cold. Its windows were black with the shadows inside, and any Godliness or sanctity had departed from it long ago. Of that I am certain. We mounted the steps, and I placed my hand on the large iron door-pull. A set, dark look passed from myself to Calvin and back again. I opened the portal. How long since that door had been touched? I would say with confidence that mine was the first in fifty years; perhaps longer. Rust-clogged hinges screamed as I opened it. The smell of rot and decay which smote us was nearly palpable. Cal made a gagging sound in his throat and twisted his head involuntarily for clearer air.

"Sir," he asked, "are you sure that you are—?"

"I'm fine," I said calmly. But I did not feel calm, Bones, no more than I do now. I believe, with Moses, with Jereboam, with Increase Mather, and with our own Hanson [when he is in a philosophical *temperament*], that there are spiritually noxious places, buildings where the milk of the cosmos has become sour and rancid. This church is such a place; I would swear to it.

We stepped into a long vestibule equipped with a dusty coat rack and shelved hymnals. It was window-less. Oil-lamps stood in niches here and there. An unre-markable room, I thought, until I heard Calvin's sharp gasp and saw what he had already noticed.

It was an obscenity.

I daren't describe that elaborately-framed picture further than this: that it was done after the fleshy style of Rubens; that it contained a grotesque travesty of a madonna and child; that strange, half-shadowed crea-tures sported and crawled in the background.

"Lord," I whispered.

"There's no Lord here," Calvin said, and his words seemed to hang in the air. I opened the door leading into the church itself, and the odor became a miasma, nearly overpowering.

In the glimmering half-light of afternoon the pews stretched ghostlike to the altar. Above them was a high, oaken pulpit and a shadow-struck narthex from which gold glimmered.

With a half-sob Calvin, that devout Protestant, made the Holy Sign, and I followed suit. For the gold was a large, beautifully-wrought cross—but it was hung upside-down, symbol of Satan's Mass.

"We must be calm," I heard myself saying. "We must be calm, Calvin. We must be calm."

But a shadow had touched my heart, and I was afraid

as I had never been. I have walked beneath death's umbrella and thought there was none darker. But there is. There is.

We walked down the aisle, our footfalls echoing above and around us. We left tracks in the dust. And at the altar there were other tenebrous *objets d'art.* I will not, cannot, let my mind dwell upon them.

I began to mount to the pulpit itself.

"Don't, Mr. Boone!" Cal cried suddenly. "I'm afraid—"

But I had gained it. A huge book lay open upon the stand, writ both in Latin and crabbed runes which looked, to my unpractised eye, either Druidic or pre-Celtic. I enclose a card with several of the symbols, redrawn from memory.

I closed the book and looked at the words stamped into the leather: *De Vermis Mysteriis.* My Latin is rusty, but serviceable enough to translate: *The Mysteries of the Worm.* As I touched it, that accursed church and Calvin's white, upturned face seemed to swim before me. It seemed that I heard low, chanting voices, full of hideous yet eager fear—and below that sound, another, filling the bowels of the earth. An hallucination, I doubt it not—but at the same moment, the church was filled with a very real sound, which I can only describe as a huge and macabre *turning* beneath my feet. The pulpit trembled beneath my fingers; the desecrated cross trembled on the wall.

We exited together, Cal and I, leaving the place to its own darkness, and neither of us dared look back until we had crossed the rude planks spanning the stream. I will not say we defiled the nineteen hundred years man has spent climbing upward from a hunkering and superstitious savage by actually running; but I would be a liar to say that we strolled.

That is my tale. You mustn't shadow your recovery by fearing that the fever has touched me again; Cal can attest to all in these pages, up to and including the hideous *noise*.

So I close, saying only that I wish I might see you [knowing that much of my bewilderment would drop away immediately], and that I remain your friend and admirer,

CHARLES.

Oct. 17, 1850.

DEAR GENTLEMEN:

In the most recent edition of your catalogue of household items (i.e., Summer, 1850), I noticed a preparation which is titled Rat's Bane. I should like to purchase one (1) 5-pound tin of this preparation at your stated price of thirty cents ($.30). I enclose return postage. Please mail to: Calvin McCann, Chapelwaite, Preacher's Corners, Cumberland County, Maine.

Thank you for your attention in this matter.

I remain, dear Gentlemen,
CALVIN McCANN.

Oct. 19, 1850.

DEAR BONES,

Developments of a disquieting nature.

The noises in the house have intensified, and I am growing more to the conclusion that rats are not all that move within our walls. Calvin and I went on another fruitless search for hidden crannies or passages, but found nothing. How poorly we would fit into one of Mrs. Radcliffe's romances! Cal claims, however, that much of the sound emanates from the cellar, and it is there we intend to explore tomorrow. It makes me no easier to know that Cousin Stephen's sister met her unfortunate end there.

Her portrait, by the by, hangs in the upstairs gallery. Marcella Boone was a sadly pretty thing, if the artist got her right, and I do know she never married. At times I think that Mrs. Cloris was right, that it *is* a bad house. It has certainly held nothing but gloom for its past inhabitants.

But I have more to say of the redoubtable Mrs. Cloris, for I have had this day a second interview with her. As the most level-headed person from the Corners that I have met thus far, I sought her out this afternoon, after an unpleasant interview which I will relate.

The wood was to have been delivered this morning, and when noon came and passed and no wood with it, I decided to take my daily walk into the town itself. My object was to visit Thompson, the man with whom Cal did business.

It has been a lovely day, full of the crisp snap of bright autumn, and by the time I reached the Thompsons' homestead [Cal, who remained home to poke further through Uncle Stephen's library, gave me adequate directions] I felt in the best mood that these last few days have seen, and quite prepared to forgive Thompson's tardiness with the wood.

The place was a massive tangle of weeds and fallen-down buildings in need of paint; to the left of the barn a huge sow, ready for November butchering, grunted and wallowed in a muddy sty, and in the littered yard between house and outbuildings a woman in a tattered gingham dress was feeding chickens from her apron. When I hailed her, she turned a pale and vapid face toward me.

The sudden change in expression from utter, doltish emptiness to one of frenzied terror was quite wonderful to behold. I can only think she took me for Stephen himself, for she raised her hand in the prong-fingered sign of the evil eye and screamed. The chicken-feed scattered on the ground and the fowls fluttered away, squawking.

Before I could utter a sound, a huge, hulking figure of a man clad only in long-handled underwear lumbered out of the house with a squirrel-rifle in one hand and a jug in the other. From the red light in his eye and unsteady manner of walking, I judged that this was Thompson the Woodcutter himself.

"A Boone!" he roared. "G— d—n your eyes!" He dropped the jug a-rolling and also made the Sign.

"I've come," I said with as much equanimity as I could muster under the circumstances, "because the wood has not. According to the agreement you struck with my man—"

"G— d—n your man too, say I!" And for the first time I noticed that beneath his bluff and bluster he was deadly afraid. I began seriously to wonder if he mightn't actually use his rifle against me in his excitement.

I began carefully: "As a gesture of courtesy, you might—"

"G— d—n your courtesy!"

"Very well, then," I said with as much dignity as I could muster. "I bid you good day until you are more in control of yourself." And with this I turned away and began down the road to the village.

"Don'tchee come back!" he screamed after me. "Stick wi' your evil up there! Cursed! Cursed! Cursed!" He pelted a stone at me, which struck my shoulder. I would not give him the satisfaction of dodging.

So I sought out Mrs. Cloris, determined to solve the mystery of Thompson's enmity, at least. She is a widow [and none of your confounded *matchmaking,* Bones; she is easily fifteen years my senior, and I'll not see forty again] and lives by herself in a charming little cottage at the ocean's very doorstep. I found the lady hanging out her wash, and she seemed genuinely pleased to see me. I found this a great relief; it is vexing almost beyond words to be branded pariah for no understandable reason.

"Mr. Boone," said she, offering a half-curtsey. "If

you've come about washing, I take none in past September. My rheumatiz pains me so that it's trouble enough to do my own."

"I wish laundry *was* the subject of my visit. I've come for help, Mrs. Cloris. I must know all you can tell me about Chapelwaite and Jerusalem's Lot and why the townfolk regard me with such fear and suspicion!"

"Jerusalem's Lot! You know about *that,* then."

"Yes," I replied, "and visited it with my companion a week ago."

"God!" She went pale as milk, and tottered. I put out a hand to steady her. Her eyes rolled horribly, and for a moment I was sure she would swoon.

"Mrs. Cloris, I am sorry if I have said anything to—"

"Come inside," she said. "You must know. Sweet Jesu, the evil days have come again!"

She would not speak more until she had brewed strong tea in her sunshiny kitchen. When it was before us, she looked pensively out at the ocean for a time. Inevitably, her eyes and mine were drawn to the jutting brow of Chapelwaite Head, where the house looked out over the water. The large bay window glittered in the rays of the westering sun like a diamond. The view was beautiful but strangely disturbing. She suddenly turned to me and declared vehemently:

"Mr. Boone, you must leave Chapelwaite immediately!"

I was flabbergasted.

"There has been an evil breath in the air since you took up residence. In the last week—since you set foot in the accursed place—there have been omens and portents. A caul over the face of the moon; flocks of whippoorwills which roost in the cemeteries; an unnatural birth. You *must* leave!"

When I found my tongue, I spoke as gently as I could. "Mrs. Cloris, these things are dreams. You must know that."

"Is it a dream that Barbara Brown gave birth to a child with no eyes? Or that Clifton Brockett found a flat, pressed trail five feet wide in the woods beyond Chapelwaite *where all had withered and gone white?* And can you, who have visited Jerusalem's Lot, say with truth that nothing still lives there?"

I could not answer; the scene in that hideous church sprang before my eyes.

She clamped her gnarled hands together in an effort to calm herself. "I know of these things only from my mother and her mother before her. Do you know the history of your family as it applies to Chapelwaite?"

"Vaguely," I said. "The house has been the home of Philip Boone's line since the 1780s; his brother Robert, my grandfather, located in Massachusetts after an argument over stolen papers. Of Philip's side I know little, except that an unhappy shadow fell over it, extending from father to son to grandchildren—Marcella died in a tragic accident and Stephen fell to his death. It was his wish that Chapelwaite become the home of me and mine, and that the family rift thus be mended."

"Never to be mended," she whispered. "You know nothing of the original quarrel?"

"Robert Boone was discovered rifling his brother's desk."

"Philip Boone was mad," she said. "A man who trafficked with the unholy. The thing which Robert Boone *attempted* to remove was a profane Bible writ in the old tongues—Latin, Druidic, others. A hell-book."

"De Vermis Mysteriis."

She recoiled as if struck. "You know of it?"

"I have seen it . . . touched it." It seemed again she might swoon. A hand went to her mouth as if to stifle an outcry. "Yes; in Jerusalem's Lot. On the pulpit of a corrupt and desecrated church."

"Still there; still there, then." She rocked in her chair. "I had hoped God in His wisdom had cast it into the pit of hell."

"What relation had Philip Boone to Jerusalem's Lot?"

"Blood relation," she said darkly. "The Mark of the Beast was on him, although he walked in the clothes of the Lamb. And on the night of October 31, 1789, Philip Boone disappeared . . . and the entire populace of that damned village with him."

She would say little more; in fact, seemed to know little more. She would only reiterate her pleas that I leave, giving as reason something about "blood calling to blood" and muttering about "those who *watch* and those who *guard*." As twilight drew on she seemed to grow more agitated rather than less, and to placate her I promised that her wishes would be taken under strong consideration.

I walked home through lengthening, gloomy shadows, my good mood quite dissipated and my head spinning with questions which still plague me. Cal greeted me with the news that our noises in the walls have grown worse still—as I can attest at this moment. I try to tell myself that I hear only rats, but then I see the terrified, earnest face of Mrs. Cloris.

The moon has risen over the sea, bloated, full, the colour of blood, staining the ocean with a noxious shade. My mind turns to that church again and

(here a line is struck out)

But you shall not see that, Bones. It is too mad. It is time I slept, I think. My thoughts go out to you.

Regards,
CHARLES.

(The following is from the pocket journal of Calvin McCann.)

Oct. 20, '50

Took the liberty this morning of forcing the lock which binds the book closed; did it before Mr. Boone arose. No help; it is all in cypher. A simple one, I believe. Perhaps I may break it as easily as the lock. A diary, I am certain, the hand oddly like Mr. Boone's own. Whose book, shelved in the most obscure corner of this library and locked across the pages? It seems old, but how to tell? The corrupting air has largely been kept from its pages. More later, if time; Mr. Boone set upon looking about the cellar. Am afraid these dreadful goings-on will be too much for his chancy health yet. I must try to persuade him—

But he comes.

Oct. 20, 1850.

BONES,

I can't write I cant *[sic]* write of this yet I I I

(From the pocket journal of Calvin McCann)

Oct. 20, '50.

As I had feared, his health has broken—

Dear God, our Father Who art in Heaven!

Cannot bear to think of it; yet it is planted, burned on my brain like a tin-type; that horror in the cellar—!

Alone now; half-past eight o'clock; house silent but—

Found him swooned over his writing table; he still sleeps; yet for those few moments how nobly he acquitted himself while I stood paralyzed and shattered!

His skin is waxy, cool. Not the fever again, God be thanked. I daren't move him or leave him to go to the village. And if I did go, who would return with me to aid him? Who would come to this cursed house?

O, the cellar! The things in the cellar that have haunted our walls!

Oct. 22, 1850.

DEAR BONES,

I am myself again, although weak, after thirty-six hours of unconsciousness. Myself again . . . what a grim and bitter joke! I shall never be myself again, never. I have come face to face with an insanity and a horror beyond the limits of human expression. And the end is not yet.

If it were not for Cal, I believe I should end my life this minute. He is one island of sanity in all this madness.

You shall know it all.

We had equipped ourselves with candles for our cellar exploration, and they threw a strong glow that was quite adequate—hellishly adequate! Calvin tried to dissuade me, citing my recent illness, saying that the most we should probably find would be some healthy rats to mark for poisoning.

I remained determined, however; Calvin fetched a sigh and answered: "Have it as you must, then, Mr. Boone."

The entrance to the cellar is by means of a trap in the kitchen floor [which Cal assures me he has since stoutly boarded over], and we raised it only with a great deal of straining and lifting.

A foetid, overpowering smell came up out of the darkness, not unlike that which pervaded the deserted town across the Royal River. The candle I held shed its glow on a steeply-slanting flight of stairs leading down into darkness. They were in a terrible state of repair—in one place an entire riser missing, leaving only a black hole—and it was easy enough to see how the unfortunate Marcella might have come to her end there.

"Be careful, Mr. Boone!" Cal said; I told him I had

no intention of being anything but, and we made the descent.

The floor was earthen, the walls of stout granite, and hardly wet. The place did not look like a rat haven at all, for there were none of the things rats like to make their nests in, such as old boxes, discarded furniture, piles of paper, and the like. We lifted our candles, gaining a small circle of light, but still able to see little. The floor had a gradual slope which seemed to run beneath the main living-room and the dining-room—i.e., to the west. It was in this direction we walked. All was in utter silence. The stench in the air grew steadily stronger, and the dark about us seemed to press like wool, as if jealous of the light which had temporarily deposed it after so many years of undisputed dominion.

At the far end, the granite walls gave way to a polished wood which seemed totally black and without reflective properties. Here the cellar ended, leaving what seemed to be an alcove off the main chamber. It was positioned at an angle which made inspection impossible without stepping around the corner.

Calvin and I did so.

It was as if a rotten spectre of this dwelling's sinister past had risen before us. A single chair stood in this alcove, and above it, fastened from a hook in one of the stout overhead beams, was a decayed noose of hemp.

"Then it was here that he hung himself," Cal muttered. "God!"

"Yes . . . with the corpse of his daughter lying at the foot of the stairs behind him."

Cal began to speak; then I saw his eyes jerked to a spot behind me; then his words became a scream.

How, Bones, can I describe the sight which fell upon our eyes? How can I tell you of the hideous tenants within our walls?

The far wall swung back, and from that darkness a face leered—a face with eyes as ebon as the Styx itself. Its mouth yawned in a toothless, agonized grin; one yellow, rotted hand stretched itself out to us. It made a hideous, mewling sound and took a shambling step forward. The light from my candle fell upon it—

And I saw the livid rope-burn about its neck!

From beyond it something else moved, something I shall dream of until the day when all dreams cease: a girl with a pallid, mouldering face and a corpse-grin; a girl whose head lolled at a lunatic angle.

They wanted us; I know it. And I know they would have drawn us into that darkness and made us their own, had I not thrown my candle directly at the thing in the partition, and followed it with the chair beneath that noose.

After that, all is confused darkness. My mind has drawn the curtain. I awoke, as I have said, in my room with Cal at my side.

If I could leave, I should fly from this house of horror with my nightdress flapping at my heels. But I cannot. I have become a pawn in a deeper, darker drama. Do not ask how I know; I only do. Mrs. Cloris was right when she spoke of blood calling to blood; and how horribly right when she spoke of those who *watch* and those who *guard.* I fear that I have wakened a Force which has slept in the tenebrous village of 'Salem's Lot for half a century, a Force which has slain my ancestors and taken them in unholy bondage as *nosferatu*—the Undead. And I have greater fears than these, Bones, but I still see only in part. If I knew . . . if I only knew all!

CHARLES.

Postscriptum—And of course I write this only for myself; we are isolated from Preacher's Corners. I daren't carry my taint there to post this, and Calvin will not leave me. Perhaps, if God is good, this will reach you in some manner.

C.

(From the pocket journal of Calvin McCann)

Oct. 23, '50

He is stronger to-day; we talked briefly of the *apparitions* in the cellar; agreed they were neither hallucinations or of an *ectoplasmic* origin, but *real.* Does Mr. Boone suspect as I do, that they have gone? Perhaps; the noises are still; yet all is ominous yet, o'ercast with a dark pall. It seems we wait in the deceptive Eye of the Storm . . .

Have found a packet of papers in an upstairs bedroom, lying in the bottom drawer of an old roll-top desk. Some correspondence & receipted bills lead me to believe the room was Robert Boone's. Yet the most interesting document is a few jottings on the back of an advertisement for gentlemen's beaver hats. At the top is writ:

Blessed are the meek.

Below, the following apparent nonsense is writ:

bke dshdermthes eak
elmsoerare shamded

I believe 'tis the key of the locked and coded book in the library. The cypher above is certainly a rustic one used in the War for Independence known as the *Fence-Rail*. When one removes the "nulls" from the second bit of scribble, the following is obtained:

besdrteek
lseaehme

Read up and down rather than across, the result is the original quotation from the Beatitudes.

Before I dare show this to Mr. Boone, I must be sure of the book's contents . . .

Oct. 24, 1850.

DEAR BONES,

An amazing occurrence—Cal, always close-mouthed until absolutely sure of himself [a rare and admirable human trait!], has found the diary of my grandfather Robert. The document was in a code which Cal himself has broken. He modestly declares that the discovery was an accident, but I suspect that perseverance and hard work had rather more to do with it.

At any rate, what a somber light it sheds on our mysteries here!

The first entry is dated June 1, 1789, the last October 27, 1789—four days before the cataclysmic disappearance of which Mrs. Cloris spoke. It tells a tale of deepening obsession—nay, of madness—and makes hideously clear the relationship between Great-uncle Philip, the town of Jerusalem's Lot, and the book which rests in that desecrated church.

The town itself, according to Robert Boone, pre-dates Chapelwaite (built in 1782) and Preacher's Corners (known in those days as Preacher's Rest and founded in 1741); it was founded by a splinter group of the Puritan faith in 1710, a sect headed by a dour religious fanatic named James Boon. What a start that name gave me! That this Boon bore relation to my family can hardly be doubted, I believe. Mrs. Cloris could not have been more right in her superstitious belief that familial bloodline is of crucial importance in this matter; and I recall with terror her answer to my question about Philip and *his* relationship to 'Salem's Lot. "Blood relation," said she, and I fear that it is so.

The town became a settled community built around the church where Boon preached—or held court. My grandfather intimates that he also held commerce with any number of ladies from the town, assuring them that this was God's way and will. As a result, the town became an anomaly which could only have existed in those isolated and queer days when belief in witches and the Virgin Birth existed hand in hand: an inter-bred, rather degenerate religious village controlled by a half-mad preacher whose twin gospels were the Bible and de Goudge's sinister *Demon Dwellings;* a community in which rites of exorcism were held regularly; a community of incest and the insanity and physical defects which so often accompany that sin. I suspect [and believe Robert Boone must have also] that one of Boon's bastard offspring must have left [or have been spirited away from] Jerusalem's Lot to seek his fortune to the south—and thus founded our present lineage. I do know, by my own family reckoning, that our clan sup-posedly originated in that part of Massachusetts which has so lately become this Sovereign State of Maine. My great-grandfather, Kenneth Boone, became a rich man as a result of the then-flourishing fur trade. It was his money, increased by time and wise investment, which built this ancestral home long after his death in 1763. His sons, Philip and Robert, built Chapelwaite. *Blood calls to blood,* Mrs. Cloris said. Could it be that Ken-neth was born of James Boon, fled the madness of his father and his father's town, only to have his sons, all-unknowing, build the Boone home *not two miles from the Boon beginnings?* If 'tis true, does it not seem that some huge and invisible Hand has guided us?

According to Robert's diary, James Boon was ancient in 1789—and he must have been. Granting him

an age of twenty-five in the year of the town's found-
ing, he would have been one hundred and four, a prodi-
gious age. The following is quoted direct from Robert
Boone's diary:

August 4, 1789.

To-day for the first time I met this Man with
whom my Brother has been so unhealthily taken;
I must admit this Boon controls a strange Mag-
netism which upset me Greatly. He is a veritable
Ancient, white-bearded, and dresses in a black
Cassock which struck me as somehow obscene.
More disturbing yet was the Fact that he was surrounded by Women, as a Sultan would be surrounded by his Harem; and P. assures me he is
active yet, although at least an Octogenarian . . .
The Village itself I had visited only once before,
and will not visit again; its Streets are silent and
filled with the Fear the old Man inspires from his
Pulpit: I fear also that Like has mated with Like,
as so many of the Faces are similar. It seemed
that each way I turned I beheld the old Man's Visage . . . all are so wan; they seem Lack-Luster,
as if sucked dry of all Vitality, I beheld Eyeless
and Noseless Children, Women who wept and
gibbered and pointed at the Sky for no Reason,
and garbled talk from the Scriptures with talk of
Demons; . . .
P. wished me to stay for Services, but the thought
of that sinister Ancient in the Pulpit before an

Audience of this Town's interbred Populace repulsed me and I made an Excuse . . .

The entries preceding and following this tell of Philip's growing fascination with James Boon. On September 1, 1789, Philip was baptized into Boon's church. His brother says: "I am aghast with Amaze and Horror—my Brother has changed before my very Eyes—he even seems to grow to resemble the wretched Man."

First mention of the book occurs on July 23. Robert's diary records it only briefly: "P. returned from the smaller Village to-night with, I thought, a rather wild Visage. Would not speak until Bedtime, when he said that Boon had enquired after a Book titled *Mysteries of the Worm*. To please P. I promised to write Johns & Goodfellow a letter of enquiry; P. almost fawningly Grateful."

On August 12, this notation: "Rec'd two Letters in the Post to-day . . . one from Johns & Goodfellow in Boston. They have Note of the Tome in which P. has expressed an Interest. Only five Copies extant in this Country. The Letter is rather cool; odd indeed. Have known Henry Goodfellow for Years."

August 13:
P. insanely excited by Goodfellow's letter; refuses to say why. He would only say that Boon is *exceedingly anxious* to obtain a Copy. Cannot think why, since by the Title it seems only a harmless gardening Treatise . . .

Am worried for Philip; he grows stranger to me Daily. I wish now we had not returned to Chapelwaite. The Summer is hot, oppressive, and filled with Omens . . .

There are only two further mentions of the infamous book in Robert's diary [he seems not to have realized the true importance of it, even at the end]. From the entry of September 4:

I have petitioned Goodfellow to act as P.'s Agent in the matter of the Purchase, although my better Judgement cries against It. What use to demur? Has he not his own Money, should I refuse? And in return I have extracted a Promise from Philip to recant this noisome Baptism . . . yet he is so Hectic; nearly Feverish; I do not trust him. I am hopelessly *at Sea* in this Matter . . .

Finally, September 16:

The Book arrived to-day, with a note from Goodfellow saying he wishes no more of my Trade . . . P. was excited to an unnatural Degree; all but snatched the Book from my Hands. It is writ in bastard Latin and a Runic Script of which I can read Nothing. The Thing seemed almost warm to the Touch, and to vibrate in my Hands, as if it contained a huge Power . . . I reminded P. of his Promise to Recant and he only laughed in

an ugly, crazed Fashion and waved that Book in
my Face, crying over and over again: "We have it!
We have it! The Worm! The Secret of the Worm!"
He is now fled, I suppose to his mad Benefactor,
and I have not seen him more this Day . . .

Of the book there is no more, but I have made certain deductions which seem at least probable. First,
that this book was, as Mrs. Cloris has said, the subject
of the falling-out between Robert and Philip; second,
that it is a repository of unholy incantation, possibly of
Druidic origin [many of the Druidic blood-rituals were
preserved in print by the Roman conquerors of Britain
in the name of scholarship, and many of these infernal
cook-books are among the world's forbidden literature];
third, that Boon and Philip intended to use the book
for their own ends. Perhaps, in some twisted way, they
intended good, but I do not believe it. I believe they had
long before bound themselves over to whatever faceless
powers exist beyond the rim of the Universe; powers
which may exist beyond the very fabric of Time. The
last entries of Robert Boone's diary lend a dim glow of
approbation to these speculations, and I allow them to
speak for themselves:

October 26, 1789
A terrific Babble in Preacher's Corners to-day;
Frawley, the Blacksmith, seized my Arm and
demanded to know "What your Brother and that
mad Antichrist are into up there." Goody Randall

claims there have been *Signs* in the Sky of *great impending Disaster.* A Cow has been born with two Heads.

As for Myself, I know not what impends; perhaps 'tis my Brother's Insanity. His Hair has gone Gray almost Overnight, his Eyes are great bloodshot Circles from which the pleasing light of Sanity seems to have departed. He grins and whispers, and, for some Reason of his Own, has begun to haunt our Cellar when not in Jerusalem's Lot.

The Whippoorwills congregate about the House and upon the Grass; their combined Calling from the Mist blends with the Sea into an unearthly Shriek that precludes all thought of Sleep.

October 27, 1789

Followed P. this Evening when he departed for Jerusalem's Lot, keeping a safe Distance to avoid Discovery. The cursed Whippoorwills flock through the Woods, filling all with a deathly, psycho-pompotic Chant. I dared not cross the Bridge; the Town all dark except for the Church, which was litten with a ghastly red Glare that seemed to transform the high, peak'd Windows into the Eyes of the Inferno. Voices rose and fell in a Devil's Litany, sometimes laughing, sometimes sobbing. The very Ground seem'd to swell and groan beneath me, as if it bore an awful Weight, and I fled, amaz'd and full of Terror, the hellish, screaming Cries of the Whippoorwills dinning in my ears as I ran through those shadow-riven Woods.

All tends to the Climax, yet unforeseen. I dare not sleep for the Dreams that come, yet not remain awake for what lunatic Terrors may come. The night is full of awful Sounds and I fear—

And yet I feel the urge to go again, to watch, *to see.* It seems that Philip himself calls me, and the old Man.

The Birds
cursed cursed cursed

Here the diary of Robert Boone ends.

Yet you must notice, Bones, near the conclusion, that he claims Philip himself seemed to call him. My final conclusion is formed by these lines, by the talk of Mrs. Cloris and the others, but most of all by those terrifying figures in the cellar, dead yet alive. Our line is yet an unfortunate one, Bones. There is a curse over us which refuses to be buried; it lives a hideous shadow-life in this house and that town. And the culmination of the cycle is drawing close again. I am the last of the Boone blood. I fear that something knows this, and that I am at the nexus of an evil endeavor beyond all sane under-standing. The anniversary is All Saints' Eve, one week from today.

How shall I proceed? If only you were here to coun-sel me, to help me! If only you were here!

I must know all; I must return to the shunned town. May God support me!

CHARLES.

(From the pocket journal of Calvin McCann)

Oct. 25, '50

Mr. Boone has slept nearly all this day. His face is pallid and much thinner. I fear recurrence of his fever is inevitable.

While refreshing his water carafe I caught sight of two unmailed letters to Mr. Granson in Florida. He plans to return to Jerusalem's Lot; 'twill be the killing of him if I allow it. Dare I steal away to Preacher's Corners and hire a buggy? I must, and yet what if he wakes? If I should return and find him gone?

The noises have begun in our walls again. Thank God he still sleeps! My mind shudders from the import of this.

Later

I brought him his dinner on a tray. He plans on rising later, and despite his evasions, I know what he plans; yet I go to Preacher's Corners. Several of the sleeping-powders prescribed to him during his late illness remained with my things; he drank one with his tea, all-unknowing. He sleeps again.

To leave him with the Things that shamble behind our walls terrifies me; to let him continue even one more day within these walls terrifies me even more greatly. I have locked him in.

God grant he should still be there, safe and sleeping, when I return with the buggy!

Still later

Stoned me! Stoned me like a wild and rabid dog! Monsters and fiends! These, that call themselves *men!* We are prisoners here—

The birds, the whippoorwills, have begun to gather.

October 26, 1850.

DEAR BONES,

It is nearly dusk, and I have just wakened, having slept nearly the last twenty-four hours away. Although Cal has said nothing, I suspect he put a sleeping-powder in my tea, having gleaned my intentions. He is a good and faithful friend, intending only the best, and I shall say nothing.

Yet my mind is set. Tomorrow is the day. I am calm, resolved, but also seem to feel the subtle onset of the fever again. If it is so, it *must* be tomorrow. Perhaps tonight would be better still; yet not even the fires of Hell itself could induce me to set foot in that village by shadowlight.

Should I write no more, may God bless and keep you, Bones.

CHARLES.

Postscriptum—The birds have set up their cry, and

the horrible shuffling sounds have begun again. Cal does not think I hear, but I do.

C.

(From the pocket journal of Calvin McCann)

Oct. 27, '50
5 *AM*

He is impersuadable. Very well. I go with him.

November 4, 1850.

DEAR BONES,

Weak, yet lucid. I am not sure of the date, yet my almanac assures me by tide and sunset that it must be correct. I sit at my desk, where I sat when I first wrote you from Chapelwaite, and look out over the dark sea from which the last of the light is rapidly fading. I shall never see more. This night is my night; I leave it for whatever shadows be.

How it heaves itself at the rocks, this sea! It throws clouds of sea-foam at the darkling sky in banners, making the floor beneath me tremble. In the window-glass I see my reflection, pallid as any vampire's. I have been without nourishment since the twenty-seventh of October, and should have been without water, had not Calvin left the carafe beside my bed on that day.

O, Cal! He is no more, Bones. He is gone in my place, in the place of this wretch with his pipestem arms and skull face who I see reflected back in the darkened glass. And yet he may be the more fortunate; for no dreams

haunt him as they have haunted me these last days—
twisted shapes that lurk in the nightmare corridors of
delirium. Even now my hands tremble; I have splotched
the page with ink.

Calvin confronted me on that morning just as I was
about to slip away—and I thinking I had been so crafty.
I had told him that I had decided we must leave, and
asked him if he would go to Tandrell, some ten miles
distant, and hire a trap where we were less notorious.
He agreed to make the hike and I watched him leave
by the sea-road. When he was out of sight I quickly
made myself ready, donning both coat and muffler [for
the weather had turned frosty; the first touch of coming
winter was on that morning's cutting breeze]. I wished
briefly for a gun, then laughed at myself for the wish.
What avails guns in such a matter?

I let myself out by the pantry-way, pausing for a last
look at sea and sky; for the smell of the fresh air against
the putrescence I knew I should smell soon enough; for
the sight of a foraging gull wheeling below the clouds.

I turned—and there stood Calvin McCann.

"You shall not go alone," said he; and his face was as
grim as ever I have seen it.

"But Calvin—" I began.

"No, not a word! We go together and do what we
must, or I return you bodily to the house. You are not
well. You shall not go alone."

It is impossible to describe the conflicting emotions
that swept over me: confusion, pique, gratefulness—yet
the greatest of them was love.

We made our way silently past the summer house and the sundial, down the weed-covered verge and into the woods. All was dead still—not a bird sang nor a wood-cricket chirruped. The world seemed cupped in a silent pall. There was only the ever-present smell of salt, and from far away, the faint tang of woodsmoke. The woods were a blazoned riot of colour, but, to my eye, scarlet seemed to predominate all.

Soon the scent of salt passed, and another, more sinister odour took its place; that rottenness which I have mentioned. When we came to the leaning bridge which spanned the Royal, I expected Cal to ask me again to defer, but he did not. He paused, looked at that grim spire which seemed to mock the blue sky above it, and then looked at me. We went on.

We proceeded with quick yet dread footsteps to James Boon's church. The door still hung ajar from our latter exit, and the darkness within seemed to leer at us. As we mounted the steps, brass seemed to fill my heart; my hand trembled as it touched the doorhandle and pulled it. The smell within was greater, more noxious than ever.

We stepped into the shadowy anteroom and, with no pause, into the main chamber.

It was a shambles.

Something vast had been at work in there, and a mighty destruction had taken place. Pews were overturned and heaped like jackstraws. The wicked cross lay against the east wall, and a jagged hole in the plaster above it testified to the force with which it had been hurled. The oil-lamps had been ripped from their high fixtures, and the reek of whale-oil mingled with the terrible stink which pervaded the town. And down the center aisle, like a ghastly bridal path, was a trail of black ichor, mingled with sinister tendrils of blood. Our eyes followed it to the pulpit—the only untouched thing in view. Atop it, staring at us from across that blasphemous Book with glazed eyes, was the butchered body of a lamb.

"God," Calvin whispered.

We approached, keeping clear of the slime on the floor. The room echoed back our footsteps and seemed to transmute them into the sound of gigantic laughter.

We mounted the narthex together. The lamb had not been torn or eaten; it appeared, rather, to have been *squeezed* until its blood-vessels had forcibly ruptured. Blood lay in thick and noisome puddles on the lectern itself, and about the base of it . . . *yet on the book it was transparent, and the crabbed runes could be read through it, as through coloured glass!*

"Must we touch it?" Cal asked, unfaltering.

"Yes. I must have it."

"What will you do?"

"What should have been done sixty years ago. I am going to destroy it."

We rolled the lamb's corpse away from the book; it struck the floor with a hideous, lolling thud. The bloodstained pages now seemed alive with a scarlet glow of their own.

My ears began to ring and hum; a low chant seemed

to emanate from the walls themselves. From the twisted look on Cal's face I knew he heard the same. The floor beneath us trembled, as if the familiar which haunted this church came now unto us, to protect its own. The fabric of sane space and time seemed to twist and crack; the church seemed filled with spectres and litten with the hell-glow of eternal cold fire. It seemed that I saw James Boon, hideous and misshapen, cavorting around the supine body of a woman, and my Grand-uncle Philip behind him, an acolyte in a black, hooded cassock, who held a knife and a bowl.

"Deum vobiscum magna vermis—"

The words shuddered and writhed on the page before me, soaked in the blood of sacrifice, prize of a creature that shambles beyond the stars—

A blind, interbred congregation swaying in mindless, daemoniac praise; deformed faces filled with hungering, nameless anticipation—

And the Latin was replaced by an older tongue, ancient when Egypt was young and the Pyramids unbuilt, ancient when this Earth still hung in an unformed, boiling firmament of empty gas:

"Gyyagin vardar Yogsoggoth! Verminis! Gyyagin! Gyyagin! Gyyagin!"

The pulpit began to rend and split, pushing upward—

Calvin screamed and lifted an arm to shield his face. The narthex trembled with a huge, tenebrous motion like a ship wracked in a gale. I snatched up the book and held it away from me; it seemed filled with the heat of the sun and I felt that I should be cindered, blinded.

"Run!" Calvin screamed. "Run!"

But I stood frozen and the alien presence filled me like an ancient vessel that had waited for years—for generations!

"Gyyagin vardar!" I screamed. "Servant of Yog-soggoth, the Nameless One! The Worm from beyond Space! Star-Eater! Blinder of Time! Verminis! Now comes the Hour of Filling, the Time of Rending! Ver-minis! Alyah! Alyah! Gyyagin!"

Calvin pushed me and I tottered, the church whirl-ing before me, and fell to the floor. My head crashed against the edge of an upturned pew, and red fire filled my head—yet seemed to clear it.

I groped for the sulphur matches I had brought.

Subterranean thunder filled the place. Plaster fell. The rusted bell in the steeple pealed a choked devil's carillon in sympathetic vibration.

My match flared. I touched it to the book just as the pulpit exploded upward in a rending explosion of wood. A huge black maw was discovered beneath; Cal tottered on the edge his hands held out, his face distended in a wordless scream that I shall hear forever.

And then there was a huge surge of gray, vibrating flesh. The smell became a nightmare tide. It was a huge outpouring of a viscid, pustulant jelly, a huge and awful form that seemed to skyrocket from the very bowels of the ground. And yet, with a sudden horrible comprehension which no man can have known, I perceived *that it was but one ring, one segment, of a monster worm that had existed eyeless for years in the chambered darkness beneath that abominated church!*

The book flared alight in my hands, and the Thing seemed to scream soundlessly above me. Calvin was struck glancingly and flung the length of the church like a doll with a broken neck.

It subsided—the thing subsided, leaving only a huge and shattered hole surrounded with black slime, and a great screaming, mewling sound that seemed to fade through colossal distances and was gone.

I looked down. The book was ashes.

I began to laugh, then to howl like a struck beast.

All sanity left me, and I sat on the floor with blood streaming from my temple, screaming and gibbering into those unhallowed shadows while Calvin sprawled in the far corner, staring at me with glazing, horror-struck eyes.

I have no idea how long I existed in that state. It is beyond all telling. But when I came again to my faculties, shadows had drawn long paths around me and I sat in twilight. Movement had caught my eye, movement from the shattered hole in the narthex floor.

A hand groped its way over the riven floorboards.

My mad laughter choked in my throat. All hysteria melted into numb bloodlessness.

With terrible, vengeful slowness, a wracked figure pulled itself up from darkness, and a half-skull peered at me. Beetles crawled over the fleshless forehead. A rotted cassock clung to the askew hollows of mouldered collarbones. Only the eyes lived—red, insane pits that glared at me with more than lunacy; they glared with the empty life of the pathless wastes beyond the edges of the Universe.

It came to take me down to darkness.

That was when I fled, screeching, leaving the body of my lifelong friend unheeded in that place of dread. I ran until the air seemed to burst like magma in my lungs and brain. I ran until I had gained this possessed and tainted house again, and my room, where I collapsed and have lain like a dead man until to-day. I ran because even in my crazed state, and even in the shattered ruin of that dead-yet-animated shape, *I had seen the family resemblance.* Yet not of Philip or of Robert, whose likenesses hang in the upstairs gallery. *That rotted visage belonged to James Boon, Keeper of the Worm!*

He still lives somewhere in the twisted, lightless wanderings beneath Jerusalem's Lot and Chapelwaite—and *It* still lives. The burning of the book thwarted *It,* but there are other copies.

Yet I am the gateway, and I am the last of the Boone blood. For the good of all humanity I must die . . . and break the chain forever.

I go to the sea now, Bones. My journey, like my story, is at an end. May God rest you and grant you all peace.

CHARLES.

The odd series of papers above was eventually received by Mr. Everett Granson, to whom they had been addressed. It is assumed that a recurrence of the unfortunate brain fever which struck him originally following the death of his wife in 1848 caused Charles Boone to lose his sanity and murder his companion and longtime friend, Mr. Calvin McCann.

The entries in Mr. McCann's pocket journal are a fascinating exercise in forgery, undoubtedly perpetrated by Charles Boone in an effort to reinforce his own paranoid delusions.

In at least two particulars, however, Charles Boone is proved wrong. First, when the town of Jerusalem's Lot was "rediscovered" (I use the term historically, of course), the floor of the narthex, although rotted, showed no sign of explosion or huge damage. Although the ancient pews *were* overturned and several windows shattered, this can be assumed to be the work of vandals from neighboring towns over the years. Among the older residents of Preacher's Corners and Tandrell there is still some idle rumor about Jerusalem's Lot (perhaps, in his day, it was this kind of harmless folk legend which started Charles Boone's mind on its fatal course), but this seems hardly relevant.

Second, Charles Boone was not the last of his line. His grandfather, Robert Boone, sired at least two bastards. One died in infancy. The second took the Boone name and located in the town of Central Falls, Rhode Island. I am the final descendant of this offshoot of the Boone line; Charles Boone's second cousin, removed by three generations. These papers have been in my committal for ten years. I offer them for publication on the occasion of my residence in the Boone ancestral home, Chapelwaite, in the hope that the reader will find sympathy in his heart for Charles Boone's poor, misguided soul. So far as I can tell, he was correct about only one thing: this place badly needs the services of an exterminator.

There are some huge rats in the walls, by the sound.

Signed,
James Robert Boone
October 2, 1971.

GRAVEYARD SHIFT

Two A.M., Friday.

Hall was sitting on the bench by the elevator, the only place on the third floor where a working joe could catch a smoke, when Warwick came up. He wasn't happy to see Warwick. The foreman wasn't supposed to show up on three during the graveyard shift; he was supposed to stay down in his office in the basement drinking coffee from the urn that stood on the corner of his desk. Besides, it was hot.

It was the hottest June on record in Gates Falls, and the Orange Crush thermometer which was also by the elevator had once rested at 94 degrees at three in the morning. God only knew what kind of hellhole the mill was on the three-to-eleven shift.

Hall worked the picker machine, a balky gadget manufactured by a defunct Cleveland firm in 1934. He had only been working in the mill since April, which meant he was still making minimum $1.78 an hour, which was still all right. No wife, no steady girl, no alimony. He was a drifter, and during the last three years he had moved on his thumb from Berkeley (college student) to Lake Tahoe (busboy) to Galveston (stevedore) to Miami (short-order cook) to Wheeling (taxi driver and dish-washer) to Gates Falls, Maine (picker-machine opera-tor). He didn't figure on moving again until the snow fell. He was a solitary person and he liked the hours from eleven to seven when the blood flow of the big mill was at its coolest, not to mention the temperature.

The only thing he did not like was the rats.

The third floor was long and deserted, lit only by the sputtering glow of the fluorescents. Unlike the other lev-els of the mill, it was relatively silent and unoccupied—at least by the humans. The rats were another matter. The only machine on three was the picker; the rest of the floor was storage for the ninety-pound bags of fiber which had yet to be sorted by Hall's long gear-toothed machine. They were stacked like link sausages in long rows, some of them (especially the discontinued mel-tons and irregular slipes for which there were no orders) years old and dirty gray with industrial wastes. They made fine nesting places for the rats, huge, fat-bellied creatures with rabid eyes and bodies that jumped with lice and vermin.

Hall had developed a habit of collecting a small arse-nal of soft-drink cans from the trash barrel during his break. He pegged them at the rats during times when work was slow, retrieving them later at his leisure. Only this time Mr. Foreman had caught him, coming up the stairs instead of using the elevator like the sneaky sonofabitch everyone said he was.

"What are you up to, Hall?"

"The rats," Hall said, realizing how lame that must sound now that all the rats had snuggled safely back into their houses. "I peg cans at 'em when I see 'em."

Warwick nodded once, briefly. He was a big beefy man with a crew cut. His shirtsleeves were rolled up and his tie was pulled down. He looked at Hall closely. "We don't pay you to chuck cans at rats, mister. Not even if you pick them up again."

"Harry hasn't sent down an order for twenty minutes," Hall answered, thinking: *Why couldn't you stay the hell put and drink your coffee?* "I can't run it through the picker if I don't have it."

Warwick nodded as if the topic no longer interested him.

"Maybe I'll take a walk up and see Wisconsky," he said. "Five to one he's reading a magazine while the crap piles up in his bins."

Hall didn't say anything.

Warwick suddenly pointed. "There's one! Get the bastard!"

Hall fired the Nehi can he had been holding with one whistling, overhand motion. The rat, which had been watching them from atop one of the fabric bags with its bright buckshot eyes, fled with one faint squeak. Warwick threw back his head and laughed as Hall went after the can.

"I came to see you about something else," Warwick said.

"Is that so?"

"Next week's Fourth of July week." Hall nodded. The mill would be shut down Monday to Saturday— vacation week for men with at least one year's tenure. Layoff week for men with less than a year. "You want to work?"

Hall shrugged. "Doing what?"

"We're going to clean the whole basement level. Nobody's touched it for twelve years. Helluva mess. We're going to use hoses."

"The town zoning committee getting on the board of directors?"

Warwick looked steadily at Hall. "You want it or not? Two an hour, double time on the fourth. We're working the graveyard shift because it'll be cooler."

Hall calculated. He could clear maybe seventy-five bucks after taxes. Better than the goose egg he had been looking forward to.

"All right."

"Report down by the dye house next Monday."

Hall watched him as he started back to the stairs. Warwick paused halfway there and turned back to look at Hall. "You used to be a college boy, didn't you?"

Hall nodded.

"Okay, college boy, I'm keeping it in mind."

He left. Hall sat down and lit another smoke, holding a soda can in one hand and watching for the rats. He could just imagine how it would be in the basement—

the sub-basement, actually, a level below the dye house. Damp, dark, full of spiders and rotten cloth and ooze from the river—and rats. Maybe even bats, the aviators of the rodent family. *Gah.*

Hall threw the can hard, then smiled thinly to himself as the faint sound of Warwick's voice came down through the overhead ducts, reading Harry Wisconsky the riot act.

Okay, college boy, I'm keeping it in mind.

He stopped smiling abruptly and butted his smoke. A few moments later Wisconsky started to send rough nylon down through the blowers, and Hall went to work. And after a while the rats came out and sat atop the bags at the back of the long room watching him with their unblinking black eyes. They looked like a jury.

———

Eleven P.M., Monday.

There were about thirty-six men sitting around when Warwick came in wearing a pair of old jeans tucked into high rubber boots. Hall had been listening to Harry Wisconsky, who was enormously fat, enormously lazy, and enormously gloomy.

"It's gonna be a mess," Wisconsky was saying when Mr. Foreman came in. "You wait and see, we're all gonna go home blacker'n midnight in Persia."

"Okay!" Warwick said. "We strung sixty lightbulbs down there, so it should be bright enough for you to see what you're doing. You guys"—he pointed to a bunch of

men that had been leaning against the drying spools—
"I want you to hook up the hoses over there to the main
water conduit by the stairwell. You can unroll them
down the stairs. We got about eighty yards for each
man, and that should be plenty. Don't get cute and spray
one of your buddies or you'll send him to the hospital.
They pack a wallop."

"Somebody'll get hurt," Wisconsky prophesied
sourly. "Wait and see."

"You other guys," Warwick said pointing to the
group that Hall and Wisconsky were a part of. "You're
the crap crew tonight. You go in pairs with an electric
wagon for each team. There's old office furniture, bags
of cloth, hunks of busted machinery, you name it. We're
gonna pile it by the airshaft at the west end. Anyone
who doesn't know how to run a wagon?"

No one raised a hand. The electric wagons were
battery-driven contraptions like miniature dump trucks.
They developed a nauseating stink after continual use
that reminded Hall of burning power lines.

"Okay," Warwick said. "We got the basement divided
up into sections, and we'll be done by Thursday. Friday
we'll chain-hoist the crap out. Questions?"

There were none. Hall studied the foreman's face
closely, and he had a sudden premonition of a strange
thing coming. The idea pleased him. He did not like
Warwick very much.

"Fine," Warwick said. "Let's get at it."

———

Two A.M., Tuesday.

Hall was bushed and very tired of listening to Wisconsky's steady patter of profane complaints. He wondered if it would do any good to belt Wisconsky. He doubted it. It would just give Wisconsky something else to bitch about.

Hall had known it would be bad, but this was murder. For one thing, he hadn't anticipated the smell. The polluted stink of the river, mixed with the odor of decaying fabric, rotting masonry, vegetable matter. In the far corner, where they had begun, Hall discovered a colony of huge white toadstools poking their way up through the shattered cement. His hands had come in contact with them as he pulled and yanked at a rusty gear-toothed wheel, and they felt curiously warm and bloated, like the flesh of a man afflicted with dropsy.

The bulbs couldn't banish the twelve-year darkness; it could only push it back a little and cast a sickly yellow glow over the whole mess. The place looked like the shattered nave of a desecrated church, with its high ceiling and mammoth discarded machinery that they would never be able to move, its wet walls overgrown with patches of yellow moss, and the atonal choir that was the water from the hoses, running in the half-clogged sewer network that eventually emptied into the river below the falls.

And the rats—huge ones that made those on third look like dwarfs. God knew what they were eating down here. They were continually overturning boards and bags to reveal huge nests of shredded newspaper, watching with atavistic loathing as the pups fled into the cracks and crannies, their eyes huge and blind with the continuous darkness.

"Let's stop for a smoke," Wisconsky said. He sounded out of breath, but Hall had no idea why; he had been goldbricking all night. Still, it was about that time, and they were currently out of sight of everyone else.

"All right." He leaned against the edge of the electric wagon and lit up.

"I never should've let Warwick talk me into this," Wisconsky said dolefully. "This ain't work for a *man*. But he was mad the other night when he caught me in the crapper up on four with my pants up. Christ, was he mad."

Hall said nothing. He was thinking about Warwick, and about the rats. Strange, how the two things seemed tied together. The rats seemed to have forgotten all about men in their long stay under the mill; they were impudent and hardly afraid at all. One of them had sat up on its hind legs like a squirrel until Hall had gotten in kicking distance, and then it had launched itself at his boot, biting at the leather. Hundreds, maybe thousands. He wondered how many varieties of disease they were carrying around in this black sumphole. And Warwick. Something about him—

"I need the money," Wisconsky said. "But Christ Jesus, buddy, this ain't no work for a *man*. Those rats." He looked around fearfully. "It almost seems like they think. You ever wonder how it'd be, if we was little and they were big—"

"Oh, shut up," Hall said.

Wisconsky looked at him, wounded. "Say, I'm sorry, buddy. It's just that . . ." He trailed off. "Jesus, this place stinks!" he cried. "This ain't no kind of *work for a man!*" A spider crawled off the edge of the wagon and scrambled up his arm. He brushed it off with a choked sound of disgust.

"Come on," Hall said, snuffing his cigarette. "The faster, the quicker."

"I suppose," Wisconsky said miserably. "I suppose."

———

Four A.M., Tuesday.

Lunchtime.

Hall and Wisconsky sat with three or four other men, eating their sandwiches with black hands that not even the industrial detergent could clean. Hall ate looking into the foreman's little glass office. Warwick was drinking coffee and eating cold hamburgers with great relish.

"Ray Upson had to go home," Charlie Brochu said.

"He puke?" someone asked. "I almost did."

"Nuh. Ray'd eat cowflop before he'd puke. Rat bit him."

Hall looked up thoughtfully from his examination of Warwick. "Is that so?" he asked.

"Yeah." Brochu shook his head. "I was teaming with him. Goddamndest thing I ever saw. Jumped out of a hole in one of those old cloth bags. Must have been big as a cat. Grabbed onto his hand and started chewing."

"Jee-*sus*," one of the men said, looking green.

"Yeah," Brochu said. "Ray screamed just like a woman, and I ain't blamin' him. He bled like a pig. Would that thing let go? No sir. I had to belt it three or four times with a board before it would. Ray was just about crazy. He stomped it until it wasn't nothing but a mess of fur. Damndest thing I ever saw. Warwick put a bandage on him and sent him home. Told him to go to the doctor tomorrow."

"That was big of the bastard," somebody said.

As if he had heard, Warwick got to his feet in his office, stretched, and then came to the door. "Time we got back with it."

The men got to their feet slowly, eating up all the time they possibly could stowing their dinner buckets, getting cold drinks, buying candy bars. Then they started down, heels clanking dispiritedly on the steel grillwork of the stair risers.

Warwick passed Hall, clapping him on the shoulder. "How's it going, college boy?" He didn't wait for an answer.

"Come on," Hall said patiently to Wisconsky, who was tying his shoelace. They went downstairs.

———

Seven A.M., Tuesday.

Hall and Wisconsky walked out together; it seemed to Hall that he had somehow inherited the fat Pole.

Wisconsky was almost comically dirty, his fat moon face smeared like that of a small boy who has just been thrashed by the town bully.

There was none of the usual rough banter from the other men, the pulling of shirttails, the cracks about who was keeping Tony's wife warm between the hours of one and four. Nothing but silence and an occasional hawking sound as someone spat on the dirty floor.

"You want a lift?" Wisconsky asked him hesitantly.

"Thanks."

They didn't talk as they rode up Mill Street and crossed the bridge. They exchanged only a brief word when Wisconsky dropped him off in front of his apartment.

Hall went directly to the shower, still thinking about Warwick, trying to place whatever it was about Mr. Foreman that drew him, made him feel that somehow they had become tied together.

He slept as soon as his head hit the pillow, but his sleep was broken and restless: he dreamed of rats.

———

One A.M., Wednesday.

It was better running the hoses.

They couldn't go in until the crap crews had finished a section, and quite often they were done hosing before the next section was clear—which meant time for a cigarette. Hall worked the nozzle of one of the long hoses and Wisconsky pattered back and forth, unsnagging lengths of the hose, turning the water on and off, moving obstructions.

Warwick was short-tempered because the work was proceeding slowly. They would never be done by Thursday, the way things were going.

Now they were working on a helter-skelter jumble of nineteenth-century office equipment that had been piled in one corner—smashed rolltop desks, moldy ledgers, reams of invoices, chairs with broken seats— and it was rat heaven. Scores of them squeaked and ran through the dark and crazy passages that honeycombed the heap, and after two men were bitten, the others refused to work until Warwick sent someone upstairs to get heavy rubberized gloves, the kind usually reserved for the dye-house crew, which had to work with acids.

Hall and Wisconsky were waiting to go in with their hoses when a sandy-haired bullneck named Carmichael began howling curses and backing away, slapping at his chest with his gloved hands.

A huge rat with gray-streaked fur and ugly, glaring eyes had bitten into his shirt and hung there, squeaking and kicking at Carmichael's belly with its back paws. Carmichael finally knocked it away with his fist, but there was a huge hole in his shirt, and a thin line of blood trickled from above one nipple. The anger faded from his face. He turned away and retched.

Hall turned the hose on the rat, which was old and moving slowly, a snatch of Carmichael's shirt still caught in its jaws. The roaring pressure drove it backward against the wall, where it smashed limply.

Warwick came over, an odd, strained smile on his lips. He clapped Hall on the shoulder. "Damn sight better than throwing cans at the little bastards, huh, college boy?"

"Some little bastard," Wisconsky said. "It's a foot long."

"Turn that hose over there." Warwick pointed at the jumble of furniture. "You guys, get out of the way!"

"With pleasure," someone muttered.

Carmichael charged up to Warwick, his face sick and twisted. "I'm gonna have compensation for this! I'm gonna—"

"Sure," Warwick said, smiling. "You got bit on the titty. Get out of the way before you get pasted down by this water."

Hall pointed the nozzle and let it go. It hit with a white explosion of spray, knocking over a desk and smashing two chairs to splinters. Rats ran everywhere, bigger than any Hall had ever seen. He could hear men crying out in disgust and horror as they fled, things with huge eyes and sleek, plump bodies. He caught a glimpse of one that looked as big as a healthy six-week puppy. He kept on until he could see no more, then shut the nozzle down.

"Okay!" Warwick called. "Let's pick it up!"

"I didn't hire out as no exterminator!" Cy Ippeston called mutinously. Hall had tipped a few with him the week before. He was a young guy, wearing a smut-stained baseball cap and a T-shirt.

"That you, Ippeston?" Warwick asked genially.

Ippeston looked uncertain, but stepped forward. "Yeah. I don't want no more of these rats. I hired to clean up, not to maybe get rabies or typhoid or somethin'. Maybe you best count me out."

There was a murmur of agreement from the others. Wisconsky stole a look at Hall, but Hall was examining the nozzle of the hose he was holding. It had a bore like a .45 and could probably knock a man twenty feet.

"You saying you want to punch your clock, Cy?"

"Thinkin' about it," Ippeston said.

Warwick nodded. "Okay. You and anybody else that wants. But this ain't no unionized shop, and never has been. Punch out now and you'll never punch back in. I'll see to it."

"Aren't you some hot ticket," Hall muttered.

Warwick swung around. "Did you say something, college boy?"

Hall regarded him blandly. "Just clearing my throat, Mr. Foreman."

Warwick smiled. "Something taste bad to you?"

Hall said nothing.

"All right, let's pick it up!" Warwick bawled.

They went back to work.

————

Two A.M., Thursday.

Hall and Wisconsky were working with the trucks

again, picking up junk. The pile by the west airshaft had grown to amazing proportions, but they were still not half done.

"Happy Fourth," Wisconsky said when they stopped for a smoke. They were working near the north wall, far from the stairs. The light was extremely dim, and some trick of acoustics made the other men seem miles away.

"Thanks." Hall dragged on his smoke. "Haven't seen many rats tonight."

"Nobody has," Wisconsky said. "Maybe they got wise."

They were standing at the end of a crazy, zigzagging alley formed by piles of old ledgers and invoices, moldy bags of cloth, and two huge flat looms of ancient vintage. "Gah," Wisconsky said, spitting. "That Warwick—"

"Where do you suppose all the rats got to?" Hall asked, almost to himself. "Not into the walls—" He looked at the wet and crumbling masonry that surrounded the huge foundation stones. "They'd drown. The river's saturated everything."

Something black and flapping suddenly dive-bombed them. Wisconsky screamed and put his hands over his head.

"A bat," Hall said, watching after it as Wisconsky straightened up.

"A bat! A bat!" Wisconsky raved. "What's a bat doing in the cellar? They're supposed to be in trees and under eaves and—"

"It was a big one," Hall said softly. "And what's a bat but a rat with wings?"

"Jesus," Wisconsky moaned. "How did it—"

"Get in? Maybe the same way the rats got out."

"What's going on back there?" Warwick shouted from somewhere behind them. "Where are you?"

"Don't sweat it," Hall said softly. His eyes gleamed in the dark.

"Was that you, college boy?" Warwick called. He sounded closer.

"It's okay!" Hall yelled. "I barked my shin!"

Warwick's short, barking laugh. "You want a Purple Heart?"

Wisconsky looked at Hall. "Why'd you say that?"

"Look." Hall knelt and lit a match. There was a square in the middle of the wet and crumbling cement. "Tap it."

Wisconsky did. "It's wood."

Hall nodded. "It's the top of a support. I've seen some other ones around here. There's another level under this part of the basement."

"God," Wisconsky said with utter revulsion.

————

Three-thirty A.M., Thursday.

They were in the northeast corner, Ippeston and Brochu behind them with one of the high-pressure hoses, when Hall stopped and pointed at the floor. "There I thought we'd come across it."

There was a wooden trapdoor with a crusted iron ringbolt set near the center.

He walked back to Ippeston and said, "Shut it off for a minute." When the hose was choked to a trickle, he raised his voice to a shout. "Hey! Hey, Warwick! Better come here a minute!"

Warwick came splashing over, looking at Hall with that same hard smile in his eyes. "Your shoelace come untied, college boy?"

"Look," Hall said. He kicked the trapdoor with his foot. "Sub-cellar."

"So what?" Warwick asked. "This isn't break time, col—"

"That's where your rats are," Hall said. "They're breeding down there. Wisconsky and I even saw a bat earlier."

Some of the other men had gathered around and were looking at the trapdoor.

"I don't care," Warwick said. "The job was the basement not—"

"You'll need about twenty exterminators, trained ones," Hall was saying. "Going to cost the management a pretty penny. Too bad."

Someone laughed. "Fat chance."

Warwick looked at Hall as if he were a bug under glass. "You're really a case, you are," he said, sounding fascinated. "Do you think I give a good goddamn how many rats there are under there?"

"I was at the library this afternoon and yesterday," Hall said. "Good thing you kept reminding me I was a college boy. I read the town zoning ordinances,

Warwick—they were set up in 1911, before this mill got big enough to co-opt the zoning board. Know what I found?"

Warwick's eyes were cold. "Take a walk, college boy. You're fired."

"I found out," Hall plowed on as if he hadn't heard, "I found out that there is a zoning law in Gates Falls about vermin. You spell that v-e-r-m-i-n, in case you wondered. It means disease-carrying animals such as bats, skunks, unlicensed dogs—and rats. Especially rats. Rats are mentioned fourteen times in two paragraphs, Mr. Foreman. So you just keep in mind that the minute I punch out I'm going straight to the town commissioner and tell him what the situation down here is."

He paused, relishing Warwick's hate-congested face. "I think that between me, him, and the town committee, we can get an injunction slapped on this place. You're going to be shut down a lot longer than just Saturday, Mr. Foreman. And I got a good idea what *your* boss is going to say when he turns up. Hope your unemployment insurance is paid up, Warwick."

Warwick's hands formed into claws. "You damned snotnose, I ought to—" He looked down at the trapdoor, and suddenly his smile reappeared. "Consider yourself rehired, college boy."

"I thought you might see the light."

Warwick nodded, the same strange grin on his face. "You're just so smart. I think maybe you ought to go down there, Hall, so we got somebody with a college education to give us an informed opinion. You and Wisconsky."

"Not me!" Wisconsky exclaimed. "Not me, I—"

Warwick looked at him. "You what?"

Wisconsky shut up.

"Good," Hall said cheerfully. "We'll need three flashlights. I think I saw a whole rack of those six-battery jobs in the main office, didn't I?"

"You want to take somebody else?" Warwick asked expansively. "Sure, pick your man."

"You," Hall said gently. The strange expression had come into his face again. "After all, the management should be represented, don't you think? Just so Wisconsky and I don't see *too* many rats down there?"

Someone (it sounded like Ippeston) laughed loudly.

Warwick looked at the men carefully. They studied the tips of their shoes. Finally he pointed at Brochu. "Brochu, go up to the office and get three flashlights. Tell the watchman I said to let you in."

"Why'd you get me into this?" Wisconsky moaned to Hall. "You know I hate those—"

"It wasn't me," Hall said, and looked at Warwick.

Warwick looked back at him, and neither would drop his eyes.

————

Four A.M., Thursday.

Brochu returned with the flashlights. He gave one to Hall, one to Wisconsky, one to Warwick.

"Ippeston! Give the hose to Wisconsky." Ippeston did so. The nozzle trembled delicately between the Pole's hands.

"All right," Warwick said to Wisconsky. "You're in the middle. If there are rats, you let them have it."

Sure, Hall thought. And if there are rats, Warwick won't see them. And neither will Wisconsky, after he finds an extra ten in his pay envelope.

Warwick pointed at two of the men. "Lift it."

One of them bent over the ringbolt and pulled. For a moment Hall didn't think it was going to give, and then it yanked free with an odd, crunching snap. The other man put his fingers on the underside to help pull, then withdrew with a cry. His hands were crawling with huge and sightless beetles.

With a convulsive grunt the man on the ringbolt pulled the trap back and let it drop. The underside was black with an odd fungus that Hall had never seen before. The beetles dropped off into the darkness below or ran across the floor to be crushed.

"Look," Hall said.

There was a rusty lock bolted on the underside, now broken. "But it shouldn't be underneath," Warwick said. "It should be on top. Why—"

"Lots of reasons," Hall said. "Maybe so nothing on this side could open it—at least when the lock was new. Maybe so nothing on that side could get up."

"But who locked it?" Wisconsky asked.

"Ah," Hall said mockingly, looking at Warwick. "A mystery."

"Listen," Brochu whispered.

"Oh, God," Wisconsky sobbed. "I ain't going down there!"

It was a soft sound, almost expectant; the whisk and patter of thousands of paws, the squeaking of rats.

"Could be frogs," Warwick said.

Hall laughed aloud.

Warwick shone his light down. A sagging flight of wooden stairs led down to the black stones of the floor beneath. There was not a rat in sight.

"Those stairs won't hold us," Warwick said with finality.

Brochu took two steps forward and jumped up and down on the first step. It creaked but showed no sign of giving way.

"I didn't ask you to do that," Warwick said.

"You weren't there when that rat bit Ray," Brochu said softly.

"Let's go," Hall said.

Warwick took a last sardonic look around at the circle of men, then walked to the edge with Hall. Wisconsky stepped reluctantly between them. They went down one at a time. Hall, then Wisconsky, then Warwick. Their flashlight beams played over the floor, which was twisted and heaved into a hundred crazy hills and valleys. The hose thumped along behind Wisconsky like a clumsy serpent.

When they got to the bottom, Warwick flashed his light around. It picked out a few rotting boxes, some barrels, little else. The seep from the river stood in puddles that came to ankle depth on their boots.

"I don't hear them anymore," Wisconsky whispered.

They walked slowly away from the trapdoor, their feet shuffling through the slime. Hall paused and shone his light on a huge wooden box with white letters on it. "Elias Varney," he read, "1841. Was the mill here then?"

"No," Warwick said. "It wasn't built until 1897. What difference?"

Hall didn't answer. They walked forward again. The sub-cellar was longer than it should have been, it seemed. The stench was stronger, a smell of decay and rot and things buried. And still the only sound was the faint, cavelike drip of water.

"What's that?" Hall asked, pointing his beam at a jut of concrete that protruded perhaps two feet into the cellar. Beyond it, the darkness continued and it seemed to Hall that he could now hear sounds up there, curiously stealthy.

Warwick peered at it. "It's . . . no, that can't be right."

"Outer wall of the mill, isn't it? And up ahead . . ."

"I'm going back," Warwick said, suddenly turning around.

Hall grabbed his neck roughly. "You're not going anywhere, Mr. Foreman."

Warwick looked up at him, his grin cutting the darkness. "You're crazy, college boy. Isn't that right? Crazy as a loon."

"You shouldn't push people, friend. Keep going."

Wisconsky moaned. "Hall—"

"Give me that." Hall grabbed the hose. He let go of Warwick's neck and pointed the hose at his head. Wisconsky turned abruptly and crashed back toward the trapdoor. Hall did not even turn. "After you, Mr. Foreman."

Warwick stepped forward, walking under the place where the mill ended above them. Hall flashed his light about, and felt a cold satisfaction—premonition fulfilled. The rats had closed in around them, silent as death. Crowded in, rank on rank. Thousands of eyes looked greedily back at him. In ranks to the wall, some fully as high as a man's shin.

Warwick saw them a moment later and came to a full stop. "They're all around us, college boy." His voice was still calm, still in control, but it held a jagged edge.

"Yes," Hall said. "Keep going."

They walked forward, the hose dragging behind. Hall looked back once and saw the rats had closed the aisle behind them and were gnawing at the heavy canvas hosing. One looked up and almost seemed to grin at him before lowering his head again. He could see the bats now, too. They were roosting from the roughhewn overheads, huge, the size of crows or rooks.

"Look," Warwick said, centering his beam about five feet ahead.

A skull, green with mold, laughed up at them. Further on Hall could see an ulna, one pelvic wing, part of a ribcage. "Keep going," Hall said. He felt something bursting up inside him, something lunatic and dark with colors. *You are going to break before I do, Mr. Foreman, so help me God.*

They walked past the bones. The rats were not crowding them; their distances appeared constant. Up ahead Hall saw one cross their path of travel. Shadows hid it, but he caught sight of a pink twitching tail as thick as a telephone cord.

Up ahead the flooring rose sharply, then dipped. Hall could hear a stealthy rustling sound, a big sound. Something that perhaps no living man had ever seen. It occurred to Hall that he had perhaps been looking for something like this through all his days of crazy wandering.

The rats were moving in, creeping on their bellies, forcing them forward. "Look," Warwick said coldly.

Hall saw. Something had happened to the rats back here, some hideous mutation that never could have survived under the eye of the sun; nature would have forbidden it. But down here, nature had taken on another ghastly face.

The rats were gigantic, some as high as three feet. But their rear legs were gone and they were blind as moles, like their flying cousins. They dragged themselves forward with hideous eagerness.

Warwick turned and faced Hall, the smile hanging on by brute willpower. Hall really had to admire him. "We can't go on, Hall. You must see that."

"The rats have business with you, I think," Hall said.

Warwick's control slipped. "Please," he said. "Please."

Hall smiled. "Keep going."

Warwick was looking over his shoulder. "They're gnawing into the hose. When they get through it, we'll never get back."

"I know. Keep going."

"You're insane—" A rat ran across Warwick's shoe and he screamed. Hall smiled and gestured with his light. They were all around, the closest of them less than a foot away now.

Warwick began to walk again. The rats drew back.

They topped the miniature rise and looked down. Warwick reached it first, and Hall saw his face go white as paper. Spit ran down his chin. "Oh, my God. Dear Jesus."

And he turned to run.

Hall opened the nozzle of the hose and the high-pressure rush of water struck Warwick squarely on the chest, knocking him back out of sight. There was a long scream that rose over the sound of the water. Thrashing sounds.

"Hall!" Grunts. A huge, tenebrous squeaking that seemed to fill the earth.

"HALL, FOR GOD'S SAKE—"

A sudden wet ripping noise. Another scream, weaker. Something huge shifted and turned. Quite distinctly Hall heard the wet snap that a fractured bone makes.

A legless rat, guided by some bastard form of sonar, lunged against him, biting. Its body was flabby, warm.

Almost absently Hall turned the hose on it, knocking it away. The hose did not have quite so much pressure now.

Hall walked to the brow of the wet hill and looked down.

The rat filled the whole gully at the far end of that noxious tomb. It was a huge and pulsating gray, eyeless, totally without legs. When Hall's light struck it, it made a hideous mewling noise. Their queen, then, the *magna mater*. A huge and nameless thing whose progeny might someday develop wings. It seemed to dwarf what remained of Warwick, but that was probably just illusion. It was the shock of seeing a rat as big as a Holstein calf.

"Goodbye, Warwick," Hall said. The rat crouched over Mr. Foreman jealously, ripping at one limp arm.

Hall turned away and began to make his way back rapidly, halting the rats with his hose, which was growing less and less potent. Some of them got through and attacked his legs above the tops of his boots with biting lunges. One hung stubbornly on at his thigh, ripping at the cloth of his corduroy pants. Hall made a fist and smashed it aside.

He was nearly three-quarters of the way back when the huge whirring filled the darkness. He looked up and the gigantic flying form smashed into his face.

The mutated bats had not lost their tails yet. It whipped around Hall's neck in a loathsome coil and squeezed as the teeth sought the soft spot under his neck. It wriggled and flapped with its membranous wings, clutching the tatters of his shirt for purchase.

Hall brought the nozzle of the hose up blindly and struck at its yielding body again and again. It fell away and he trampled it beneath his feet, dimly aware that he was screaming. The rats ran in a flood over his feet, up his legs.

He broke into a staggering run, shaking some off. The others bit at his belly, his chest. One ran up his shoulder and pressed its questing muzzle into the cup of his ear.

He ran into the second bat. It roosted on his head for a moment, squealing, and then ripped away a flap of Hall's scalp.

He felt his body growing numb. His ears filled with the screech and yammer of many rats. He gave one last heave, stumbled over furry bodies, fell to his knees. He began to laugh, a high, screaming sound.

———

Five A.M., Thursday.

"Somebody better go down there," Brochu said tentatively.

"Not me," Wisconsky whispered. "Not me."

"No, not you, jelly belly," Ippeston said with contempt.

"*Well, let's go,*" Brogan said, bringing up another hose. "Me, Ippeston, Dangerfield, Nedeau. Stevenson, go up to the office and get a few more lights."

Ippeston looked down into the darkness thought-fully. "Maybe they stopped for a smoke," he said. "A few rats, what the hell."

Stevenson came back with the lights; a few moments later they started down.

NIGHT SURF

After the guy was dead and the smell of his burning flesh was off the air, we all went back down to the beach. Corey had his radio, one of those suitcase-sized transistor jobs that take about forty batteries and also make and play tapes. You couldn't say the sound reproduction was great, but it sure was loud. Corey had been well-to-do before A6, but stuff like that didn't matter anymore. Even his big radio/tape-player was hardly more than a nice-looking hunk of junk. There were only two radio stations left on the air that we could get. One was WKDM in Portsmouth—some backwoods deejay who had gone nutty-religious. He'd play a Perry Como record, say a prayer, bawl, play a Johnny Ray record, read from Psalms (complete with each "selah," just like James Dean in *East of Eden*), then bawl some more. Happy-time stuff like that. One day he sang "Bringing in the Sheaves" in a cracked, moldy voice that sent Needles and me into hysterics.

The Massachusetts station was better, but we could only get it at night. It was a bunch of kids. I guess they took over the transmitting facilities of WRKO or WBZ after everybody left or died. They only gave gag call letters, like WDOPE or KUNT or WA6 or stuff like that. Really funny, you know—you could die laughing. That was the one we were listening to on the way back to the beach. I was holding hands with Susie; Kelly and Joan were ahead of us, and Needles was already over the brow of the Point and out of sight. Corey was bringing up the rear, swinging his radio. The Stones were singing "Angie."

"Do you *love* me?" Susie was asking. "That's all I want to know, do you *love* me?" Susie needed constant reassurance. I was her teddy bear.

"No," I said. She was getting fat, and if she lived long enough, which wasn't likely, she would get really flabby. She was already mouthy.

"You're rotten," she said, and put a hand to her face. Her lacquered fingernails twinkled dimly with the half-moon that had risen about an hour ago.

"Are you going to cry again?"

"Shut up!" She sounded like she was going to cry again, all right.

We came over the ridge and I paused. I always have to pause. Before A6, this had been a public beach. Tourists, picnickers, runny-nosed kids and fat baggy grandmothers with sunburned elbows. Candy wrappers and popsicle sticks in the sand, all the beautiful people necking on their beach blankets, intermingled stench of exhaust from the parking lot, seaweed, and Coppertone oil.

But now all the dirt and all the crap was gone. The ocean had eaten it, all of it, as casually as you might eat a handful of Cracker Jacks. There were no people to come back and dirty it again. Just us, and we weren't enough to make much mess. We loved the beach too, I guess—hadn't we just offered it a kind of sacrifice? Even Susie, little bitch Susie with her fat ass and her cranberry bellbottoms.

The sand was white and duned, marked only by the high-tide line—twisted skein of seaweed, kelp, hunks of driftwood. The moonlight stitched inky crescent-shaped shadows and folds across everything. The deserted lifeguard tower stood white and skeletal some fifty yards from the bathhouse, pointing toward the sky like a finger bone.

And the surf, the night surf, throwing up great bursts of foam, breaking against the headlands for as far as we could see in endless attacks. Maybe that water had been halfway to England the night before.

" 'Angie,' by the Stones," the cracked voice on Corey's radio said. "I'm sureya dug that one, a blast from the past that's a golden gas, straight from the grooveyard, a platta that mattas. I'm Bobby. This was supposed to be Fred's night, but Fred got the flu. He's all swelled up." Susie giggled then, with the first tears still on her eyelashes. I started toward the beach a little faster to keep her quiet.

"Wait up!" Corey called. "Bernie? Hey, Bernie, wait up!"

The guy on the radio was reading some dirty limericks, and a girl in the background asked him where did he put the beer. He said something back, but by that time we were on the beach. I looked back to see how Corey was doing. He was coming down on his backside, as usual, and he looked so ludicrous I felt a little sorry for him.

"Run with me," I said to Susie.

"Why?"

I slapped her on the can and she squealed. "Just because it feels good to run."

We ran. She fell behind, panting like a horse and calling for me to slow down, but I put her out of my head. The wind rushed past my ears and blew the hair off my forehead. I could smell the salt in the air, sharp and tart. The surf pounded. The waves were like foamed black glass. I kicked off my rubber sandals and pounded across the sand barefoot, not minding the sharp digs of an occasional shell. My blood roared.

And then there was the lean-to with Needles already inside and Kelly and Joan standing beside it, holding hands and looking at the water. I did a forward roll, feeling sand go down the back of my shirt, and fetched up against Kelly's legs. He fell on top of me and rubbed my face in the sand while Joan laughed.

We got up and grinned at each other. Susie had given up running and was plodding toward us. Corey had almost caught up to her.

"Some fire," Kelly said.

"Do you think he came all the way from New York, like he said?" Joan asked.

"I don't know." I couldn't see that it mattered anyway. He had been behind the wheel of a big Lincoln when we found him, semi-conscious and raving. His head was bloated to the size of a football and his neck looked like a sausage. He had Captain Trips and not far to go, either. So we took him up to the Point that overlooks the beach and burned him. He said his name was Alvin Sackheim. He kept calling for his grandmother. He thought Susie was his grandmother. This struck her funny, God knows why. The strangest things strike Susie funny.

It was Corey's idea to burn him up, but it started off as a joke. He had read all those books about witchcraft and black magic at college, and he kept leering at us in the dark beside Alvin Sackheim's Lincoln and telling us that if we made a sacrifice to the dark gods, maybe the spirits would keep protecting us against A6.

Of course none of us really believed that bullshit, but the talk got more and more serious. It was a new thing to do, and finally we went ahead and did it. We tied him to the observation gadget up there—you put a dime in it and on a clear day you can see all the way to Portland Headlight. We tied him with our belts, and then we went rooting around for dry brush and hunks of driftwood like kids playing a new kind of hide-and-seek. All the time we were doing it Alvin Sackheim just sort of leaned there and mumbled to his grandmother. Susie's eyes got very bright and she was breathing fast. It was really turning her on. When we were down in the ravine on the other side of the outcrop she leaned against me and kissed me. She was wearing too much lipstick and it was like kissing a greasy plate.

I pushed her away and that was when she started pouting.

We went back up, all of us, and piled dead branches and twigs up to Alvin Sackheim's waist. Needles lit the pyre with his Zippo, and it went up fast. At the end, just before his hair caught on fire, the guy began to scream. There was a smell just like sweet Chinese pork.

"Got a cigarette, Bernie?" Needles asked.

"There's about fifty cartons right behind you."

He grinned and slapped a mosquito that was probing his arm. "Don't want to move."

I gave him a smoke and sat down. Susie and I met Needles in Portland. He was sitting on the curb in front of the State Theater, playing Leadbelly tunes on a big old Gibson guitar he had looted someplace. The sound had echoed up and down Congress Street as if he were playing in a concert hall.

Susie stopped in front of us, still out of breath. "You're rotten, Bernie."

"Come on, Sue. Turn the record over. That side stinks."

"Bastard. Stupid, unfeeling son of a bitch. *Creep!*"

"Go away," I said, "or I'll black your eye, Susie. See if I don't."

She started to cry again. She was really good at it. Corey came up and tried to put an arm around her. She elbowed him in the crotch and he spit in her face.

"I'll *kill* you!" She came at him, screaming and weeping, making propellers with her hands. Corey backed off, almost fell, then turned tail and ran. Susie followed him, hurling hysterical obscenities. Needles put back his head and laughed. The sound of Corey's radio came back to us faintly over the surf.

Kelly and Joan had wandered off. I could see them down by the edge of the water, walking with their arms around each other's waist. They looked like an ad in a travel agent's window—*Fly to Beautiful St. Lorca.* It was all right. They had a good thing.

"Bernie?"

"What?" I sat and smoked and thought about Needles flipping back the top of his Zippo, spinning the wheel, making fire with flint and steel like a caveman.

"I've got it," Needles said.

"Yeah?" I looked at him. "Are you sure?"

"Sure I am. My head aches. My stomach aches. Hurts to piss."

"Maybe it's just Hong Kong flu. Susie had Hong Kong flu. She wanted a Bible." I laughed. That had been while we were still at the University, about a week before they closed it down for good, a month before they started carrying bodies away in dump trucks and burying them in mass graves with payloaders.

"Look." He lit a match and held it under the angle of

his jaw. I could see the first triangular smudges, the first swelling. It was A6, all right.

"Okay," I said.

"I don't feel so bad," he said. "In my mind, I mean. You, though. You think about it a lot. I can tell."

"No I don't." A lie.

"Sure you do. Like that guy tonight. You're thinking about that, too. We probably did him a favor, when you get right down to it. I don't think he even knew it was happening."

"He knew."

He shrugged and turned on his side. "It doesn't matter.

We smoked and I watched the surf come in and go out. Needles had Captain Trips. That made everything real all over again. It was late August already, and in a couple of weeks the first chill of fall would be creeping in. Time to move inside someplace. Winter. Dead by Christmas, maybe, all of us. In somebody's front room with Corey's expensive radio/tape-player on top of a bookcase full of Reader's Digest Condensed Books and the weak winter sun lying on the rug in meaningless windowpane patterns.

The vision was clear enough to make me shudder. Nobody should think about winter in August. It's like a goose walking over your grave.

Needles laughed. "See? You *do* think about it."

What could I say? I stood up. "Going to look for Susie."

"Maybe we're the last people on earth, Bernie. Did you ever think of that?" In the faint moonlight he already looked half dead, with circles under his eyes and pallid, unmoving fingers like pencils.

I walked down to the water and looked out across it. There was nothing to see but the restless, moving humps of the waves, topped by delicate curls of foam. The thunder of the breakers was tremendous down here, bigger than the world. Like standing inside a thunderstorm. I closed my eyes and rocked on my bare feet. The sand was cold and damp and packed. And if we were the last people on earth, so what? This would go on as long as there was a moon to pull the water.

Susie and Corey were up the beach. Susie was riding him as if he were a bucking bronc, pounding his head into the running boil of the water. Corey was flailing and splashing. They were both soaked. I walked down and pushed her off with my foot. Corey splashed away on all fours, spluttering and whoofing.

"I *hate you!*" Susie screamed at me. Her mouth was a dark grinning crescent. It looked like the entrance to a fun house. When I was a kid my mother used to take us kids to Harrison State Park and there was a fun house with a big clown face on the front, and you walked in through the mouth.

"Come on, Susie. Up, Fido." I held out my hand. She took it doubtfully and stood up. There was damp sand clotted on her blouse and skin.

"You didn't have to push me, Bernie. You don't ever—"

"Come on." She wasn't like a jukebox; you never had to put in a dime and she never came unplugged.

We walked up the beach toward the main concession. The man who ran the place had had a small overhead apartment. There was a bed. She didn't really deserve a bed, but Needles was right about that. It didn't matter. No one was really scoring the game anymore.

The stairs went up the side of the building, but I paused for just a minute to look in the broken window at the dusty wares inside that no one had cared enough about to loot—stacks of sweatshirts ("Anson Beach" and a picture of sky and waves printed on the front), glittering bracelets that would green the wrist on the second day, bright junk earrings, beachballs, dirty greeting cards, badly painted ceramic madonnas, plastic vomit (*So realistic! Try it on your wife!*), Fourth of July sparklers for a Fourth that never was, beach towels with a voluptuous girl in a bikini standing amid the names of a hundred famous resort areas, pennants (*Souvenir of Anson Beach and Park*), balloons, bathing suits. There was a snack bar up front with a big sign saying TRY OUR CLAM CAKE SPECIAL.

I used to come to Anson Beach a lot when I was still in high school. That was seven years before A6, and I was going with a girl named Maureen. She was a big girl. She had a pink checked bathing suit. I used to tell her it looked like a tablecloth. We had walked along the boardwalk in front of this place, barefoot, the boards hot and sandy beneath our heels. We had never tried the clam cake special.

"What are you looking at?"

"Nothing. Come on."

———

I had sweaty, ugly dreams about Alvin Sackheim. He was propped behind the wheel of his shiny yellow Lincoln, talking about his grandmother. He was nothing but a bloated, blackened head and a charred skeleton. He smelled burnt. He talked on and on, and after a while I couldn't make out a single word. I woke up breathing hard.

Susie was sprawled across my thighs, pale and bloated. My watch said 3:50, but it had stopped. It was still dark out. The surf pounded and smashed. High tide. Make it 4:15. Light soon. I got out of bed and went to the doorway. The sea breeze felt fine against my hot body. In spite of it all I didn't want to die.

I went over in the corner and grabbed a beer. There were three or four cases of Bud stacked against the wall. It was warm, because there was no electricity. I don't mind warm beer like some people do, though. It just foams a little more. Beer is beer. I went back out on the landing and sat down and pulled the ring tab and drank up.

So here we were, with the whole human race wiped out, not by atomic weapons or bio-warfare or pollution or anything *grand* like that. *Just the flu.* I'd like to put down a huge plaque somewhere, in the Bonneville Salt Flats, maybe. Bronze Square. Three miles on a side.

And in big raised letters it would say, for the benefit of any landing aliens: JUST THE FLU.

I tossed the beer can over the side. It landed with a hollow clank on the cement walk that went around the building. The lean-to was a dark triangle on the sand. I wondered if Needles was awake. I wondered if I would be.

"Bernie?"

She was standing in the doorway wearing one of my shirts. I hate that. She sweats like a pig.

"You don't like me much anymore, do you, Bernie?"

I didn't say anything. There were times when I could still feel sorry for everything. She didn't deserve me any more than I deserved her.

"Can I sit down with you?"

"I doubt if it would be wide enough for both of us."

She made a choked hiccupping noise and started to go back inside.

"Needles has got A6," I said.

She stopped and looked at me. Her face was very still. "Don't joke, Bernie."

I lit a cigarette.

"He can't! He had—"

"Yes, he had A2. Hong Kong flu. Just like you and me and Corey and Kelly and Joan."

"But that would mean he isn't—"

"Immune."

"Yes. Then we could get it."

"Maybe he lied when he said he had A2. So we'd take him along with us that time," I said.

Relief spilled across her face. "Sure, that's it. I would have lied if it had been me. Nobody likes to be alone, do they?" She hesitated. "Coming back to bed?"

"Not just now."

She went inside. I didn't have to tell her that A2 was no guarantee against A6. She knew that. She had just blocked it out. I sat and watched the surf. It was really up. Years ago, Anson had been the only halfway decent surfing spot in the state. The Point was a dark, jutting hump against the sky. I thought I could see the upright that was the observation post, but it probably was just imagination. Sometimes Kelly took Joan up to the Point. I didn't think they were up there tonight.

I put my face in my hands and clutched it, feeling the skin, its grain and texture. It was all narrowing so swiftly, and it was all so mean—there was no dignity in it.

The surf coming in, coming in, coming in. Limitless. Clean and deep. We had come here in the summer, Maureen and I, the summer after high school, the summer before college and reality and A6 coming out of Southeast Asia and covering the world like a pall, July, we had eaten pizza and listened to her radio, I had put oil on her back, she had put oil on mine, the air had been hot, the sand bright, the sun like a burning glass.

I AM THE DOORWAY

Richard and I sat on my porch, looking out over the dunes to the Gulf. The smoke from his cigar drifted mellowly in the air, keeping the mosquitoes at a safe distance. The water was a cool aqua, the sky a deeper, truer blue. It was a pleasant combination.

"You are the doorway," Richard repeated thoughtfully. "You are sure you killed the boy—you didn't just dream it?"

"I didn't dream it. And I didn't kill him, either—I told you that. They did. I am the doorway."

Richard sighed. "You buried him?"

"Yes."

"You remember where?"

"Yes." I reached into my breast pocket and got a cigarette. My hands were awkward with their covering of bandages. They itched abominably. "If you want to see it, you'll have to get the dune buggy. You can't roll this"—I indicated my wheelchair—"through the sand."

Richard's dune buggy was a 1959 VW with pillow-sized

tires. He collected driftwood in it. Ever since he retired from the real estate business in Maryland he had been living on Key Caroline and building driftwood sculptures which he sold to the winter tourists at shameless prices.

He puffed his cigar and looked out at the Gulf. "Not yet. Will you tell me once more?"

I sighed and tried to light my cigarette. He took the matches away from me and did it himself. I puffed twice, dragging deep. The itch in my fingers was maddening.

"All right," I said. "Last night at seven I was out here, looking at the Gulf and smoking, just like now, and—"

"Go further back," he invited.

"Further?"

"Tell me about the flight."

I shook my head. "Richard, we've been through it and through it. There's nothing—"

The seamed and fissured face was as enigmatic as one of his own driftwood sculptures. "You may remember," he said. "Now you may remember."

"Do you think so?"

"Possibly. And when you're through, we can look for the grave."

"The grave," I said. It had a hollow, horrible ring, darker than anything, darker even than all that terrible ocean Cory and I had sailed through five years ago. Dark, dark, dark.

Beneath the bandages, my new eyes stared blindly

into the darkness the bandages forced on them. They itched.

———

Cory and I were boosted into orbit by the Saturn 16, the one all the commentators called the Empire State Building booster. It was a big beast, all right. It made the old Saturn 1-B look like a Redstone, and it took off from a bunker two hundred feet deep—it had to, to keep from taking half of Cape Kennedy with it.

We swung around the Earth, verifying all our systems, and then did our inject. Headed out for Venus. We left a Senate fighting over an appropriations bill for further deep-space exploration, and a bunch of NASA people praying that we would find something, anything.

"It don't matter what," Don Lovinger, Project Zeus' private whiz kid, was very fond of saying when he'd had a few. "You got all the gadgets, plus five souped-up TV cameras and a nifty little telescope with a zillion lenses and filters. Find some gold or platinum. Better yet, find some nice, dumb little blue men for us to study and exploit and feel superior to. Anything. Even the ghost of Howdy Doody would be a start."

Cory and I were anxious enough to oblige, if we could. Nothing had worked for the deep-space program. From Borman, Anders, and Lovell, who orbited the moon in '68 and found an empty, forbidding world that looked like dirty beach sand, to Markhan and Jacks, who touched down on Mars eleven years later to find an arid wasteland of frozen sand and a few struggling lichens, the deep-space program had been an expensive bust. And there had been casualties—Pedersen and Lederer, eternally circling the sun when all at once nothing worked on the second-to-last Apollo flight. John Davis, whose little orbiting observatory was holed by a meteoroid in a one-in-a-thousand fluke. No, the space program was hardly swinging along. The way things looked, the Venus orbit might be our last chance to say we told you so.

It was sixteen days out—we ate a lot of concentrates, played a lot of gin, and swapped a cold back and forth—and from the tech side it was a milk run. We lost an air-moisture converter on the third day out, went to backup, and that was all, except for nits and nats, until re-entry. We watched Venus grow from a star to a quarter to a milky crystal ball, swapped jokes with Huntsville Control, listened to tapes of Wagner and the Beatles, tended to automated experiments which had to do with everything from measurements of the solar wind to deep-space navigation. We did two midcourse corrections, both of them infinitesimal, and nine days into the flight Cory went outside and banged on the retractable DESA until it decided to operate. There was nothing else out of the ordinary until . . .

"DESA," Richard said. "What's that?"

"An experiment that didn't pan out. NASA-ese for Deep Space Antenna—we were broadcasting pi in high-frequency pulses for anyone who cared to listen." I rubbed my fingers against my pants, but it was no good; if anything, it made it worse. "Same idea as that radio telescope in West Virginia—you know, the one that listens to the stars. Only instead of listening, we were transmitting, primarily to the deeper space planets— Jupiter, Saturn, Uranus. If there's any intelligent life out there, it was taking a nap."

"Only Cory went out?"

"Yes. And if he brought in any interstellar plague, the telemetry didn't show it."

"Still—"

"It doesn't matter," I said crossly. "Only the here and now matters. They killed the boy last night, Richard. It wasn't a nice thing to watch—or feel. His head . . . it exploded. As if someone had scooped out his brains and put a hand grenade in his skull."

"Finish the story," he said.

I laughed hollowly. "What's to tell?"

We went into an eccentric orbit around the planet. It was radical and deteriorating, three twenty by seventy-six miles. That was on the first swing. The second swing our apogee was even higher, the perigee lower. We had a max of four orbits. We made all four. We got a good look at the planet. Also over six hundred stills and God knows how many feet of film.

The cloud cover is equal parts methane, ammonia, dust, and flying shit. The whole planet looks like the

Grand Canyon in a wind tunnel. Cory estimated wind-speed at about 600 mph near the surface. Our probe beeped all the way down and then went out with a squawk. We saw no vegetation and no sign of life. Spectroscope indicated only traces of the valuable minerals. And that was Venus. Nothing but nothing—except it scared me. It was like circling a haunted house in the middle of deep space. I know how unscientific that sounds, but I was scared gutless until we got out of there. I think if our rockets hadn't gone off, I would have cut my throat on the way down. It's not like the moon. The moon is desolate but somehow antiseptic. That world we saw was utterly unlike anything that anyone has ever seen. Maybe it's a good thing that cloud cover is there. It was like a skull that's been picked clean—that's the closest I can get.

On the way back we heard the Senate had voted to halve space-exploration funds. Cory said something like "looks like we're back in the weather-satellite business, Artie." But I was almost glad. Maybe we don't belong out there.

Twelve days later Cory was dead and I was crippled for life. We bought all our trouble on the way down. The chute was fouled. How's that for life's little ironies? We'd been in space for over a month, gone further than any humans had ever gone, and it all ended the way it did because some guy was in a hurry for his coffee break and let a few lines get fouled.

We came down hard. A guy that was in one of the copters said it looked like a gigantic baby falling out of the sky, with the placenta trailing after it. I lost consciousness when we hit.

I came to when they were taking me across the deck of the *Portland*. They hadn't even had a chance to roll up the red carpet we were supposed to've walked on. I was bleeding. Bleeding and being hustled up to the infirmary over a red carpet that didn't look anywhere near as red as I did . . .

———

". . . I was in Bethesda for two years. They gave me the Medal of Honor and a lot of money and this wheelchair. I came down here the next year. I like to watch the rockets take off."

"I know," Richard said. He paused. "Show me your hands."

"No." It came out very quickly and sharply. "I can't let them see. I've told you that."

"It's been five years," Richard said. "Why now, Arthur? Can you tell me that?"

"I don't know. I don't know! Maybe whatever it is has a long gestation period. Or who's to say I even got it out there? Whatever it was might have entered me in Fort Lauderdale. Or right here on this porch, for all I know."

Richard sighed and looked out over the water, now reddish with the late-evening sun. "I'm trying. Arthur, I don't want to think that you are losing your mind."

"If I have to, I'll show you my hands," I said. It cost me an effort to say it. "But only if I have to."

Richard stood up and found his cane. He looked old and frail. "I'll get the dune buggy. We'll look for the boy."

"Thank you, Richard."

He walked out toward the rutted dirt track that led to his cabin—I could just see the roof of it over the Big Dune, the one that runs almost the whole length of Key Caroline. Over the water toward the Cape, the sky had gone an ugly plum color, and the sound of thunder came faintly to my ears.

———

I didn't know the boy's name but I saw him every now and again, walking along the beach at sunset, with his sieve under his arm. He was tanned almost black by the sun, and all he was ever clad in was a frayed pair of denim cutoffs. On the far side of Key Caroline there is a public beach, and an enterprising young man can make perhaps as much as five dollars on a good day, patiently sieving the sand for buried quarters or dimes. Every now and then I would wave to him and he would wave back, both of us noncommittal, strangers yet brothers, year-round dwellers set against a sea of money spending, Cadillac-driving, loud-mouthed tourists. I imagine he lived in the small village clustered around the post office about a half mile further down.

When he passed by that evening I had already been on the porch for an hour, immobile, watching. I had taken off the bandages earlier. The itching had been intolerable, and it was always better when they could look through their eyes.

It was a feeling like no other in the world—as if I were a portal just slightly ajar through which they were peeking at a world which they hated and feared. But the worst part was that I could see, too, in a way. Imagine your mind transported into a body of a housefly, a housefly looking into your own face with a thousand eyes. Then perhaps you can begin to see why I kept my hands bandaged even when there was no one around to see them.

It began in Miami. I had business there with a man named Cresswell, an investigator from the Navy Department. He checks up on me once a year—for a while I was as close as anyone ever gets to the classified stuff our space program has. I don't know just what it is he looks for; a shifty gleam in the eye, maybe, or maybe a scarlet letter on my forehead. God knows why. My pension is large enough to be almost embarrassing.

Cresswell and I were sitting on the terrace of his hotel room, sipping drinks and discussing the future of the U.S. space program. It was about three-fifteen. My fingers began to itch. It wasn't a bit gradual. It was switched on like electric current. I mentioned it to Cresswell.

"So you picked up some poison ivy on that scrofulous little island," he said, grinning.

"The only foliage on Key Caroline is a little palmetto scrub," I said. "Maybe it's the seven-year itch." I looked down at my hands. Perfectly ordinary hands. But itchy.

Later in the afternoon I signed the same old paper ("I do solemnly swear that I have neither received nor disclosed and divulged information which would . . .") and drove myself back to the Key. I've got an old Ford, equipped with hand-operated brake and accelerator. I love it—it makes me feel self-sufficient.

It's a long drive back, down Route 1, and by the time I got off the big road and onto the Key Caroline exit ramp, I was nearly out of my mind. My hands itched maddeningly. If you have ever suffered through the healing of a deep cut or a surgical incision, you may have some idea of the kind of itch I mean. Live things seemed to be crawling and boring in my flesh.

The sun was almost down and I looked at my hands carefully in the glow of the dash lights. The tips of them were red now, red in tiny, perfect circlets, just above the pad where the fingerprint is, where you get calluses if you play guitar. There were also red circles of infection on the space between the first and second joint of each thumb and finger, and on the skin between the second joint and the knuckle. I pressed my right fingers to my lips and withdrew them quickly, with a sudden loathing. A feeling of dumb horror had risen in my throat, woolen and choking. The flesh where the red spots had appeared was hot, feverish, and the flesh was soft and gelid, like the flesh of an apple gone rotten.

I drove the rest of the way trying to persuade myself that I had indeed caught poison ivy somehow. But in the back of my mind there was another ugly thought. I had an aunt, back in my childhood, who lived the last ten years of her life closed off from the world in an upstairs room. My mother took her meals up, and her name was a forbidden topic. I found out later that she had Hansen's disease—leprosy.

When I got home I called Dr. Flanders on the mainland. I got his answering service instead. Dr. Flanders was on a fishing cruise, but if it was urgent, Dr. Ballanger—

"When will Dr. Flanders be back?"

"Tomorrow afternoon at the latest. Would that—"

"Sure."

I hung up slowly, then dialed Richard. I let it ring a dozen times before hanging up. After that I sat indecisive for a while. The itching had deepened. It seemed to emanate from the flesh itself.

I rolled my wheelchair over to the bookcase and pulled down the battered medical encyclopedia that I'd had for years. The book was maddeningly vague. It could have been anything, or nothing.

I leaned back and closed my eyes. I could hear the old ship's clock ticking on the shelf across the room. There was the high, thin drone of a jet on its way to Miami. There was the soft whisper of my own breath.

I was still looking at the book.

The realization crept on me, then sank home with a frightening rush. My eyes were closed, but I was still looking at the book. What I was seeing was smeary and monstrous, the distorted, fourth-dimensional counterpart of a book, yet unmistakable for all that.

And I was not the only one watching.

I snapped my eyes open, feeling the constriction of my heart. The sensation subsided a little, but not entirely. I was looking at the book, seeing the print and diagrams with my own eyes, perfectly normal everyday experience, and I was also seeing it from a different, lower angle and seeing it with other eyes. Seeing not a book but an alien thing, something of monstrous shape and ominous intent.

I raised my hands slowly to my face, catching an eerie vision of my living room turned into a horror house.

I screamed.

There were eyes peering up at me through splits in the flesh of my fingers. And even as I watched the flesh was dilating, retreating, as they pushed their mindless way up to the surface.

But that was not what made me scream. I had looked into my own face and seen a monster.

———

The dune buggy nosed over the hill and Richard brought it to a halt next to the porch. The motor gunned and roared choppily. I rolled my wheelchair down the inclined plane to the right of the regular steps and Richard helped me in.

"All right, Arthur," he said. "It's your party. Where to?"

I pointed down toward the water, where the Big Dune finally begins to peter out. Richard nodded. The rear wheels spun sand and we were off. I usually found time to rib Richard about his driving, but I didn't bother tonight. There was too much else to think about—and to feel: they didn't want the dark, and I could feel them straining to see through the bandages, willing me to take them off.

The dune buggy bounced and roared through the sand toward the water, seeming almost to take flight from the tops of the small dunes. To the left the sun was going down in bloody glory. Straight ahead and across the water, the thunderclouds were beating their way toward us. Lightning forked at the water.

"Off to your right," I said. "By that lean-to."

Richard brought the dune buggy to a sand-spraying halt beside the rotted remains of the lean-to, reached into the back, and brought out a spade. I winced when I saw it. "Where?" Richard asked expressionlessly.

"Right there." I pointed to the place.

He got out and walked slowly through the sand to the spot, hesitated for a second, then plunged the shovel into the sand. It seemed that he dug for a very long time. The sand he was throwing back over his shoulder looked damp and moist. The thunderheads were darker, higher, and the water looked angry and implacable under their shadow and the reflected glow of the sunset.

I knew long before he stopped digging that he was not going to find the boy. They had moved him. I hadn't bandaged my hands last night, so they could see—and act. If they had been able to use me to kill the boy, they could use me to move him, even while I slept.

"There's no boy, Arthur." He threw the dirty shovel

into the dune buggy and sat tiredly on the seat. The coming storm cast marching, crescent-shaped shadows along the sand. The rising breeze rattled sand against the buggy's rusted body. My fingers itched.

"They used me to move him," I said dully. "They're getting the upper hand, Richard. They're forcing their doorway open, a little at a time. A hundred times a day I find myself standing in front of some perfectly familiar object—a spatula, a picture, even a can of beans—with no idea how I got there, holding my hands out, showing it to them, seeing it as they do, as an obscenity, something twisted and grotesque—"

"Arthur," he said. "Arthur, don't. Don't." In the failing light his face was wan with compassion. "*Standing* in front of something, you said. *Moving* the boy's body, you said. *But you can't walk, Arthur.* You're dead from the waist down."

I touched the dashboard of the dune buggy. "This is dead, too. But when you enter it, you can make it go. You could make it kill. It couldn't stop you even if it wanted to." I could hear my voice rising hysterically. "I am the doorway, can't you understand that? They killed the boy, Richard! They moved the body!"

"I think you'd better see a medical man," he said quietly. "Let's go back. Let's—"

"Check! Check on the boy, then! Find out—"

"You said you didn't even know his name."

"He must have been from the village. It's a small village. Ask—"

"I talked to Maud Harrington on the phone when I

got the dune buggy. If anyone in the state has a longer nose, I've not come across her. I asked if she'd heard of anyone's boy not coming home last night. She said she hadn't."

"But he's a local! He has to be!"

He reached for the ignition switch, but I stopped him. He turned to look at me and I began to unwrap my hands.

From the Gulf, thunder muttered and growled.

———

I didn't go to the doctor and I didn't call Richard back. I spent three weeks with my hands bandaged every time I went out. Three weeks just blindly hoping it would go away. It wasn't a rational act; I can admit that. If I had been a whole man who didn't need a wheelchair for legs or who had spent a normal life in a normal occupation, I might have gone to Doc Flanders or to Richard. I still might have, if it hadn't been for the memory of my aunt, shunned, virtually a prisoner, being eaten alive by her own failing flesh. So I kept a desperate silence and prayed that I would wake up some morning and find it had been an evil dream.

And little by little, I felt them. Them. An anonymous intelligence. I never really wondered what they looked like or where they had come from. It was moot. I was their doorway, and their window on the world. I got enough feedback from them to feel their revulsion and horror, to know that our world was very different from theirs. Enough feedback to feel their blind hate. But still they watched. Their flesh was embedded in my own. I began to realize that they were using me, actually manipulating me.

When the boy passed, raising one hand in his usual noncommittal salute, I had just about decided to get in touch with Cresswell at his Navy Department number. Richard had been right about one thing—I was certain that whatever had gotten hold of me had done it in deep space or in that weird orbit around Venus. The Navy would study me, but they would not freakify me. I wouldn't have to wake up anymore into the creaking darkness and stifle a scream as I felt them watching, watching, watching.

My hands went out toward the boy and I realized that I had not bandaged them. I could see the eyes in the dying light, watching silently. They were large, dilated, golden-irised. I had poked one of them against the tip of a pencil once, and had felt excruciating agony slam up my arm. The eye seemed to glare at me with a chained hatred that was worse than physical pain. I did not poke again.

And now they were watching the boy. I felt my mind sideslip. A moment later my control was gone. The door was open. I lurched across the sand toward him, legs scissoring nervelessly, so much driven deadwood. My own eyes seemed to close and I saw only with those alien eyes—saw a monstrous alabaster seascape over-topped with a sky like a great purple way, saw a leaning, eroded shack that might have been the carcass of some unknown, flesh-devouring creature, saw an abominated creature that moved and respired and carried a device of wood and wire under its arm, a device constructed of geometrically impossible right angles.

I wonder what he thought, that wretched, unnamed boy with his sieve under his arm and his pockets bulging with an odd conglomerate of sandy tourist coins, what he thought when he saw me lurching at him like a blind conductor stretching out his hands over a lunatic orchestra, what he thought as the last of the light fell across my hands, red and split and shining with their burden of eyes, what he thought when the hands made that sudden, flailing gesture in the air, just before his head burst.

I know what I thought.

I thought I had peeked over the rim of the universe and into the fires of hell itself.

————

The wind pulled at the bandages and made them into tiny, whipping streamers as I unwrapped them. The clouds had blottered the red remnants of the sunset, and the dunes were dark and shadow-cast. The clouds raced and boiled above us.

"You must promise me one thing, Richard," I said over the rising wind. "You must run if it seems I might try . . . to hurt you. Do you understand that?"

"Yes." His open-throated shirt whipped and rippled with the wind. His face was set, his own eyes little more than sockets in early dark.

The last of the bandages fell away.

I looked at Richard and they looked at Richard. I saw a face I had known for five years and come to love. They saw a distorted, living monolith.

"You see them," I said hoarsely. "Now you see them."

He took an involuntary step backward. His face became stained with a sudden unbelieving terror. Lightning slashed out of the sky. Thunder walked in the clouds and the water had gone black as the river Styx.

"Arthur—"

How hideous he was! How could I have lived near him, spoken with him? He was not a creature, but mute pestilence. He was—

"Run! Run, Richard!"

And he did run. He ran in huge, bounding leaps. He became a scaffold against the looming sky. My hands flew up, flew over my head in a screaming, orlesque gesture, the fingers reaching to the only familiar thing in this nightmare world—reaching to the clouds.

And the clouds answered.

There was a huge, blue-white streak of lightning that seemed like the end of the world. It struck Richard, it enveloped him. The last thing I remember is the electric stench of ozone and burnt flesh.

When I awoke I was sitting calmly on my porch, looking out toward the Big Dune. The storm had passed and the air was pleasantly cool. There was a tiny sliver of moon. The sand was virginal—no sign of Richard or of the dune buggy.

I looked down at my hands. The eyes were open but glazed. They had exhausted themselves. They dozed.

I knew well enough what had to be done. Before the door could be wedged open any further, it had to be locked. Forever. Already I could notice the first signs of structural change in the hands themselves. The fingers were beginning to shorten . . . and to change.

There was a small hearth in the living room, and in season I had been in the habit of lighting a fire against the damp Florida cold. I lit one now, moving with haste. I had no idea when they might wake up to what I was doing.

When it was burning well I went out back to the kerosene drum and soaked both hands. They came awake immediately, screaming with agony. I almost didn't make it back to the living room, and to the fire.

But I did make it.

———

That was all seven years ago.

I'm still here, still watching the rockets take off. There have been more of them lately. This is a space-minded administration. There has even been talk of another series of manned Venus probes.

I found out the boy's name, not that it matters. He was from the village, just as I thought. But his mother had expected him to stay with a friend on the mainland that night, and the alarm was not raised until the following Monday. Richard—well, everyone thought Richard was an odd duck, anyway. They suspect he may have gone back to Maryland or taken up with some woman.

As for me, I'm tolerated, although I have quite a reputation for eccentricity myself. After all, how many ex-astronauts regularly write their elected Washington officials with the idea that space-exploration money could be better spent elsewhere?

I get along just fine with these hooks. There was terrible pain for the first year or so, but the human body can adjust to almost anything. I shave with them and even tie my own shoelaces. And as you can see, my typing is nice and even. I don't expect to have any trouble putting the shotgun into my mouth or pulling the trigger. It started again three weeks ago, you see.

There is a perfect circle of twelve golden eyes on my chest.

THE MANGLER

Officer Hunton got to the laundry just as the ambulance was leaving—slowly, with no siren or flashing lights. Ominous. Inside, the office was stuffed with milling, silent people, some of them weeping. The plant itself was empty; the big automatic washers at the far end had not even been shut down. It made Hunton very wary. The crowd should be at the scene of the accident, not in the office. It was the way things worked—the human animal had a built-in urge to view the remains. A very bad one, then. Hunton felt his stomach tighten as it always did when the accident was very bad. Fourteen years of cleaning human litter from highways and streets and the sidewalks at the bases of very tall buildings had not been able to erase that little hitch in the belly, as if something evil had clotted there.

A man in a white shirt saw Hunton and walked toward him reluctantly. He was a buffalo of a man with head thrust forward between shoulders, nose and cheeks vein-broken either from high blood pressure or too many conversations with the brown bottle. He was trying to frame words, but after two tries Hunton cut him off briskly:

"Are you the owner? Mr. Gartley?"

"No . . . no. I'm Stanner. The foreman. God, this—"

Hunton got out his notebook. "Please show me the scene of the accident, Mr. Stanner, and tell me what happened."

Stanner seemed to grow even more white; the blotches on his nose and cheeks stood out like birthmarks. "D-do I have to?"

Hunton raised his eyebrows. "I'm afraid you do. The call I got said it was serious."

"Serious—" Stanner seemed to be battling with his gorge; for a moment his Adam's apple went up and down like a monkey on a stick. "Mrs. Frawley is dead. Jesus, I wish Bill Gartley *was* here."

"What happened?"

Stanner said, "You better come over here."

He led Hunton past a row of hand presses, a shirt-folding unit, and then stopped by a laundry-marking machine. He passed a shaky hand across his forehead. "You'll have to go over by yourself, Officer. I can't look at it again. It makes me . . . I can't. I'm sorry."

Hunton walked around the marking machine with a mild feeling of contempt for the man. They run a loose shop, cut corners, run live steam through home-welded pipes, they work with dangerous cleaning chemicals without the proper protection, and finally, someone gets hurt. Or gets dead. Then they can't look. They can't—

Hunton saw it.

The machine was still running. No one had shut it off. The machine he later came to know intimately: the Hadley-Watson Model-6 Speed Ironer and Folder. A long and clumsy name. The people who worked here in the steam and the wet had a better name for it. The mangler.

Hunton took a long, frozen look, and then he performed a first in his fourteen years as a law-enforcement officer: he turned around, put a convulsive hand to his mouth, and threw up.

———

"You didn't eat much," Jackson said.

The women were inside, doing dishes and talking babies while John Hunton and Mark Jackson sat in lawn chairs near the aromatic barbecue. Hunton smiled slightly at the understatement. He had eaten nothing.

"There was a bad one today," he said. "The worst."

"Car crash?"

"No. Industrial."

"Messy?"

Hunton did not reply immediately, but his face made an involuntary, writhing grimace. He got a beer out of the cooler between them, opened it, and emptied half of it. "I suppose you college profs don't know anything about industrial laundries?"

Jackson chuckled. "This one does. I spent a summer working in one as an undergraduate."

"Then you know the machine they call the speed ironer?"

Jackson nodded. "Sure. They run damp flatwork through them, mostly sheets and linen. A big, long machine."

"That's it," Hunton said. "A woman named Adelle Frawley got caught in it at the Blue Ribbon Laundry crosstown. It sucked her right in."

Jackson looked suddenly ill. "But . . . that can't happen, Johnny. There's a safety bar. If one of the women feeding the machine accidentally gets a hand under it, the bar snaps up and stops the machine. At least that's how I remember it."

Hunton nodded. "It's a state law. But it happened."

Hunton closed his eyes and in the darkness he could see the Hadley-Watson speed ironer again, as it had been that afternoon. It formed a long, rectangular box in shape, thirty feet by six. At the feeder end, a moving canvas belt moved under the safety bar, up at a slight angle, and then down. The belt carried the damp-dried, wrinkled sheets in continuous cycle over and under sixteen huge revolving cylinders that made up the main body of the machine. Over eight and under eight, pressed between them like thin ham between layers of superheated bread. Steam heat in the cylinders could be adjusted up to 300 degrees for maximum drying. The pressure on the sheets that rode the moving canvas belt was set at 800 pounds per square foot to get out every wrinkle.

And Mrs. Frawley, somehow, had been caught and

dragged in. The steel, asbestos-jacketed pressing cylinders had been as red as barn paint, and the rising steam from the machine had carried the sickening stench of hot blood. Bits of her white blouse and blue slacks, even ripped segments of her bra and panties, had been torn free and ejected from the machine's far end thirty feet down, the bigger sections of cloth folded with grotesque and bloodstained neatness by the automatic folder. But not even that was the worst.

———

"It tried to fold everything," he said to Jackson, tasting bile in his throat. "But a person isn't a sheet, Mark. What I saw . . . what was left of her . . ." Like Stanner, the hapless foreman, he could not finish. "They took her out in a basket," he said softly.

Jackson whistled. "Who's going to get it in the neck? The laundry or the state inspectors?"

"Don't know yet," Hunton said. The malign image still hung behind his eyes, the image of the mangler wheezing and thumping and hissing, blood dripping down the green sides of the long cabinet in runnels, the burning *stink* of her . . . "It depends on who okayed that goddamn safety bar and under what circumstances."

"If it's the management, can they wiggle out of it?"

Hunton smiled without humor. "The woman died, Mark. If Gartley and Stanner were cutting corners on the speed ironer's maintenance, they'll go to jail. No matter who they know on the City Council."

"Do you think they were cutting corners?"

Hunton thought of the Blue Ribbon Laundry, badly lighted, floors wet and slippery, some of the machines incredibly ancient and creaking. "I think it's likely," he said quietly.

They got up to go in the house together. "Tell me how it comes out, Johnny," Jackson said. "I'm interested."

———

Hunton was wrong about the mangler; it was clean as a whistle.

Six state inspectors went over it before the inquest, piece by piece. The net result was absolutely nothing. The inquest verdict was death by misadventure.

Hunton, dumbfounded, cornered Roger Martin, one of the inspectors, after the hearing. Martin was a tall drink of water with glasses as thick as the bottoms of shot glasses. He fidgeted with a ball-point pen under Hunton's questions.

"Nothing? Absolutely nothing doing with the machine?"

"Nothing," Martin said. "Of course, the safety bar was the guts of the matter. It's in perfect working order. You heard that Mrs. Gillian testify. Mrs. Frawley must have pushed her hand too far. No one saw that; they were watching their own work. She started screaming. Her hand was gone already, and the machine was taking her arm. They tried to pull her out instead of shutting it down—pure panic. Another woman, Mrs. Keene, said she *did* try to shut it off, but it's a fair assumption that she hit the start button rather than the stop in the confusion. By then it was too late."

"Then the safety bar malfunctioned," Hunton said flatly. "Unless she put her hand over it rather than under?"

"You can't. There's a stainless-steel facing above the safety bar. And the bar itself didn't malfunction. It's circuited into the machine itself. If the safety bar goes on the blink, the machine shuts down."

"Then how did it happen, for Christ's sake?"

"We don't know. My colleagues and I are of the opinion that the only way the speed ironer could have killed Mrs. Frawley was for her to have fallen into it from above. And she had both feet on the floor when it happened. A dozen witnesses can testify to that."

"You're describing an impossible accident," Hunton said.

"No. Only one we don't understand." He paused, hesitated, and then said: "I will tell you one thing, Hunton, since you seem to have taken this case to heart. If you mention it to anyone else, I'll deny I said it. But I didn't like that machine. It seemed . . . almost to be mocking us. I've inspected over a dozen speed ironers in the last five years on a regular basis. Some of them are in such bad shape that I wouldn't leave a dog unleashed around them—the state law is lamentably lax. But they were only machines for all that. But this one . . . it's a spook.

I don't know why, but it is. I think if I'd found one thing, even a technicality, that was off whack, I would have ordered it shut down. Crazy, huh?"

"I felt the same way," Hunton said.

"Let me tell you about something that happened two years ago in Milton," the inspector said. He took off his glasses and began to polish them slowly on his vest. "Fella had parked an old icebox out in his backyard. The woman who called us said her dog had been caught in it and suffocated. We got the state policeman in the area to inform him it had to go to the town dump. Nice enough fella, sorry about the dog. He loaded it into his pickup and took it to the dump the next morning. That afternoon a woman in the neighborhood reported her son missing."

"God," Hunton said.

"The icebox was at the dump and the kid was in it, dead. A smart kid, according to his mother. She said he'd no more play in an empty icebox than he would take a ride with a strange man. Well, he did. We wrote it off. Case closed?"

"I guess," Hunton said.

"No. The dump caretaker went out next day to take the door off the thing. City Ordinance No. 58 on the maintenance of public dumping places." Martin looked at him expressionlessly. "He found six dead birds inside. Gulls, sparrows, a robin. And he said the door closed on his arm while he was brushing them out. Gave him a hell of a jump. That mangler at the Blue Ribbon strikes me like that, Hunton. I don't like it."

They looked at each other wordlessly in the empty inquest chamber, some six city blocks from where the Hadley-Watson Model-6 Speed Ironer and Folder sat in the busy laundry, steaming and fuming over its sheets.

———

The case was driven out of his mind in the space of a week by the press of more prosaic police work. It was only brought back when he and his wife dropped over to Mark Jackson's house for an evening of bid whist and beer.

Jackson greeted him with: "Have you ever wondered if that laundry machine you told me about is haunted, Johnny?"

Hunton blinked, at a loss. "What?"

"The speed ironer at the Blue Ribbon Laundry, I guess you didn't catch the squeal this time."

"What squeal?" Hunton asked, interested.

Jackson passed him the evening paper and pointed to an item at the bottom of page two. The story said that a steam line had let go on the large speed ironer at the Blue Ribbon Laundry, burning three of the six women working at the feeder end. The accident had occurred at 3:45 P.M. and was attributed to a rise in steam pressure from the laundry's boiler. One of the women, Mrs. Annette Gillian, had been held at City Receiving Hospital with second-degree burns.

"Funny coincidence," he said, but the memory of Inspector Martin's words in the empty inquest chamber suddenly recurred: *It's a spook* . . . And the story about the dog and the boy and the birds caught in the discarded refrigerator.

He played cards very badly that night.

———

Mrs. Gillian was propped up in bed reading *Screen Secrets* when Hunton came into the four-bed hospital room. A large bandage blanketed one arm and the side of her neck. The room's other occupant, a young woman with a pallid face, was sleeping.

Mrs. Gillian blinked at the blue uniform and then smiled tentatively. "If it was for Mrs. Cherinikov, you'll have to come back later. They just gave her medication."

"No, it's for you, Mrs. Gillian." Her smile faded a little. "I'm here unofficially—which means I'm curious about the accident at the laundry. John Hunton." He held out his hand.

It was the right move. Mrs. Gillian's smile became brilliant and she took his grip awkwardly with her unburnt hand. "Anything I can tell you, Mr. Hunton. God, I thought my Andy was in trouble at school again."

"What happened?"

"We was running sheets and the ironer just blew up—or it seemed that way. I was thinking about going home an' getting off my dogs when there's this great big bang, like a bomb. Steam is everywhere and this hissing noise . . . awful." Her smile trembled on the verge of extinction. "It was like the ironer was breathing. Like a dragon, it was. And Alberta—that's Alberta Keene—shouted that something was exploding and everyone was running and screaming and Ginny Jason started yelling she was burnt. I started to run away and I fell down. I didn't know I got it worst until then. God forbid it was no worse than it was. That live steam is three hundred degrees."

"The paper said a steam line let go. What does that mean?"

"The overhead pipe comes down into this kinda flexible line that feeds the machine. George—Mr. Stanner—said there must have been a surge from the boiler or something. The line split wide open."

Hunton could think of nothing else to ask. He was making ready to leave when she said reflectively:

"We never used to have these things on that machine. Only lately. The steam line breaking. That awful, awful accident with Mrs. Frawley, God rest her. And little things. Like the day Essie got her dress caught in one of the drive chains. That could have been dangerous if she hadn't ripped it right out. Bolts and things fall off. Oh, Herb Diment—he's the laundry repairman—has had an awful time with it. Sheets get caught in the folder. George says that's because they're using too much bleach in the washers, but it never used to happen. Now the girls hate to work on it. Essie even says there are still little bits of Adelle Frawley caught in it and it's sacrilege or something. Like it had a curse. It's been that way ever since Sherry cut her hand on one of the clamps."

"Sherry?" Hunton asked.

"Sherry Ouelette. Pretty little thing, just out of high school. Good worker. But clumsy sometimes. You know how young girls are."

"She cut her hand on something?"

"Nothing strange about *that*. There are clamps to tighten down the feeder belt, see. Sherry was adjusting them so we could do a heavier load and probably dreaming about some boy. She cut her finger and bled all over everything." Mrs. Gillian looked puzzled. "It wasn't until after that the bolts started falling off. Adelle was . . . you know . . . about a week later. As if the machine had tasted blood and found it liked it. Don't women get funny ideas sometimes, Officer Hinton?"

"Hunton," he said absently, looking over her head and into space.

————

Ironically, he had met Mark Jackson in a washateria in the block that separated their houses, and it was there that the cop and the English professor still had their most interesting conversations.

Now they sat side by side in bland plastic chairs, their clothes going round and round behind the glass portholes of the coin-op washers. Jackson's paperback copy of Milton's collected works lay neglected beside him while he listened to Hunton tell Mrs. Gillian's story.

When Hunton had finished, Jackson said, "I asked you once if you thought the mangler might be haunted. I was only half joking. I'll ask you again now."

"No," Hunton said uneasily. "Don't be stupid."

Jackson watched the turning clothes reflectively. "Haunted is a bad word. Let's say possessed. There are almost as many spells for casting demons in as there are for casting them out. Frazier's *Golden Bough* is replete with them. Druidic and Aztec lore contain others. Even older ones, back to Egypt. Almost all of them can be reduced to startlingly common denominators. The most common, of course, is the blood of a virgin." He looked at Hunton. "Mrs. Gillian said the trouble started after this Sherry Ouelette accidentally cut herself."

"Oh, come on," Hunton said.

"You have to admit she sounds just the type," Jackson said.

"I'll run right over to her house," Hunton said with a small smile. "I can see it. 'Miss Ouelette, I'm Officer John Hunton. I'm investigating an ironer with a bad case of demon possession and would like to know if you're a virgin.' Do you think I'd get a chance to say goodbye to Sandra and the kids before they carted me off to the booby hatch?"

"I'd be willing to bet you'll end up saying something just like that," Jackson said without smiling. "I'm serious, Johnny. That machine scares the hell out of me and I've never seen it."

"For the sake of conversation," Hunton said, "what are some of the other so-called common denominators?"

Jackson shrugged. "Hard to say without study. Most Anglo-Saxon hex formulas specify graveyard dirt or the eye of a toad. European spells often mention the hand of glory, which can be interpreted as the actual hand of a dead man or one of the hallucinogenics used in connection with the Witches' Sabbath—usually belladonna or a psilocybin derivative. There could be others."

"And you think all those things got into the Blue Ribbon ironer? Christ, Mark, I'll bet there isn't any belladonna within a five-hundred-mile radius. Or do you think someone whacked off their Uncle Fred's hand and dropped it in the folder?"

"If seven hundred monkeys typed for seven hundred years—"

"One of them would turn out the works of Shakespeare," Hunton finished sourly. "Go to hell. Your turn to go across to the drugstore and get some dimes for the dryers."

———

It was very funny how George Stanner lost his arm in the mangler.

Seven o'clock Monday morning the laundry was deserted except for Stanner and Herb Diment, the maintenance man. They were performing the twice-yearly function of greasing the mangler's bearings before the laundry's regular day began at seven-thirty. Diment was at the far end, greasing the four secondaries and thinking of how unpleasant this machine made him feel lately, when the mangler suddenly roared into life.

He had been holding up four of the canvas exit belts

to get at the motor beneath and suddenly the belts were running in his hands, ripping the flesh off his palms, dragging him along.

He pulled free with a convulsive jerk seconds before the belts would have carried his hands into the folder.

"What the Christ, George!" he yelled. "Shut the frigging thing *off!*"

George Stanner began to scream.

It was a high, wailing, blood-maddened sound that filled the laundry, echoing off the steel faces of the washers, the grinning mouths of the steam presses, the vacant eyes of the industrial dryers. Stanner drew in a great, whooping gasp of air and screamed again: "*Oh God of Christ I'm caught I'M CAUGHT—*"

The rollers began to produce rising steam. The folder gnashed and thumped. Bearings and motors seemed to cry out with a hidden life of their own.

Diment raced to the other end of the machine.

The first roller was already going a sinister red. Diment made a moaning, gobbling noise in his throat. The mangler howled and thumped and hissed.

A deaf observer might have thought at first that Stanner was merely bent over the machine at an odd angle. Then even a deaf man would have seen the pallid, eye-bulging rictus of his face, mouth twisted open in a continuous scream. The arm was disappearing under the safety bar and beneath the first roller; the fabric of his shirt had torn away at the shoulder seam and his upper arm bulged grotesquely as the blood was pushed steadily backward.

"Turn it off!" Stanner screamed. There was a snap as his elbow broke.

Diment thumbed the off button.

The mangler continued to hum and growl and turn.

Unbelieving, he slammed the button again and again—nothing. The skin of Stanner's arm had grown shiny and taut. Soon it would split with the pressure the roll was putting on it; and still he was conscious and screaming. Diment had a nightmare cartoon image of a man flattened by a steamroller, leaving only a shadow.

"Fuses—" Stanner screeched. His head was being pulled down, down, as he was dragged forward.

Diment whirled and ran to the boiler room, Stanner's screams chasing him like lunatic ghosts. The mixed stench of blood and steam rose in the air.

On the left wall were three heavy gray boxes containing all the fuses for the laundry's electricity. Diment yanked them open and began to pull the long, cylindrical fuses like a crazy man, throwing them back over his shoulders. The overhead lights went out; then the air compressor; then the boiler itself, with a huge dying whine.

And still the mangler turned. Stanner's screams had been reduced to bubbly moans.

Diment's eye happened on the fire ax in its glassed-in box. He grabbed it with a small, gagging whimper and ran back. Stanner's arm was gone almost to the shoulder. Within seconds his bent and straining neck would be snapped against the safety bar.

"I can't," Diment blubbered, holding the ax. "Jesus, George, I can't, I can't, I—"

The machine was an abattoir now. The folder spat out pieces of shirt sleeve, scraps of flesh, a finger. Stanner gave a huge, whooping scream and Diment swung the ax up and brought it down in the laundry's shadowy lightlessness. Twice. Again.

Stanner fell away, unconscious and blue, blood jetting from the stump just below the shoulder. The mangler sucked what was left into itself . . . and shut down.

Weeping, Diment pulled his belt out of its loops and began to make a tourniquet.

———

Hunton was talking on the phone with Roger Martin, the inspector. Jackson watched him while he patiently rolled a ball back and forth for three-year-old Patty Hunton to chase.

"He pulled *all* the fuses?" Hunton was asking. "And the off button just didn't function, huh? . . . Has the ironer been shut down? . . . Good. Great. Huh? . . . No, not official." Hunton frowned, then looked sideways at Jackson. "Are you still reminded of that refrigerator, Roger? . . . Yes. Me too. Goodbye."

He hung up and looked at Jackson. "Let's go see the girl, Mark."

———

She had her own apartment (the hesitant yet proprietary way she showed them in after Hunton had flashed his buzzer made him suspect that she hadn't had it long), and she sat uncomfortably across from them in the carefully decorated, postage-stamp living room.

"I'm Officer Hunton and this is my associate, Mr. Jackson. It's about the accident at the laundry." He felt hugely uncomfortable with this dark, shyly pretty girl.

"Awful," Sherry Ouelette murmured. "It's the only place I've ever worked. Mr. Gartley is my uncle. I liked it because it let me have this place and my own friends. But now . . . it's so *spooky.*"

"The State Board of Safety has shut the ironer down pending a full investigation," Hunton said. "Did you know that?"

"Sure." She sighed restlessly. "I don't know what I'm going to do—"

"Miss Ouelette," Jackson interrupted, "you had an accident with the ironer, didn't you? Cut your hand on a clamp, I believe?"

"Yes, I cut my finger." Suddenly her face clouded. "That was the first thing." She looked at them woefully. "Sometimes I feel like the girls don't like me so much anymore . . . as if I were to blame."

"I have to ask you a hard question," Jackson said slowly. "A question you won't like. It seems absurdly personal and off the subject, but I can only tell you it is not. Your answers won't ever be marked down in a file or record."

She looked frightened. "D-did I do something?"

Jackson smiled and shook his head; she melted. *Thank God for Mark,* Hunton thought.

"I'll add this, though: the answer may help you keep your nice little flat here, get your job back, and make things at the laundry the way they were before."

"I'd answer anything to have that," she said.

"Sherry, are you a virgin?"

She looked utterly flabbergasted, utterly shocked, as if a priest had given communion and then slapped her. Then she lifted her head, made a gesture at her neat efficiency apartment, as if asking them how they could believe it might be a place of assignation.

"I'm saving myself for my husband," she said simply.

Hunton and Jackson looked calmly at each other, and in that tick of a second, Hunton knew that it was all true: a devil had taken over the inanimate steel and cogs and gears of the mangler and had turned it into something with its own life.

"Thank you," Jackson said quietly.

"What now?" Hunton asked bleakly as they rode back. "Find a priest to exorcise it?"

Jackson snorted. "You'd go a far piece to find one that wouldn't hand you a few tracts to read while he phoned the booby hatch. It has to be our play, Johnny."

"Can we do it?"

"Maybe. The problem is this: We know something is in the mangler. We don't know *what*." Hunton felt cold, as if touched by a fleshless finger. "There are a great many demons. Is the one we're dealing with in the circle of Bubastis or Pan? Baal? Or the Christian deity we call Satan? We don't know. If the demon had been deliberately cast, we would have a better chance. But this seems to be a case of random possession."

Jackson ran his fingers through his hair. "The blood of a virgin, yes. But that narrows it down hardly at all. We have to be sure, very sure."

"Why?" Hunton asked bluntly. "Why not just get a bunch of exorcism formulas together and try them out?"

Jackson's face went cold. "This isn't cops 'n' robbers, Johnny. For Christ's sake, don't think it is. The rite of exorcism is horribly dangerous. It's like controlled nuclear fission, in a way. We could make a mistake and destroy ourselves. The demon is caught in that piece of machinery. But give it a chance and—"

"It could get out?"

"It would love to get out," Jackson said grimly. "And it likes to kill."

When Jackson came over the following evening, Hunton had sent his wife and daughter to a movie. They had the living room to themselves, and for this Hunton was relieved. He could still barely believe what he had become involved in.

"I canceled my classes," Jackson said, "and spent the day with some of the most god-awful books you can imagine. This afternoon I fed over thirty recipes for calling demons into the tech computer. I've got a number of common elements. Surprisingly few."

He showed Hunton the list: blood of a virgin, graveyard dirt, hand of glory, bat's blood, night moss, horse's hoof, eye of toad.

There were others, all marked secondary.

"Horse's hoof," Hunton said thoughtfully. "Funny—"

"Very common. In fact—"

"Could these things—any of them—be interpreted loosely?" Hunton interrupted.

"If lichens picked at night could be substituted for night moss, for instance?"

"Yes."

"It's very likely," Jackson said. "Magical formulas are often ambiguous and elastic. The black arts have always allowed plenty of room for creativity."

"Substitute Jell-O for horse's hoof," Hunton said. "Very popular in bag lunches. I noticed a little container of it sitting under the ironer's sheet platform on the day the Frawley woman died. Gelatin is made from horses' hooves."

Jackson nodded. "Anything else?"

"Bat's blood . . . well, it's a big place. Lots of unlighted nooks and crannies. Bats seem likely, although I doubt if the management would admit to it. One could conceivably have been trapped in the mangler."

Jackson tipped his head back and knuckled bloodshot eyes. "It fits . . . it all fits."

"It does?"

"Yes. We can safely rule out the hand of glory, I think. Certainly no one dropped a hand into the ironer *before* Mrs. Frawley's death, and belladonna is definitely not indigenous to the area."

"Graveyard dirt?"

"What do you think?"

"It would have to be a hell of a coincidence," Hunton said. "Nearest cemetery is Pleasant Hill, and that's five miles from the Blue Ribbon."

"Okay," Jackson said. "I got the computer operator—who thought I was getting ready for Halloween—to run a positive breakdown of all the primary and secondary elements on the list. Every possible combination. I threw out some two dozen which were completely meaningless. The others fall into fairly clearcut categories. The elements we've isolated are in one of those."

"What is it?"

Jackson grinned. "An easy one. The mythos centers in South America with branches in the Caribbean. Related to voodoo. The literature I've got looks on the deities as strictly bush league, compared to some of the real heavies, like Saddath or He-Who-Cannot-Be-Named. The thing in that machine is going to slink away like the neighborhood bully."

"How do we do it?"

"Holy water and a smidgen of the Holy Eucharist ought to do it. And we can read some of the Leviticus to it. Strictly Christian white magic."

"You're sure it's not worse?"

"Don't see how it can be," Jackson said pensively. "I don't mind telling you I was worried about that hand of glory. That's very black juju. Strong magic."

"Holy water wouldn't stop it?"

"A demon called up in conjunction with the hand of glory could eat a stack of Bibles for breakfast. We would be in bad trouble messing with something like that at all. Better to pull the goddamn thing apart."

"Well, are you completely sure—"

"No, but fairly sure. It all fits too well."

"When?"

"The sooner, the better," Jackson said. "How do we get in? Break a window?"

Hunton smiled, reached into his pocket, and dangled a key in front of Jackson's nose.

"Where'd you get that? Gartley?"

"No," Hunton said. "From a state inspector named Martin."

"He know what we're doing?"

"I think he suspects. He told me a funny story a couple of weeks ago."

"About the mangler?"

"No," Hunton said. "About a refrigerator. Come on."

———

Adelle Frawley was dead; sewed together by a patient undertaker, she lay in her coffin. Yet something of her spirit perhaps remained in the machine, and if it did, it cried out. She would have known, could have warned them. She had been prone to indigestion, and for this common ailment she had taken a common stomach tablet called E-Z Gel, purchasable over the counter of any drugstore for seventy-nine cents. The side panel holds a printed warning: People with glaucoma must not take E-Z Gel, because the active ingredient causes an aggravation of that condition. Unfortunately, Adelle Frawley did not have that condition. She might have remembered the day, shortly before Sherry Ouelette cut her hand, that she had dropped a full box of E-Z Gel tablets into the mangler by accident. But she was dead, unaware that the active ingredient which soothed her heartburn was a chemical derivative of belladonna, known quaintly in some European countries as the hand of glory.

There was a sudden ghastly burping noise in the spectral silence of the Blue Ribbon Laundry—a bat fluttered madly for its hole in the insulation above the dryers where it had roosted, wrapping wings around its blind face.

It was a noise almost like a chuckle.

The mangler began to run with a sudden, lurching grind—belts hurrying through the darkness, cogs meeting and meshing and grinding, heavy pulverizing rollers rotating on and on.

It was ready for them.

———

When Hunton pulled into the parking lot it was shortly after midnight and the moon was hidden behind a raft of moving clouds. He jammed on the brakes and switched off the lights in the same motion; Jackson's forehead almost slammed against the padded dash.

He switched off the ignition and the steady thump-hiss-thump became louder. "It's the mangler," he said slowly. "It's the mangler. Running by itself. In the middle of the night."

They sat for a moment in silence, feeling the fear crawl up their legs.

Hunton said, "All right. Let's do it."

They got out and walked to the building, the sound of the mangler growing louder. As Hunton put the key into the lock of the service door, he thought that the machine *did* sound alive—as if it were breathing in great hot gasps and speaking to itself in hissing, sardonic whispers.

"All of a sudden I'm glad I'm with a cop," Jackson said. He shifted the brown bag he held from one arm to the other. Inside was a small jelly jar filled with holy water wrapped in waxed paper, and a Gideon Bible.

They stepped inside and Hunton snapped up the light switches by the door. The fluorescents flickered into cold life. At the same instant the mangler shut off.

A membrane of steam hung over its rollers. It waited for them in its new ominous silence.

"God, it's an ugly thing," Jackson whispered.

"Come on," Hunton said. "Before we lose our nerve."

They walked over to it. The safety bar was in its down position over the belt which fed the machine.

Hunton put out a hand. "Close enough, Mark. Give me the stuff and tell me what to do."

"But—"

"No argument."

Jackson handed him the bag and Hunton put it on the sheet table in front of the machine. He gave Jackson the Bible.

"I'm going to read," Jackson said. "When I point at you, sprinkle the holy water on the machine with your fingers. You say: In the name of the Father, and of the Son, and of the Holy Ghost, get thee from this place, thou unclean. Got it?"

"Yes."

"The second time I point, break the wafer and repeat the incantation again."

"How will we know if it's working?"

"You'll know. The thing is apt to break every window in the place getting out. If it doesn't work the first time, we keep doing it until it does."

"I'm scared green," Hunton said.

"As a matter of fact, so am I."

"If we're wrong about the hand of glory—"

"We're not," Jackson said. "Here we go."

He began. His voice filled the empty laundry with spectral echoes. "Turnest not thou aside to idols, nor make molten gods for yourself. I am the Lord thy God . . ." The words fell like stones into a silence that had suddenly become filled with a creeping, tomblike cold. The mangler remained still and silent under the fluorescents, and to Hunton it still seemed to grin.

". . . and the land will vomit you out for having

defiled it, as it vomited out nations before you." Jackson looked up, his face strained, and pointed.

Hunton sprinkled holy water across the feeder belt.

There was a sudden, gnashing scream of tortured metal. Smoke rose from the canvas belts where the holy water had touched and took on writhing, red-tinged shapes. The mangler suddenly jerked into life.

"We've got it!" Jackson cried above the rising clamor. "It's on the run!"

He began to read again, his voice rising over the sound of the machinery. He pointed to Hunton again, and Hunton sprinkled some of the host. As he did so he was suddenly swept with a bone-freezing terror, a sudden vivid feeling that it had gone wrong, that the machine had called their bluff—and was the stronger.

Jackson's voice was still rising, approaching climax.

Sparks began to jump across the arc between the main motor and the secondary; the smell of ozone filled the air, like the copper smell of hot blood. Now the main motor was smoking; the mangler was running at an insane, blurred speed: a finger touched to the central belt would have caused the whole body to be hauled in and turned to a bloody rag in the space of five seconds. The concrete beneath their feet trembled and thrummed.

A main bearing blew with a searing flash of purple light, filling the chill air with the smell of thunderstorms, and still the mangler ran, faster and faster, belts and rollers and cogs moving at a speed that made them seem to blend and merge, change, melt, transmute—

Hunton, who had been standing almost hypnotized, suddenly took a step backward. "Get away!" he screamed over the blaring racket.

"We've almost got it!" Jackson yelled back. "Why—"

There was a sudden indescribable ripping noise and a fissure in the concrete floor suddenly raced toward them and past, widening. Chips of ancient cement flew up in a starburst.

Jackson looked at the mangler and screamed.

It was trying to pull itself out of the concrete, like a dinosaur trying to escape a tar pit. And it wasn't precisely an ironer anymore. It was still changing, melting. The 550-volt cable fell, spitting blue fire, into the rollers and was chewed away. For a moment two fireballs glared at them like lambent eyes, eyes filled with a great and cold hunger.

Another fault line tore open. The mangler leaned toward them, within an ace of being free of the concrete moorings that held it. It leered at them; the safety bar had slammed up and what Hunton saw was a gaping, hungry mouth filled with steam.

They turned to run and another fissure opened at their feet. Behind them, a great screaming roar as the thing came free. Hunton leaped over, but Jackson stumbled and fell sprawling.

Hunton turned to help and a huge, amorphous shadow fell over him, blocking the fluorescents.

It stood over Jackson, who lay on his back, staring up in a silent rictus of terror—the perfect sacrifice. Hunton had only a confused impression of something black and moving that bulked to a tremendous height above them both, something with glaring electric eyes the size of footballs, an open mouth with a moving canvas tongue.

He ran; Jackson's dying scream followed him.

———

When Roger Martin finally got out of bed to answer the doorbell, he was still only a third awake; but when Hunton reeled in, shock slapped him fully into the world with a rough hand.

Hunton's eyes bulged madly from his head, and his hands were claws as he scratched at the front of Martin's robe. There was a small oozing cut on his cheek and his face was splashed with dirty gray specks of powdered cement.

His hair had gone dead white.

"Help me . . . for Jesus' sake, help me. Mark is dead. Jackson is dead."

"Slow down," Martin said. "Come in the living room."

Hunton followed him, making a thick whining noise in his throat, like a dog.

Martin poured him a two-ounce knock of Jim Beam and Hunton held the glass in both hands, downing the raw liquor in a choked gulp. The glass fell unheeded to the carpet and his hands, like wandering ghosts, sought Martin's lapels again.

"The mangler killed Mark Jackson. It . . . it . . . oh God, it might get out! We can't let it get out! We can't . . . we . . . oh—" He began to scream, a crazy, whooping sound that rose and fell in jagged cycles.

Martin tried to hand him another drink but Hunton knocked it aside. "We have to burn it," he said. "Burn it before it can get out. Oh, what if it gets out? Oh Jesus, what if—" His eyes suddenly flickered, glazed, rolled up to show the whites, and he fell to the carpet in a stonelike faint.

Mrs. Martin was in the doorway, clutching her robe to her throat. "Who is he, Rog? Is he crazy? I thought—" She shuddered.

"I don't think he's crazy." She was suddenly frightened by the sick shadow of fear on her husband's face. "God, I hope he came quick enough."

He turned to the telephone, picked up the receiver, froze.

There was a faint, swelling noise from the east of the house, the way that Hunton had come. A steady, grinding clatter, growing louder. The living-room window stood half open and now Martin caught a dark smell on the breeze. An odor of ozone . . . or blood.

He stood with his hand on the useless telephone as it grew louder, louder, gnashing and fuming, something in the streets that was hot and steaming. The blood stench filled the room.

His hand dropped from the telephone.

It was already out.

THE BOOGEYMAN

"I came to you because I want to tell my story," the man on Dr. Harper's couch was saying. The man was Lester Billings from Waterbury, Connecticut. According to the history taken from Nurse Vickers, he was twenty-eight, employed by an industrial firm in New York, divorced, and the father of three children. All deceased.

"I can't go to a priest because I'm not Catholic. I can't go to a lawyer because I haven't done anything to consult a lawyer about. All I did was kill my kids. One at a time. Killed them all."

Dr. Harper turned on the tape recorder.

Billings lay straight as a yardstick on the couch, not giving it an inch of himself. His feet protruded stiffly over the end. Picture of a man enduring necessary humiliation. His hands were folded corpselike on his chest. His face was carefully set. He looked at the plain white composition ceiling as if seeing scenes and pictures played out there.

"Do you mean you actually killed them, or—"

"No." Impatient flick of the hand. "But I was responsible. Denny in 1967. Shirl in 1971. And Andy this year. I want to tell you about it."

Dr. Harper said nothing. He thought that Billings looked haggard and old. His hair was thinning, his complexion sallow. His eyes held all the miserable secrets of whiskey.

"They were murdered, see? Only no one believes that. If they would, things would be all right."

"Why is that?"

"Because . . ."

Billings broke off and darted up on his elbows, staring across the room. "What's that?" he barked. His eyes had narrowed to black slots.

"What's what?"

"That door."

"The closet," Dr. Harper said. "Where I hang my coat and leave my overshoes."

"Open it. I want to see."

Dr. Harper got up wordlessly, crossed the room, and opened the closet. Inside, a tan raincoat hung on one of four or five hangers. Beneath that was a pair of shiny galoshes. The New York *Times* had been carefully tucked into one of them. That was all.

"All right?" Dr. Harper said.

"All right." Billings removed the props of his elbows and returned to his previous position.

"You were saying," Dr. Harper said as he went back to his chair, "that if the murder of your three children could be proved, all your troubles would be over. Why is that?"

"I'd go to jail," Billings said immediately. "For life. And you can see into all the rooms in a jail. All the rooms." He smiled at nothing.

"How were your children murdered?"

"Don't try to jerk it out of me!"

Billings twitched around and stared balefully at Harper.

"I'll tell you, don't worry. I'm not one of your freaks strutting around and pretending to be Napoleon or explaining that I got hooked on heroin because my mother didn't love me. I know you won't believe me. I don't care. It doesn't matter. Just to tell will be enough."

"All right." Dr. Harper got out his pipe.

"I married Rita in 1965—I was twenty-one and she was eighteen. She was pregnant. That was Denny." His lips twisted in a rubbery, frightening grin that was gone in a wink. "I had to leave college and get a job, but I didn't mind. I loved both of them. We were very happy.

"Rita got pregnant just a little while after Denny was born, and Shirl came along in December of 1966. Andy came in the summer of 1969, and Denny was already dead by then. Andy was an accident. That's what Rita said. She said sometimes that birth-control stuff doesn't work. I think that it was more than an accident. Children tie a man down, you know. Women like that, especially when the man is brighter than they. Don't you find that's true?"

Harper grunted noncommittally.

"It doesn't matter, though. I loved him anyway." He said it almost vengefully, as if he had loved the child to spite his wife.

"Who killed the children?" Harper asked.

"The boogeyman," Lester Billings answered immediately. "The boogeyman killed them all. Just came out of the closet and killed them." He twisted around and grinned. "You think I'm crazy, all right. It's written all over you. But I don't care. All I want to do is tell you and then get lost."

"I'm listening," Harper said.

"It started when Denny was almost two and Shirl was just an infant. He started crying when Rita put him to bed. We had a two-bedroom place, see. Shirl slept in a crib in our room. At first I thought he was crying because he didn't have a bottle to take to bed anymore. Rita said don't make an issue of it, let it go, let him have it and he'll drop it on his own. But that's the way kids start off bad. You get permissive with them, spoil them. Then they break your heart. Get some girl knocked up, you know, or start shooting dope. Or they get to be sissies. Can you imagine waking up some morning and finding your kid—your *son*—is a sissy?

"After a while, though, when he didn't stop, I started putting him to bed myself. And if he didn't stop crying I'd give him a whack. Then Rita said he was saying 'light' over and over again. Well, I didn't know. Kids that little, how can you tell what they're saying. Only a mother can tell.

"Rita wanted to put in a nightlight. One of those wall-plug things with Mickey Mouse or Huckleberry Hound or something on it. I wouldn't let her. If a kid doesn't get over being afraid of the dark when he's little, he never gets over it.

"Anyway, he died the summer after Shirl was born. I put him to bed that night and he started to cry right off. I heard what he said that time. He pointed right at the closet when he said it. 'Boogeyman,' the kid says. 'Boogeyman, Daddy.'

"I turned off the light and went into our room and asked Rita why she wanted to teach the kid a word like that. I was tempted to slap her around a little, but I didn't. She said she never taught him to say that. I called her a goddamn liar.

"That was a bad summer for me, see. The only job I could get was loading Pepsi-Cola trucks in a warehouse, and I was tired all the time. Shirl would wake up and cry every night and Rita would pick her up and sniffle. I tell you, sometimes I felt like throwing them both out a window. Christ, kids drive you crazy sometimes. You could kill them.

"Well, the kid woke me at three in the morning, right on schedule. I went to the bathroom, only a quarter awake, you know, and Rita asked me if I'd check on Denny. I told her to do it herself and went back to bed. I was almost asleep when she started to scream.

"I got up and went in. The kid was dead on his back. Just as white as flour except for where the blood had . . . had sunk. Back of the legs, the head, the a—

the buttocks. His eyes were open. That was the worst, you know. Wide open and glassy, like the eyes you see on a moosehead some guy put over his mantel. Like pictures you see of those gook kids over in Nam. But an American kid shouldn't look like that. Dead on his back. Wearing diapers and rubber pants because he'd been wetting himself again the last couple of weeks. Awful, I loved that kid."

Billings shook his head slowly, then offered the rubbery, frightening grin again. "Rita was screaming her head off. She tried to pick Denny up and rock him, but I wouldn't let her. The cops don't like you to touch any of the evidence. I know that—"

"Did you know it was the boogeyman then?" Harper asked quietly.

"Oh, no. Not then. But I did see one thing. It didn't mean anything to me then, but my mind stored it away."

"What was that?"

"The closet door was open. Not much. Just a crack. But I knew I left it shut, see. There's dry-cleaning bags in there. A kid messes around with one of those and bango. Asphyxiation. You know that?"

"Yes. What happened then?"

Billings shrugged. "We planted him." He looked morbidly at his hands, which had thrown dirt on three tiny coffins.

"Was there an inquest?"

"Sure." Billings' eyes flashed with sardonic brilliance. "Some back-country fuckhead with a stethoscope and a black bag full of Junior Mints and a sheepskin from some cow college. Crib death, he called it! You ever hear such a pile of yellow manure? The kid was three years old!"

"Crib death is most common during the first year," Harper said carefully, "but that diagnosis has gone on death certificates for children up to age five for want of a better—"

"*Bullshit!*" Billings spat out violently.

Harper relit his pipe.

"We moved Shirl into Denny's old room a month after the funeral. Rita fought it tooth and nail, but I had the last word. It hurt me, of course it did. Jesus, I loved having the kid in with us. But you can't get overprotective. You make a kid a cripple that way. When I was a kid my mom used to take me to the beach and then scream herself hoarse. 'Don't go out so far! Don't go there! It's got an undertow! You only ate an hour ago! Don't go over your head!' Even to watch out for sharks, before God. So what happens? I can't even go near the water now. It's the truth. I get the cramps if I go near a beach. Rita got me to take her and the kids to Savin Rock once when Denny was alive. I got sick as a dog. I know, see? You can't overprotect kids. And you can't coddle yourself either. Life goes on. Shirl went right into Denny's crib. We sent the old mattress to the dump, though. I didn't want my girl to get any germs.

"So a year goes by. And one night when I'm putting Shirl into her crib she starts to yowl and scream and cry. 'Boogeyman, Daddy, boogeyman, boogeyman!'

"That threw a jump into me. It was just like Denny.

And I started to remember about that closet door, open just a crack when we found him. I wanted to take her into our room for the night."

"Did you?"

"No." Billings regarded his hands and his face twitched. "How could I go to Rita and admit I was wrong? I *had* to be strong. She was always such a jellyfish . . . look how easy she went to bed with me when we weren't married."

Harper said, "On the other hand, look how easily *you* went to bed with *her*."

Billings froze in the act of rearranging his hands and slowly turned his head to look at Harper. "Are you trying to be a wise guy?"

"No, indeed," Harper said.

"Then let me tell it my way," Billings snapped. "I came here to get this off my chest. To tell my story. I'm not going to talk about my sex life, if that's what you expect. Rita and I had a very normal sex life, with none of that dirty stuff. I know it gives some people a charge to talk about that, but I'm not one of them."

"Okay," Harper said.

"Okay," Billings echoed with uneasy arrogance. He seemed to have lost the thread of his thought, and his eyes wandered uneasily to the closet door, which was firmly shut.

"Would you like that open?" Harper asked.

"No!" Billings said quickly. He gave a nervous little laugh. "What do I want to look at your overshoes for?

"The boogeyman got her, too," Billings said. He

brushed at his forehead, as if sketching memories. "A month later. But something happened before that. I heard a noise in there one night. And then she screamed. I opened the door real quick—the hall light was on—and . . . she was sitting up in the crib crying and . . . something *moved*. Back in the shadows, by the closet. Something *slithered*."

"Was the closet door open?"

"A little. Just a crack." Billings licked his lips. "Shirl was screaming about the boogeyman. And something else that sounded like 'claws.' Only she said 'craws,' you know. Little kids have trouble with that 'l' sound. Rita ran upstairs and asked what the matter was. I said she got scared by the shadows of the branches moving on the ceiling."

"Crawset?" Harper said.

"Huh?"

"Crawset . . . closet. Maybe she was trying to say 'closet.' "

"Maybe," Billings said. "Maybe that was it. But I don't think so. I think it was 'claws.' " His eyes began seeking the closet door again. "Claws, long claws." His voice had sunk to a whisper.

"Did you look in the closet?"

"Y-yes." Billings' hands were laced tightly across his chest, laced tightly enough to show a white moon at each knuckle.

"Was there anything in there? Did you see the—"

"*I didn't see anything!*" Billings screamed suddenly. And the words poured out as if a black cork had been pulled from the bottom of his soul: "When she died I found her, see. And she was black. All black. She swallowed her own tongue and she was just as black as a nigger in a minstrel show and she was staring at me. Her eyes, they looked like those eyes you see on stuffed animals, all shiny and awful, like live marbles, and they were saying it got me, Daddy, you let it get me, you killed me, you helped it kill me . . ." His words trailed off. One single tear very large and silent, ran down the side of his cheek.

"It was a brain convulsion, see? Kids get those sometimes. A bad signal from the brain. They had an autopsy at Hartford Receiving and they told us she choked on her tongue from the convulsion. And I had to go home alone because they kept Rita under sedation. She was out of her mind. I had to go back to that house all alone, and I know a kid don't just get convulsions because their brain frigged up. You can scare a kid into convulsions. And I had to go back to the house where *it* was."

He whispered, "I slept on the couch. With the light on."

"Did anything happen?"

"I had a dream," Billings said. "I was in a dark room and there was something I couldn't . . . couldn't quite see, in the closet. It made a noise . . . a squishy noise. It reminded me of a comic book I read when I was a kid. *Tales from the Crypt,* you remember that? Christ! They had a guy named Graham Ingles; he could draw every god-awful thing in the world—and some out of it. Anyway, in this story this woman drowned her husband, see? Put cement blocks on his feet and dropped him into a quarry. Only he came back. He was all rotted and black-green and the fish had eaten away one of his eyes and there was seaweed in his hair. He came back and killed her. And when I woke up in the middle of the night, I thought that would be leaning over me. With claws . . . long claws . . ."

Dr. Harper looked at the digital clock inset into his desk. Lester Billings had been speaking for nearly half an hour. He said, "When your wife came back home, what was her attitude toward you?"

"She still loved me," Billings said with pride. "She still wanted to do what I told her. That's the wife's place, right? This women's lib only makes sick people. The most important thing in life is for a person to know his place. His . . . his . . . uh . . ."

"Station in life?"

"That's it!" Billings snapped his fingers. "That's it exactly. And a wife should follow her husband. Oh, she was sort of colorless the first four or five months after— dragged around the house, didn't sing, didn't watch the TV, didn't laugh. I knew she'd get over it. When they're that little, you don't get so attached to them. After a while you have to go to the bureau drawer and look at a picture to even remember exactly what they looked like.

"She wanted another baby," he added darkly. "I told her it was a bad idea. Oh, not forever, but for a while. I told her it was a time for us to get over things and begin to enjoy each other. We never had a chance to do that before. If you wanted to go to a movie, you had to hassle around for a baby-sitter. You couldn't go into town to see the Mets unless her folks would take the kids, because my mom wouldn't have anything to do with us. Denny was born too soon after we were married, see? She said Rita was just a tramp, a common little corner-walker. Corner-walker is what my mom always called them. Isn't that a sketch? She sat me down once and told me diseases you can get if you went to a cor . . . to a prostitute. How your pri . . . your penis has just a little tiny sore on it one day and the next day it's rotting right off. She wouldn't even come to the wedding."

Billings drummed his chest with his fingers.

"Rita's gynecologist sold her on this thing called an IUD—interuterine device. Foolproof, the doctor said. He just sticks it up the woman's . . . her place, and that's it. If there's anything in there, the egg can't fertilize. You don't even know it's there." He smiled at the ceiling with dark sweetness. "No one knows if it's there or not. And next year she's pregnant again. Some foolproof."

"No birth-control method is perfect," Harper said. "The pill is only ninety-eight percent. The IUD may be ejected by cramps, strong menstrual flow, and, in exceptional cases, by evacuation."

"Yeah. Or you can take it out."

"That's possible."

"So what's next? She's knitting little things, singing in the shower, and eating pickles like crazy. Sitting on my lap and saying things about how it must have been God's will. *Piss.*"

"The baby came at the end of the year after Shirl's death?"

"That's right. A boy. She named it Andrew Lester Billings. I didn't want anything to do with it, at least at first. My motto was she screwed up, so let her take care of it. I know how that sounds but you have to remember that I'd been through a lot.

"But I warmed up to him, you know it? He was the only one of the litter that looked like me, for one thing. Denny looked like his mother, and Shirl didn't look like anybody, except maybe my Grammy Ann. But Andy was the spitting image of me.

"I'd get to playing around with him in his playpen when I got home from work. He'd grab only my finger and smile and gurgle. Nine weeks old and the kid was grinning up at his old dad. You believe that?

"Then one night, here I am coming out of a drugstore with a mobile to hang over the kid's crib. Me! Kids don't appreciate presents until they're old enough to say thank you, that was always my motto. But there I was, buying him silly crap and all at once I realize I love him the most of all. I had another job by then, a pretty good one, selling drill bits for Cluett and Sons. I did real well, and when Andy was one, we moved to Waterbury. The old place had too many bad memories.

"And too many closets.

"That next year was the best one for us. I'd give every finger on my right hand to have it back again. Oh, the war in Vietnam was still going on, and the hippies were still running around with no clothes on, and the niggers were yelling a lot, but none of that touched us. We were on a quiet street with nice neighbors. We were happy," he summed up simply. "I asked Rita once if she wasn't worried. You know, bad luck comes in threes and all that. She said not for us. She said Andy was special. She said God had drawn a ring around him."

Billings looked morbidly at the ceiling.

"Last year wasn't so good. Something about the house changed. I started keeping my boots in the hall because I didn't like to open the closet door anymore. I kept thinking: Well, what if it's in there? All crouched down and ready to spring the second I open the door? And I'd started thinking I could hear squishy noises, as if something black and green and wet was moving around in there just a little.

"Rita asked me if I was working too hard, and I started to snap at her, just like the old days. I got sick to my stomach leaving them alone to go to work, but I was glad to get out. God help me, I was glad to get out. I started to think, see, that it lost us for a while when we moved. It had to hunt around, slinking through the streets at night and maybe creeping in the sewers. Smelling for us. It took a year, but it found us. It's back. It wants Andy and it wants me. I started to think, maybe if you think of a thing long enough, and believe in it, it gets real. Maybe all the monsters we were scared of when we were kids, Frankenstein and Wolfman and Mummy, maybe they were real. Real enough to kill the kids that were supposed to have fallen into gravel pits or drowned in lakes or were just never found. Maybe . . ."

"Are you backing away from something, Mr. Billings?"

Billings was silent for a long time—two minutes clicked off the digital clock. Then he said abruptly: "Andy died in February. Rita wasn't there. She got a call from her father. Her mother had been in a car crash the day after New Year's and wasn't expected to live. She took a bus back that night.

"Her mother didn't die, but she was on the critical list for a long time—two months. I had a very good woman who stayed with Andy days. We kept house nights. And closet doors kept coming open."

Billings licked his lips. "The kid was sleeping in the room with me. It's funny, too. Rita asked me once when he was two if I wanted to move him into another room. Spock or one of those other quacks claims it's bad for kids to sleep with their parents, see? Supposed to give them traumas about sex and all that. But we never did it unless the kid was asleep. And I didn't want to move him. I was afraid to, after Denny and Shirl."

"But you did move him, didn't you?" Dr. Harper asked.

"Yeah," Billings said. He smiled a sick, yellow smile. "I did."

Silence again. Billings wrestled with it.

"I had to!" he barked finally. "I had to! It was all right when Rita was there, but when she was gone, it started to get bolder. It started . . ." He rolled his eyes at Harper and bared his teeth in a savage grin. "Oh, you won't believe it. I know what you think, just another goofy for your casebook, I know that, but you weren't there, you lousy smug head-peeper.

"One night every door in the house blew wide open. One morning I got up and found a trail of mud and filth across the hall between the coat closet and the front door. Was it going out? Coming in? I don't know! Before Jesus, I just don't know! Records all scratched up and covered with slime, mirrors broken . . . and the sounds . . . the sounds . . ."

He ran a hand through his hair. "You'd wake up at three in the morning and look into the dark and at first you'd say, 'It's only the clock.' But underneath it you could hear something moving in a stealthy way. But not too stealthy, because it wanted you to hear it. A slimy sliding sound like something from the kitchen drain. Or a clicking sound, like claws being dragged lightly over the staircase banister. And you'd close your eyes, knowing that hearing it was bad, but if you *saw* it . . .

"And always you'd be afraid that the noises might stop for a little while, and then there would be a laugh right over your face and a breath of air like stale cabbage on your face, and then hands on your throat."

Billings was pallid and trembling.

"So I moved him. I knew it would go for him, see. Because he was weaker. And it did. That very first night he screamed in the middle of the night and finally, when I got up the cojones to go in, he was standing up in bed and screaming. 'The boogeyman, Daddy . . . boogeyman . . . wanna go wif Daddy, go wif Daddy.' " Billings' voice had become a high treble, like a child's. His eyes seemed to fill his entire face; he almost seemed to shrink on the couch.

"But I couldn't," the childish breaking treble continued, "I couldn't. And an hour later there was a scream. An awful, gurgling scream. And I knew how much I loved him because I ran in, I didn't even turn on the light, I ran, ran, *ran,* oh, Jesus God Mary, it had him; it was shaking him, shaking him just like a terrier shakes a piece of cloth and I could see something with awful slumped shoulders and a scarecrow head and I could smell something like a dead mouse in a pop bottle and I heard . . ." He trailed off, and then his voice clicked back into an adult range. "I heard it when Andy's neck broke." Billings' voice was cool and dead. "It made a sound like ice cracking when you're skating on a country pond in winter."

"Then what happened?"

"Oh, I ran," Billings said in the same cool, dead voice. "I went to an all-night diner. How's that for complete cowardice? Ran to an all-night diner and drank six cups of coffee. Then I went home. It was already dawn. I called the police even before I went upstairs. He was lying on the floor and staring at me. Accusing me. A tiny bit of blood had run out of one ear. Only a drop, really. And the closet door was open—but just a crack."

The voice stopped. Harper looked at the digital clock. Fifty minutes had passed.

"Make an appointment with the nurse," he said. "In fact, several of them. Tuesdays and Thursdays?"

"I only came to tell my story," Billings said. "To get it off my chest. I lied to the police, see? Told them the kid must have tried to get out of his crib in the night and . . . they swallowed it. Course they did. That's just what it looked like. Accidental, like the others. But Rita knew. Rita . . . finally . . . knew . . ."

He covered his eyes with his right arm and began to weep.

"Mr. Billings, there is a great deal to talk about," Dr. Harper said after a pause. "I believe we can remove some of the guilt you've been carrying, but first you have to want to get rid of it."

"Don't you believe I *do?*" Billings cried, removing his arm from his eyes. They were red, raw, wounded.

"Not yet," Harper said quietly. "Tuesdays and Thursdays?"

After a long silence, Billings muttered, "Goddamn shrink. All right. All right."

"Make an appointment with the nurse, Mr. Billings. And have a good day."

Billings laughed emptily and walked out of the office quickly, without looking back.

The nurses' station was empty. A small sign on the desk blotter said: BACK IN A MINUTE.

Billings turned and went back into the office. "Doctor, your nurse is—"

The room was empty.

But the closet door was open. Just a crack.

"So nice," the voice from the closet said. "So nice." The words sounded as if they might have come through a mouthful of rotted seaweed.

Billings stood rooted to the spot as the closet door swung open. He dimly felt warmth at his crotch as he wet himself.

"So nice," the boogeyman said as it shambled out.

It still held its Dr. Harper mask in one rotted, spade-claw hand.

GRAY MATTER

They had been predicting a norther all week and along
about Thursday we got it, a real screamer that piled
up eight inches by four in the afternoon and showed no
signs of slowing down. The usual five or six were gathered around the Reliable in Henry's Nite-Owl, which
is the only little store on this side of Bangor that stays
open right around the clock.

Henry don't do a huge business—mostly, it amounts
to selling the college kids their beer and wine—but he
gets by and it's a place for us old duffers on Social Security to get together and talk about who's died lately and
how the world's going to hell.

This afternoon Henry was at the counter; Bill Pelham, Bertie Connors, Carl Littlefield, and me was
tipped up by the stove. Outside, not a car was moving
on Ohio Street, and the plows was having hard going.
The wind was socking drifts across that looked like the
backbone on a dinosaur.

Henry'd only had three customers all afternoon—

that is, if you want to count in blind Eddie. Eddie's about seventy, and he ain't completely blind. Runs into things, mostly. He comes in once or twice a week and sticks a loaf of bread under his coat and walks out with an expression on his face like: *there, you stupid sons-abitches, fooled you again.*

Bertie once asked Henry why he never put a stop to it.

"I'll tell you," Henry said. "A few years back the Air Force wanted twenty million dollars to rig up a flyin' model of an airplane they had planned out. Well, it cost them seventy-five million and then the damn thing wouldn't fly. That happened ten years ago, when blind Eddie and myself were considerably younger, and I voted for the woman who sponsored that bill. Blind Eddie voted against her. And since then I've been buyin' his bread."

Bertie didn't look like he quite followed all of that, but he sat back to muse over it.

Now the door opened again, letting in a blast of the cold gray air outside, and a young kid came in, stamping snow off his boots. I placed him after a second. He was Richie Grenadine's kid, and he looked like he'd just kissed the wrong end of the baby. His Adam's apple was going up and down and his face was the color of old oilcloth.

"Mr. Parmalee," he says to Henry, his eyeballs rolling around in his head like ball bearings, "you got to come. You got to take him his beer and come. I can't stand to go back there. I'm scared."

"Now slow down," Henry says, taking off his white butcher's apron and coming around the counter. "What's the matter? Your dad been on a drunk?"

I realized when he said that that Richie hadn't been in for quite some time. Usually he'd be by once a day to pick up a case of whatever beer was going cheapest at that time, a big fat man with jowls like pork butts and ham-hock arms. Richie always was a pig about his beer, but he handled it okay when he was working at the sawmill out in Clifton. Then something happened—a pulper piled a bad load, or maybe Richie just made it out that way—and Richie was off work, free an' easy, with the sawmill company paying him compensation. Something in his back. Anyway, he got awful fat. He hadn't been in lately, although once in a while I'd seen his boy come in for Richie's nightly case. Nice enough boy. Henry sold him the beer, for he knew it was only the boy doing as his father said.

"He's been on a drunk," the boy was saying now, "but that ain't the trouble. It's . . . it's . . . oh Lord, it's *awful!*"

Henry saw he was going to bawl, so he says real quick: "Carl, will you watch things for a minute?"

"Sure."

"Now, Timmy, you come back into the stockroom and tell me what's what."

He led the boy away, and Carl went around behind the counter and sat on Henry's stool. No one said anything for quite a while. We could hear 'em back there, Henry's deep, slow voice and then Timmy Grenadine's high one, speaking very fast. Then the boy commenced to cry, and Bill Pelham cleared his throat and started filling up his pipe.

"I ain't seen Richie for a couple months," I said.

Bill grunted. "No loss."

"He was in . . . oh, near the end of October," Carl said. "Near Halloween. Bought a case of Schlitz beer. He was gettin' awful meaty."

There wasn't much more to say. The boy was still crying, but he was talking at the same time. Outside the wind kept on whooping and yowling and the radio said we'd have another six inches or so by morning. It was mid-January and it made me wonder if anyone had seen Richie since October—besides his boy, that is.

The talking went on for quite a while, but finally Henry and the boy came back out. The boy had taken his coat off, but Henry had put his on. The boy was kinda hitching in his chest the way you do when the worst is past, but his eyes was red and when he glanced at you, he'd look down at the floor.

Henry looked worried. "I thought I'd send Timmy here upstairs an' have my wife cook him up a toasted cheese or somethin'. Maybe a couple of you fellas'd like to go around to Richie's place with me. Timmy says he wants some beer. He gave me the money." He tried to smile, but it was a pretty sick affair and he soon gave up.

"Sure," Bertie says. "What kind of beer? I'll go fetch her."

"Get Harrow's Supreme," Henry said. "We got some cutdown boxes back there."

I got up, too. It would have to be Bertie and me. Carl's arthritis gets something awful on days like this, and Billy Pelham don't have much use of his right arm anymore.

Bertie got four six-packs of Harrow's and I packed them into a box while Henry took the boy upstairs to the apartment, overhead.

Well, he straightened that out with his missus and came back down, looking over his shoulder once to make sure the upstairs door was closed. Billy spoke up, fairly busting: "What's up? Has Richie been workin' the kid over?"

"No," Henry said. "I'd just as soon not say anything just yet. It'd sound crazy. I will show you somethin', though. The money Timmy had to pay for the beer with." He shed four dollar bills out of his pocket, holding them by the corner, and I don't blame him. They was all covered with a gray, slimy stuff that looked like the scum on top of bad preserves. He laid them down on the counter with a funny smile and said to Carl; "Don't let anybody touch 'em. Not if what the kid says is even half right!"

And he went around to the sink by the meat counter and washed his hands.

I got up, put on my pea coat and scarf and buttoned up. It was no good taking a car; Richie lived in an apartment building down on Curve Street, which is as close to straight up an' down as the law allows, and it's the last place the plows touch.

As we were going out, Bill Pelham called after us: "Watch out, now."

Henry just nodded and put the case of Harrow's on the little handcart he keeps by the door, and out we trundled.

The wind hit us like a sawblade, and right away I pulled my scarf up over my ears. We paused in the doorway just for a second while Bertie pulled on his gloves. He had a pained sort of a wince on his face, and I knew how he felt. It's all well for younger fellows to go out skiing all day and running those goddamn wasp-wing snowmobiles half the night, but when you get up over seventy without an oil change, you feel that northeast wind around your heart.

"I don't want to scare you boys," Henry said, with that queer, sort of revolted smile still on his mouth, "but I'm goin' to show you this all the same. And I'm goin' to tell you what the boy told me while we walk up there . . . because I want you to know, you see!"

And he pulled a .45-caliber hogleg out of his coat pocket—the pistol he'd kept loaded and ready under the counter ever since he went to twenty-four hours a day back in 1958. I don't know where he got it, but I do know the one time he flashed it at a stickup guy, the fella just turned around and bolted right out the door. Henry was a cool one, all right. I saw him throw out a college kid that came in one time and gave him a hard time about cashing a check. That kid walked away like his ass was on sideways and he had to crap.

Well, I only tell you that because Henry wanted Bertie and me to know he meant business, and we did, too.

So we set out, bent into the wind like washerwomen, Henry trundling that cart and telling us what the boy had said. The wind was trying to rip the words away before we could hear 'em, but we got most of it—more'n we wanted to. I was damn glad Henry had his Frenchman's pecker stowed away in his coat pocket.

The kid said it must have been the beer—you know how you can get a bad can every now and again. Flat or smelly or green as the peestains in an Irishman's underwear. A fella once told me that all it takes is a tiny hole to let in bacteria that'll do some damn strange things. The hole can be so small that the beer won't hardly dribble out, but the bacteria can get in. And beer's good food for some of those bugs.

Anyway, the kid said Richie brought back a case of Golden Light just like always that night in October and sat down to polish it off while Timmy did his homework.

Timmy was just about ready for bed when he hears Richie say, "Christ Jesus, that ain't right."

And Timmy says, "What's that, Pop?"

"That beer," Richie says. "God, that's the *worst* taste I ever had in my mouth."

Most people would wonder why in the name of God he drank it if it tasted so bad, but then, most people have never seen Richie Grenadine go to his beer. I was down in Wally's Spa one afternoon, and I saw him win the goddamndest bet. He bet a fella he could drink twenty two-bit glasses of beer in one minute. Nobody local would take him up, but this salesman from Montpelier laid down a twenty-dollar bill and Richie covered him. He drank all twenty with seven seconds to spare—although when he walked out he was more'n three sails into the wind. So I expect Richie had most of that bad can in his gut before his brain could warn him.

"I'm gonna puke," Richie says. "Look out!"

But by the time he got to the head it had passed off, and that was the end of it. The boy said he smelt the can, and it smelt like something crawled in there and died. There was a little gray dribble around the top, too.

Two days later the boy comes home from school and there's Richie sitting in front of the TV and watching the afternoon tearjerkers with every goddamn shade in the place pulled down.

"What's up?" Timmy asks, for Richie don't hardly ever roll in before nine.

"I'm watchin' the TV," Richie says. "I didn't seem to want to go out today."

Timmy turned on the light over the sink, and Richie yelled at him: "And turn off that friggin' light!"

So Timmy did, not asking how he's gonna do his homework in the dark. When Richie's in that mood, you don't ask him nothing.

"An' go out an' get me a case," Richie says. "Money's on the table."

When the kid gets back, his dad's still sitting in the dark, only now it's dark outside, too. And the TV's off. The kid starts getting the creeps—well, who wouldn't?

Nothing but a dark flat and your daddy setting in the corner like a big lump.

So he puts the beer on the table, knowing that Richie don't like it so cold it spikes his forehead, and when he gets close to his old man he starts to notice a kind of rotten smell, like an old cheese someone left standing on the counter over the weekend. He don't say shit or go blind, though, as the old man was never what you'd call a cleanly soul. Instead he goes into his room and shuts the door and does his homework, and after a while he hears the TV start to go and Richie's popping the top in his first of the evening.

And for two weeks or so, that's the way things went. The kid got up in the morning and went to school an' when he got home Richie'd be in front of the television, and beer money on the table.

The flat was smelling ranker and ranker, too. Richie wouldn't have the shades up at all, and about the middle of November he made Timmy stop studying in his room. Said he couldn't abide the light under the door. So Timmy started going down the block to a friend's house after getting his dad the beer.

Then one day when Timmy came home from school— it was four o'clock and pretty near dark already—Richie says, "Turn on the light."

The kid turns on the light over the sink, and damn if Richie ain't all wrapped up in a blanket.

"Look," Richie says, and one hand creeps out from under the blanket. Only it ain't a hand at all. *Something gray,* is all the kid could tell Henry. *Didn't look like a hand at all. Just a gray lump.*

Well, Timmy Grenadine was scared bad. He says, "Pop, what's happening to you?"

And Richie says, "I dunno. But it don't hurt. It feels . . . kinda nice."

So, Timmy says, "I'm gonna call Dr. Westphail."

And the blanket starts to tremble all over, like something awful was shaking—*all over*—under there. And Richie says, "Don't you dare. If you do I'll touch ya and you'll end up just like this." And he slides the blanket down over his face for just a minute.

By then we were up to the corner of Harlow and Curve Street, and I was even colder than the temperature had been on Henry's Orange Crush thermometer when we came out. A person doesn't hardly want to believe such things, and yet there's still strange things in the world.

I once knew a fella named George Kelso, who worked for the Bangor Public Works Department. He spent fifteen years fixing water mains and mending electricity cables and all that, an' then one day he just up an' quit, not two years before his retirement. Frankie Haldeman, who knew him, said George went down into a sewer pipe on Essex laughing and joking just like always and came up fifteen minutes later with his hair just as white as snow and his eyes staring like he just looked through a window into hell. He walked straight down to the BPW garage and punched his clock and went down to Wally's Spa and started drinking. It killed him two years later. Frankie said he tried to talk to him about it and George said something one time, and that was when he was pretty well blotto. Turned around on his stool, George did, an' asked Frankie Haldeman if he'd ever seen a spider as big as a good-sized dog setting in a web full of kitties an' such all wrapped up in silk thread. Well, what could he say to that? I'm not saying there's any truth in it, but I am saying that there's things in the corners of the world that would drive a man insane to look 'em right in the face.

So we just stood on the corner a minute, in spite of the wind that was whooping up the street.

"What'd he see?" Bertie asked.

"He said he could still see his dad," Henry answered, "but he said it was like he was buried in gray jelly . . . and it was all kinda mashed together. He said his clothes were all stickin' in and out of his skin, like they was melted to his body."

"Holy Jesus," Bertie said.

"Then he covered right up again and started screaming at the kid to turn off the light."

"Like he was a fungus," I said.

"Yes," Henry said. "Sorta like that."

"You keep that pistol handy," Bertie said.

"Yes, I think I will." And with that, we started to trundle up Curve Street.

The apartment house where Richie Grenadine had his flat was almost at the top of the hill, one of those big Victorian monsters that were built by the pulp an' paper barons at the turn of the century. They've just about all been turned into apartment houses now. When Bertie got his breath he told us Richie lived on the third floor under that top gable that jutted out like an eyebrow. I took the chance to ask Henry what happened to the kid after that.

Along about the third week in November the kid came back one afternoon to find Richie had gone one further than just pulling the shades down. He'd taken and nailed blankets across every window in the place. It was starting to stink worse, too—kind of a mushy stink, the way fruit gets when it goes to ferment with yeast.

A week or so after that, Richie got the kid to start heating his beer on the stove. Can you feature that? The kid all by himself in that apartment with his dad turning into . . . well, into something . . . an' heating his beer and then having to listen to him—it—drinking it with awful thick slurping sounds, the way an old man eats his chowder: Can you imagine it?

And that's the way things went on until today, when the kid's school let out early because of the storm.

"The boy says he went right home," Henry told us. "There's no light in the upstairs hall at all—the boy claims his dad musta snuck out some night and broke it—so he had to sort of creep down to his door.

"Well, he heard somethin' moving around in there, and it suddenly pops into his mind that he don't know what Richie does all day through the week. He ain't seen his dad stir out of that chair for almost a month, and a man's got to sleep and go to the bathroom sometime.

"There's a Judas hole in the middle of the door, and it's supposed to have a latch on the inside to fasten it shut, but it's been busted ever since they lived there. So the kid slides up to the door real easy and pushed it open a bit with his thumb and pokes his eye up to it."

By now we were at the foot of the steps and the house was looming over us like a high, ugly face, with those windows on the third floor for eyes. I looked up there and sure enough those two windows were just as black as pitch. Like somebody'd put blankets over 'em or painted 'em up.

"It took him a minute to get his eye adjusted to the gloom. An' then he seen a great big gray lump, not like a man at all, slitherin' over the floor, leavin' a gray, slimy trail behind it. An' then it sort of snaked out an arm—or something like an arm—and pried a board off'n the wall. And took out a cat." Henry stopped for a second. Bertie was beating his hands together and it was god-awful cold out there on the street, but none of us was ready to go up just yet. "A dead cat," Henry recommenced, "that had putrefacted. The boy said it looked all swole up stiff . . . and there was little white things crawlin' all over it . . ."

"Stop," Bertie said. "For Christ's sake."

"And then his dad ate it."

I tried to swallow and something tasted greasy in my throat.

"That's when Timmy closed the peephole," Henry finished softly. "And ran."

"I don't think I can go up there," Bertie said.

Henry didn't say nothing, just looked from Bertie to me and back again.

"I guess we better," I said. "We got Richie's beer."

Bertie didn't say anything to that, so we went up the steps and in through the front hall door. I smelled it right off.

Do you know how a cider house smells in summer? You never get the smell of apples out, but in the fall it's all right because it smells tangy and sharp enough to ream your nose right out. But in the summer, it just smells mean, this smell was like that, but a little bit worse.

There was one light on in the lower hall, a mean yellow thing in a frosted glass that threw a glow as thin as buttermilk. And those stairs that went up into the shadows.

Henry bumped the cart to a stop, and while he was lifting out the case of beer, I thumbed the button at the foot of the stairs that controlled the second-floor-landing bulb. But it was busted, just as the boy said.

Bertie quavered: "I'll lug the beer. You just take care of that pistol."

Henry didn't argue. He handed it over and we started up, Henry first, then me, then Bertie with the case in his arms. By the time we had fetched the second-floor landing, the stink was just that much worse. Rotted apples, all fermented, and under that an even uglier stink.

When I lived out in Levant I had a dog one time— Rex, his name was—and he was a good mutt but not very wise about cars. He got hit a lick one afternoon while I was at work and he crawled under the house and died there. My Christ, what a stink. I finally had to go under and haul him out with a pole. That other stench was like that; flyblown and putrid and just as dirty as a borin' cob.

Up till then I had kept thinking that maybe it was some sort of joke, but I saw it wasn't. "Lord, why don't the neighbors kick up Harry?" I asked.

"What neighbors?" Henry asked, and he was smiling that queer smile again.

I looked around and saw that the hall had a sort of dusty, unused look and the door of all three second-floor apartments was closed and locked up.

"Who's the landlord, I wonder?" Bertie asked, resting the case on the newel post and getting his breath. "Gaiteau? Surprised he don't kick 'im out."

"Who'd go up there and evict him?" Henry asked. "You?"

Bertie didn't say nothing.

Presently we started up the next flight, which was even narrower and steeper than the last. It was getting hotter, too. It sounded like every radiator in the place was clanking and hissing. The smell was awful, and I started to feel like someone was stirring my guts with a stick.

At the top was a short hall, and one door with a little Judas hole in the middle of it.

Bertie made a soft little cry an' whispered out: "Look what we're walkin' in!"

I looked down and saw all this slimy stuff on the hall

floor, in little puddles. It looked like there'd been a carpet once, but the gray stuff had eaten it all away.

Henry walked down to the door, and we went after him. I don't know about Bertie, but I was shaking in my shoes. Henry never hesitated, though; he raised up that gun and beat on the door with the butt of it.

"Richie?" he called, and his voice didn't sound a bit scared, although his face was deadly pale. "This is Henry Parmalee from down at the Nite-Owl. I brought your beer."

There wasn't any answer for p'raps a full minute, and then a voice said, "Where's Timmy? Where's my boy?"

I almost ran right then. That voice wasn't human at all. It was queer an' low an' bubbly, like someone talking through a mouthful of suet.

"He's at my store," Henry said, "havin' a decent meal. He's just as skinny as a slat cat, Richie."

There wasn't nothing for a while, and then some horrible squishing noises, like a man in rubber boots walking through mud. Then that decayed voice spoke right through the other side of the door.

"Open the door an' shove that beer through," it said. "Only you got to pull all the ring tabs first. I can't."

"In a minute," Henry said. "What kind of shape you in, Richie?"

"Never mind that," the voice said, and it was horribly eager. "Just push in the beer and go!"

"It ain't just dead cats anymore, is it?" Henry said, and he sounded sad. He wasn't holdin' the gun butt-up anymore; now it was business end first.

And suddenly, in a flash of light, I made the mental connection Henry had already made, perhaps even as Timmy was telling his story. The smell of decay and rot seemed to double in my nostrils when I remembered. Two young girls and some old Salvation Army wino had disappeared in town during the last three weeks or so—all after dark.

"Send it in or I'll come out an' get it," the voice said.

Henry gestured us back, and we went.

"I guess you better, Richie." He cocked his piece.

There was nothing then, not for a long time. To tell the truth, I began to feel as if it was all over. Then that door burst open, so sudden and so hard that it actually *bulged* before slamming out against the wall. And out came Richie.

It was just a second, just a second before Bertie and me was down those stairs like schoolkids, four an' five at a time, and out the door into the snow, slipping an' sliding.

Going down we heard Henry fire three times, the reports loud as grenades in the closed hallways of that empty, cursed house.

What we saw in that one or two seconds will last me a lifetime—or whatever's left of it. It was like a huge gray wave of jelly, jelly that looked like a man, and leaving a trail of slime behind it.

But that wasn't the worst. Its eyes were flat and yellow and wild, with no human soul in 'em. Only there wasn't two. There were four, an' right down the center of the thing, betwixt the two pairs of eyes, was a white, fibrous line with a kind of pulsing pink flesh showing through like a slit in a hog's belly.

It was dividing, you see. Dividing in two.

Bertie and I didn't say nothing to each other going back to the store. I don't know what was going through his mind, but I know well enough what was in mine: the multiplication table. Two times two is four, four times two is eight, eight times two is sixteen, sixteen times two is—

We got back. Carl and Bill Pelham jumped up and started asking questions right off. We wouldn't answer, neither of us. We just turned around and waited to see if Henry was gonna walk in outta the snow. I was up to 32,768 times two is the end of the human race and so we sat there cozied up to all that beer and waited to see which one was going to finally come back; and here we still sit.

I hope it's Henry. I surely do.

BATTLEGROUND

"**M**r. Renshaw?"

The desk clerk's voice caught him halfway to the elevator, and Renshaw turned back impatiently, shifting his flight bag from one hand to the other. The envelope in his coat pocket, stuffed with twenties and fifties, crackled heavily. The job had gone well and the pay had been excellent—even after the Organization's 15 percent finder's fee had been skimmed off the top. Now all he wanted was a hot shower and a gin and tonic and sleep.

"What is it?"

"Package, sir. Would you sign the slip?"

Renshaw signed and looked thoughtfully at the rectangular package. His name and the building's address were written on the gummed label in a spiky backhand script that seemed familiar. He rocked the package on the imitation-marble surface of the desk, and something clanked faintly inside.

"Should I have that sent up, Mr. Renshaw?"

"No, I've got it." It was about eighteen inches on a side and fitted clumsily under his arm. He put it on the plush carpet that covered the elevator floor and twisted his key in the penthouse slot above the regular rack of buttons. The car rose smoothly and silently. He closed his eyes and let the job replay itself on the dark screen of his mind.

First, as always, a call from Cal Bates: "You available, Johnny?"

He was available twice a year, minimum fee $10,000. He was very good, very reliable, but what his customers really paid for was the infallible predator's talent. John Renshaw was a human hawk, constructed by both genetics and environment to do two things superbly: kill and survive.

After Bates' call, a buff-colored envelope appeared in Renshaw's box. A name, an address, a photograph. All committed to memory; then down the garbage disposal with the ashes of envelope and contents.

This time the face had been that of a sallow Miami businessman named Hans Morris, founder and owner of the Morris Toy Company. Someone had wanted Morris out of the way and had gone to the Organization. The Organization, in the person of Calvin Bates, had talked to John Renshaw. *Pow.* Mourners please omit flowers.

The doors slid open, he picked up his package and stepped out. He unlocked the suite and stepped in. At this time of day, just after 3 P.M., the spacious living room was splashed with April sunshine. He paused for a moment, enjoying it, then put the package on the end table by the door and loosened his tie. He dropped the envelope on top of it and walked over to the terrace.

He pushed open the sliding glass door and stepped out. It was cold, and the wind knifed through his thin topcoat. Yet he paused a moment, looking over the city the way a general might survey a captured country. Traffic crawled beetlelike in the streets. Far away, almost buried in the golden afternoon haze, the Bay Bridge glittered like a madman's mirage. To the east, all but lost behind the downtown high rises, the crammed and dirty tenements with their stainless-steel forests of TV aerials. It was better up here. Better than in the gutters.

He went back inside, slid the door closed, and went into the bathroom for a long, hot shower.

When he sat down forty minutes later to regard his package, drink in hand, the shadows had marched halfway across the wine-colored carpet and the best of the afternoon was past.

It was a bomb.

Of course it wasn't, but one proceeded as if it were. That was why one had remained upright and taking nourishment while so many others had gone to that great unemployment office in the sky.

If it was a bomb, it was clockless. It sat utterly silent; bland and enigmatic. Plastique was more likely these days, anyway. Less temperamental than the clocksprings manufactured by Westclox and Big Ben.

Renshaw looked at the postmark. Miami, April 15. Five days ago. So the bomb was not time-set. It would have gone off in the hotel safe in that case.

Miami. Yes. And that spiky backhand writing. There had been a framed photograph on the sallow businessman's desk. The photo had been of an even sallower old crone wearing a babushka. The script slanted across the bottom had read: "Best from your number-one idea girl—Mom."

What kind of a number-one idea is this, Mom? A do-it-yourself extermination kit?

He regarded the package with complete concentration, not moving, his hands folded. Extraneous questions, such as how Morris' number-one idea girl might have discovered his address, did not occur to him. They were for later, for Cal Bates. Unimportant now.

With a sudden, almost absent move, he took a small celluloid calendar out of his wallet and inserted it deftly under the twine that crisscrossed the brown paper. He slid it under the Scotch tape that held one end flap. The flap came loose, relaxing against the twine.

He paused for a time, observing, then leaned close and sniffed. Cardboard, paper, string. Nothing more. He walked around the box, squatted easily on his haunches, and repeated the process. Twilight was invading his apartment with gray, shadowy fingers.

One of the flaps popped free of the restraining twine, showing a dull green box beneath. Metal. Hinged. He produced a pocket knife and cut the twine. It fell away, and a few helping prods with the tip of the knife revealed the box.

It was green with black markings, and stenciled on the front in white letters were the words: G.I. JOE VIET-

NAM FOOTLOCKER. Below that: *20 Infantrymen, 10 Heli-copters, 2 BAR Men, 2 Bazooka Men, 2 Medics, 4 Jeeps.* Below that: a flag decal. Below that, in the corner: *Morris Toy Company, Miami, Fla.*

He reached out to touch it, then withdrew his hand. Something inside the footlocker had moved.

Renshaw stood up, not hurrying, and backed across the room toward the kitchen and the hall. He snapped on the lights.

The Vietnam Footlocker was rocking, making the brown paper beneath it rattle. It suddenly overbalanced and fell to the carpet with a soft thud, landing on one end. The hinged top opened a crack of perhaps two inches.

Tiny foot soldiers, about an inch and a half tall, began to crawl out. Renshaw watched them, unblinking. His mind made no effort to cope with the real or unreal aspect of what he was seeing—only with the possible consequences for his survival.

The soldiers were wearing minuscule army fatigues, helmets, and field packs. Tiny carbines were slung across their shoulders. Two of them looked briefly across the room at Renshaw. Their eyes, no bigger than pencil points, glittered.

Five, ten, twelve, then all twenty. One of them was gesturing, ordering the others. They lined themselves up along the crack that the fall had produced and began to push. The crack began to widen.

Renshaw picked one of the large pillows off the couch and began to walk toward them. The command-ing officer turned and gestured. The others whirled and unslung their carbines. There were tiny, almost delicate popping sounds, and Renshaw felt suddenly as if he had been stung by bees.

He threw the pillow. It struck them, knocking them sprawling, then hit the box and knocked it wide open. Insectlike, with a faint, high whirring noise like chiggers, a cloud of miniature helicopters, painted jungle green, rose out of the box.

Tiny *phut! phut!* sounds reached Renshaw's ears and he saw pinprick-sized muzzle flashes coming from the open copter doors. Needles pricked his belly, his right arm, the side of his neck. He clawed out and got one— sudden pain in his fingers; blood welling. The whirling blades had chopped them to the bone in diagonal scarlet hash marks. The others whirled out of range, circling him like horseflies. The stricken copter thumped to the rug and lay still.

Sudden excruciating pain in his foot made him cry out. One of the foot soldiers was standing on his shoe and bayoneting his ankle. The tiny face looked up, panting and grinning.

Renshaw kicked at it and the tiny body flew across the room to splatter on the wall. It did not leave blood but a viscid purple smear.

There was a tiny, coughing explosion and blinding agony ripped his thigh. One of the bazooka men had come out of the footlocker. A small curl of smoke rose lazily from his weapon. Renshaw looked down at his leg and saw a blackened, smoking hole in his pants the size of a quarter. The flesh beneath was charred.

The little bastard shot me!

He turned and ran into the hall, then into his bedroom. One of the helicopters buzzed past his cheek, blades whirring busily. The small stutter of a BAR. Then it darted away.

The gun beneath his pillow was a .44 Magnum, big enough to put a hole the size of two fists through anything it hit. Renshaw turned, holding the pistol in both hands. He realized coolly that he would be shooting at a moving target not much bigger than a flying lightbulb.

Two of the copters whirred in. Sitting on the bed, Renshaw fired once. One of the helicopters exploded into nothingness. That's two, he thought. He drew a bead on the second . . . squeezed the trigger . . .

It jigged! Goddamnit, it jigged!

The helicopter swooped at him in a sudden deadly arc, fore and aft overhead props whirring with blinding speed. Renshaw caught a glimpse of one of the BAR men crouched at the open bay door, firing his weapon in short, deadly bursts, and then he threw himself to the floor and rolled.

My eyes, the bastard was going for my eyes!

He came up on his back at the far wall, the gun held at chest level. But the copter was retreating. It seemed to pause for a moment, and dip in recognition of Renshaw's superior firepower. Then it was gone, back toward the living room.

Renshaw got up, wincing as his weight came down on the wounded leg. It was bleeding freely. And why not? he thought grimly. It's not everybody who gets hit point-blank with a bazooka shell and lives to tell about it.

So Mom was his number-one idea girl, was she? She was all that and a bit more.

He shook a pillowcase free of the tick and ripped it into a bandage for his leg, then took his shaving mirror from the bureau and went to the hallway door. Kneeling, he shoved it out onto the carpet at an angle and peered in.

They were bivouacking by the footlocker, damned if they weren't. Miniature soldiers ran hither and thither, setting up tents. Jeeps two inches high raced about importantly. A medic was working over the soldier Renshaw had kicked. The remaining eight copters flew in a protective swarm overhead, at coffee-table level.

Suddenly they became aware of the mirror, and three of the foot soldiers dropped to one knee and began firing. Seconds later the mirror shattered in four places. *Okay, okay, then.*

Renshaw went back to the bureau and got the heavy mahogany odds-and-ends box Linda had given him for Christmas. He hefted it once, nodded, and went to the doorway and lunged through. He wound up and fired like a pitcher throwing a fast ball. The box described a swift, true vector and smashed little men like ninepins. One of the jeeps rolled over twice. Renshaw advanced to the doorway of the living room, sighted on one of the sprawling soldiers, and gave it to him.

Several of the others had recovered. Some were kneeling and firing formally. Others had taken cover. Still others had retreated back into the footlocker.

The bee stings began to pepper his legs and torso, but none reached higher than his rib cage. Perhaps the range was too great. It didn't matter; he had no intention of being turned away. This was it.

He missed with his next shot—they were so goddamn small—but the following one sent another soldier into a broken sprawl.

The copters were buzzing toward him ferociously. Now the tiny bullets began to splat into his face, above and below his eyes. He potted the lead copter, then the second. Jagged streaks of pain silvered his vision.

The remaining six split into two retreating wings. His face was wet with blood and he swiped at it with his forearm. He was ready to start firing again when he paused. The soldiers who had retreated inside the footlocker were trundling something out. Something that looked like . . .

There was a blinding sizzle of yellow fire, and a sudden gout of wood and plaster exploded from the wall to his left.

. . . a rocket launcher!

He squeezed off one shot at it, missed, wheeled and ran for the bathroom at the far end of the corridor. He slammed the door and locked it. In the bathroom mirror an Indian was staring back at him with dazed and haunted eyes, a battle-crazed Indian with thin streamers of red paint drawn from holes no bigger than grains of pepper. A ragged flap of skin dangled from one cheek. There was a gouged furrow in his neck.

I'm losing!

He ran a shaking hand through his hair. The front door was cut off. So was the phone and the kitchen extension. They had a goddamn rocket launcher and a direct hit would tear his head off.

Damn it, that wasn't even listed on the box!

He started to draw in a long breath and let it out in a sudden grunt as a fist-sized section of the door blew in with a charred burst of wood. Tiny flames glowed briefly around the ragged edges of the hole, and he saw the brilliant flash as they launched another round. More wood blew inward, scattering burning slivers on the bathroom rug. He stamped them out and two of the copters buzzed angrily through the hole. Minuscule BAR slugs stitched his chest.

With a whining groan of rage he smashed one out of the air barehanded, sustaining a picket fence of deep slashes across his palm. In sudden desperate invention, he slung a heavy bath towel over the other. It fell, writhing, to the floor, and he stamped the life out of it. His breath was coming in hoarse whoops. Blood ran into one eye, hot and stinging, and he wiped it away.

There, goddamnit. There. That'll make them think.

Indeed, it did seem to be making them think. There was no movement for fifteen minutes. Renshaw sat on the edge of the tub, thinking feverishly. There had to be a way out of this blind alley. There *had* to be. If there was only a way to flank them . . .

He suddenly turned and looked at the small window over the tub. There was a way. Of course there was.

His eyes dropped to the can of lighter fluid on top of the medicine cabinet. He was reaching for it when the rustling noise came.

He whirled, bringing the Magnum up . . . but it was only a tiny scrap of paper shoved under the crack of the door. The crack, Renshaw noted grimly, was too narrow for even one of *them* to get through.

There was one tiny word written on the paper:

Surrender

Renshaw smiled grimly and put the lighter fluid in his breast pocket. There was a chewed stub of pencil beside it. He scrawled one word on the paper and shoved it back under the door. The word was:

NUTS

There was a sudden blinding barrage of rocket shells, and Renshaw backed away. They arched through the hole in the door and detonated against the pale blue tiles above the towel rack, turning the elegant wall into a pocket lunar landscape. Renshaw threw a hand over his eyes as plaster flew in a hot rain of shrapnel. Burning holes ripped through his shirt and his back was peppered.

When the barrage stopped, Renshaw moved. He climbed on top of the tub and slid the window open.

Cold stars looked in at him. It was a narrow window, and a narrow ledge beyond it. But there was no time to think of that.

He boosted himself through, and the cold air slapped his lacerated face and neck like an open hand. He was leaning over the balance point of his hands, staring straight down. Forty stories down. From this height the street looked no wider than a child's train track. The bright, winking lights of the city glittered madly below him like thrown jewels.

With the deceptive ease of a trained gymnast, Renshaw brought his knees up to rest on the lower edge of the window. If one of those wasp-sized copters flew through that hole in the door now, one shot in the ass would send him straight down, screaming all the way.

None did.

He twisted, thrust one leg out, and one reaching hand grabbed the overhead cornice and held. A moment later he was standing on the ledge outside the window.

Deliberately not thinking of the horrifying drop below his heels, not thinking of what would happen if one of the helicopters buzzed out after him, Renshaw edged toward the corner of the building.

Fifteen feet . . . ten . . . There. He paused, his chest pressed against the wall, hands splayed out on the rough surface. He could feel the lighter fluid in his breast pocket and the reassuring weight of the Magnum jammed in his waistband.

Now to get around the goddamn corner.

Gently, he eased one foot around and slid his weight

onto it. Now the right angle was pressed razorlike into his chest and gut. There was a smear of bird guano in front of his eyes on the rough stone. Christ, he thought crazily. I didn't know they could fly this high.

His left foot slipped.

For a weird, timeless moment he tottered over the brink, right arm backwatering madly for balance, and then he was clutching the two sides of the building in a lover's embrace, face pressed against the hard corner, breath shuddering in and out of his lungs.

A bit at a time, he slid the other foot around.

Thirty feet away, his own living-room terrace jutted out.

He made his way down to it, breath sliding in and out of his lungs with shallow force. Twice he was forced to stop as sharp gusts of wind tried to pick him off the ledge.

Then he was there, gripping the ornamented iron railings.

He hoisted himself over noiselessly. He had left the curtains half drawn across the sliding glass partition, and now he peered in cautiously. They were just the way he wanted them—ass to.

Four soldiers and one copter had been left to guard the footlocker. The rest would be outside the bathroom door with the rocket launcher.

Okay. In through the opening like gangbusters. Wipe out the ones by the footlocker, then out the door. Then a quick taxi to the airport. Off to Miami to find Morris' number-one idea girl. He thought he might just burn her face off with a flame thrower. That would be poetic justice.

He took off his shirt and ripped a long strip from one sleeve. He dropped the rest to flutter limply by his feet, and bit off the plastic spout on the can of lighter fluid. He stuffed one end of the rag inside, withdrew it, and stuffed the other end in so only a six-inch strip of saturated cotton hung free.

He got out his lighter, took a deep breath, and thumbed the wheel. He tipped it to the cloth and as it sprang alight he rammed open the glass partition and plunged through.

The copter reacted instantly, kamikaze-diving him as he charged across the rug, dripping tiny splatters of liquid fire. Renshaw straight-armed it, hardly noticing the jolt of pain that ran up his arm as the turning blades chopped his flesh open.

The tiny foot soldiers scattered into the footlocker.

After that, it all happened very rapidly.

Renshaw threw the lighter fluid. The can caught, mushrooming into a licking fireball. The next instant he was reversing, running for the door.

He never knew what hit him.

It was like the thud that a steel safe would make when dropped from a respectable height. Only this thud ran through the entire high-rise apartment building, thrumming in its steel frame like a tuning fork.

The penthouse door blew off its hinges and shattered against the far wall.

A couple who had been walking hand in hand below

looked up in time to see a very large white flash, as though a hundred flashguns had gone off at once.

"Somebody blew a fuse," the man said. "I guess—"

"What's that?" his girl asked.

Something was fluttering lazily down toward them; he caught it in one outstretched hand. "Jesus, some guy's shirt. All full of little holes. Bloody, too."

"I don't like it," she said nervously. "Call a cab, huh, Ralph? We'll have to talk to the cops if something happened up there, and I ain't supposed to be out with you."

"Sure, yeah."

He looked around, saw a taxi, and whistled. Its brake lights flared and they ran across to get it.

Behind them, unseen, a tiny scrap of paper floated down and landed near the remains of John Renshaw's shirt. Spiky backhand script read:

Hey, kids! Special in this Vietnam Footlocker!

    (For a Limited Time Only)
    1 Rocket Launcher
    20 Surface-to-Air "Twister" Missiles
    1 Scale-Model Thermonuclear Weapon

TRUCKS

The guy's name was Snodgrass and I could see him getting ready to do something crazy. His eyes had gotten bigger, showing a lot of the whites, like a dog getting ready to fight. The two kids who had come skidding into the parking lot in the old Fury were trying to talk to him, but his head was cocked as though he was hearing other voices. He had a tight little potbelly encased in a good suit that was getting a little shiny in the seat. He was a salesman and he kept his display bag close to him, like a pet dog that had gone to sleep.

"Try the radio again," the truck driver at the counter said.

The short-order cook shrugged and turned it on. He flipped it across the band and got nothing but static.

"You went too fast," the trucker protested. "You might have missed something."

"Hell," the short-order cook said. He was an elderly black man with a smile of gold and he wasn't looking at the trucker. He was looking through the diner-length picture window at the parking lot.

Seven or eight heavy trucks were out there, engines rumbling in low, idling roars that sounded like big cats purring. There were a couple of Macks, a Hemingway, and four or five Reos. Trailer trucks, interstate haulers with a lot of license plates and CB whip antennas on the back.

The kids' Fury was lying on its roof at the end of long, looping skid marks in the loose crushed rock of the parking lot. It had been battered into senseless junk. At the entrance to the truck stop's turnaround, there was a blasted Cadillac. Its owner stared out of the star-shattered windshield like a gutted fish. Horn-rimmed glasses hung from one ear.

Halfway across the lot from it lay the body of a girl in a pink dress. She had jumped from the Caddy when she saw it wasn't going to make it. She had hit running but never had a chance. She was the worst, even though she was face down. There were flies around her in clouds.

Across the road an old Ford station wagon had been slammed through the guardrails. That had happened an hour ago. No one had been by since then. You couldn't see the turnpike from the window and the phone was out.

"You went too fast," the trucker was protesting. "You oughta—"

That was when Snodgrass bolted. He turned the table over getting up, smashing coffee cups and sending sugar in a wild spray. His eyes were wilder than ever, and his mouth hung loosely and he was blabbering: "We gotta get outta here we gotta getouttahere wegottaget-outtahere—"

The kid shouted and his girl friend screamed.

I was on the stool closest to the door and I got a handful of his shirt, but he tore loose. He was cranked up all the way. He would have gone through a bank-vault door.

He slammed out the door and then he was sprinting across the gravel toward the drainage ditch on the left. Two of the trucks lunged after him, smokestacks blowing diesel exhaust dark brown against the sky, huge rear wheels machine-gunning gravel up in sprays.

He couldn't have been any more than five or six running steps from the edge of the flat parking lot when he turned back to look, fear scrawled on his face. His feet tangled each other and he faltered and almost fell down. He got his balance again, but it was too late.

One of the trucks gave way and the other charged down, huge front grille glittering savagely in the sun. Snodgrass screamed, the sound high and thin, nearly lost under the Reo's heavy diesel roar.

It didn't drag him under. As things turned out, it would have been better if it had. Instead it drove him up and out, the way a punter kicks a football. For a moment he was silhouetted against the hot afternoon sky like a crippled scarecrow, and then he was gone into the drainage ditch.

The big truck's brakes hissed like dragon's breath,

its front wheels locked, digging grooves into the gravel skin of the lot, and it stopped inches from jackknifing in. The bastard.

The girl in the booth screamed. Both hands were clamped into her cheeks, dragging the flesh down, turning it into a witch's mask.

Glass broke. I turned my head and saw that the trucker had squeezed his glass hard enough to break it. I don't think he knew it yet. Milk and a few drops of blood fell onto the counter.

The black counterman was frozen by the radio, a dishcloth in hand, looking amazed. His teeth glittered. For a moment there was no sound but the buzzing West-clox and the rumbling of the Reo's engine as it returned to its fellows. Then the girl began to cry and it was all right—or at least better.

My own car was around the side, also battered to junk. It was a 1971 Camaro and I had still been paying on it, but I didn't suppose that mattered now.

There was no one in the trucks.

The sun glittered and flashed on empty cabs. The wheels turned themselves. You couldn't think about it too much. You'd go insane if you thought about it too much. Like Snodgrass.

Two hours passed. The sun began to go down. Outside, the trucks patrolled in slow circles and figure eights. Their parking lights and running lights had come on.

I walked the length of the counter twice to get the kinks out of my legs and then sat in a booth by the long front window. It was a standard truck stop, close to the major thruway, a complete service facility out back, gas and diesel fuel both. The truckers came here for coffee and pie.

"Mister?" The voice was hesitant.

I looked around. It was the two kids from the Fury. The boy looked about nineteen. He had long hair and a beard that was just starting to take hold. His girl looked younger.

"Yeah?"

"What happened to you?"

I shrugged. "I was coming up the interstate to Pelson," I said. "A truck came up behind me—I could see it in the mirror a long way off—really highballing. You could hear it a mile down the road. It whipped out around a VW Beetle and just snapped it off the road with the whiplash of the trailer, the way you'd snap a ball of paper off a table with your finger. I thought the truck would go, too. No driver could have held it with the trailer whipping that way. But it didn't go. The VW flopped over six or seven times and exploded. And the truck got the next one coming up the same way. It was coming up on me and I took the exit ramp in a hurry." I laughed but my heart wasn't in it. "Right into a truck stop, of all places. From the frying pan into the fire."

The girl swallowed. "We saw a Greyhound going north in the southbound lane. It was . . . plowing . . . through cars. It exploded and burned but before it did . . . slaughter."

A Greyhound bus. That was something new. And bad.

Outside, all the headlights suddenly popped on in unison, bathing the lot in an eerie, depthless glare. Growling, they cruised back and forth. The headlights seemed to give them eyes, and in the growing gloom, the dark trailer boxes looked like the hunched, squared-off shoulders of prehistoric giants.

The counterman said, "Is it safe to turn on the lights?"

"Do it," I said, "and find out."

He flipped the switches and a series of flyspecked globes overhead came on. At the same time a neon sign out front stuttered into life: CONANT'S TRUCK STOP & DINER—GOOD EATS. Nothing happened. The trucks continued their patrol.

"I can't understand it," the trucker said. He had gotten down from his stool and was walking around, his hand wrapped in a red engineer's bandanna. "I ain't had no problems with my rig. She's a good old girl. I pulled in here a little past one for a spaghetti dinner and this happens." He waved his arms and the bandanna flapped. "My own rig's out there right now, the one with the weak left taillight. Been driving her for six years. But if I stepped out that door—"

"It's just starting," the counterman said. His eyes were hooded and obsidian. "It must be bad if that radio's gone. It's just starting."

The girl had drained as pale as milk. "Never mind that," I said to the counterman. "Not yet."

"What would do it?" The trucker was worrying.

"Electrical storms in the atmosphere? Nuclear testing? What?"

"Maybe they're mad," I said.

———

Around seven o'clock I walked over to the counterman. "How are we fixed here? I mean, if we have to stay awhile?"

His brow wrinkled. "Not so bad. Yest'y was delivery day. We got two-three hunnert hamburg patties, canned fruit and vegetables, dry cereal, aigs . . . no more milk than what's in the cooler, but the water's from the well. If we had to, the five of us cud get on for a month or more."

The trucker came over and blinked at us. "I'm dead out of cigarettes. Now that cigarette machine . . ."

"It ain't my machine," the counterman said. "No sir."

The trucker had a steel pinch bar he'd gotten in the supply room out back. He went to work on the machine.

The kid went down to where the jukebox glittered and flashed and plugged in a quarter. John Fogarty began to sing about being born on the bayou.

I sat down and looked out the window. I saw something I didn't like right away. A Chevy light pickup had joined the patrol, like a Shetland pony amid Percherons. I watched it until it rolled impartially over the body of the girl from the Caddy and then I looked away.

"We *made* them!" the girl cried out with sudden wretchedness. "They *can't!*"

Her boy friend told her to hush. The trucker got the cigarette machine open and helped himself to six or eight packs of Viceroys. He put them in different pockets and then ripped one pack open. From the intent expression on his face, I wasn't sure if he was going to smoke them or eat them up.

Another record came on the juke. It was eight o'clock.

At eight-thirty the power went off.

When the lights went, the girl screamed, a cry that stopped suddenly, as if her boy friend had put his hand over her mouth. The jukebox died with a deepening, unwinding sound.

"What the *Christ!*" the trucker said.

"Counterman!" I called. "You got any candles?"

"I think so. Wait . . . yeah. Here's a few."

I got up and took them. We lit them and started placing them around. "Be careful," I said. "If we burn the place down there's the devil to pay."

He chuckled morosely. "You know it."

When we were done placing the candles, the kid and his girl were huddled together and the trucker was by the back door, watching six more heavy trucks weaving in and out between the concrete fuel islands. "This changes things, doesn't it?" I said.

"Damn right, if the power's gone for good."

"How bad?"

"Hamburg'll go over in three days. Rest of the meat and aigs'll go by about as quick. The cans will be okay, an' the dry stuff. But that ain't the worst. We ain't gonna have no water without the pump."

"How long?"

"Without no water? A week."

"Fill every empty jug you've got. Fill them till you can't draw anything but air. Where are the toilets? There's good water in the tanks."

"Employees' res'room is in the back. But you have to go outside to get to the lady's and gent's."

"Across to the service building?" I wasn't ready for that. Not yet.

"No. Out the side door an' up a ways."

"Give me a couple of buckets."

He found two galvanized pails. The kid strolled up.

"What are you doing?"

"We have to have water. All we can get."

"Give me a bucket then."

I handed him one.

"Jerry!" the girl cried. "You—"

He looked at her and she didn't say anything else, but she picked up a napkin and began to tear at the corners. The trucker was smoking another cigarette and grinning at the floor. He didn't speak up.

We walked over to the side door where I'd come in that afternoon and stood there for a second, watching the shadows wax and wane as the trucks went back and forth.

"Now?" the kid said. His arm brushed mine and the muscles were jumping and humming like wires. If anyone bumped him he'd go straight up to heaven.

"Relax," I said.

He smiled a little. It was a sick smile, but better than none.

"Okay."

We slipped out.

The night air had cooled. Crickets chirred in the grass, and frogs thumped and croaked in the drainage ditch. Out here the rumble of the trucks was louder, more menacing, the sound of beasts. From inside it was a movie. Out here it was real, you could get killed.

We slid along the tiled outer wall. A slight overhang gave us some shadow. My Camaro was huddled against the cyclone fence across from us, and faint light from the roadside sign glinted on broken metal and puddles of gas and oil.

"You take the lady's," I whispered. "Fill your bucket from the toilet tank and wait."

Steady diesel rumblings. It was tricky; you thought they were coming, but it was only echoes bouncing off the building's odd corners. It was only twenty feet, but it seemed much farther.

He opened the lady's-room door and went in. I went past and then I was inside the gent's. I could feel my muscles loosen and a breath whistled out of me. I caught a glimpse of myself in the mirror, strained white face with dark eyes.

I got the porcelain tank cover off and dunked the bucket full. I poured a little back to keep from sloshing and went to the door. "Hey?"

"Yeah," he breathed.

"You ready?"

"Yeah."

We went out again. We got maybe six steps before lights blared in our faces. It had crept up, big wheels barely turning on the gravel. It had been lying in wait and now it leaped at us, electric headlamps glowing in savage circles, the huge chrome grille seeming to snarl.

The kid froze, his face stamped with horror, his eyes blank, the pupils dilated down to pinpricks. I gave him a hard shove, spilling half his water.

"Go!"

The thunder of that diesel engine rose to a shriek. I reached over the kid's shoulder to yank the door open, but before I could it was shoved from inside. The kid lunged in and I dodged after him. I looked back to see the truck—a big cabover Peterbilt—kiss off the tiled outside wall, peeling away jagged hunks of tile. There was an ear-grinding squealing noise, like gigantic fingers scraping a blackboard. Then the right mudguard and the corners of the grille smashed into the still-open door, sending glass in a crystal spray and snapping the door's steel-gauge hinges like tissue paper. The door flew into the night like something out of a Dali painting and the truck accelerated toward the front parking lot, its exhaust racketing like machine-gun fire. It had a disappointed, angry sound.

The kid put his bucket down and collapsed into the girl's arms, shuddering.

My heart was thudding heavily in my chest and my calves felt like water. And speaking of water, we had brought back about a bucket and a quarter between us. It hardly seemed worth it.

"I want to block up that doorway," I said to the counterman. "What will do the trick?"

"Well—"

The trucker broke in: "Why? One of those big trucks couldn't get a wheel in through there."

"It's not the big trucks I'm worried about."

The trucker began hunting for a smoke.

"We got some sheet sidin' out in the supply room," the counterman said. "Boss was gonna put up a shed to store butane gas."

"We'll put them across and prop them with a couple of booths."

"It'll help," the trucker said.

It took about an hour and by the end we'd all gotten into the act, even the girl. It was fairly solid. Of course, fairly solid wasn't going to be good enough, not if something hit it at full speed. I think they all knew that.

There were still three booths ranged along the big glass picture window and I sat down in one of them. The clock behind the counter had stopped at 8:32, but it felt like ten. Outside the trucks prowled and growled. Some left, hurrying off to unknown missions, and others came. There were three pickup trucks now, circling importantly amid their bigger brothers.

I was starting to doze, and instead of counting sheep I counted trucks. How many in the state, how many in America? Trailer trucks, pickup trucks, flatbeds, day-haulers, three-quarter-tons, army convoy trucks by the tens of thousands, and buses. Nightmare vision of a city bus, two wheels in the gutter and two wheels on the pavement roaring along and plowing through screaming pedestrians like ninepins.

I shook it off and fell into a light, troubled sleep.

———

It must have been early morning when Snodgrass began to scream. A thin new moon had risen and was shining icily through a high scud of cloud. A new clattering note had been added, counterpointing the throaty, idling roar of the big rigs. I looked for it and saw a hay baler circling out by the darkened sign. The moonlight glanced off the sharp, turning spokes of its packer.

The scream came again, unmistakably from the drainage ditch: "Help . . . *meeeee* . . ."

"What was that?" It was the girl. In the shadows her eyes were wide and she looked horribly frightened.

"Nothing," I said.

"Help . . . *meeeee* . . ."

"He's alive," she whispered. "Oh, God. *Alive.*"

I didn't have to see him. I could imagine it all too well. Snodgrass lying half in and half out of the drainage ditch, back and legs broken, carefully pressed suit caked with mud, white, gasping face turned up to the indifferent moon . . .

"I don't hear anything," I said. "Do you?"

She looked at me. "How can you? How?"

"Now if you woke him up," I said, jerking a thumb

at the kid, "*he* might hear something. He might go out there. Would you like that?"

Her face began to twitch and pull as if stitched by invisible needles. "Nothing," she whispered. "Nothing out there."

She went back to her boy friend and pressed her head against his chest. His arms came up around her in his sleep.

No one else woke up. Snodgrass cried and wept and screamed for a long time, and then he stopped.

Dawn.

Another truck had arrived, this one a flatbed with a giant rack for hauling cars. It was joined by a bulldozer. That scared me.

The trucker came over and twitched my arm. "Come on back," he whispered excitedly. The others were still sleeping. "Come look at this."

I followed him back to the supply room. About ten trucks were patrolling out there. At first I didn't see anything new.

"See?" he said, and pointed. "Right there."

Then I saw. One of the pickups was stopped dead. It was sitting there like a lump, all of the menace gone out of it.

"Out of gas?"

"That's right, buddy. *And they can't pump their own.*

We got it knocked. All we have to do is wait." He smiled and fumbled for a cigarette.

It was about nine o'clock and I was eating a piece of yesterday's pie for breakfast when the air horn began— long, rolling blasts that rattled your skull. We went over to the windows and looked out. The trucks were sitting still, idling. One trailer truck, a huge Reo with a red cab, had pulled up almost to the narrow verge of grass between the restaurant and the parking lot. At this distance the square grille was huge and murderous. The tires would stand to a man's chest cavity.

The horn began to blare again; hard, hungry blasts that traveled off in straight, flat lines and echoed back. There was a pattern. Shorts and longs in some kind of rhythm.

"That's Morse!" the kid, Jerry, suddenly exclaimed.

The trucker looked at him. "How would you know?"

The kid went a little red. "I learned it in the Boy Scouts."

"You?" the trucker said. "*You?* Wow." He shook his head.

"Never mind," I said. "Do you remember enough to—"

"Sure. Let me listen. Got a pencil?"

The counterman gave him one, and the kid began to write letters on a napkin. After a while he stopped. "It's just saying 'Attention' over and over again. Wait."

We waited. The air horn beat its longs and shorts into the still morning air. Then the pattern changed and the kid started to write again. We hung over his shoulders and watched the message form. "Someone must pump fuel. Someone will not be harmed. All fuel must be pumped. This shall be done now. Now someone will pump fuel."

The air blasts kept up, but the kid stopped writing. "It's just repeating 'Attention' again," he said.

The truck repeated its message again and again. I didn't like the look of the words, printed on the napkin in block style. They looked machinelike, ruthless. There would be no compromise with those words. You did or you didn't.

"Well," the kid said, "what do we do?"

"Nothing," the trucker said. His face was excited and working. "All we have to do is wait. They must all be low on fuel. One of the little ones out back has already stopped. All we have to do—"

The air horn stopped. The truck backed up and joined its fellows. They waited in a semicircle, headlights pointed in toward us.

"There's a bulldozer out there," I said.

Jerry looked at me. "You think they'll rip the place down?"

"Yes."

He looked at the counterman. "They couldn't do that, could they?"

The counterman shrugged.

"We oughta vote," the trucker said. "No blackmail, damn it. All we gotta do is wait." He had repeated it three times now, like a charm.

"Okay," I said. "Vote."

"Wait," the trucker said immediately.

"I think we ought to fuel them," I said. "We can wait for a better chance to get away. Counterman?"

"Stay in here," he said. "You want to be their slaves? That's what it'll come to. You want to spend the rest of your life changin' oil filters every time one of those . . . *things* blats its horn? Not me." He looked darkly out the window. "Let them starve."

I looked at the kid and the girl.

"I think he's right," he said. "That's the only way to stop them. If someone was going to rescue us, they would have. God knows what's going on in other places." And the girl, with Snodgrass in her eyes, nodded and stepped closer to him.

"That's it then," I said.

I went over to the cigarette machine and got a pack without looking at the brand. I'd stopped smoking a year ago, but this seemed like a good time to start again. The smoke rasped harsh in my lungs.

Twenty minutes crawled by. The trucks out front waited. In back, they were lining up at the pumps.

"I think it was all a bluff," the trucker said. "Just—"

Then there was a louder, harsher, choppier note, the sound of an engine revving up and falling off, then revving up again. The bulldozer.

It glittered like a yellowjacket in the sun, a Caterpillar with clattering steel treads. Black smoke belched from its short stack as it wheeled around to face us.

"It's going to charge," the trucker said. There was a

look of utter surprise on his face. "It's going to charge!"

"Get back," I said. "Behind the counter."

The bulldozer was still revving. Gear-shift levers moved themselves. Heat shimmer hung over its smoking stack. Suddenly the dozer blade lifted, a heavy steel curve clotted with dried dirt. Then, with a screaming howl of power, it roared straight at us.

"The *counter!*" I gave the trucker a shove, and that started them.

There was a small concrete verge between the parking lot and the grass. The dozer charged over it, blade lifting for a moment, and then it rammed the front wall head on. Glass exploded inward with a heavy, coughing roar and the wood frame crashed into splinters. One of the overhead light globes fell, splashing more glass. Crockery fell from the shelves. The girl was screaming but the sound was almost lost beneath the steady, pounding roar of the Cat's engine.

It reversed, clanked across the chewed strip of lawn, and lunged forward again, sending the remaining booths crashing and spinning. The pie case fell off the counter, sending pie wedges skidding across the floor.

The counterman was crouching with his eyes shut, and the kid was holding his girl. The trucker was walleyed with fear.

"We gotta stop it," he gibbered. "Tell 'em we'll do it, we'll do anything—"

"A little late, isn't it?"

The Cat reversed and got ready for another charge. New nicks in its blade glittered and heliographed in the sun. It lurched forward with a bellowing roar and this time it took down the main support to the left of what had been the window. That section of the roof fell in with a grinding crash. Plaster dust billowed up.

The dozer pulled free. Beyond it I could see the group of trucks, waiting.

I grabbed the counterman. "Where are the oil drums?" The cookstoves ran on butane gas, but I had seen vents for a warm-air furnace.

"Back of the storage room," he said.

I grabbed the kid. "Come on."

We got up and ran into the storage room. The bulldozer hit again and the building trembled. Two or three more hits and it would be able to come right up to the counter for a cup of coffee.

There were two large fifty-gallon drums with feeds to the furnace and turn spigots. There was a carton of empty ketchup bottles near the back door. "Get those, Jerry."

While he did, I pulled off my shirt and yanked it to rags. The dozer hit again and again, and each hit was accompanied by the sound of more breakage.

I filled four of the ketchup bottles from the spigots, and he stuffed rags into them. "You play football?" I asked him.

"In high school."

"Okay. Pretend you're going in from the five."

We went out into the restaurant. The whole front wall was open to the sky. Sprays of glass glittered like diamonds. One heavy beam had fallen diagonally across the opening. The dozer was backing up to take it out and I thought that this time it would keep coming, ripping through the stools and then demolishing the counter itself.

We knelt down and thrust the bottles out. "Light them up," I said to the trucker.

He got his matches out, but his hands were shaking too badly and he dropped them. The counterman picked them up, struck one, and the hunks of shirt blazed greasily alight.

"Quick," I said.

We ran, the kid a little in the lead. Glass crunched and gritted underfoot. There was a hot, oily smell in the air. Everything was very loud, very bright.

The dozer charged.

The kid dodged out under the beam and stood silhouetted in front of that heavy tempered steel blade. I went out to the right. The kid's first throw fell short. His second hit the blade and the flame splashed harmlessly.

He tried to turn and then it was on him, a rolling juggernaut, four tons of steel. His hands flew up and then he was gone, chewed under.

I buttonhooked around and lobbed one bottle into the open cab and the second right into the works. They exploded together in a leaping shout of flame.

For a moment the dozer's engine rose in an almost human squeal of rage and pain. It wheeled in a maddened half-circle, ripping out the left corner of the diner, and rolled drunkenly toward the drainage ditch.

The steel treads were streaked and dotted with gore

and where the kid had been there was something that looked like a crumpled towel.

The dozer got almost to the ditch, flames boiling from under its cowling and from the cockpit, and then it exploded in a geyser.

I stumbled backward and almost fell over a pile of rubble. There was a hot smell that wasn't just oil. It was burning hair. I was on fire.

I grabbed a tablecloth, jammed it on my head, ran behind the counter, and plunged my head into the sink hard enough to crack it on the bottom. The girl was screaming Jerry's name over and over in a shrieking insane litany.

I turned around and saw the huge car-carrier slowly rolling toward the defenseless front of the diner.

The trucker screamed and broke for the side door.

"Don't!" the counterman cried. "Don't do that—"

But he was out and sprinting for the drainage ditch and the open field beyond.

The truck must have been standing sentry just out of sight of that side door—a small panel job with "Wong's Cash-and-Carry Laundry" written on the side. It ran him down almost before you could see it happen. Then it was gone and only the trucker was left, twisted into the gravel. He had been knocked out of his shoes.

The car-carrier rolled slowly over the concrete verge, onto the grass, over the kid's remains, and stopped with its huge snout poking into the diner.

Its air horn let out a sudden, shattering honk, followed by another, and another.

"Stop!" the girl whimpered. "Stop, oh stop, please—"

But the honks went on a long time. It took only a minute to pick up the pattern. It was the same as before. It wanted someone to feed it and the others.

"I'll go," I said. "Are the pumps unlocked?"

The counterman nodded. He had aged fifty years.

"No!" the girl screamed. She threw herself at me. "You've got to stop them! Beat them, burn them, break them—" Her voice wavered and broke into a harsh bray of grief and loss.

The counterman held her. I went around the corner of the counter, picking my way through the rubble, and out through the supply room. My heart was thudding heavily when I stepped out into the warm sun. I wanted another cigarette, but you don't smoke around fuel islands.

The trucks were still lined up. The laundry truck was crouched across the gravel from me like a hound dog, growling and rasping. A funny move and it would cream me. The sun glittered on its blank windshield and I shuddered. It was like looking into the face of an idiot.

I switched the pump to "on" and pulled out the nozzle; unscrewed the first gas cap and began to pump fuel.

It took me half an hour to pump the first tank dry and then I moved on to the second island. I was alternating between gas and diesel. Trucks marched by endlessly. I was beginning to understand now. I was beginning to see. People were doing this all over the country or they were lying dead like the trucker, knocked out of their boots with heavy treadmarks mashed across their guts.

The second tank was dry then and I went to the third. The sun was like a hammer and my head was starting to ache with the fumes. There were blisters in the soft webbing between thumb and index finger. But they wouldn't know about that. They would know about leaky manifolds and bad gaskets and frozen universal joints, but not about blisters or sunstroke or the need to scream. They needed to know only one thing about their late masters, and they knew it. We bleed.

The last tank was sucked dry and I threw the nozzle on the ground. Still there were more trucks, lined up around the corner. I twisted my head to relieve a crick in my neck and stared. The line went out of the front parking lot and up the road and out of sight, two and three lanes deep. It was like a nightmare of the Los Angeles Freeway at rush hour. The horizon shimmered and danced with their exhaust; the air stank of carburization.

"No," I said. "Out of gas. All gone, fellas."

And there was a heavier rumble, a bass note that shook the teeth. A huge silvery truck was pulling up, a tanker. Written on the side was: "Fill Up with Phillips 66—The Jetport Fuel"!

A heavy hose dropped out of the rear.

I went over, took it, flipped up the feeder plate on the first tank, and attached the hose. The truck began to pump. The stench of petroleum sank into me—the same stink that the dinosaurs must have died smelling as they went down into the tar pits. I filled the other two tanks and then went back to work.

Consciousness twinkled away to a point where I

lost track of time and trucks. I unscrewed, rammed the nozzle into the hole, pumped until the hot, heavy liquid splurted out, then replaced the cap. My blisters broke, trickling pus down to my wrists. My head was pounding like a rotted tooth and my stomach rolled helplessly with the stench of hydrocarbons.

I was going to faint. I was going to faint and that would be the end of it. I would pump until I dropped.

Then there were hands on my shoulders, the dark hands of the counterman. "Go in," he said. "Rest yourself. I'll take over till dark. Try to sleep."

I handed him the pump.

But I can't sleep.

The girl is sleeping. She's sprawled over in the corner with her head on a tablecloth and her face won't unknot itself even in sleep. It's the timeless, ageless face of the warhag. I'm going to get her up pretty quick. It's twilight and the counterman has been out there for five hours.

Still they keep coming. I look out through the wrecked window and their headlights stretch for a mile or better, twinkling like yellow sapphires in the growing darkness. They must be backed up all the way to the turnpike, maybe further.

The girl will have to take her turn. I can show her how. She'll say she can't, but she will. She wants to live.

You want to be their slaves? the counterman had

said. *That's what it'll come to. You want to spend the rest of your life changin' oil filters every time one of those things blats its horn?*

We could run, maybe. It would be easy to make the drainage ditch now, the way they're stacked up. Run through the fields, through the marshy places where trucks would bog down like mastodons and go—

—back to the caves.

Drawing pictures in charcoal. This is the moon god. This is a tree. This is a Mack semi overwhelming a hunter.

Not even that. So much of the world is paved now. Even the playgrounds are paved. And for the fields and marshes and deep woods there are tanks, half-tracks, flatbeds equipped with lasers, masers, heat-seeking radar. And little by little, they can make it into the world they want.

I can see great convoys of trucks filling the Okefenokee Swamp with sand, the bulldozers ripping through the national parks and wildlands, grading the earth flat, stamping it into one great flat plain. And then the hot-top trucks arriving.

But they're machines. No matter what's happened to them, what mass consciousness we've given them, *they can't reproduce.* In fifty or sixty years they'll be rusting hulks with all menace gone out of them, moveless carcasses for free men to stone and spit at.

And if I close my eyes I can see the production lines in Detroit and Dearborn and Youngstown and Mackinac, new trucks being put together by blue-collars who no longer even punch a clock but only drop and are replaced.

The counterman is staggering a little now. He's an old bastard, too. I've got to wake the girl.

Two planes are leaving silver contrails etched across the darkening eastern horizon.

I wish I could believe there are people in them.

SOMETIMES THEY COME BACK

Jim Norman's wife had been waiting for him since two, and when she saw the car pull up in front of their apartment building, she came out to meet him. She had gone to the store and bought a celebration meal—a couple of steaks, a bottle of Lancer's, a head of lettuce, and Thousand Island dressing. Now, watching him get out of the car, she found herself hoping with some desperation (and not for the first time that day) that there was going to be something to celebrate.

He came up the walk, holding his new briefcase in one hand and four texts in the other. She could see the title of the top one—*Introduction to Grammar*. She put her hands on his shoulder and asked, "How did it go?"

And he smiled.

But that night, he had the old dream for the first time in a very long time and woke up sweating, with a scream behind his lips.

————

His interview had been conducted by the principal of Harold Davis High School and the head of the English Department. The subject of his breakdown had come up. He had expected it would.

The principal, a bald and cadaverous man named Fenton, had leaned back and looked at the ceiling. Simmons, the English head, lit his pipe.

"I was under a great deal of pressure at the time," Jim Norman said. His fingers wanted to twist about in his lap, but he wouldn't let them.

"I think we understand that," Fenton said, smiling. "And while we have no desire to pry, I'm sure we'd all agree that teaching is a pressure occupation, especially at the high-school level. You're onstage five periods out of seven, and you're playing to the toughest audience in the world. That's why," he finished with some pride, "teachers have more ulcers than any other professional group, with the exception of air-traffic controllers."

Jim said, "The pressures involved in my breakdown were . . . extreme."

Fenton and Simmons nodded noncommittal encouragement, and Simmons clicked his lighter open to rekindle his pipe. Suddenly the office seemed very tight, very close. Jim had the queer sensation that someone had just turned on a heat lamp over the back of his neck. His fingers were twisting in his lap, and he made them stop.

"I was in my senior year and practice teaching. My mother had died the summer before—cancer—and in my last conversation with her, she asked me to go right on and finish. My brother, my older brother, died when we were both quite young. He had been planning to teach and she thought . . ."

He could see from their eyes that he was wandering and thought: *God, I'm making a botch of this.*

"I did as she asked," he said, leaving the tangled relationship of his mother and his brother Wayne—poor, murdered Wayne—and himself behind. "During the second week of my intern teaching, my fiancée was involved in a hit-and-run accident. She was the hit part of it. Some kid in a hot rod . . . they never caught him."

Simmons made a soft noise of encouragement.

"I went on. There didn't seem to be any other course. She was in a great deal of pain—a badly broken leg and four fractured ribs—but no danger. I don't think I really knew the pressure I was under."

Careful now. This is where the ground slopes away.

"I interned at Center Street Vocational Trades High," Jim said.

"Garden spot of the city," Fenton said. "Switchblades, motorcycle boots, zip guns in the lockers, lunch-money protection rackets, and every third kid selling dope to the other two. I know about Trades."

"There was a kid named Mack Zimmerman," Jim said. "Sensitive boy. Played the guitar. I had him in a composition class, and he had talent. I came in one morning and two boys were holding him while a third smashed his Yamaha guitar against the radiator. Zimmerman was screaming. I yelled for them to stop and give me the guitar. I started for them and someone slugged me." Jim shrugged. "That was it. I had a breakdown. No screaming meemies or crouching in the corner. I just couldn't go back. When I got near Trades, my chest would tighten up. I couldn't breathe right, I got cold sweat—"

"That happens to me, too," Fenton said amiably.

"I went into analysis. A community therapy deal. I couldn't afford a psychiatrist. It did me good. Sally and I are married. She has a slight limp and a scar, but otherwise, good as new." He looked at them squarely. "I guess you could say the same for me."

Fenton said, "You actually finished your practice teaching requirement at Cortez High School, I believe."

"That's no bed of roses, either," Simmons said.

"I wanted a hard school," Jim said. "I swapped with another guy to get Cortez."

"A's from your supervisor and critic teacher," Fenton commented.

"Yes."

"And a four-year average of 3.88. Damn close to straight A's."

"I enjoyed my college work."

Fenton and Simmons glanced at each other, then stood up. Jim got up.

"We'll be in touch, Mr. Norman," Fenton said. "We do have a few more applicants to interview—"

"Yes, of course."

"—but speaking for myself, I'm impressed by your academic records and personal candor."

"It's nice of you to say so."

"Sim, perhaps Mr. Norman would like a coffee before he goes."

They shook hands.

In the hall, Simmons said, "I think you've got the job if you want it. That's off the record, of course."

Jim nodded. He had left a lot off the record himself.

———

Davis High was a forbidding rockpile that housed a remarkably modern plant—the science wing alone had been funded at 1.5 million in last year's budget. The classrooms, which still held the ghosts of the WPA workers who had built them and the postwar kids who had first used them, were furnished with modern desks and soft-glare blackboards. The students were clean, well dressed, vivacious, affluent. Six out of ten seniors owned their own cars. All in all, a good school. A fine school to teach in during the Sickie Seventies. It made Center Street Vocational Trades look like darkest Africa.

But after the kids were gone, something old and brooding seemed to settle over the halls and whisper in the empty rooms. Some black, noxious beast, never quite in view. Sometimes, as he walked down the Wing 4 corridor toward the parking lot with his new briefcase in one hand, Jim Norman thought he could almost hear it breathing.

———

He had the dream again near the end of October, and that time he did scream. He clawed his way into waking reality to find Sally sitting up in bed beside him, holding his shoulder. His heart was thudding heavily.

"God," he said, and scrubbed a hand across his face.

"Are you all right?"

"Sure. I yelled, didn't I?"

"Boy, did you. Nightmare?"

"Yes."

"Something from when those boys broke that fellow's guitar?"

"No," he said. "Much older than that. Sometimes it comes back, that's all. No sweat."

"Are you sure?"

"Yes."

"Do you want a glass of milk?" Her eyes were dark with concern.

He kissed her shoulder. "No. Go to sleep."

She turned off the light and he lay there, looking into the darkness.

———

He had a good schedule for the new teacher on the staff. Period one was free. Two and three were freshman comp, one group dull, one kind of fun. Period four was his best class: American Lit with college-bound seniors who got a kick out of bashing the ole masters around for a period each day. Period five was a "consultation period," when he was supposed to see students with personal or academic problems. There were very few who seemed to have either (or who wanted to discuss them with him), and he spent most of those periods with a good novel. Period six was a grammar course, dry as chalkdust.

Period seven was his only cross. The class was called Living with Literature, and it was held in a small box of a classroom on the third floor. The room was hot in the early fall and cold as the winter approached. The class itself was an elective for what school catalogues coyly call "the slow learner."

There were twenty-seven "slow learners" in Jim's class, most of them school jocks. The kindest thing you could accuse them of would be disinterest, and some of them had a streak of outright malevolence. He walked in one day to find an obscene and cruelly accurate caricature of himself on the board, with "Mr. Norman" unnecessarily chalked under it. He wiped it off without comment and proceeded with the lesson in spite of the snickers.

He worked up interesting lesson plans, included a/v materials, and ordered several high-interest, high-comprehension texts—all to no avail. The classroom mood veered between unruly hilarity and sullen silence. Early in November, a fight broke out between two boys during a discussion of *Of Mice and Men*. Jim broke it up and sent both boys to the office. When he opened his book to where he had left off, the words "Bite It" glared up at him.

He took the problem to Simmons, who shrugged and lit his pipe. "I don't have any real solution, Jim. Last period is always a bitch. And for some of them, a D grade in your class means no more football or basketball. And they've had the other gut English courses, so they're stuck with it."

"And me, too," Jim said glumly.

Simmons nodded. "Show them you mean business, and they'll buckle down, if only to keep their sports eligibility."

But period seven remained a constant thorn in his side.

One of the biggest problems in Living with Lit was a huge, slow-moving moose named Chip Osway. In early December, during the brief hiatus between football and basketball (Osway played both), Jim caught him with a crib sheet and ran him out of the classroom.

"If you flunk me, we'll get you, you son of a bitch!" Osway yelled down the dim third-floor corridor. "You hear me?"

"Go on," Jim said. "Don't waste your breath."

"We'll get you, creepo!"

Jim went back into the classroom. They looked up at him blandly, faces betraying nothing. He felt a surge of unreality, like the feeling that had washed over him before . . . before . . .

We'll get you, creepo.

He took his grade book out of his desk, opened it to the page titled "Living with Literature," and carefully lettered an F in the exam slot next to Chip Osway's name.

———

That night he had the dream again.

The dream was always cruelly slow. There was time to see and feel everything. And there was the added horror of reliving events that were moving toward a known conclusion, as helpless as a man strapped into a car going over a cliff.

In the dream he was nine and his brother Wayne was twelve. They were going down Broad Street in Stratford, Connecticut, bound for the Stratford Library. Jim's books were two days overdue, and he had hooked four cents from the cupboard bowl to pay the fine. It was summer vacation. You could smell the freshly cut grass. You could hear a ballgame floating out of some second-floor apartment window, Yankees leading the Red Sox six to nothing in the top of the eighth, Ted Williams batting, and you could see the shadows from the Burrets Building Company slowly lengthening across the street as the evening turned slowly toward dark.

Beyond Teddy's Market and Burrets, there was a railroad overpass, and on the other side, a number of the local losers hung around a closed gas station—five or six boys in leather jackets and pegged jeans. Jim hated to go by them. They yelled out hey four-eyes and hey shit-heels and hey you got an extra quarter and once they chased them half a block. But Wayne would not take the long way around. That would be chicken.

In the dream, the overpass loomed closer and closer, and you began to feel dread struggling in your throat like a big black bird. You saw everything: the Burrets neon sign, just starting to stutter on and off; the flakes of rust on the green overpass; the glitter of broken glass in the cinders of the railroad bed; a broken bike rim in the gutter.

You try to tell Wayne you've been through this before, a hundred times. The local losers aren't hanging around the gas station this time; they're hidden in the shadows under the trestle. But it won't come out. You're helpless.

Then you're underneath, and some of the shadows detach themselves from the walls and a tall kid with a blond crew cut and a broken nose pushes Wayne up against the sooty cinderblocks and says: *Give us some money.*

Let me alone.

You try to run, but a fat guy with greasy black hair grabs you and throws you against the wall next to your brother. His left eyelid is jittering up and down nervously and he says: *Come on, kid, how much you got?*

F-four cents.

You fuckin' liar.

Wayne tries to twist free and a guy with odd, orange-colored hair helps the blond one to hold him. The guy with the jittery eyelid suddenly bashes you one in the mouth. You feel a sudden heaviness in your groin, and a dark patch appears on your jeans.

Look, Vinnie, he wet himself!

Wayne's struggles become frenzied, and he almost—not quite—gets free. Another guy, wearing black chinos and a white T-shirt, throws him back. There is a small strawberry birthmark on his chin. The stone throat of the overpass is beginning to tremble. The metal girders pick up a thrumming vibration. Train coming.

Someone strikes the books out of your hands and the kid with the birthmark on his chin kicks them into the gutter. Wayne suddenly kicks out with his right foot, and it connects with the crotch of the kid with the jittery face. He screams.

Vinnie, he's gettin' away!

The kid with the jittery face is screaming about his nuts, but even his howls are lost in the gathering, shaking roar of the approaching train. Then it is over them, and its noise fills the world.

Light flashes on switchblades. The kid with the blond crew cut is holding one and Birthmark has the other. You can't hear Wayne, but his words are in the shape of his lips:

Run Jimmy run.

You slip to your knees and the hands holding you are gone and you skitter between a pair of legs like a frog. A hand slaps down on your back, groping for purchase, and gets none. Then you are running back the way you came, with all of the horrible sludgy slowness of dreams. You look back over your shoulder and see—

He woke in the dark, Sally sleeping peacefully beside him. He bit back the scream, and when it was throttled, he fell back.

When he had looked back, back into the yawning darkness of the overpass, he had seen the blond kid and the birthmarked kid drive their knives into his brother—Blondie's below the breastbone, and Birthmark's directly into his brother's groin.

He lay in the darkness, breathing harshly, waiting for that nine-year-old ghost to depart, waiting for honest sleep to blot it all away.

An unknown time later, it did.

———

The Christmas vacation and semester break were combined in the city's school district, and the holiday was almost a month long. The dream came twice, early on, and did not come again. He and Sally went to visit her sister in Vermont, and skied a great deal. They were happy.

Jim's Living with Lit problem seemed inconsequential and a little foolish in the open, crystal air. He went back to school with a winter tan, feeling cool and collected.

———

Simmons caught him on the way to his period-two class and handed him a folder. "New student, period seven. Name is Robert Lawson. Transfer."

"Hey, I've got twenty-seven in there right now, Sim. I'm overloaded."

"You've still got twenty-seven. Bill Stearns got killed the Tuesday after Christmas. Car accident. Hit-and-run."

"Billy?"

The picture formed in his mind in black and white, like a senior photograph. William Stearns, Key Club 1, Football 1, 2, *Pen & Lance,* 2. He had been one of the few good ones in Living with Lit. Quiet, consistent A's and B's on his exams. Didn't volunteer often, but usually summoned the correct answers (laced with a pleasing dry wit) when called on. Dead? Fifteen years old. His own mortality suddenly whispered through his bones like a cold draft under a door.

"Christ, that's awful. Do they know what happened?"

"Cops are checking into it. He was downtown exchanging a Christmas present. Started across Rampart Street and an old Ford sedan hit him. No one got the license number, but the words 'Snake Eyes' were written on the side door . . . the way a kid would do it."

"Christ," Jim said again.

"There's the bell," Simmons said.

He hurried away, pausing to break up a crowd of kids around a drinking fountain. Jim went toward his class, feeling empty.

During his free period he flipped open Robert Lawson's folder. The first page was a green sheet from Milford High, which Jim had never heard of. The second was a student personality profile. Adjusted IQ of 78. Some manual skills, not many. Antisocial answers to the Barnett-Hudson personality test. Poor aptitude scores. Jim thought sourly that he was a Living with Lit kid all the way.

The next page was a disciplinary history, the yellow sheet. The Milford sheet was white with a black border, and it was depressingly well filled. Lawson had been in a hundred kinds of trouble.

He turned the next page, glanced down at a school photo of Robert Lawson, then looked again. Terror suddenly crept into the pit of his belly and coiled there, warm and hissing.

Lawson was staring antagonistically into the camera, as if posing for a police mug shot rather than a school photographer. There was a small strawberry birthmark on his chin.

————

By period seven, he had brought all the civilized rationalizations into play. He told himself there must be thousands of kids with red birthmarks on their chins. He told himself that the hood who had stabbed his brother that day sixteen long dead years ago would now be at least thirty-two.

But, climbing to the third floor, the apprehension remained. And another fear to go with it: *This is how you felt when you were cracking up.* He tasted the bright steel of panic in his mouth.

The usual group of kids was horsing around the door of Room 33, and some of them went in when they saw Jim coming. A few hung around, talking in undertones and grinning. He saw the new boy standing beside Chip Osway. Robert Lawson was wearing blue jeans and heavy yellow tractor boots—all the rage this year.

"Chip, go on in."

"That an order?" He smiled vacuously over Jim's head.

"Sure."

"You flunk me on that test?"

"Sure."

"Yeah, that's . . ." The rest was an under-the-breath mumble.

Jim turned to Robert Lawson. "You're new," he said. "I just wanted to tell you how we run things around here."

"Sure, Mr. Norman." His right eyebrow was split with a small scar, a scar Jim knew. There could be no mistake. It was crazy, it was lunacy, but it was also a fact. Sixteen years ago, this kid had driven a knife into his brother.

Numbly, as if from a great distance, he heard himself beginning to outline the class rules and regulations. Robert Lawson hooked his thumbs into his garrison belt, listened, smiled, and began to nod, as if they were old friends.

"Jim?"

"Hmmm?"

"Is something wrong?"

"No."

"Those Living with Lit boys still giving you a hard time?"

No answer.

"Jim?"

"No."

"Why don't you go to bed early tonight?"

But he didn't.

———

The dream was very bad that night. When the kid with the strawberry birthmark stabbed his brother with his knife, he called after Jim: "You next, kid. Right through the bag."

He woke up screaming.

———

He was teaching *Lord of the Flies* that week, and talking about symbolism when Lawson raised his hand.

"Robert?" he said evenly.

"Why do you keep starin' at me?" Jim blinked and felt his mouth go dry.

"You see somethin' green? Or is my fly unzipped?"

A nervous titter from the class.

Jim replied evenly: "I wasn't staring at you, Mr. Lawson. Can you tell us why Ralph and Jack disagreed over—"

"You were *starin'* at me."

"Do you want to talk about it with Mr. Fenton?"

Lawson appeared to think it over. "Naw."

"Good. Now can you tell us why Ralph and Jack—"

"I didn't read it. I think it's a dumb book."

Jim smiled tightly. "Do you, now? You want to remember that while you're judging the book, the book is also judging you. Now can anyone else tell me why they disagreed over the existence of the beast?"

Kathy Slavin raised her hand timidly, and Lawson gave her a cynical once-over and said something to Chip Osway. The words leaving his lips looked like "nice tits." Chip nodded.

"Kathy?"

"Isn't it because Jack wanted to hunt the beast?"

"Good." He turned and began to write on the board. At the instant his back was turned, a grapefruit smashed against the board beside his head.

He jerked backward and wheeled around. Some class members laughed, but Osway and Lawson only looked at Jim innocently.

Jim stooped and picked up the grapefruit. "Someone," he said, looking toward the back of the room, "ought to have this jammed down his goddamn throat."

Kathy Slavin gasped.

He tossed the grapefruit in the wastebasket and turned back to the blackboard.

He opened the morning paper, sipping his coffee, and saw the headline about halfway down. "God!" he said, splitting his wife's easy flow of morning chatter. His belly felt suddenly filled with splinters—

"Teen-Age Girl Falls to Her Death: Katherine Slavin, a seventeen-year-old junior at Harold Davis High School, either fell or was pushed from the roof of her downtown apartment house early yesterday evening. The girl, who kept a pigeon coop on the roof, had gone up with a sack of feed, according to her mother.

"Police said an unidentified woman in a neighboring development had seen three young boys running across the roof at 6:45 P.M., just minutes after the girl's body (continued page 3—"

(continued page 3—"

"Jim, was she one of yours?"

But he could only look at her mutely.

Two weeks later, Simmons met him in the hall after the lunch bell with a folder in his hand, and Jim felt a terrible sinking in his belly.

"New student," he said flatly to Simmons. "Living with Lit."

Sim's eyebrows went up. "How did you know that?"

Jim shrugged and held his hand out for the folder.

"Got to run," Simmons said. "Department heads are

meeting on course evaluations. You look a little run-down. Feeling okay?"

That's right, a little run-down. Like Billy Stearns.

"Sure," he said.

"That's the stuff," Simmons said, and clapped him on the back.

When he was gone, Jim opened the folder to the picture, wincing in advance, like a man about to be hit.

But the face wasn't instantly familiar. Just a kid's face. Maybe he'd seen it before, maybe not. The kid, David Garcia, was a hulking, dark-haired boy with rather negroid lips and dark, slumbering eyes. The yellow sheet said he was also from Milford High and that he had spent two years in Granville Reformatory. Car theft.

Jim closed the folder with hands that trembled slightly.

———

"Sally?"

She looked up from her ironing. He had been staring at a TV basketball game without really seeing it.

"Nothing," he said. "Forgot what I was going to say."

"Must have been a lie."

He smiled mechanically and looked at the TV again. It had been on the tip of his tongue to spill everything. But how could he? It was worse than crazy. Where would you start? The dream? The breakdown? The appearance of Robert Lawson?

No. With Wayne—your brother.

But he had never told anyone about that, not even in analysis. His thoughts turned to David Garcia, and the dreamy terror that had washed over him when they had looked at each other in the hall. Of course, he had only looked vaguely familiar in the picture. Pictures don't move . . . or twitch.

Garcia had been standing with Lawson and Chip Osway, and when he looked up and saw Jim Norman, he smiled and his eyelids began to jitter up and down and voices spoke in Jim's mind with unearthly clarity:

Come on, kid, how much you got?

F-four cents.

You fuckin' liar . . . look, Vinnie, he wet himself!

"Jim? Did you say something?"

"No." But he wasn't sure if he had or not. He was getting very scared.

One day after school in early February there was a knock on the teachers'-room door, and when Jim opened it, Chip Osway stood there. He looked frightened. Jim was alone; it was ten after four and the last of the teachers had gone home an hour before. He was correcting a batch of American Lit themes.

"Chip?" he said evenly.

Chip shuffled his feet. "Can I talk to you for a minute, Mr. Norman?"

"Sure. But if it's about that test, you're wasting your—"

"It's not about that. Uh, can I smoke in here?"

"Go ahead."

He lit his cigarette with a hand that trembled slightly. He didn't speak for perhaps as long as a minute. It seemed that he couldn't. His lips twitched, his hands came together, and his eyes slitted, as if some inner self was struggling to find expression.

He suddenly burst out: "If they do it, I want you to know I wasn't in on it! I don't like those guys! They're creeps!"

"What guys, Chip?"

"Lawson and that Garcia creep."

"Are they planning to get me?" The old dreamy terror was on him, and he knew the answer.

"I liked them at first," Chip said. "We went out and had a few beers. I started bitchin' about you and that test. About how I was gonna get you. But that was just talk! I swear it!"

"What happened?"

"They took me right up on it. Asked what time you left school, what kind of car you drove, all that stuff. I said what have you got against him and Garcia said they knew you a long time ago . . . hey, are you all right?"

"The cigarette," he said thickly. "Haven't ever gotten used to the smoke."

Chip ground it out. "I asked them when they knew

you and Bob Lawson said I was still pissin' my didies then. But they're seventeen, the same as me."

"Then what?"

"Well, Garcia leans over the table and says you can't want to get him very bad if you don't even know when he leaves the fuckin' school. What was you gonna do? So I says I was gonna matchstick your tires and leave you with four flats." He looked at Jim with pleading eyes. "I wasn't even gonna do that. I said it because . . ."

"You were scared?" Jim asked quietly.

"Yeah, and I'm still scared."

"What did they think of your idea?"

Chip shuddered. "Bob Lawson says, is that what you was gonna do, you cheap prick? And I said, tryin' to be tough, what was you gonna do, off him? And Garcia—his eyelids start to go up and down—he takes something out of his pocket and clicked it open and it's a switchknife. That's when I took off."

"When was this, Chip?"

"Yesterday. I'm scared to sit with those guys now, Mr. Norman."

"Okay," Jim said. "Okay." He looked down at the papers he had been correcting without seeing them.

"What are you going to do?"

"I don't know," Jim said. "I really don't."

On Monday morning he still didn't know. His first thought had been to tell Sally everything, starting with his brother's murder sixteen years ago. But it was impossible. She would be sympathetic but frightened and unbelieving.

Simmons? Also impossible. Simmons would think he was mad. And maybe he was. A man in a group encounter session he had attended had said having a breakdown was like breaking a vase and then gluing it back together. You could never trust yourself to handle that vase again with any surety. You couldn't put a flower in it because flowers need water and water might dissolve the glue.

Am I crazy, then?

If he was, Chip Osway was, too. That thought came to him as he was getting into his car, and a bolt of excitement went through him.

Of course! Lawson and Garcia had threatened him in Chip Osway's presence. That might not stand up in court, but it would get the two of them suspended if he could get Chip to repeat his story in Fenton's office. And he was almost sure he could get Chip to do that. Chip had his own reasons for wanting them far away.

He was driving into the parking lot when he thought about what had happened to Billy Stearns and Kathy Slavin.

During his free period, he went up to the office and leaned over the registration secretary's desk. She was doing the absence list.

"Chip Osway here today?" he asked casually.

"Chip . . . ?" She looked at him doubtfully.

"Charles Osway," Jim amended. "Chip's a nickname."

She leafed through a pile of slips, glanced at one, and pulled it out. "He's absent, Mr. Norman."

"Can you get me his phone number?"

She pushed her pencil into her hair and said, "Certainly." She dug it out of the O file and handed it to him. Jim dialed the number on an office phone.

The phone rang a dozen times and he was about to hang up when a rough, sleep-blurred voice said, "Yeah?"

"Mr. Osway?"

"Barry Osway's been dead six years. I'm Gary Denkinger."

"Are you Chip Osway's stepfather?"

"What'd he do?"

"Pardon?"

"He's run off. I want to know what he did."

"So far as I know, nothing. I just wanted to talk with him. Do you have any idea where he might be?"

"Naw, I work nights. I don't know none of his friends."

"Any idea at a—"

"Nope. He took the old suitcase and fifty bucks he saved up from stealin' car parts or sellin' dope or whatever these kids do for money. Gone to San Francisco to be a hippie for all I know."

"If you hear from him, will you call me at school? Jim Norman, English wing."

"Sure will."

Jim put the phone down. The registration secretary

looked up and offered a quick meaningless smile. Jim
didn't smile back.

———

Two days later, the words "left school" appeared
after Chip Osway's name on the morning attendance
slip. Jim began to wait for Simmons to show up with a
new folder. A week later he did.

He looked dully down at the picture. No question
about this one. The crew cut had been replaced by long
hair, but it was still blond. And the face was the same,
Vincent Corey. Vinnie, to his friends and intimates. He
stared up at Jim from the picture, an insolent grin on
his lips.

When he approached his period-seven class, his
heart was thudding gravely in his chest. Lawson and
Garcia and Vinnie Corey were standing by the bulletin
board outside the door—they all straightened when he
came toward them.

Vinnie smiled his insolent smile, but his eyes were as
cold and dead as ice floes. "You must be Mr. Norman.
Hi, Norm."

Lawson and Garcia tittered.

"I'm Mr. Norman," Jim said, ignoring the hand that
Vinnie had put out. "You'll remember that?"

"Sure, I'll remember it. How's your brother?"

Jim froze. He felt his bladder loosen, and as if from
far away, from down a long corridor somewhere in his

cranium, he heard a ghostly voice: *Look, Vinnie, he wet himself!*

"What do you know about my brother?" he asked thickly.

"Nothin'," Vinnie said. "Nothin' much." They smiled at him with their empty dangerous smiles.

The bell rang and they sauntered inside.

———

Drugstore phone booth, ten o'clock that night.

"Operator, I want to call the police station in Stratford, Connecticut. No, I don't know the number."

Clickings on the line. Conferences.

The policeman had been Mr. Nell. In those days he had been white-haired, perhaps in his mid-fifties. Hard to tell when you were just a kid. Their father was dead, and somehow Mr. Nell had known that.

Call me Mr. Nell, boys.

Jim and his brother met at lunchtime every day and they went into the Stratford Diner to eat their bag lunches. Mom gave them each a nickel to buy milk—that was before school milk programs started. And sometimes Mr. Nell would come in, his leather belt creaking with the weight of his belly and his .38 revolver, and buy them each a pie à la mode.

Where were you when they stabbed my brother, Mr. Nell?

A connection was made. The phone rang once.

"Stratford Police."

"Hello. My name is James Norman, Officer. I'm calling long-distance." He named the city. "I want to know if you can give me a line on a man who would have been on the force around 1957."

"Hold the line a moment, Mr. Norman."

A pause, then a new voice.

"I'm Sergeant Morton Livingston, Mr. Norman. Who are you trying to locate?"

"Well," Jim said, "us kids just called him Mr. Nell. Does that—"

"Hell, yes! Don Nell's retired now. He's seventy-three or -four."

"Does he still live in Stratford?"

"Yes, over on Barnum Avenue. Would you like the address?"

"And the phone number, if you have it."

"Okay. Did you know Don?"

"He used to buy my brother and me apple pie à la mode down at the Stratford Diner."

"Christ, that's been gone ten years. Wait a minute." He came back on the phone and read an address and a phone number. Jim jotted them down, thanked Livingston, and hung up.

He dialed 0 again, gave the number, and waited. When the phone began to ring, a sudden hot tension filled him and he leaned forward, turning instinctively away from the drugstore soda fountain, although there was no one there but a plump teen-age girl reading a magazine.

The phone was picked up and a rich, masculine

voice, sounding not at all old, said, "Hello?" That single word set off a dusty chain reaction of memories and emotions, as startling as the Pavlovian reaction that can be set off by hearing an old record on the radio.

"Mr. Nell? Donald Nell?"

"Yes."

"My name is James Norman, Mr. Nell. Do you remember me, by any chance?"

"Yes," the voice responded immediately. "Pie à la mode. Your brother was killed . . . knifed. A shame. He was a lovely boy."

———

Jim collapsed against one of the booth's glass walls. The tension's sudden departure left him as weak as a stuffed toy. He found himself on the verge of spilling everything, and he bit the urge back desperately.

"Mr. Nell, those boys were never caught."

"No," Nell said. "We did have suspects. As I recall, we had a lineup at a Bridgeport police station."

"Were those suspects identified to me by name?"

"No. The procedure at a police showup was to address the participants by number. What's your interest in this now, Mr. Norman?"

"Let me throw some names at you," Jim said. "I want to know if they ring a bell in connection with the case."

"Son, I wouldn't—"

"You might," Jim said, beginning to feel a trifle desperate. "Robert Lawson, David Garcia, Vincent Corey. Do any of those—"

"Corey," Mr. Nell said flatly. "I remember him. Vinnie the Viper. Yes, we had him up on that. His mother alibied him. I don't get anything from Robert Lawson. That could be anyone's name. But Garcia . . . that rings a bell. I'm not sure why. Hell. I'm old." He sounded disgusted.

"Mr. Nell, is there any way you could check on those boys?"

"Well, of course, they wouldn't be boys anymore."

Oh, yeah?

"Listen, Jimmy. Has one of those boys popped up and started harassing you?"

"I don't know. Some strange things have been happening. Things connected with the stabbing of my brother."

"What things?"

"Mr. Nell, I can't tell you. You'd think I was crazy."

His reply, quick, firm, interested: "Are you?"

Jim paused. "No," he said.

"Okay, I can check the names through Stratford R&I. Where can I get in touch?"

Jim gave his home number. "You'd be most likely to catch me on Tuesday night." He was in almost every night, but on Tuesday evenings Sally went to her pottery class.

"What are you doing these days, Jimmy?"

"Teaching school."

"Good. This might take a few days, you know. I'm retired now."

"You sound just the same."

"Ah, but if you could see me!" He chuckled. "D'you still like a good piece of pie à la mode, Jimmy?"

"Sure," Jim said. It was a lie. He hated pie à la mode.

"I'm glad to hear that. Well, if there's nothing else, I'll—"

"There is one more thing. Is there a Milford High in Stratford?"

"Not that I know of."

"That's what I—"

"Only thing name of Milford around here is Milford Cemetery out on the Ash Heights Road. And no one ever graduated from there." He chuckled dryly, and to Jim's ears it sounded like the sudden rattle of bones in a pit.

"Thank you," he heard himself saying. "Goodbye."

Mr. Nell was gone. The operator asked him to deposit sixty cents, and he put it in automatically. He turned, and stared into a horrid, squashed face plastered up against the glass, framed in two spread hands, the splayed fingers flattened white against the glass, as was the tip of the nose.

It was Vinnie, grinning at him.

Jim screamed.

———

Class again.

Living with Lit was doing a composition, and most of

them were bent sweatily over their papers, putting their thoughts grimly down on the page, as if chopping wood. All but three. Robert Lawson, sitting in Billy Stearns's seat, David Garcia in Kathy Slavin's, Vinnie Corey in Chip Osway's. They sat with their blank papers in front of them, watching him.

A moment before the bell, Jim said softly, "I want to talk to you for a minute after class, Mr. Corey."

"Sure, Norm."

Lawson and Garcia tittered noisily, but the rest of the class did not. When the bell rang, they passed in their papers and fairly bolted through the door. Lawson and Garcia lingered, and Jim felt his belly tighten.

Is it going to be now?

Then Lawson nodded at Vinnie. "See you later."

"Yeah."

They left. Lawson closed the door, and from beyond the frosted glass, David Garcia suddenly yelled hoarsely, "*Norm eats it!*" Vinnie looked at the door, then back at Jim. He smiled.

He said, "I was wondering if you'd ever get down to it."

"Really?" Jim said.

"Scared you the other night in the phone booth, right, dad?"

"No one says dad anymore, Vinnie. It's not cool. Like cool's not cool. It's as dead as Buddy Holly."

"I talk the way I want," Vinnie said.

"Where's the other one? The guy with the funny red hair."

"Split, man." But under his studied unconcern, Jim sensed a wariness.

"He's alive, isn't he? That's why he's not here. He's alive and he's thirty-two or -three, the way you would be if—"

"Bleach was always a drag. He's nothin'." Vinnie sat up behind his desk and put his hands down flat on the old graffiti. His eyes glittered. "Man, I remember you at that lineup. You looked ready to piss your little old corduroy pants. I seen you lookin' at me and Davie. I put the hex on you."

"I suppose you did," Jim said. "You gave me sixteen years of bad dreams. Wasn't that enough? Why now? Why me?"

Vinnie looked puzzled, and then smiled again. "Because you're unfinished business, man. You got to be cleaned up."

"Where were you?" Jim asked. "Before."

Vinnie's lips thinned. "We ain't talkin' about that. Dig?"

"They dug *you* a hole, didn't they, Vinnie? Six feet deep. Right in the Milford Cemetery. Six feet of—"

"You shut up!"

He was on his feet. The desk fell over in the aisle.

"It's not going to be easy," Jim said. "I'm not going to make it easy for you."

"We're gonna kill you, dad. You'll find out about that hole."

"Get out of here."

"Maybe that little wifey of yours, too."

"You goddamn punk, if you touch her—" He started forward blindly, feeling violated and terrified by the mention of Sally.

Vinnie grinned and started for the door. "Just be cool. Cool as a fool." He tittered.

"If you touch my wife, I'll kill you."

Vinnie's grin widened. "Kill me? Man, I thought you knew, I'm already dead."

He left. His footfalls echoed in the corridor for a long time.

———

"What are you reading, hon?"

Jim held the binding of the book, *Raising Demons*, out for her to read.

"Yuck." She turned back to the mirror to check her hair.

"Will you take a taxi home?" he asked.

"It's only four blocks. Besides, the walk is good for my figure."

"Someone grabbed one of my girls over on Summer Street," he lied. "She thinks the object was rape."

"Really? Who?"

"Dianne Snow," he said, making a name up at random. "She's a levelheaded girl. Treat yourself to a taxi, okay?"

"Okay," she said. She stopped at his chair, knelt, put her hands on his cheeks and looked into his eyes. "What's the matter, Jim?"

"Nothing."

"Yes. Something is."

"Nothing I can't handle."

"Is it something . . . about your brother?"

A draft of terror blew over him, as if an inner door had been opened. "Why do you say that?"

"You were moaning his name in your sleep last night. *Wayne, Wayne,* you were saying. *Run, Wayne.*"

"It's nothing."

But it wasn't. They both knew it. He watched her go.

Mr. Nell called at quarter past eight. "You don't have to worry about those guys," he said. "They're all dead."

"Is that so?" He was holding his place in *Raising Demons* with his index finger as he talked.

"Car smash. Six months after your brother was killed. A cop was chasing them. Frank Simon was the cop, as a matter of fact. He works out at Sikorsky now. Probably makes a lot more money."

"And they crashed."

"The car left the road at more than a hundred miles an hour and hit a main power pole. When they finally got the power shut off and scraped them out, they were cooked medium rare."

Jim closed his eyes. "You saw the report?"

"Looked at it myself."

"Anything on the car?"

"It was a hot rod."

"Any description?"

"Black 1954 Ford sedan with 'Snake Eyes' written on the side. Fitting enough. They really crapped out."

"They had a sidekick, Mr. Nell. I don't know his name, but his nickname was Bleach."

"That would be Charlie Sponder," Mr. Nell said without hesitation. "He bleached his hair with Clorox one time. I remember that. It went streaky-white, and he tried to dye it back. The streaks went orange."

"Do you know what he's doing now?"

"Career army man. Joined up in fifty-eight or -nine, after he got a local girl pregnant."

"Could I get in touch with him?"

"His mother lives in Stratford. She'd know."

"Can you give me her address?"

"I won't, Jimmy. Not until you tell me what's eating you."

"I can't, Mr. Nell. You'd think I was crazy."

"Try me."

"I can't."

"All right, son."

"Will you—" But the line was dead.

"You bastard," Jim said, and put the phone in the cradle. It rang under his hand and he jerked away from it as if it had suddenly burned him. He looked at it, breathing heavily. It rang three times, four. He picked it up. Listened. Closed his eyes.

———

A cop pulled him over on his way to the hospital, then went ahead of him, siren screaming. There was a young doctor with a toothbrush mustache in the emergency room. He looked at Jim with dark, emotionless eyes.

"Excuse me, I'm James Norman and—"

"I'm sorry, Mr. Norman. She died at 9:04 P.M.

He was going to faint. The world went far away and swimmy, and there was a high buzzing in his ears. His eyes wandered without purpose, seeing green tiled walls, a wheeled stretcher glittering under the overhead fluorescents, a nurse with her cap on crooked. *Time to freshen up, honey.* An orderly was leaning against the wall outside Emergency Room No. 1. Wearing dirty whites with a few drops of drying blood splattered across the front. Cleaning his fingernails with a knife. The orderly looked up and grinned into Jim's eyes. The orderly was David Garcia.

Jim fainted.

———

Funeral. Like a dance in three acts. The house. The funeral parlor. The graveyard. Faces coming out of nowhere, whirling close, whirling off into the darkness again. Sally's mother, her eyes streaming tears behind a black veil. Her father, looking shocked and old. Simmons. Others. They introduced themselves and shook his hand. He nodded, not remembering their names. Some of the women brought food, and one lady brought an apple pie and someone ate a piece and when he went out in the kitchen he saw it sitting on the counter, cut wide open and drooling juice into the pie plate like amber blood and he thought: *Should have a big scoop of vanilla ice cream right on top.*

He felt his hands and legs trembling, wanting to go across to the counter and throw the pie against the wall.

And then they were going and he was watching himself, the way you watch yourself in a home movie, as he shook hands and nodded and said: Thank you . . . Yes, I will . . . Thank you . . . I'm sure she is . . . Thank you . . .

When they were gone, the house was his again. He went over to the mantel. It was cluttered with souvenirs of their marriage. A stuffed dog with jeweled eyes that she had won at Coney Island on their honeymoon. Two leather folders—his diploma from B.U. and hers from U. Mass. A giant pair of styrofoam dice she had given him as a gag after he had dropped sixteen dollars in Pinky Silverstein's poker game a year or so before. A thin china cup she had bought in a Cleveland junk shop last year. In the middle of the mantel, their wedding picture. He turned it over and then sat down in his chair and looked at the blank TV set. An idea began to form behind his eyes.

———

An hour later the phone rang, jolting him out of a light doze. He groped for it.

"You're next, Norm."

"Vinnie?"

"Man, she was like one of those clay pigeons in a shooting gallery. Wham and splatter."

"I'll be at the school tonight, Vinnie. Room 33. I'll leave the lights off. It'll be just like the overpass that day. I think I can even provide the train."

"Just want to end it all, is that right?"

"That's right," Jim said. "You be there."

"Maybe."

"You'll be there," Jim said, and hung up.

It was almost dark when he got to the school. He parked in his usual slot, opened the back door with his passkey, and went first to the English Department office on the second floor. He let himself in, opened the record cabinet, and began to flip through the records. He paused about halfway through the stack and took out one called *Hi-Fi Sound Effects*. He turned it over. The third cut on the A side was "Freight Train: 3:04." He put the album on top of the department's portable stereo and took *Raising Demons* out of his overcoat pocket. He turned to a marked passage, read something, and nodded. He turned out the lights.

———

Room 33.

He set up the stereo system, stretching the speakers to their widest separation, and then put on the freight-train cut. The sound came swelling up out of nothing until it filled the whole room with the harsh clash of diesel engines and steel on steel.

With his eyes closed, he could almost believe he was under the Broad Street trestle, driven to his knees, watching as the savage little drama worked to its inevitable conclusion . . .

He opened his eyes, rejected the record, then reset it. He sat behind his desk and opened *Raising Demons* to a chapter entitled "Malefic Spirits and How to Call Them." His lips moved as he read, and he paused at intervals to take objects out of his pocket and lay them on his desk.

First, an old and creased Kodak of him and his brother, standing on the lawn in front of the Broad Street apartment house where they had lived. They both had identical crew cuts, and both of them were smiling shyly into the camera. Second, a small bottle of blood. He had caught a stray alley cat and slit its throat with his pocketknife. Third, the pocketknife itself. Last, a sweatband ripped from the lining of an old Little League baseball cap. Wayne's cap. Jim had kept it in secret hopes that someday he and Sally would have a son to wear it.

He got up, went to the window, looked out. The parking lot was empty.

He began to push the school desks toward the walls, leaving a rough circle in the middle of the room. When that was done he got chalk from his desk drawer and, following the diagram in the book exactly and using a yardstick, he drew a pentagram on the floor.

His breath was coming harder now. He turned off the lights, gathered his objects in one hand, and began to recite.

"Dark Father, hear me for my soul's sake. I am one who promises sacrifice. I am one who begs a dark boon for sacrifice. I am one who seeks vengeance of the left hand. I bring blood in promise of sacrifice."

He screwed the cap off the jar, which had originally held peanut butter, and splashed it within the pentagram.

Something happened in the darkened schoolroom. It was not possible to say exactly what, but the air became heavier. There was a thickness in it that seemed to fill the throat and the belly with gray steel. The deep silence grew, swelled with something unseen.

He did as the old rites instructed.

Now there was a feeling in the air that reminded Jim of the time he had taken a class to visit a huge power station—a feeling that the very air was crammed with electric potential and was vibrating. And then a voice, curiously low and unpleasant, spoke to him.

"What do you require?"

He could not tell if he was actually hearing it or only thinking that he did. He spoke two sentences.

"It is a small boon. What do you offer?"

Jim spoke two words.

"Both," the voice whispered. "Right and left. Agreed?"

"Yes."

"Then give me what is mine."

He opened his pocketknife, turned to his desk, laid his right hand down flat, and hacked off his right index finger with four hard chops. Blood flew across the blotter in dark patterns. It didn't hurt at all. He brushed the finger aside and switched the pocketknife to his right hand. Cutting off the left finger was harder. His right hand felt awkward and alien with the missing finger, and the knife kept slipping. At last, with an impatient grunt, he threw the knife away, snapped the bone, and ripped the finger free. He picked them both up like breadsticks and threw them into the pentagram. There was a bright flash of light, like an old-fashioned photographer's flashpowder. No smoke, he noted. No smell of brimstone.

"What objects have you brought?"

"A photograph. A band of cloth that has been dipped in his sweat."

"Sweat is precious," the voice remarked, and there was a cold greed in the tone that made Jim shiver. "Give them to me."

Jim threw them into the pentagram. The light flashed.

"It is good," the voice said.

"If they come," Jim said.

There was no response. The voice was gone—if it had ever been there. He leaned closer to the pentagram. The picture was still there, but blackened and charred. The sweatband was gone.

In the street there was a noise, faint at first, then swelling. A hot rod equipped with glasspack mufflers, first turning onto Davis Street, then approaching. Jim sat down, listening to hear if it would go by or turn in.

It turned in.

Footfalls on the stairs, echoing.

Robert Lawson's high-pitched giggle, then someone going "Shhhhh!" and then Lawson's giggle again. The footfalls came closer, lost their echo, and then the glass door at the head of the stairs banged open.

"Yoo-hoo, Normie!" David Garcia called, falsetto.

"You there, Normie?" Lawson whispered, and then giggled. "Vas you dere, Cholly?"

Vinnie didn't speak, but as they advanced up the hall, Jim could see their shadows. Vinnie's was the tallest, and he was holding a long object in one hand. There was a light snick of sound, and the long object became longer still.

They were standing by the door, Vinnie in the middle. They were all holding knives.

"Here we come, man," Vinnie said softly. "Here we come for your ass."

Jim turned on the record player.

"Jesus!" Garcia called out, jumping. "What's that?"

The freight train was coming closer. You could almost feel the walls thrumming with it.

The sound no longer seemed to be coming out of the speakers but from down the hall, from down tracks someplace far away in time as well as space.

"I don't like this, man," Lawson said.

"It's too late," Vinnie said. He stepped forward and gestured with the knife. "Give us your money, dad."

. . . let us go . . .

Garcia recoiled. "What the hell—"

But Vinnie never hesitated. He motioned the others to spread out, and the thing in his eyes might have been relief.

"Come on, kid, how much you got?" Garcia asked suddenly.

"Four cents," Jim said. It was true. He had picked them out of the penny jar in the bedroom. The most recent date was 1956.

"You fuckin' liar."

. . . leave him alone . . .

Lawson glanced over his shoulder and his eyes widened. The walls had become misty, insubstantial. The freight train wailed. The light from the parking-lot streetlamp had reddened, like the neon Burrets Building Company sign, stuttering against the twilight sky.

Something was walking out of the pentagram, something with the face of a small boy perhaps twelve years old. A boy with a crew cut.

Garcia darted forward and punched Jim in the mouth. He could smell mixed garlic and pepperoni on his breath. It was all slow and painless.

Jim felt a sudden heaviness, like lead, in his groin, and his bladder let go. He looked down and saw a dark patch appear and spread on his pants.

"Look, Vinnie, he wet himself!" Lawson cried out. The tone was right, but the expression on his face was one of horror—the expression of a puppet that has come to life only to find itself on strings.

"Let him alone," the Wayne-thing said, but it was not Wayne's voice—it was the cold, greedy voice of the thing from the pentagram. "Run, Jimmy! Run! Run! Run!"

Jim slipped to his knees and a hand slapped down on his back, groping for purchase, and found none.

He looked up and saw Vinnie, his face stretched into a caricature of hatred, drive his knife into the Wayne-thing just below the breastbone . . . and then scream, his face collapsing in on itself, charring, blackening, becoming awful.

Then he was gone.

Garcia and Lawson struck a moment later, writhed, charred, and disappeared.

Jim lay on the floor, breathing harshly. The sound of the freight train faded.

His brother was looking down at him.

"Wayne?" he breathed.

And the face changed. It seemed to melt and run together. The eyes went yellow, and a horrible, grinning malignancy looked out at him.

"I'll come back, Jim," the cold voice whispered.

And it was gone.

He got up slowly and turned off the record player with one mangled hand. He touched his mouth. It was bleeding from Garcia's punch. He went over and turned on the lights. The room was empty. He looked out into the parking lot and that was empty, too, except for one hubcap that reflected the moon in idiot pantomime. The classroom air smelled old and stale—the atmosphere of tombs. He erased the pentagram on the floor and then began to straighten up the desks for the substitute the next day. His fingers hurt very badly—*what fingers?* He would have to see a doctor. He closed the door and went downstairs slowly, holding his hands to his chest. Half-way down, something—a shadow, or perhaps only an intuition—made him whirl around.

Something unseen seemed to leap back.

Jim remembered the warning in *Raising Demons*— the danger involved. You could perhaps summon them, perhaps cause them to do your work. You could even get rid of them.

But sometimes they come back.

He walked down the stairs again, wondering if the nightmare was over after all.

STRAWBERRY SPRING

Springheel Jack . . .

I saw those two words in the paper this morning and my God, how they take me back. All that was eight years ago, almost to the day. Once, while it was going on, I saw myself on nationwide TV—the Walter Cronkite Report. Just a hurrying face in the general background behind the reporter, but my folks picked me out right away. They called long-distance. My dad wanted my analysis of the situation; he was all bluff and hearty and man-to-man. My mother just wanted me to come home. But I didn't want to come home. I was enchanted.

Enchanted by that dark and mist-blown strawberry spring, and by the shadow of violent death that walked through it on those nights eight years ago. The shadow of Springheel Jack.

In New England they call it a strawberry spring. No one knows why; it's just a phrase the old-timers use. They say it happens once every eight or ten years. What happened at New Sharon Teachers' College that particular strawberry spring . . . there may be a cycle for that, too, but if anyone has figured it out, they've never said.

At New Sharon, the strawberry spring began on March 16, 1968. The coldest winter in twenty years broke on that day. It rained and you could smell the sea twenty miles west of the beaches. The snow, which had been thirty-five inches deep in places, began to melt and the campus walks ran with slush. The Winter Carnival snow sculptures, which had been kept sharp and clearcut for two months by the subzero temperatures, at last began to sag and slouch. The caricature of Lyndon Johnson in front of the Tep fraternity house cried melted tears. The dove in front of Prashner Hall lost its frozen feathers and its plywood skeleton showed sadly through in places.

And when night came the fog came with it, moving silent and white along the narrow college avenues and thoroughfares. The pines on the mall poked through it like counting fingers and it drifted, slow as cigarette smoke, under the little bridge down by the Civil War cannons. It made things seem out of joint, strange, magical. The unwary traveler would step out of the juke-thumping, brightly lit confusion of the Grinder, expecting the hard clear starriness of winter to clutch him . . . and instead he would suddenly find himself in a silent, muffled world of white drifting fog, the only sound his own footsteps and the soft drip of water from the ancient gutters. You half expected to see Gollum or Frodo and Sam go hurrying past, or to turn and see that the Grinder was gone, vanished, replaced by a foggy panorama of moors and yew trees and perhaps a Druid-circle or a sparkling fairy ring.

The jukebox played "Love Is Blue" that year. It played "Hey, Jude" endlessly, endlessly. It played "Scarborough Fair."

And at ten minutes after eleven on that night a junior named John Dancey on his way back to his dormitory began screaming into the fog, dropping books on and between the sprawled legs of the dead girl lying in a shadowy corner of the Animal Sciences parking lot, her throat cut from ear to ear but her eyes open and almost seeming to sparkle as if she had just successfully pulled off the funniest joke of her young life—Dancey, an education major and a speech minor, screamed and screamed and screamed.

The next day was overcast and sullen, and we went to classes with questions eager in our mouths—who? why? when do you think they'll get him? And always the final thrilled question: Did you know her? Did you know her?

Yes, I had an art class with her.

Yes, one of my roommate's friends dated her last term.

Yes, she asked me for a light once in the Grinder. She was at the next table.

Yes,

Yes, I

Yes . . . yes . . . oh yes, I

We all knew her. Her name was Gale Cerman (pronounced Kerr-man), and she was an art major. She wore granny glasses and had a good figure. She was well liked but her roommates had hated her. She had never gone out much even though she was one of the most promiscuous girls on campus. She was ugly but cute. She had been a vivacious girl who talked little and smiled seldom. She had been pregnant and she had had leukemia. She was a lesbian who had been murdered by her boyfriend. It was strawberry spring, and on the morning of March 17 we all knew Gale Cerman.

Half a dozen State Police cars crawled onto the campus, most of them parked in front of Judith Franklin Hall, where the Cerman girl had lived. On my way past there to my ten o'clock class I was asked to show my student ID. I was clever. I showed him the one without the fangs.

"Do you carry a knife?" the policeman asked cunningly.

"Is it about Gale Cerman?" I asked, after I told him that the most lethal thing on my person was a rabbit's-foot key chain.

"What makes you ask?" He pounced.

I was five minutes late to class.

It was strawberry spring and no one walked by themselves through the half-academical, half-fantastical campus that night. The fog had come again, smelling of the sea, quiet and deep.

Around nine o'clock my roommate burst into our room, where I had been busting my brains on a Milton essay since seven. "They caught him," he said. "I heard it over at the Grinder."

"From who?"

"I don't know. Some guy. Her boyfriend did it. His name is Carl Amalara."

I settled back, relieved and disappointed. With a name like that it had to be true. A lethal and sordid little crime of passion.

"Okay," I said. "That's good."

He left the room to spread the news down the hall. I reread my Milton essay, couldn't figure out what I had been trying to say, tore it up and started again.

It was in the papers the next day. There was an incongruously neat picture of Amalara—probably a high-school graduation picture—and it showed a rather sad-looking boy with an olive complexion and dark eyes and pockmarks on his nose. The boy had not confessed yet, but the evidence against him was strong. He and Gale Cerman had argued a great deal in the last month or so, and had broken up the week before. Amalara's roomie said he had been "despondent." In a footlocker under his bed, police had found a seven-inch hunting knife from L. L. Bean's and a picture of the girl that had apparently been cut up with a pair of shears.

Beside Amalara's picture was one of Gale Cerman. It blurrily showed a dog, a peeling lawn flamingo, and a rather mousy blond girl wearing spectacles. An uncomfortable smile had turned her lips up and her eyes were squinted. One hand was on the dog's head. It was true then. It had to be true.

The fog came again that night, not on little cat's feet but in an improper silent sprawl. I walked that night. I had a headache and I walked for air, smelling the wet, misty smell of the spring that was slowly wiping away the reluctant snow, leaving lifeless patches of last year's grass bare and uncovered, like the head of a sighing old grandmother.

For me, that was one of the most beautiful nights I can remember. The people I passed under the haloed streetlights were murmuring shadows, and all of them seemed to be lovers, walking with hands and eyes linked. The melting snow dripped and ran, dripped and ran, and from every dark storm drain the sound of the sea drifted up, a dark winter sea now strongly ebbing.

I walked until nearly midnight, until I was thoroughly mildewed, and I passed many shadows, heard many footfalls clicking dreamily off down the winding paths. Who is to say that one of those shadows was not the man or the thing that came to be known as Springheel Jack? Not I, for I passed many shadows but in the fog I saw no faces.

The next morning the clamor in the hall woke me. I blundered out to see who had been drafted, combing my hair with both hands and running the fuzzy caterpillar that had craftily replaced my tongue across the dry roof of my mouth.

"He got another one," someone said to me, his face pallid with excitement. "They had to let him go."

"Who go?"

"Amalara!" someone else said gleefully. "He was sitting in jail when it happened."

"When what happened?" I asked patiently. Sooner or later I would get it. I was sure of that.

"The guy killed somebody else last night. And now they're hunting all over for it."

"For what?"

The pallid face wavered in front of me again. "Her head. Whoever killed her took her head with him."

———

New Sharon isn't a big school now, and was even smaller then—the kind of institution the public relations people chummily refer to as a "community college." And it really was like a small community, at least in those days; between you and your friends, you probably had at least a nodding acquaintance with everybody else and their friends. Gale Cerman had been the type of girl you just nodded to, thinking vaguely that you had seen her around.

We all knew Ann Bray. She had been the first runner-up in the Miss New England pageant the year before, her talent performance consisting of twirling a flaming baton to the tune of "Hey, Look Me Over." She was brainy, too; until the time of her death she had been editor of the school newspaper (a once-weekly rag with a lot of political cartoons and bombastic letters), a member of the student dramatics society, and president of the National Service Sorority, New Sharon Branch.

In the hot, fierce bubblings of my freshman youth I had submitted a column idea to the paper and asked for a date—turned down on both counts.

And now she was dead . . . worse than dead.

I walked to my afternoon classes like everyone else, nodding to people I knew and saying hi with a little more force than usual, as if that would make up for the close way I studied their faces. Which was the same way they were studying mine. There was someone dark among us, as dark as the paths which twisted across the mall or wound among the hundred-year-old oaks on the quad in back of the gymnasium. As dark as the hulking Civil War cannons seen through a drifting membrane of fog. We looked into each other's faces and tried to read the darkness behind one of them.

This time the police arrested no one. The blue beetles patrolled the campus ceaselessly on the foggy spring nights of the eighteenth, nineteenth, and twentieth, and spotlights stabbed into dark nooks and crannies with erratic eagerness. The administration imposed a mandatory nine o'clock curfew. A foolhardy couple discovered necking in the landscaped bushes north of the Tate Alumni Building were taken to the New Sharon police station and grilled unmercifully for three hours.

There was a hysterical false alarm on the twentieth when a boy was found unconscious in the same parking lot where the body of Gale Cerman had been found. A gibbering campus cop loaded him into the back of his cruiser and put a map of the county over his face without bothering to hunt for a pulse and started toward the local hospital, siren wailing across the deserted campus like a seminar of banshees.

Halfway there the corpse in the back seat had risen and asked hollowly, "Where the hell am I?" The cop shrieked and ran off the road. The corpse turned out to be an undergrad named Donald Morris who had been in bed the last two days with a pretty lively case of flu—was it Asian that year? I can't remember. Anyway, he fainted in the parking lot on his way to the Grinder for a bowl of soup and some toast.

The days continued warm and overcast. People clustered in small groups that had a tendency to break up and re-form with surprising speed. Looking at the same set of faces for too long gave you funny ideas about some of them. And the speed with which rumors swept from one end of the campus to the other began to approach the speed of light; a well-liked history professor had been overheard laughing and weeping down by the small bridge; Gale Cerman had left a cryptic two-word message written in her own blood on the black-top of the Animal Sciences parking lot; both murders were actually political crimes, ritual murders that had been performed by an offshoot of the SDS to protest the war. This was really laughable. The New Sharon SDS had seven members. One fair-sized offshoot would have bankrupted the whole organization. This fact brought an even more sinister embellishment from the campus right-wingers: outside agitators. So during those queer, warm days we all kept our eyes peeled for them.

The press, always fickle, ignored the strong resem-

blance our murderer bore to Jack the Ripper and dug
further back—all the way to 1819. Ann Bray had been
found on a soggy path of ground some twelve feet from
the nearest sidewalk, and yet there were no footprints,
not even her own. An enterprising New Hampshire
newsman with a passion for the arcane christened the
killer Springheel Jack, after the infamous Dr. John
Hawkins of Bristol, who did five of his wives to death
with odd pharmaceutical knickknacks. And the name,
probably because of that soggy yet unmarked ground,
stuck.

On the twenty-first it rained again, and the mall and
quadrangle became quagmires. The police announced
that they were salting plainclothes detectives, men and
women, about, and took half the police cars off duty.

The campus newspaper published a strongly indig-
nant, if slightly incoherent, editorial protesting this.
The upshot of it seemed to be that, with all sorts of cops
masquerading as students, it would be impossible to tell
a real outside agitator from a false one.

Twilight came and the fog with it, drifting up the
tree-lined avenues slowly, almost thoughtfully, blotting
out the buildings one by one. It was soft, insubstantial
stuff, but somehow implacable and frightening. Springheel Jack was a man, no one seemed to doubt that, but
the fog was his accomplice and it was female . . . or so
it seemed to me. It was as if our little school was caught
between them, squeezed in some crazy lovers' embrace,
part of a marriage that had been consummated in blood.
I sat and smoked and watched the lights come on in the

growing darkness and wondered if it was all over. My roommate came in and shut the door quietly behind him.

"It's going to snow soon," he said.

I turned around and looked at him. "Does the radio say that?"

"No," he said. "Who needs a weatherman? Have you ever heard of strawberry spring?"

"Maybe," I said. "A long time ago. Something grandmothers talk about, isn't it?"

He stood beside me, looking out at the creeping dark.

"Strawberry spring is like Indian summer," he said, "only much more rare. You get a good Indian summer in this part of the country once every two or three years. A spell of weather like we've been having is supposed to come only every eight or ten. It's a false spring, a lying spring, like Indian summer is a false summer. My own grandmother used to say strawberry spring means the worst norther of the winter is still on the way—and the longer this lasts, the harder the storm."

"Folk tales," I said. "Never believe a word." I looked at him. "But I'm nervous. Are you?"

He smiled benevolently and stole one of my cigarettes from the open pack on the window ledge. "I suspect everyone but me and thee," he said, and then the smile faded a little. "And sometimes I wonder about thee. Want to go over to the Union and shoot some eight-ball? I'll spot you ten."

"Trig prelim next week. I'm going to settle down with a magic marker and a hot pile of notes."

For a long time after he was gone, I could only look out the window. And even after I had opened my book and started in, part of me was still out there, walking in the shadows where something dark was now in charge.

That night Adelle Parkins was killed. Six police cars and seventeen collegiate-looking plainclothesmen (eight of them were women imported all the way from Boston) patrolled the campus. But Springheel Jack killed her just the same, going unerringly for one of our own. The false spring, the lying spring, aided and abetted him— he killed her and left her propped behind the wheel of her 1964 Dodge to be found the next morning and they found part of her in the back seat and part of her in the trunk. And written in blood on the windshield—this time fact instead of rumor—were two words: HA! HA!

The campus went slightly mad after that; all of us and none of us had known Adelle Parkins. She was one of those nameless, harried women who worked the break-back shift in the Grinder from six to eleven at night, facing hordes of hamburger-happy students on study break from the library across the way. She must have had it relatively easy those last three foggy nights of her life; the curfew was being rigidly observed, and after nine the Grinder's only patrons were hungry cops and happy janitors—the empty buildings had improved their habitual bad temper considerably.

There is little left to tell. The police, as prone to hysteria as any of us and driven against the wall, arrested an innocuous homosexual sociology graduate student named Hanson Gray, who claimed he "could not remember" where he had spent several of the lethal evenings. They charged him, arraigned him, and let him go to scamper hurriedly back to his native New Hampshire town after the last unspeakable night of strawberry spring when Marsha Curran was slaughtered on the mall.

Why she had been out and alone is forever beyond knowing—she was a fat, sadly pretty thing who lived in an apartment in town with three other girls. She had slipped on campus as silently and as easily as Spring-heel Jack himself. What brought her? Perhaps her need was as deep and as ungovernable as her killer's, and just as far beyond understanding. Maybe a need for one desperate and passionate romance with the warm night, the warm fog, the smell of the sea, and the cold knife.

———

That was on the twenty-third. On the twenty-fourth the president of the college announced that spring break would be moved up a week, and we scattered, not joyfully but like frightened sheep before a storm, leaving the campus empty and haunted by the police and one dark specter.

I had my own car on campus, and I took six people downstate with me, their luggage crammed in helter-skelter. It wasn't a pleasant ride. For all any of us knew, Springheel Jack might have been in the car with us.

That night the thermometer dropped fifteen degrees,

and the whole northern New England area was belted by a shrieking norther that began in sleet and ended in a foot of snow. The usual number of old duffers had heart attacks shoveling it away—and then, like magic, it was April. Clean showers and starry nights.

They called it strawberry spring, God knows why, and it's an evil, lying time that only comes once every eight or ten years. Springheel Jack left with the fog, and by early June, campus conversation had turned to a series of draft protests and a sit-in at the building where a well-known napalm manufacturer was holding job interviews. By June, the subject of Springheel Jack was almost unanimously avoided—at least aloud. I suspect there were many who turned it over and over privately, looking for the one crack in the seamless egg of madness that would make sense of it all.

That was the year I graduated, and the next year was the year I married. A good job in a local publishing house. In 1971 we had a child, and now he's almost school age. A fine and questing boy with my eyes and her mouth.

Then, today's paper.

Of course I knew it was here. I knew it yesterday morning when I got up and heard the mysterious sound of snowmelt running down the gutters, and smelled the salt tang of the ocean from our front porch, nine miles from the nearest beach. I knew strawberry spring had come again when I started home from work last night and had to turn on my headlights against the mist that was already beginning to creep out of the fields and hollows, blurring the lines of the buildings and putting fairy haloes around the streetlamps.

This morning's paper says a girl was killed on the New Sharon campus near the Civil War cannons. She was killed last night and found in a melting snowbank. She was not . . . she was not all there.

My wife is upset. She wants to know where I was last night. I can't tell her because I don't remember. I remember starting home from work, and I remember putting my headlights on to search my way through the lovely creeping fog, but that's all I remember.

I've been thinking about that foggy night when I had a headache and walked for air and passed all the lovely shadows without shape or substance. And I've been thinking about the trunk of my car—such an ugly word, *trunk*—and wondering why in the world I should be afraid to open it.

I can hear my wife as I write this, in the next room, crying. She thinks I was with another woman last night.

And oh dear God, I think so too.

THE LEDGE

"**G**o on," Cressner said again. "Look in the bag."

We were in his penthouse apartment, forty-three stories up. The carpet was deep-cut pile, burnt orange. In the middle, between the Basque sling chair where Cressner sat and the genuine leather couch where no one at all sat, there was a brown shopping bag.

"If it's a payoff, forget it," I said. "I love her."

"It's money, but it's not a payoff. Go on. Look." He was smoking a Turkish cigarette in an onyx holder. The air-circulation system allowed me just a dry whiff of the tobacco and then whipped it away. He was wearing a silk dressing gown on which a dragon was embroidered. His eyes were calm and intelligent behind his glasses. He looked just like what he was: an A-number-one, 500-carat, dyed-in-the-wool son of a bitch. I loved his wife, and she loved me. I had expected him to make trouble, and I knew this was it, but I just wasn't sure what brand it was.

I went to the shopping bag and tipped it over. Banded

bundles of currency tumbled out on the rug. All twenties. I picked one of the bundles up and counted. Ten bills to a bundle. There were a lot of bundles.

"Twenty thousand dollars," he said, and puffed on his cigarette.

I stood up. "Okay."

"It's for you."

"I don't want it."

"My wife comes with it."

I didn't say anything. Marcia had warned me how it would be. He's like a cat, she had said. An old tom full of meanness. He'll try to make you a mouse.

"So you're a tennis pro," he said. "I don't believe I've ever actually seen one before."

"You mean your detectives didn't get any pictures?"

"Oh, yes." He waved the cigarette holder negligently. "Even a motion picture of the two of you in that Bayside Motel. A camera was behind the mirror. But pictures are hardly the same, are they?"

"If you say so."

He'll keep changing tacks, Marcia had said. It's the way he puts people on the defensive. Pretty soon he'll have you hitting out at where you think he's going to be, and he'll get you someplace else. Say as little as possible, Stan. And remember that I love you.

"I invited you up because I thought we should have a little man-to-man chat, Mr. Norris. Just a pleasant conversation between two civilized human beings, one of whom has made off with the other's wife."

I started to answer but decided not to.

"Did you enjoy San Quentin?" Cressner said, puffing lazily.

"Not particularly."

"I believe you passed three years there. A charge of breaking and entering, if I'm correct."

"Marcia knows about it," I said, and immediately wished I hadn't. I was playing his game, just what Marcia had warned against. Hitting soft lobs for him to smash back.

"I've taken the liberty of having your car moved," he said, glancing out the window at the far end of the room. It really wasn't a window at all: the whole wall was glass. In the middle was a sliding-glass door. Beyond it, a balcony the size of a postage stamp. Beyond that, a very long drop. There was something strange about the door. I couldn't quite put my finger on it.

"This is a very pleasant building," Cressner said. "Good security. Closed-circuit TV and all that. When I knew you were in the lobby, I made a telephone call. An employee then hotwired the ignition of your car and moved it from the parking area here to a public lot several blocks away." He glanced up at the modernistic sunburst clock above the couch. It was 8:05. "At 8:20 the same employee will call the police from a public phone booth concerning your car. By 8:30, at the latest, the minions of the law will have discovered over six ounces of heroin hidden in the spare tire of your trunk. You will be eagerly sought after, Mr. Norris."

He had set me up. I had tried to cover myself as well as I could, but in the end I had been child's play for him.

"These things will happen unless I call my employee and tell him to forget the phone call."

"And all I have to do is tell you where Marcia is," I said. "No deal, Cressner, I don't know. We set it up this way just for you."

"My men had her followed."

"I don't think so. I think we lost them at the airport."

Cressner sighed, removed the smoldering cigarette holder, and dropped it into a chromium ashtray with a sliding lid. No fuss, no muss. The used cigarette and Stan Norris had been taken care of with equal ease.

"Actually," he said, "you're right. The old ladies'-room vanishing act. My operatives were extremely vexed to have been taken in by such an ancient ruse. I think it was so old they never expected it."

I said nothing. After Marcia had ditched Cressner's operatives at the airport, she had taken the bus shuttle back to the city and then to the bus station; that had been the plan. She had two hundred dollars, all the money that had been in my savings account. Two hundred dollars and a Greyhound bus could take you anyplace in the country.

"Are you always so uncommunicative?" Cressner asked, and he sounded genuinely interested.

"Marcia advised it."

A little more sharply, he said: "Then I imagine you'll stand on your rights when the police take you in. And the next time you see my wife could be when she's a little old grandmother in a rocker. Have you gotten that through your head? I understand that possession of six ounces of heroin could get you forty years."

"That won't get you Marcia back."

He smiled thinly. "And that's the nub of it, isn't it? Shall I review where we are? You and my wife have fallen in love. You have had an affair . . . if you want to call a series of one-nighters in cheap motels an affair. My wife has left me. However, I have you. And you are in what is called a bind. Does that summarize it adequately?"

"I can understand why she got tired of you," I said.

To my surprise, he threw back his head and laughed. "You know, I rather like you, Mr. Norris. You're vulgar and you're a piker, but you seem to have heart. Marcia said you did. I rather doubted it. Her judgment of character is lax. But you do have a certain . . . verve. Which is why I've set things up the way I have. No doubt Marcia has told you that I am fond of wagering."

"Yes." Now I knew what was wrong with the door in the middle of the glass wall. It was the middle of winter, and no one was going to want to take tea on a balcony forty-three stories up. The balcony had been cleared of furniture. And the screen had been taken off the door. Now why would Cressner have done that?

"I don't like my wife very much," Cressner said, fixing another cigarette carefully in the holder. "That's no secret. I'm sure she's told you as much. And I'm sure a man of your . . . experience knows that contented wives do not jump into the hay with the local tennis-club pro at the drop of a racket. In my opinion, Marcia is a prissy, whey-faced little prude, a whiner, a weeper, a bearer of tales, a—"

"That's about enough," I said.

He smiled coldly. "I beg your pardon. I keep forgetting we are discussing your beloved. It's 8:16. Are you nervous?"

I shrugged.

"Tough to the end," he said, and lit his cigarette. "At any rate, you may wonder why, if I dislike Marcia so much, I do not simply give her her freedom—"

"No, I don't wonder at all."

He frowned at me.

"You're a selfish, grasping, egocentric son of a bitch. That's why. No one takes what's yours. Not even if you don't want it anymore."

He went red and then laughed. "One for you, Mr. Norris. Very good."

I shrugged again.

"I'm going to offer you a wager. If you win, you leave here with the money, the woman, and your freedom. On the other hand, if you lose, you lose your life."

I looked at the clock. I couldn't help it. It was 8:19.

"All right," I said. What else? It would buy time, at least. Time for me to think of some way to beat it out of here, with or without the money.

Cressner picked up the telephone beside him and dialed a number.

"Tony? Plan two. Yes." He hung up.

"What's plan two?" I asked.

"I'll call Tony back in fifteen minutes, and he will remove the . . . offending substance from the trunk of your car and drive it back here. If I don't call, he will get in touch with the police."

"Not very trusting, are you?"

"Be sensible, Mr. Norris. There is twenty thousand dollars on the carpet between us. In this city murder has been committed for twenty cents."

"What's the bet?"

He looked genuinely pained. "Wager, Mr. Norris, wager. Gentlemen make wagers. Vulgarians place bets."

"Whatever you say."

"Excellent. I've seen you looking at my balcony."

"The screen's off the door."

"Yes. I had it taken off this afternoon. What I propose is this: that you walk around my building on the ledge that juts out just below the penthouse level. If you circumnavigate the building successfully, the jackpot is yours."

"You're crazy."

"On the contrary. I have proposed this wager six times to six different people during my dozen years in this apartment. Three of the six were professional athletes, like you—one of them a notorious quarterback more famous for his TV commercials than his passing game, one a baseball player, one a rather famous jockey who made an extraordinary yearly salary and who was also afflicted with extraordinary alimony problems. The other three were more ordinary citizens who had differing professions but two things in common: a need for money and a certain degree of body grace." He puffed his cigarette thoughtfully and then continued. "The wager was declined five times out of hand. On the other occasion, it was accepted. The terms were twenty thousand dollars against six months' service to me. I collected. The fellow took one look over the edge of the balcony and nearly fainted." Cressner looked amused and contemptuous. "He said everything down there looked so small. That was what killed his nerve."

"What makes you think—"

He cut me off with an annoyed wave of his hand. "Don't bore me, Mr. Norris. I think you will do it because you have no choice. It's my wager on the one hand or forty years in San Quentin on the other. The money and my wife are only added fillips, indicative of my good nature."

"What guarantee do I have that you won't double-cross me? Maybe I'd do it and find out you'd called Tony and told him to go ahead anyway."

He sighed. "You are a walking case of paranoia, Mr. Norris. I don't love my wife. It is doing my storied ego no good at all to have her around. Twenty thousand dollars is a pittance to me. I pay four times that every week to be given to police bagmen. As for the wager, however . . ." His eyes gleamed. "That is beyond price."

I thought about it, and he left me. I suppose he knew that the real mark always convinces himself. I was a thirty-six-year-old tennis bum, and the club had been thinking of letting me go when Marcia applied a little gentle pressure. Tennis was the only profession I knew, and without it, even getting a job as a janitor would be tough—especially with a record. It was kid stuff, but employers don't care.

And the funny thing was that I really loved Marcia Cressner. I had fallen for her after two nine-o'clock tennis lessons, and she had fallen for me just as hard. It was a case of Stan Norris luck, all right. After thirty-six years of happy bachelorhood, I had fallen like a sack of mail for the wife of an Organization overlord.

The old tom sitting there and puffing his imported Turkish cigarette knew all that, of course. And something else, as well. I had no guarantee that he wouldn't turn me in if I accepted his wager and won, but I knew damn well that I'd be in the cooler by ten o'clock if I didn't. And the next time I'd be free would be at the turn of the century.

"I want to know one thing," I said.

"What might that be, Mr. Norris?"

"Look me right in the face and tell me if you're a welsher or not."

He looked at me directly. "Mr. Norris," he said quietly, "I never welsh."

"All right," I said. What other choice was there?

He stood up, beaming. "Excellent! Really excellent! Approach the door to the balcony with me, Mr. Norris."

We walked over together. His face was that of a man who had dreamed this scene hundreds of times and was enjoying its actuality to the fullest.

"The ledge is five inches wide," he said dreamily. "I've measured it myself. In fact, I've stood on it, holding on to the balcony, of course. All you have to do is lower yourself over the wrought-iron railing. You'll be chest-high. But, of course, beyond the railing there are no handgrips. You'll have to inch your way along, being very careful not to overbalance."

My eye had fastened on something else outside the window . . . something that made my blood temperature sink several degrees. It was a wind gauge. Cressner's apartment was quite close to the lake, and it was high enough so there were no higher buildings to act as a windbreak. That wind would be cold, and it would cut like a knife. The needle was standing at ten pretty steadily, but a gust would send the needle almost up to twenty-five for a few seconds before dropping off.

"Ah, I see you've noticed my wind gauge," Cressner said jovially. "Actually, it's the other side which gets the prevailing wind; so the breeze may be a little stronger on that side. But actually this is a fairly still night. I've seen evenings when the wind has gusted up to eighty-five . . . you can actually feel the building rock a little. A bit like being on a ship, in the crow's nest. And it's quite mild for this time of year."

He pointed, and I saw the lighted numerals atop a bank skyscraper to the left. They said it was forty-four degrees. But with the wind, that would have made the chill factor somewhere in the mid-twenties.

"Have you got a coat?" I asked. I was wearing a light jacket.

"Alas, no." The lighted figures on the bank switched to show the time. It was 8:32. "And I think you had better get started, Mr. Norris, so I can call Tony and put plan three into effect. A good boy but apt to be impulsive. You understand."

I understood, all right. Too damn well.

But the thought of being with Marcia, free from Cressner's tentacles and with enough money to get started at something made me push open the sliding-glass door and step out onto the balcony. It was cold and damp; the wind ruffled my hair into my eyes.

"Bon soir," Cressner said behind me, but I didn't bother to look back. I approached the railing, but I didn't look down. Not yet. I began to do deep-breathing.

It's not really an exercise at all but a form of self-hypnosis. With every inhale-exhale, you throw a distraction out of your mind, until there's nothing left but the match ahead of you. I got rid of the money with one breath and Cressner himself with two. Marcia took longer—her face kept rising in my mind, telling me not to be stupid, not to play his game, that maybe Cressner never welshed, but he always hedged his bets. I didn't listen. I couldn't afford to. If I lost this match, I wouldn't have to buy the beers and take the ribbing; I'd be so much scarlet sludge splattered for a block of Deakman Street in both directions.

When I thought I had it, I looked down.

The building sloped away like a smooth chalk cliff to the street far below. The cars parked there looked like those matchbox models you can buy in the five-and-dime. The ones driving by the building were just tiny pinpoints of light. If you fell that far, you would have plenty of time to realize just what was happening, to see the wind blowing your clothes as the earth pulled you back faster and faster. You'd have time to scream a long, long scream. And the sound you made when you hit the pavement would be like the sound of an overripe watermelon.

I could understand why that other guy had chickened out. But he'd only had six months to worry about. I was staring forty long, gray, Marcia-less years in the eye.

I looked at the ledge. It looked small, I had never seen five inches that looked so much like two. At least the building was fairly new; it wouldn't crumble under me.

I hoped.

I swung over the railing and carefully lowered myself until I was standing on the ledge. My heels were out over the drop. The floor on the balcony was about chest-high, and I was looking into Cressner's penthouse through the wrought-iron ornamental bars. He was standing inside the door, smoking, watching me the way a scientist watches a guinea pig to see what the latest injection will do.

"Call," I said, holding on to the railing.

"What?"

"Call Tony. I don't move until you do."

He went back into the living room—it looked amazingly warm and safe and cozy—and picked up the phone. It was a worthless gesture, really. With the wind, I couldn't hear what he was saying. He put the phone down and returned. "Taken care of, Mr. Norris."

"It better be."

"Goodbye, Mr. Norris. I'll see you in a bit . . . perhaps."

It was time to do it. Talking was done. I let myself think of Marcia one last time, her light-brown hair, her wide gray eyes, her lovely body, and then put her out of my mind for good. No more looking down, either. It would have been too easy to get paralyzed, looking down through that space. Too easy to just freeze up until you lost your balance or just fainted from fear. It was time for tunnel vision. Time to concentrate on nothing but left foot, right foot.

I began to move to the right, holding on to the balcony's railing as long as I could. It didn't take long to see I was going to need all the tennis muscle my ankles had. With my heels beyond the edge, those tendons would be taking all my weight.

I got to the end of the balcony, and for a moment I didn't think I was going to be able to let go of that safety. I forced myself to do it. Five inches, hell, that was plenty of room. If the ledge were only a foot off the ground instead of 400 feet, you could breeze around this building in four minutes flat, I told myself. So just pretend it is.

Yeah, and if you fall from a ledge a foot off the ground, you just say rats, and try again. Up here you get only one chance.

I slid my right foot farther and then brought my left foot next to it. I let go of the railing. I put my open hands up, allowing the palms to rest against the rough stone of the apartment building. I caressed the stone. I could have kissed it.

A gust of wind hit me, snapping the collar of my jacket against my face, making my body sway on the ledge. My heart jumped into my throat and stayed there until the wind had died down. A strong enough gust would have peeled me right off my perch and sent me flying down into the night. And the wind would be stronger on the other side.

I turned my head to the left, pressing my cheek against the stone. Cressner was leaning over the balcony, watching me.

"Enjoying yourself?" he asked affably.

He was wearing a brown camel's-hair overcoat.

"I thought you didn't have a coat," I said.

"I lied," he answered equably. "I lie about a lot of things."

"What's that supposed to mean?"

"Nothing . . . nothing at all. Or perhaps it does mean something. A little psychological warfare, eh, Mr. Norris? I should tell you not to linger overlong. The ankles grow tired, and if they should give way . . ." He took an apple out of his pocket, bit into it, and then tossed it over the edge. There was no sound for a long time. Then, a faint and sickening plop. Cressner chuckled.

He had broken my concentration, and I could feel panic nibbling at the edges of my mind with steel teeth. A torrent of terror wanted to rush in and drown me. I turned my head away from him and did deep-breathing, flushing the panic away. I was looking at the lighted bank sign, which now said: 8:46, Time to Save at Mutual!

By the time the lighted numbers read 8:49, I felt that I had myself under control again. I think Cressner must have decided I'd frozen, and I heard a sardonic patter of applause when I began to shuffle toward the corner of the building again.

I began to feel the cold. The lake had whetted the edge of the wind; its clammy dampness bit at my skin like an auger. My thin jacket billowed out behind me as I shuffled along. I moved slowly, cold or not. If I was going to do this, I would have to do it slowly and deliberately. If I rushed, I would fall.

The bank clock read 8:52 when I reached the corner. It didn't appear to be a problem—the ledge went right around, making a square corner—but my right hand told me that there was a crosswind. If I got caught leaning the wrong way, I would take a long ride very quickly.

I waited for the wind to drop, but for a long time it refused to, almost as though it were Cressner's willing ally. It slapped against me with vicious, invisible fingers, prying and poking and tickling. At last, after a particularly strong gust had made me rock on my toes, I knew that I could wait forever and the wind would never drop all the way off.

So the next time it sank a little, I slipped my right foot around and, clutching both walls with my hands, made the turn. The crosswind pushed me two ways at once, and I tottered. For a second I was sickeningly sure that Cressner had won his wager. Then I slid a step farther along and pressed myself tightly against the wall, a held breath slipping out of my dry throat.

That was when the raspberry went off, almost in my ear.

Startled, I jerked back to the very edge of balance. My hands lost the wall and pinwheeled crazily for balance. I think that if one of them had hit the stone face of the building, I would have been gone. But after what seemed an eternity, gravity decided to let me return to the wall instead of sending me down to the pavement forty-three stories below.

My breath sobbed out of my lungs in a pained whistle. My legs were rubbery. The tendons in my ankles were humming like high-voltage wires. I had never felt so mortal. The man with the sickle was close enough to read over my shoulder.

I twisted my neck, looked up, and there was Cressner, leaning out of his bedroom window four feet above me. He was smiling, in his right hand he held a New Year's Eve noisemaker.

"Just keeping you on your toes," he said.

I didn't waste my breath. I couldn't have spoken above a croak anyway. My heart was thudding crazily in my chest. I sidled five or six feet along, just in case he was thinking about leaning out and giving me a good shove. Then I stopped and closed my eyes and deep-breathed until I had my act back together again.

I was on the short side of the building now. On my

right only the highest towers of the city bulked above me. On the left, only the dark circle of the lake, with a few pinpricks of light which floated on it. The wind whooped and moaned.

The crosswind at the second corner was not so tricky, and I made it around with no trouble. And then something bit me.

I gasped and jerked. The shift of balance scared me, and I pressed tightly against the building. I was bitten again. No . . . not bitten but pecked. I looked down.

There was a pigeon standing on the ledge, looking up with bright, hateful eyes.

You get used to pigeons in the city; they're as common as cab drivers who can't change a ten. They don't like to fly, and they give ground grudgingly, as if the sidewalks were theirs by squatters' rights. Oh, yes, and you're apt to find their calling cards on the hood of your car. But you never take much notice. They may be occasionally irritating, but they're interlopers in our world.

But I was in his, and I was nearly helpless, and he seemed to know it. He pecked my tired right ankle again, sending a bright dart of pain up my leg.

"Get," I snarled at it. "Get out."

The pigeon only pecked me again. I was obviously in what he regarded as his home; this section of the ledge was covered with droppings, old and new.

A muted cheeping from above.

I cricked my neck as far back as it would go and looked up. A beak darted at my face, and I almost recoiled. If I had, I might have become the city's first pigeon-induced casualty. It was Mama Pigeon, protecting a bunch of baby pigeons just under the slight overhang of the roof. Too far up to peck my head, thank God.

Her husband pecked me again, and now blood was flowing. I could feel it. I began to inch my way along again, hoping to scare the pigeon off the ledge. No way. Pigeons don't scare, not city pigeons, anyway. If a moving van only makes them amble a little faster, a man pinned on a high ledge isn't going to upset them at all.

The pigeon backpedaled as I shuffled forward, his bright eyes never leaving my face except when the sharp beak dipped to peck my ankle. And the pain was getting more intense now; the bird was pecking at raw flesh . . . and eating it, for all I knew.

I kicked at it with my right foot. It was a weak kick, the only kind I could afford. The pigeon only fluttered its wings a bit and then returned to the attack. I, on the other hand, almost went off the side.

The pigeon pecked me again, again, again. A cold blast of wind struck me, rocking me to the limit of balance; pads of my fingers scraped at the bland stone, and I came to rest with my left cheek pressed against the wall, breathing heavily.

Cressner couldn't have conceived of worse torture if he had planned it for ten years. One peck was not so bad. Two or three were little more. But that damned bird must have pecked me sixty times before I reached the wrought-iron railing of the penthouse opposite Cressner's.

Reaching that railing was like reaching the gates

of heaven. My hands curled sweetly around the cold uprights and held on as if they would never let go.

Peck.

The pigeon was staring up at me almost smugly with its bright eyes, confident of my impotence and its own invulnerability. I was reminded of Cressner's expression when he had ushered me out onto the balcony on the other side of the building.

Gripping the iron bars more tightly, I lashed out with a hard, strong kick and caught the pigeon squarely. It emitted a wholly satisfying squawk and rose into the air, wings flapping. A few feathers, dove gray, settled back to the ledge or disappeared slowly down into the darkness, swan-boating back and forth in the air.

Gasping, I crawled up onto the balcony and collapsed there. Despite the cold, my body was dripping with sweat. I don't know how long I lay there, recuperating. The building hid the bank clock, and I don't wear a watch.

I sat up before my muscles could stiffen up on me and gingerly rolled down my sock. The right ankle was lacerated and bleeding, but the wound looked superficial. Still, I would have to have it taken care of, if I ever got out of this. God knows what germs pigeons carry around. I thought of bandaging the raw skin but decided not to. I might stumble on a tied bandage. Time enough later. Then I could buy twenty thousand dollars' worth of bandages.

I got up and looked longingly into the darkened penthouse opposite Cressner's. Barren, empty, unlived in.

The heavy storm screen was over this door. I might have been able to break in, but that would have been forfeiting the bet. And I had more to lose than money.

When I could put it off no longer, I slipped over the railing and back onto the ledge. The pigeon, a few feathers worse for wear, was standing below his mate's nest, where the guano was thickest, eyeing me balefully. But I didn't think he'd bother me, not when he saw I was moving away.

It was very hard to move away—much harder than it had been to leave Cressner's balcony. My mind knew I had to, but my body, particularly my ankles, was screaming that it would be folly to leave such a safe harbor. But I did leave, with Marcia's face in the darkness urging me on.

I got to the second short side, made it around the corner, and shuffled slowly across the width of the building. Now that I was getting close, there was an almost ungovernable urge to hurry, to get it over with. But if I hurried, I would die. So I forced myself to go slowly.

The crosswind almost got me again on the fourth corner, and I slipped around it thanks to luck rather than skill. I rested against the building, getting my breath back. But for the first time I knew that I was going to make it, that I was going to win. My hands felt like half-frozen steaks, my ankles hurt like fire (especially the pigeon-pecked right ankle), sweat kept trickling in my eyes, but I knew I was going to make it. Halfway down the length of the building, warm yellow light spilled out on Cressner's balcony. Far beyond I could see the bank sign glowing like a welcome-home banner. It was 10:48, but it seemed that I had spent my whole life on those five inches of ledge.

And God help Cressner if he tried to welsh. The urge to hurry was gone. I almost lingered. It was 11:09 when I put first my right hand on the wrought-iron balcony railing and then my left. I hauled myself up, wriggled over the top, collapsed thankfully on the floor . . . and felt the cold steel muzzle of a .45 against my temple.

I looked up and saw a goon ugly enough to stop Big Ben dead in its clockwork. He was grinning.

"Excellent!" Cressner's voice said from within. "I applaud you, Mr. Norris!" He proceeded to do just that. "Bring him in, Tony."

Tony hauled me up and set me on my feet so abruptly that my weak ankles almost buckled. Going in, I staggered against the balcony door.

Cressner was standing by the living-room fireplace, sipping brandy from a goblet the size of a fishbowl. The money had been replaced in the shopping bag. It still stood in the middle of the burnt-orange rug.

I caught a glimpse of myself in a small mirror on the other side of the room. The hair was disheveled, the face pallid except for two bright spots of color on the cheeks. The eyes looked insane.

I got only a glimpse, because the next moment I was flying across the room. I hit the Basque chair and fell over it, pulling it down on top of me and losing my wind.

When I got some of it back, I sat up and managed: "You lousy welsher. You had this planned."

"Indeed I did," Cressner said, carefully setting his brandy on the mantel. "But I'm not a welsher, Mr. Norris. Indeed no. Just an extremely poor loser. Tony is here only to make sure you don't do anything . . . ill-advised." He put his fingers under his chin and tittered a little. He didn't look like a poor loser. He looked more like a cat with canary feathers on its muzzle. I got up, suddenly feeling more frightened than I had on the ledge.

"You fixed it," I said slowly. "Somehow, you fixed it."

"Not at all. The heroin has been removed from your car. The car itself is back in the parking lot. The money is over there. You may take it and go."

"Fine," I said.

Tony stood by the glass door to the balcony, still looking like a leftover from Halloween. The .45 was in his hand. I walked over to the shopping bag, picked it up, and walked toward the door on my jittery ankles, fully expecting to be shot down in my tracks. But when I got the door open, I began to have the same feeling that I'd had on the ledge when I rounded the fourth corner: I was going to make it.

Cressner's voice, lazy and amused, stopped me.

"You don't really think that old ladies'-room dodge fooled anyone, do you?"

I turned back slowly, the shopping bag in my arms. "What do you mean?"

"I told you I never welsh, and I never do. You won three things, Mr. Norris. The money, your freedom, my wife. You have the first two. You can pick up the third at the county morgue."

I stared at him, unable to move, frozen in a soundless thunderclap of shock.

"You didn't really think I'd let you have her?" he asked me pityingly. "Oh, no. The money, yes. Your freedom, yes. But not Marcia. Still, I don't welsh. And after you've had her buried—"

I didn't go near him. Not then. He was for later. I walked toward Tony, who looked slightly surprised until Cressner said in a bored voice: "Shoot him, please."

I threw the bag of money. It hit him squarely in the gun hand, and it struck him hard. I hadn't been using my arms and wrists out there, and they're the best part of any tennis player. His bullet went into the burnt-orange rug, and then I had him.

His face was the toughest part of him. I yanked the gun out of his hand and hit him across the bridge of the nose with the barrel. He went down with a single very weary grunt, looking like Rondo Hatton.

Cressner was almost out the door when I snapped a shot over his shoulder and said, "Stop right there, or you're dead."

He thought about it and stopped. When he turned around, his cosmopolitan world-weary act had curdled a little around the edges. It curdled a little more when he saw Tony lying on the floor and choking on his own blood.

"She's not dead," he said quickly. "I had to salvage something, didn't I?" He gave me a sick, cheese-eating grin.

"I'm a sucker, but I'm not that big a sucker," I said.

My voice sounded lifeless, dead. Why not? Marcia had been my life, and this man had put her on a slab.

With a finger that trembled slightly, Cressner pointed at the money tumbled around Tony's feet. "That," he said, "that's chickenfeed. I can get you a hundred thousand. Or five. Or how about a million, all of it in a Swiss bank account? How about that? How about—"

"I'll make you a bet," I said slowly.

He looked from the barrel of the gun to my face. "A—"

"A bet," I repeated. "Not a wager. Just a plain old bet. I'll bet you can't walk around this building on the ledge out there."

His face went dead pale. For a moment I thought he was going to faint. "You . . ." he whispered.

"These are the stakes," I said in my dead voice. "If you make it, I'll let you go. How's that?"

"No," he whispered. His eyes were huge, staring.

"Okay," I said, and cocked the pistol.

"No!" he said, holding his hands out. "No! Don't! I . . . all right." He licked his lips.

I motioned with the gun, and he preceded me out onto the balcony. "You're shaking," I told him. "That's going to make it harder."

"Two million," he said, and he couldn't get his voice above a husky whine. "Two million in unmarked bills."

"No," I said. "Not for ten million. But if you make it, you go free. I'm serious."

A minute later he was standing on the ledge. He was

shorter than I; you could just see his eyes over the edge, wide and beseeching, and his white-knuckled hands gripping the iron rail like prison bars.

"Please," he whispered. "Anything."

"You're wasting time," I said. "It takes it out of the ankles."

But he wouldn't move until I had put the muzzle of the gun against his forehead. Then he began to shuffle to the right, moaning. I glanced up at the bank clock. It was 11:29.

I didn't think he was going to make it to the first corner. He didn't want to budge at all, and when he did, he moved jerkily, taking risks with his center of gravity, his dressing gown billowing into the night.

He disappeared around the corner and out of sight at 12:01, almost forty minutes ago. I listened closely for the diminishing scream as the crosswind got him, but it didn't come. Maybe the wind had dropped. I do remember thinking the wind was on his side, when I was out there. Or maybe he was just lucky. Maybe he's out on the other balcony now, quivering in a heap, afraid to go any farther.

But he probably knows that if I catch him there when I break into the other penthouse, I'll shoot him down like a dog. And speaking of the other side of the building, I wonder how he likes that pigeon.

Was that a scream? I don't know. It might have been the wind. It doesn't matter. The bank clock says 12:44. Pretty soon I'll break into the other apartment and check the balcony, but right now I'm just sitting here on Cressner's balcony with Tony's .45 in my hand. Just on the off chance that he might come around that last corner with his dressing gown billowing out behind him.

Cressner said he's never welshed on a bet.

But I've been known to.

THE LAWNMOWER MAN

In previous years, Harold Parkette had always taken pride in his lawn. He had owned a large silver Lawn-boy and paid the boy down the block five dollars per cutting to push it. In those days Harold Parkette had followed the Boston Red Sox on the radio with a beer in his hand and the knowledge that God was in his heaven and all was right with the world, including his lawn. But last year, in mid-October, fate had played Harold Parkette a nasty trick. While the boy was mowing the grass for the last time of the season, the Castonmeyers' dog had chased the Smiths' cat under the mower.

Harold's daughter had thrown up half a quart of cherry Kool-Aid into the lap of her new jumper, and his wife had nightmares for a week afterward. Although she had arrived after the fact, she *had* arrived in time to see Harold and the green-faced boy cleaning the blades. Their daughter and Mrs. Smith stood over them, weeping, although Alicia had taken time enough to change her jumper for a pair of blue jeans and one of those disgusting skimpy sweaters. She had a crush on the boy who mowed the lawn.

After a week of listening to his wife moan and gobble in the next bed, Harold decided to get rid of the mower. He didn't really *need* a mower anyway, he supposed. He had hired a boy this year; next year he would just hire a boy *and* a mower. And maybe Carla would stop moaning in her sleep. He might even get laid again.

So he took the silver Lawnboy down to Phil's Sunoco, and he and Phil dickered over it. Harold came away with a brand-new Kelly blackwall tire and a tankful of hi-test, and Phil put the silver Lawnboy out on one of the pump islands with a hand-lettered FOR SALE sign on it.

And this year, Harold just kept putting off the necessary hiring. When he finally got around to calling last year's boy, his mother told him Frank had gone to the state university. Harold shook his head in wonder and went to the refrigerator to get a beer. Time certainly flew, didn't it? My God, yes.

He put off hiring a new boy as first May and then June slipped past him and the Red Sox continued to wallow in fourth place. He sat on the back porch on the weekends and watched glumly as a never ending progression of young boys he had never seen before popped out to mutter a quick hello before taking his buxom daughter off to the local passion pit. And the grass thrived and grew in a marvelous way. It was a good summer for grass; three days of shine followed by one of gentle rain, almost like clockwork.

By mid-July, the lawn looked more like a meadow

than a suburbanite's backyard, and Jack Castonmeyer had begun to make all sorts of extremely unfunny jokes, most of which concerned the price of hay and alfalfa. And Don Smith's four-year-old daughter Jenny had taken to hiding in it when there was oatmeal for breakfast or spinach for supper.

One day in late July, Harold went out on the patio during the seventh-inning stretch and saw a woodchuck sitting perkily on the overgrown back walk. The time had come, he decided. He flicked off the radio, picked up the paper, and turned to the classifieds. And halfway down the Part Time column, he found this: *Lawns mowed. Reasonable. 776-2390.*

Harold called the number, expecting a vacuuming housewife who would yell outside for her son. Instead, a briskly professional voice said, "Pastoral Greenery and Outdoor Services . . . how may we help you?"

Cautiously, Harold told the voice how Pastoral Greenery could help him. Had it come to this, then? Were lawncutters starting their own businesses and hiring office help? He asked the voice about rates, and the voice quoted him a reasonable figure.

Harold hung up with a lingering feeling of unease and went back to the porch. He sat down, turned on the radio, and stared out over his glandular lawn at the Saturday clouds moving slowly across the Saturday sky. Carla and Alicia were at his mother-in-law's and the house was his. It would be a pleasant surprise for them if the boy who was coming to cut the lawn finished before they came back.

He cracked a beer and sighed as Dick Drago was touched for a double and then hit a batter. A little breeze shuffled across the screened-in porch. Crickets hummed softly in the long grass. Harold grunted something unkind about Dick Drago and then dozed off.

He was jarred awake a half hour later by the doorbell. He knocked over his beer getting up to answer it.

A man in grass-stained denim overalls stood on the front stoop, chewing a toothpick. He was fat. The curve of his belly pushed his faded blue overall out to a point where Harold half suspected he had swallowed a basketball.

"Yes?" Harold Parkette asked, still half asleep.

The man grinned, rolled his toothpick from one corner of his mouth to the other, tugged at the seat of his overalls, and then pushed his green baseball cap up a notch on his forehead. There was a smear of fresh engine oil on the bill of his cap. And there he was, smelling of grass, earth, and oil, grinning at Harold Parkette.

"Pastoral sent me, buddy," he said jovially, scratching his crotch. "You called, right? Right, buddy?" He grinned on endlessly.

"Oh. The lawn. You?" Harold stared stupidly.

"Yep, me." The lawnmower man bellowed fresh laughter into Harold's sleep-puffy face.

Harold stood helplessly aside and the lawnmower man tromped ahead of him down the hall, through the living room and kitchen, and onto the back porch. Now Harold had placed the man and everything was all right.

He had seen the type before, working for the sanitation department and the highway repair crews out on the turnpike. Always with a spare minute to lean on their shovels and smoke Lucky Strikes or Camels, looking at you as if they were the salt of the earth, able to hit you for five or sleep with your wife anytime they wanted to. Harold had always been slightly afraid of men like this; they were always tanned dark brown, there were always nets of wrinkles around their eyes, and they always knew what to do.

"The back lawn's the real chore," he told the man, unconsciously deepening his voice. "It's square and there are no obstructions, but it's pretty well grown up." His voice faltered back into its normal register and he found himself apologizing: "I'm afraid I've let it go."

"No sweat, buddy. No strain. Great-great-great." The lawnmower man grinned at him with a thousand traveling-salesman jokes in his eyes. "The taller, the better. Healthy soil, that's what you got there, by Circe. That's what I always say."

By Circe?

The lawnmower man cocked his head at the radio. Yastrzemski had just struck out. "Red Sox fan? I'm a Yankees man, myself." He clumped back into the house and down the front hall. Harold watched him bitterly.

He sat back down and looked accusingly for a moment at the puddle of beer under the table with the overturned Coors can in the middle of it. He thought of getting the mop from the kitchen and decided it would keep.

No sweat. No strain.

He opened his paper to the financial section and cast a judicious eye at the closing stock quotations. As a good Republican, he considered the Wall Street executives behind the columned type to be at least minor demigods—

(By Circe??)

—and he had wished many times that he could better understand the Word, as handed down from the mount not on stone tablets but in such enigmatic abbreviations as pct. and Kdk and 3.28 up ⅔. He had once bought a judicious three shares in a company called Midwest Bisonburgers, Inc., that had gone broke in 1968. He had lost his entire seventy-five-dollar investment. Now, he understood, bisonburgers were quite the coming thing. The wave of the future. He had discussed this often with Sonny, the bartender down at the Goldfish Bowl. Sonny told Harold his trouble was that he was five years ahead of his time, and he should . . .

A sudden racketing roar startled him out of the new doze he had just been slipping into.

Harold jumped to his feet, knocking his chair over and staring around wildly.

"That's a lawnmower?" Harold Parkette asked the kitchen. "My God, *that's* a lawnmower?"

He rushed through the house and stared out the front door. There was nothing out there but a battered green van with the words PASTORAL GREENERY, INC. painted on the side. The roaring sound was in back now. Harold rushed through his house again, burst onto the back porch, and stood frozen.

It was obscene.

It was a travesty.

The aged red power mower the fat man had brought in his van was running on its own. No one was pushing it; in fact, no one was within five feet of it. It was running at a fever pitch, tearing through the unfortunate grass of Harold Parkette's back lawn like an avenging red devil straight from hell. It screamed and bellowed and farted oily blue smoke in a crazed kind of mechanical madness that made Harold feel ill with terror. The overripe smell of cut grass hung in the air like sour wine.

But the lawnmower man was the true obscenity.

The lawnmower man had removed his clothes— every stitch. They were folded neatly in the empty birdbath that was at the center of the back lawn. Naked and grass-stained, he was crawling along about five feet behind the mower, eating the cut grass. Green juice ran down his chin and dripped onto his pendulous belly. And every time the lawnmower whirled around a corner, he rose and did an odd, skipping jump before prostrating himself again.

"Stop!" Harold Parkette screamed. *"Stop that!"*

But the lawnmower man took no notice, and his screaming scarlet familiar never slowed. If anything, it seemed to speed up. Its nicked steel grille seemed to grin sweatily at Harold as it raved by.

Then Harold saw the mole. It must have been hiding in stunned terror just ahead of the mower, in the swath of grass about to be slaughtered. It bolted across the cut band of lawn toward safety under the porch, a panicky brown streak.

The lawnmower swerved.

Blatting and howling, it roared over the mole and spat it out in a string of fur and entrails that reminded Harold of the Smiths' cat. The mole destroyed, the lawnmower rushed back to the main job.

The lawnmower man crawled rapidly by, eating grass. Harold stood paralyzed with horror, stocks, bonds, and bisonburgers completely forgotten. He could actually see that huge, pendulous belly expanding. *The lawnmower man swerved and ate the mole.*

That was when Harold Parkette leaned out the screen door and vomited into the zinnias. The world went gray, and suddenly he realized he was fainting, *had* fainted. He collapsed backward onto the porch and closed his eyes . . .

—————

Someone was shaking him. Carla was shaking him. He hadn't done the dishes or emptied the garbage and Carla was going to be very angry but that was all right. As long as she was waking him up, taking him out of the horrible dream he had been having, back into the normal world, nice normal Carla with her Playtex Living Girdle and her buck teeth—

Buck teeth, yes. But not Carla's buck teeth. Carla had weak-looking chipmunk buck teeth. But these teeth were—

Hairy.

Green hair was growing on these buck teeth. It almost looked like—

Grass?

"Oh my God," Harold said.

"You fainted, buddy, right, huh?" The lawnmower man was bending over him, grinning with his hairy teeth. His lips and chin were hairy, too. Everything was hairy. And green. The yard stank of grass and gas and too sudden silence.

Harold bolted up to a sitting position and stared at the dead mower. All the grass had been neatly cut. And there would be no need to rake this job, Harold observed sickly. If the lawnmower man had missed a single cut blade, he couldn't see it. He squinted obliquely at the lawnmower man and winced. He was still naked, still fat, still terrifying. Green trickles ran from the corners of his mouth.

"What is this?" Harold begged.

The man waved an arm benignly at the lawn. "This? Well, it's a new thing the boss has been trying. It works out real good. Real good, buddy. We're killing two birds with one stone. We keep getting along toward the final stage, and we're making money to support our other operations to boot. See what I mean? Of course every now and then we run into a customer who doesn't understand—some people got no respect for efficiency, right?—but the boss is always agreeable to a sacrifice. Sort of keeps the wheels greased, if you catch me."

Harold said nothing. One word knelled over and over in his mind, and that word was "sacrifice." In his mind's eye he saw the mole spewing out from under the battered red mower.

He got up slowly, like a palsied old man. "Of course," he said, and could only come up with a line from one of Alicia's folk-rock records. "God bless the grass."

The lawnmower man slapped one summer-apple-colored thigh. "That's pretty good, buddy. In fact, that's damned good. I can see you got the right spirit. Okay if I write that down when I get back to the office? Might mean a promotion."

"Certainly," Harold said, retreating toward the back door and striving to keep his melting smile in place. "You go right ahead and finish. I think I'll take a little nap—"

"Sure, buddy," the lawnmower man said, getting ponderously to his feet. Harold noticed the unusually deep split between the first and second toes, almost as if the feet were . . . well, cloven.

"It hits everybody kinda hard at first," the lawnmower man said. "You'll get used to it." He eyed Harold's portly figure shrewdly. "In fact, you might even want to give it a whirl yourself. The boss has always got an eye out for new talent."

"The boss," Harold repeated faintly.

The lawnmower man paused at the bottom of the steps and gazed tolerantly up at Harold Parkette. "Well, say, buddy. I figured you must have guessed . . . God bless the grass and all."

Harold shook his head carefully and the lawnmower man laughed.

"Pan. Pan's the boss." And he did a half hop, half shuffle in the newly cut grass and the lawnmower screamed into life and began to trundle around the house.

"The neighbors—" Harold began, but the lawnmower man only waved cheerily and disappeared.

Out front the lawnmower blatted and howled. Harold Parkette refused to look, as if by refusing he could deny the grotesque spectacle that the Castonmeyers and Smiths—wretched Democrats both—were probably drinking in with horrified but no doubt righteously I-told-you-so eyes.

Instead of looking, Harold went to the telephone, snatched it up, and dialed police headquarters from the emergency decal pasted on the phone's handset.

"Sergeant Hall," the voice at the other end said.

Harold stuck a finger in his free ear and said, "My name is Harold Parkette. My address is 1421 East Endicott Street. I'd like to report . . ." What? What would he like to report? A man is in the process of raping and murdering my lawn and he works for a fellow named Pan and has cloven feet?

"Yes, Mr. Parkette?"

Inspiration struck. "I'd like to report a case of indecent exposure."

"Indecent exposure," Sergeant Hall repeated.

"Yes. There's a man mowing my lawn. He's in the, uh, altogether."

"You mean he's naked?" Sergeant Hall asked, politely incredulous.

"Naked!" Harold agreed, holding tightly to the frayed ends of his sanity. "Nude. Unclothed. Bare-assed. On my front lawn. Now will you get somebody the hell over here?"

"That address was 1421 West Endicott?" Sergeant Hall asked bemusedly.

"East!" Harold yelled. "For God's sake—"

"And you say he's definitely naked? You are able to observe his, uh, genitals and so on?"

Harold tried to speak and could only gargle. The sound of the insane lawnmower seemed to be growing louder and louder, drowning out everything in the universe. He felt his gorge rise.

"Can you speak up?" Sergeant Hall buzzed. "There's an awfully noisy connection there at your end—"

The front door crashed open.

Harold looked around and saw the lawnmower man's mechanized familiar advancing through the door. Behind it came the lawnmower man himself, still quite naked. With something approaching true insanity, Harold saw the man's pubic hair was a rich fertile green. He was twirling his baseball cap on one finger.

"That was a mistake, buddy," the lawnmower man said reproachfully. "You shoulda stuck with God bless the grass."

"Hello? Hello, Mr. Parkette—"

The telephone dropped from Harold's nerveless fingers as the lawnmower began to advance on him, cutting through the nap of Carla's new Mohawk rug and spitting out brown hunks of fiber as it came.

Harold stared at it with a kind of bird-and-snake fascination until it reached the coffee table. When the mower shunted it aside, shearing one leg into sawdust and splinters as it did so, he climbed over the back of his chair and began to retreat toward the kitchen, dragging the chair in front of him.

"That won't do any good, buddy," the lawnmower man said kindly. "Apt to be messy, too. Now if you was just to show me where you keep your sharpest butcher knife, we could get this sacrifice business out of the way real painless . . . I think the birdbath would do . . . and then—"

Harold shoved the chair at the lawnmower, which had been craftily flanking him while the naked man drew his attention, and bolted through the doorway. The lawnmower roared around the chair, jetting out exhaust, and as Harold smashed open the porch screen door and leaped down the steps, he heard it—smelled it, felt it—right at his heels.

The lawnmower roared off the top step like a skier going off a jump. Harold sprinted across his newly cut back lawn, but there had been too many beers, too many afternoon naps. He could sense it nearing him, then on his heels, and then he looked over his shoulder and tripped over his own feet.

The last thing Harold Parkette saw was the grinning

grill of the charging lawnmower, rocking back to reveal its flashing, green-stained blades, and above it the fat face of the lawnmower man, shaking his head in good-natured reproof.

———

"Hell of a thing," Lieutenant Goodwin said as the last of the photographs were taken. He nodded to the two men in white, and they trundled their basket across the lawn. "He reported some naked guy on his lawn not two hours ago."

"Is that so?" Patrolman Cooley asked.

"Yeah. One of the neighbors called in, too. Guy named Castonmeyer. He thought it was Parkette himself. Maybe it was, Cooley. Maybe it was."

"Sir?"

"Crazy with the heat," Lieutenant Goodwin said gravely, and tapped his temple. "Schizo-fucking-phrenia."

"Yes sir," Cooley said respectfully.

"Where's the rest of him?" one of the white-coats asked.

"The birdbath," Goodwin said. He looked profoundly up at the sky.

"Did you say the birdbath?" the white-coat asked.

"Indeed I did," Lieutenant Goodwin agreed. Patrolman Cooley looked at the birdbath and suddenly lost most of his tan.

"Sex maniac," Lieutenant Goodwin said. "Must have been."

"Prints?" Cooley asked thickly.

"You might as well ask for footprints," Goodwin said. He gestured at the newly cut grass.

Patrolman Cooley made a strangled noise in his throat.

Lieutenant Goodwin stuffed his hands into his pockets and rocked back on his heels. "The world," he said gravely, "is full of nuts. Never forget that, Cooley. Schizos. Lab boys say somebody chased Parkette through his own living room with a lawnmower. Can you imagine that?"

"No sir," Cooley said.

Goodwin looked out over Harold Parkette's neatly manicured lawn. "Well, like the man said when he saw the blackhaired Swede, it surely is a Norse of a different color."

Goodwin strolled around the house and Cooley followed him. Behind them, the scent of newly mown grass hung pleasantly in the air.

QUITTERS, INC.

Morrison was waiting for someone who was hung up in the air traffic jam over Kennedy International when he saw a familiar face at the end of the bar and walked down.

"Jimmy? Jimmy McCann?"

It was. A little heavier than when Morrison had seen him at the Atlanta Exhibition the year before, but otherwise he looked awesomely fit. In college he had been a thin, pallid chain smoker buried behind huge horn-rimmed glasses. He had apparently switched to contact lenses.

"Dick Morrison?"

"Yeah. You look great." He extended his hand and they shook.

"So do you," McCann said, but Morrison knew it was a lie. He had been overworking, overeating, and smoking too much. "What are you drinking?"

"Bourbon and bitters," Morrison said. He hooked his

feet around a bar stool and lighted a cigarette. "Meeting someone, Jimmy?"

"No. Going to Miami for a conference. A heavy client. Bills six million. I'm supposed to hold his hand because we lost out on a big special next spring."

"Are you still with Crager and Barton?"

"Executive veep now."

"Fantastic! Congratulations! When did all this happen?" He tried to tell himself that the little worm of jealousy in his stomach was just acid indigestion. He pulled out a roll of antacid pills and crunched one in his mouth.

"Last August. Something happened that changed my life." He looked speculatively at Morrison and sipped his drink. "You might be interested."

My God, Morrison thought with an inner wince. Jimmy McCann's got religion.

"Sure," he said, and gulped at his drink when it came.

"I wasn't in very good shape," McCann said. "Personal problems with Sharon, my dad died—heart attack—and I'd developed this hacking cough. Bobby Crager dropped by my office one day and gave me a fatherly little pep talk. Do you remember what those are like?"

"Yeah." He had worked at Crager and Barton for eighteen months before joining the Morton Agency. "Get your butt in gear or get your butt out."

McCann laughed. "You know it. Well, to put the capper on it, the doc told me I had an incipient ulcer. He told me to quit smoking." McCann grimaced. "Might as well tell me to quit breathing."

Morrison nodded in perfect understanding. Non-smokers could afford to be smug. He looked at his own cigarette with distaste and stubbed it out, knowing he would be lighting another in five minutes.

"Did you quit?" he asked.

"Yes, I did. At first I didn't think I'd be able to—I was cheating like hell. Then I met a guy who told me about an outfit over on Forty-sixth Street. Specialists. I said what do I have to lose and went over. I haven't smoked since."

Morrison's eyes widened. "What did they do? Fill you full of some drug?"

"No." He had taken out his wallet and was rummaging through it. "Here it is. I knew I had one kicking around." He laid a plain white business card on the bar between them.

QUITTERS, INC.
Stop Going Up in Smoke!
237 East 46th Street
Treatments by Appointment

"Keep it, if you want," McCann said. "They'll cure you. Guaranteed."

"How?"

"I can't tell you," McCann said.

"Huh? Why not?"

"It's part of the contract they make you sign. Anyway, they tell you how it works when they interview you."

"You signed a *contract?*"

McCann nodded.

"And on the basis of that—"

"Yep." He smiled at Morrison, who thought: Well, it's happened. Jim McCann has joined the smug bastards.

"Why the great secrecy if this outfit is so fantastic? How come I've never seen any spots on TV, billboards, magazine ads—"

"They get all the clients they can handle by word of mouth."

"You're an advertising man, Jimmy. You can't believe that."

"I do," McCann said. "They have a ninety-eight percent cure rate."

"Wait a second," Morrison said. He motioned for another drink and lit a cigarette. "Do these guys strap you down and make you smoke until you throw up?"

"No."

"Give you something so that you get sick every time you light—"

"No, it's nothing like that. Go and see for yourself." He gestured at Morrison's cigarette. "You don't really like that, do you?"

"Nooo, but—"

"Stopping really changed things for me," McCann said. "I don't suppose it's the same for everyone, but with me it was just like dominoes falling over. I felt better and my relationship with Sharon improved. I had more energy, and my job performance picked up."

"Look, you've got my curiosity aroused. Can't you just—"

"I'm sorry, Dick. I really can't talk about it." His voice was firm.

"Did you put on any weight?"

For a moment he thought Jimmy McCann looked almost grim. "Yes. A little too much, in fact. But I took it off again. I'm about right now. I was skinny before."

"Flight 206 now boarding at Gate 9," the loudspeaker announced.

"That's me," McCann said, getting up. He tossed a five on the bar. "Have another, if you like. And think about what I said, Dick. Really." And then he was gone, making his way through the crowd to the escalators. Morrison picked up the card, looked at it thoughtfully, then tucked it away in his wallet and forgot it.

———

The card fell out of his wallet and onto another bar a month later. He had left the office early and had come here to drink the afternoon away. Things had not been going so well at the Morton Agency. In fact, things were bloody horrible.

He gave Henry a ten to pay for his drink, then picked up the small card and reread it—237 East Forty-sixth Street was only two blocks over; it was a cool, sunny October day outside, and maybe, just for chuckles—

When Henry brought his change, he finished his drink and then went for a walk.

———————

Quitters, Inc., was in a new building where the monthly rent on office space was probably close to Morrison's yearly salary. From the directory in the lobby, it looked to him like their offices took up one whole floor, and that spelled money. Lots of it.

He took the elevator up and stepped off into a lushly carpeted foyer and from there into a gracefully appointed reception room with a wide window that looked out on the scurrying bugs below. Three men and one woman sat in the chairs along the walls, reading magazines. Business types, all of them. Morrison went to the desk.

"A friend gave me this," he said, passing the card to the receptionist. "I guess you'd say he's an alumnus."

She smiled and rolled a form into her typewriter. "What is your name, sir?"

"Richard Morrison."

Clack-clackety-clack. But very muted clacks; the typewriter was an IBM.

"Your address?"

"Twenty-nine Maple Lane, Clinton, New York."

"Married?"

"Yes."

"Children?"

"One." He thought of Alvin and frowned slightly. "One" was the wrong word. "A half" might be better.

His son was mentally retarded and lived at a special school in New Jersey.

"Who recommended us to you, Mr. Morrison?"

"An old school friend. James McCann."

"Very good. Will you have a seat? It's been a very busy day."

"All right."

He sat between the woman, who was wearing a severe blue suit, and a young executive type wearing a herringbone jacket and modish sideburns. He took out his pack of cigarettes, looked around, and saw there were no ashtrays.

He put the pack away again. That was all right. He would see this little game through and then light up while he was leaving. He might even tap some ashes on their maroon shag rug if they made him wait long enough. He picked up a copy of *Time* and began to leaf through it.

He was called a quarter of an hour later, after the woman in the blue suit. His nicotine center was speaking quite loudly now. A man who had come in after him took out a cigarette case, snapped it open, saw there were no ashtrays, and put it away—looking a little guilty, Morrison thought. It made him feel better.

At last the receptionist gave him a sunny smile and said, "Go right in, Mr. Morrison."

Morrison walked through the door beyond her desk and found himself in an indirectly lit hallway. A heavyset man with white hair that looked phony shook his hand, smiled affably, and said, "Follow me, Mr. Morrison."

He led Morrison past a number of closed, unmarked doors and then opened one of them about halfway down the hall with a key. Beyond the door was an austere little room walled with drilled white cork panels. The only furnishings were a desk with a chair on either side. There was what appeared to be a small oblong window in the wall behind the desk, but it was covered with a short green curtain. There was a picture on the wall to Morrison's left—a tall man with iron-gray hair. He was holding a sheet of paper in one hand. He looked vaguely familiar.

"I'm Vic Donatti," the heavyset man said. "If you decide to go ahead with our program, I'll be in charge of your case."

"Pleased to know you," Morrison said. He wanted a cigarette very badly.

"Have a seat."

Donatti put the receptionist's form on the desk, and then drew another form from the desk drawer. He looked directly into Morrison's eyes. "Do you want to quit smoking?"

Morrison cleared his throat, crossed his legs, and tried to think of a way to equivocate. He couldn't. "Yes," he said.

"Will you sign this?" He gave Morrison the form. He scanned it quickly. The undersigned agrees not to divulge the methods or techniques or et cetera, et cetera.

"Sure," he said, and Donatti put a pen in his hand. He scratched his name, and Donatti signed below it. A moment later the paper disappeared back into the desk drawer. Well, he thought ironically, I've taken the pledge. He had taken it before. Once it had lasted for two whole days.

"Good," Donatti said. "We don't bother with propaganda here, Mr. Morrison. Questions of health or expense or social grace. We have no interest in why you want to stop smoking. We are pragmatists."

"Good," Morrison said blankly.

"We employ no drugs. We employ no Dale Carnegie people to sermonize you. We recommend no special diet. And we accept no payment until you have stopped smoking for one year."

"My God," Morrison said.

"Mr. McCann didn't tell you that?"

"No."

"How is Mr. McCann, by the way? Is he well?"

"He's fine."

"Wonderful. Excellent. Now . . . just a few questions, Mr. Morrison. These are somewhat personal, but I assure you that your answers will be held in strictest confidence."

"Yes?" Morrison asked noncommittally.

"What is your wife's name?"

"Lucinda Morrison. Her maiden name was Ramsey."

"Do you love her?"

Morrison looked up sharply, but Donatti was looking at him blandly. "Yes, of course," he said.

"Have you ever had marital problems? A separation, perhaps?"

"What has that got to do with kicking the habit?"

Morrison asked. He sounded a little angrier than he had intended, but he wanted—hell, he *needed*—a cigarette.

"A great deal," Donatti said. "Just bear with me."

"No. Nothing like that." Although things *had* been a little tense just lately.

"You just have the one child?"

"Yes. Alvin. He's in a private school."

"And which school is it?"

"That," Morrison said grimly, "I'm not going to tell you."

"All right," Donatti said agreeably. He smiled disarmingly at Morrison. "All your questions will be answered tomorrow at your first treatment."

"How nice," Morrison said, and stood.

"One final question," Donatti said. "You haven't had a cigarette for over an hour. How do you feel?"

"Fine," Morrison lied. "Just fine."

"Good for you!" Donatti exclaimed. He stepped around the desk and opened the door. "Enjoy them tonight. After tomorrow, you'll never smoke again."

"Is that right?"

"Mr. Morrison," Donatti said solemnly, "we guarantee it."

───────

He was sitting in the outer office of Quitters, Inc., the next day promptly at three. He had spent most of the day swinging between skipping the appointment the receptionist had made for him on the way out and going in a spirit of mulish cooperation—*Throw your best pitch at me, buster.*

In the end, something Jimmy McCann had said convinced him to keep the appointment—*It changed my whole life.* God knew his own life could do with some changing. And then there was his own curiosity. Before going up in the elevator, he smoked a cigarette down to the filter. Too damn bad if it's the last one, he thought. It tasted horrible.

The wait in the outer office was shorter this time. When the receptionist told him to go in, Donatti was waiting. He offered his hand and smiled, and to Morrison the smile looked almost predatory. He began to feel a little tense, and that made him want a cigarette.

"Come with me," Donatti said, and led the way down to the small room. He sat behind the desk again, and Morrison took the other chair.

"I'm very glad you came," Donatti said. "A great many prospective clients never show up again after the initial interview. They discover they don't want to quit as badly as they thought. It's going to be a pleasure to work with you on this."

"When does the treatment start?" Hypnosis, he was thinking. It must be hypnosis.

"Oh, it already has. It started when we shook hands in the hall. Do you have cigarettes with you, Mr. Morrison?"

"Yes."

"May I have them, please?"

Shrugging, Morrison handed Donatti his pack. There were only two or three left in it, anyway.

Donatti put the pack on the desk. Then, smiling into Morrison's eyes, he curled his right hand into a fist and began to hammer it down on the pack of cigarettes, which twisted and flattened. A broken cigarette end flew out. Tobacco crumbs spilled. The sound of Donatti's fist was very loud in the closed room. The smile remained on his face in spite of the force of the blows, and Morrison was chilled by it. Probably just the effect they want to inspire, he thought.

At last Donatti ceased pounding. He picked up the pack, a twisted and battered ruin. "You wouldn't believe the pleasure that gives me," he said, and dropped the pack into the wastebasket. "Even after three years in the business, it still pleases me."

"As a treatment, it leaves something to be desired," Morrison said mildly. "There's a newsstand in the lobby of this very building. And they sell all brands."

"As you say," Donatti said. He folded his hands. "Your son, Alvin Dawes Morrison, is in the Paterson School for Handicapped Children. Born with cranial brain damage. Tested IQ of 46. Not quite in the educable retarded category. Your wife—"

"How did you find that out?" Morrison barked. He was startled and angry. "You've got no goddamn right to go poking around my—"

"We know a lot about you," Donatti said smoothly. "But, as I said, it will all be held in strictest confidence."

"I'm getting out of here," Morrison said thinly. He stood up.

"Stay a bit longer."

Morrison looked at him closely. Donatti wasn't upset. In fact, he looked a little amused. The face of a man who has seen this reaction scores of times—maybe hundreds.

"All right. But it better be good."

"Oh, it is." Donatti leaned back. "I told you we were pragmatists here. As pragmatists, we have to start by realizing how difficult it is to cure an addiction to tobacco. The relapse rate is almost eighty-five percent. The relapse rate for heroin addicts is lower than that. It is an extraordinary problem. *Extraordinary.*"

Morrison glanced into the wastebasket. One of the cigarettes, although twisted, still looked smokeable. Donatti laughed good-naturedly, reached into the wastebasket, and broke it between his fingers.

"State legislatures sometimes hear a request that the prison systems do away with the weekly cigarette ration. Such proposals are invariably defeated. In a few cases where they have passed, there have been fierce prison riots. *Riots,* Mr. Morrison. Imagine it."

"I," Morrison said, "am not surprised."

"But consider the implications. When you put a man in prison you take away any normal sex life, you take away his liquor, his politics, his freedom of movement. No riots—or few in comparison to the number of prisons. But when you take away his *cigarettes*—wham! bam!" He slammed his fist on the desk for emphasis.

"During World War I, when no one on the German home front could get cigarettes, the sight of German aristocrats picking butts out of the gutter was a common one. During World War II, many American women turned to pipes when they were unable to obtain cigarettes. A fascinating problem for the true pragmatist, Mr. Morrison."

"Could we get to the treatment?"

"Momentarily. Step over here, please." Donatti had risen and was standing by the green curtains Morrison had noticed yesterday. Donatti drew the curtains, discovering a rectangular window that looked into a bare room. No, not quite bare. There was a rabbit on the floor, eating pellets out of a dish.

"Pretty bunny," Morrison commented.

"Indeed. Watch him." Donatti pressed a button by the windowsill. The rabbit stopped eating and began to hop about crazily. It seemed to leap higher each time its feet struck the floor. Its fur stood out spikily in all directions. Its eyes were wild.

"Stop that! You're electrocuting him!"

Donatti released the button. "Far from it. There's a very low-yield charge in the floor. Watch the rabbit, Mr. Morrison!"

The rabbit was crouched about ten feet away from the dish of pellets. His nose wriggled. All at once he hopped away into a corner.

"If the rabbit gets a jolt often enough while he's eating," Donatti said, "he makes the association very quickly. Eating causes pain. Therefore, he won't eat. A few more shocks, and the rabbit will starve to death in front of his food. It's called aversion training."

Light dawned in Morrison's head.

"No, thanks." He started for the door.

"Wait, please, Mr. Morrison."

Morrison didn't pause. He grasped the door-knob . . . and felt it slip solidly through his hand. "Unlock this."

"Mr. Morrison, if you'll just sit down—"

"Unlock this door or I'll have the cops on you before you can say Marlboro Man."

"Sit down." The voice was as cold as shaved ice.

Morrison looked at Donatti. His brown eyes were muddy and frightening. My God, he thought, I'm locked in here with a psycho. He licked his lips. He wanted a cigarette more than he ever had in his life.

"Let me explain the treatment in more detail," Donatti said.

"You don't understand," Morrison said with counter-feit patience. "I don't want the treatment. I've decided against it."

"No, Mr. Morrison. *You're* the one who doesn't under-stand. You don't have any choice. When I told you the treatment had already begun, I was speaking the literal truth. I would have thought you'd tipped to that by now."

"You're crazy," Morrison said wonderingly.

"No. Only a pragmatist. Let me tell you all about the treatment."

"Sure," Morrison said. "As long as you understand that as soon as I get out of here I'm going to buy five packs of cigarettes and smoke them all on the way to the police station." He suddenly realized he was biting his thumbnail, sucking on it, and made himself stop.

"As you wish. But I think you'll change your mind when you see the whole picture."

Morrison said nothing. He sat down again and folded his hands.

"For the first month of the treatment, our operatives will have you under constant supervision," Donatti said. "You'll be able to spot some of them. Not all. But they'll always be with you. *Always.* If they see you smoke a cigarette, I get a call."

"And I suppose you bring me here and do the old rabbit trick," Morrison said. He tried to sound cold and sarcastic, but he suddenly felt horribly frightened. This was a nightmare.

"Oh, no," Donatti said. "Your wife gets the rabbit trick, not you."

Morrison looked at him dumbly.

Donatti smiled. "You," he said, "get to watch."

———

After Donatti let him out, Morrison walked for over two hours in a complete daze. It was another fine day, but he didn't notice. The monstrousness of Donatti's smiling face blotted out all else.

"You see," he had said, "a pragmatic problem demands pragmatic solutions. You must realize we have your best interests at heart."

Quitters, Inc., according to Donatti, was a sort of foundation—a nonprofit organization begun by the man in the wall portrait. The gentleman had been extremely successful in several family businesses—including slot machines, massage parlors, numbers, and a brisk (although clandestine) trade between New York and Turkey. Mort "Three-Fingers" Minelli had been a heavy smoker—up in the three-pack-a-day range. The paper he was holding in the picture was a doctor's diagnosis: lung cancer. Mort had died in 1970, after endowing Quitters, Inc., with family funds.

"We try to keep as close to breaking even as possible," Donatti had said. "But we're more interested in helping our fellow man. And of course, it's a great tax angle."

The treatment was chillingly simple. A first offense and Cindy would be brought to what Donatti called "the rabbit room." A second offense, and Morrison would get the dose. On a third offense, both of them would be brought in together. A fourth offense would show grave cooperation problems and would require sterner measures. An operative would be sent to Alvin's school to work the boy over.

"Imagine," Donatti said, smiling, "how horrible it will be for the boy. He wouldn't understand it even if someone explained. He'll only know someone is hurting him because Daddy was bad. He'll be very frightened."

"You bastard," Morrison said helplessly. He felt close to tears. "You dirty, filthy bastard."

"Don't misunderstand," Donatti said. He was smiling sympathetically. "I'm sure it won't happen. Forty percent of our clients never have to be disciplined at all—and only ten percent have more than three falls from grace. Those are reassuring figures, aren't they?"

Morrison didn't find them reassuring. He found them terrifying.

"Of course, if you transgress a *fifth* time—"

"What do you mean?"

Donatti beamed. "The room for you and your wife, a second beating for your son, and a beating for your wife."

Morrison, driven beyond the point of rational consideration, lunged over the desk at Donatti. Donatti moved with amazing speed for a man who had apparently been completely relaxed. He shoved the chair backward and drove both of his feet over the desk and into Morrison's belly. Gagging and coughing, Morrison staggered backward.

"Sit down, Mr. Morrison," Donatti said benignly. "Let's talk this over like rational men."

When he could get his breath, Morrison did as he was told. Nightmares had to end sometime, didn't they?

Quitters, Inc., Donatti had explained further, operated on a ten-step punishment scale. Steps six, seven, and eight consisted of further trips to the rabbit room (and increased voltage) and more serious beatings. The ninth step would be the breaking of his son's arms.

"And the tenth?" Morrison asked, his mouth dry.

Donatti shook his head sadly. "Then we give up, Mr. Morrison. You become part of the unregenerate two percent."

"You really give up?"

"In a manner of speaking." He opened one of the desk drawers and laid a silenced .45 on the desk. He smiled into Morrison's eyes. "But even the unregenerate two percent never smoke again. We guarantee it."

The Friday Night Movie was *Bullitt,* one of Cindy's favorites, but after an hour of Morrison's mutterings and fidgetings, her concentration was broken.

"What's the matter with you?" she asked during station identification.

"Nothing . . . everything," he growled. "I'm giving up smoking."

She laughed. "Since when? Five minutes ago?"

"Since three o'clock this afternoon."

"You really haven't had a cigarette since then?"

"No," he said, and began to gnaw his thumbnail. It was ragged, down to the quick.

"That's wonderful! What ever made you decide to quit?"

"You," he said. "And . . . and Alvin."

Her eyes widened, and when the movie came back on, she didn't notice. Dick rarely mentioned their retarded son. She came over, looked at the empty ashtray by his right hand, and then into his eyes. "Are you really trying to quit, Dick?"

"Really." And if I go to the cops, he added mentally,

the local goon squad will be around to rearrange your face, Cindy.

"I'm glad. Even if you don't make it, we both thank you for the thought, Dick."

"Oh, I think I'll make it," he said, thinking of the muddy, homicidal look that had come into Donatti's eyes when he kicked him in the stomach.

———————

He slept badly that night, dozing in and out of sleep. Around three o'clock he woke up completely. His craving for a cigarette was like a low-grade fever. He went downstairs and to his study. The room was in the middle of the house. No windows. He slid open the top drawer of his desk and looked in, fascinated by the cigarette box. He looked around and licked his lips.

Constant supervision during the first month, Donatti had said. Eighteen hours a day during the next two—but he would never know *which* eighteen. During the fourth month, the month when most clients backslid, the "service" would return to twenty-four hours a day. Then twelve hours of broken surveillance each day for the rest of the year. After that? Random surveillance for the rest of the client's life.

For the rest of his life.

"We may audit you every other month," Donatti said. "Or every other day. Or constantly for one week two years from now. The point is, *you won't know.* If you smoke, you'll be gambling with loaded dice. Are they watching? Are they picking up my wife or sending a man after my son right now? Beautiful, isn't it? And if you do sneak a smoke, it'll taste awful. It will taste like your son's blood."

But they couldn't be watching now, in the dead of night, in his own study. The house was grave-quiet.

He looked at the cigarettes in the box for almost two minutes, unable to tear his gaze away. Then he went to the study door, peered out into the empty hall, and went back to look at the cigarettes some more. A horrible picture came: his life stretching before him and not a cigarette to be found. How in the name of God was he ever going to be able to make another tough presentation to a wary client, without that cigarette burning nonchalantly between his fingers as he approached the charts and layouts? How would he be able to endure Cindy's endless garden shows without a cigarette? How could he even get up in the morning and face the day without a cigarette to smoke as he drank his coffee and read the paper?

He cursed himself for getting into this. He cursed Donatti. And most of all, he cursed Jimmy McCann. How could he have done it? The son of a bitch had *known*. His hands trembled in their desire to get hold of Jimmy Judas McCann.

Stealthily, he glanced around the study again. He reached into the drawer and brought out a cigarette. He caressed it, fondled it. What was that old slogan? *So round, so firm, so fully packed.* Truer words had never been spoken. He put the cigarette in his mouth and then paused, cocking his head.

Had there been the slightest noise from the closet? A faint shifting? Surely not. But—

Another mental image—that rabbit hopping crazily in the grip of electricity. The thought of Cindy in that room—

He listened desperately and heard nothing. He told himself that all he had to do was go to the closet door and yank it open. But he was too afraid of what he might find. He went back to bed but didn't sleep for a long time.

———

In spite of how lousy he felt in the morning, breakfast tasted good. After a moment's hesitation, he followed his customary bowl of cornflakes with scrambled eggs. He was grumpily washing out the pan when Cindy came downstairs in her robe.

"Richard Morrison! You haven't eaten an egg for breakfast since Hector was a pup."

Morrison grunted. He considered *since Hector was a pup* to be one of Cindy's stupider sayings, on a par with *I should smile and kiss a pig.*

"Have you smoked yet?" she asked, pouring orange juice.

"No."

"You'll be back on them by noon," she proclaimed airily.

"Lot of goddamn help you are!" he rasped, rounding on her. "You and anyone else who doesn't smoke, you all think . . . ah, never mind."

He expected her to be angry, but she was looking at him with something like wonder. "You're really serious," she said. "You really are."

"You bet I am." *You'll never know* how *serious. I hope.*

"Poor baby," she said, going to him. "You look like death warmed over. But I'm very proud."

Morrison held her tightly.

———

Scenes from the life of Richard Morrison, October–November:

Morrison and a crony from Larkin Studios at Jack Dempsey's bar. Crony offers a cigarette. Morrison grips his glass a little more tightly and says: *I'm quitting.* Crony laughs and says: *I give you a week.*

Morrison waiting for the morning train, looking over the top of the *Times* at a young man in a blue suit. He sees the young man almost every morning now, and sometimes at other places. At Onde's, where he is meeting a client. Looking at 45s in Sam Goody's, where Morrison is looking for a Sam Cooke album. Once in a foursome behind Morrison's group at the local golf course.

Morrison getting drunk at a party, wanting a cigarette—but not quite drunk enough to take one.

Morrison visiting his son, bringing him a large ball

that squeaked when you squeezed it. His son's slobbering, delighted kiss. Somehow not as repulsive as before. Hugging his son tightly, realizing what Donatti and his colleagues had so cynically realized before him: love is the most pernicious drug of all. Let the romantics debate its existence. Pragmatists accept it and use it.

Morrison losing the physical compulsion to smoke little by little, but never quite losing the psychological craving, or the need to have something in his mouth—cough drops, Life Savers, a toothpick. Poor substitutes, all of them.

And finally, Morrison hung up in a colossal traffic jam in the Midtown Tunnel. Darkness. Horns blaring. Air stinking. Traffic hopelessly snarled. And suddenly, thumbing open the glove compartment and seeing the half-open pack of cigarettes in there. He looked at them for a moment, then snatched one and lit it with the dashboard lighter. If anything happens, it's Cindy's fault, he told himself defiantly. I told her to get rid of all the damn cigarettes.

The first drag made him cough smoke out furiously. The second made his eyes water. The third made him feel lightheaded and swoony. It tastes awful, he thought.

And on the heels of that: My God, what am I doing?

Horns blatted impatiently behind him. Ahead, the traffic had begun to move again. He stubbed the cigarette out in the ashtray, opened both front windows, opened the vents, and then fanned the air helplessly like a kid who has just flushed his first butt down the john.

He joined the traffic flow jerkily and drove home.

"Cindy?" he called. "I'm home."

No answer.

"Cindy? Where are you, hon?"

The phone rang, and he pounced on it. "Hello? Cindy?"

"Hello, Mr. Morrison," Donatti said. He sounded pleasantly brisk and businesslike. "It seems we have a small business matter to attend to. Would five o'clock be convenient?"

"Have you got my wife?"

"Yes, indeed." Donatti chuckled indulgently.

"Look, let her go," Morrison babbled. "It won't happen again. It was a slip, just a slip, that's all. I only had three drags and for God's sake *it didn't even taste good!*"

"That's a shame. I'll count on you for five then, shall I?"

"Please," Morrison said, close to tears. "Please—"

He was speaking to a dead line.

At 5 P.M. the reception room was empty except for the secretary, who gave him a twinkly smile that ignored Morrison's pallor and disheveled appearance. "Mr. Donatti?" she said into the intercom. "Mr. Morrison to see you." She nodded to Morrison. "Go right in."

Donatti was waiting outside the unmarked room with a man who was wearing a SMILE sweatshirt and carrying a .38. He was built like an ape.

"Listen," Morrison said to Donatti. "We can work something out, can't we? I'll pay you. I'll—"

"Shaddap," the man in the SMILE sweatshirt said.

"It's good to see you," Donatti said. "Sorry it has to be under such adverse circumstances. Will you come with me? We'll make this as brief as possible. I can assure you your wife won't be hurt . . . this time."

Morrison tensed himself to leap at Donatti.

"Come, come," Donatti said, looking annoyed. "If you do that, Junk here is going to pistol-whip you and your wife is still going to get it. Now where's the percentage in that?"

"I hope you rot in hell," he told Donatti.

Donatti sighed. "If I had a nickel for every time someone expressed a similar sentiment, I could retire. Let it be a lesson to you, Mr. Morrison. When a romantic tries to do a good thing and fails, they give him a medal. When a pragmatist succeeds, they wish him in hell. Shall we go?"

Junk motioned with the pistol.

Morrison preceded them into the room. He felt numb. The small green curtain had been pulled. Junk prodded him with the gun. This is what being a witness at the gas chamber must have been like, he thought.

He looked in. Cindy was there, looking around bewilderedly.

"Cindy!" Morrison called miserably. "Cindy, they—"

"She can't hear or see you," Donatti said. "One-way glass. Well, let's get it over with. It really was a very small slip. I believe thirty seconds should be enough. Junk?"

Junk pressed the button with one hand and kept the pistol jammed firmly into Morrison's back with the other.

It was the longest thirty seconds of his life.

When it was over, Donatti put a hand on Morrison's shoulder and said, "Are you going to throw up?"

"No," Morrison said weakly. His forehead was against the glass. His legs were jelly. "I don't think so." He turned around and saw that Junk was gone.

"Come with me," Donatti said.

"Where?" Morrison asked apathetically.

"I think you have a few things to explain, don't you?"

"How can I face her? How can I tell her that I . . . I . . ."

"I think you're going to be surprised," Donatti said.

———

The room was empty except for a sofa. Cindy was on it, sobbing helplessly.

"Cindy?" he said gently.

She looked up, her eyes magnified by tears. "Dick?" she whispered. "Dick? Oh . . . Oh God . . ." He held her tightly. "Two men," she said against his chest. "In the house and at first I thought they were burglars and then I thought they were going to rape me and then they took me someplace with a blindfold over my eyes and . . . and . . . oh it was *h-horrible*—"

"Shhh," he said. "Shhh."

"But why?" she asked, looking up at him. "Why would they—"

"Because of me," he said. "I have to tell you a story, Cindy—"

———

When he had finished he was silent a moment and then said, "I suppose you hate me. I wouldn't blame you."

He was looking at the floor, and she took his face in both hands and turned it to hers. "No," she said. "I don't hate you."

He looked at her in mute surprise.

"It was worth it," she said. "God bless these people. They've let you out of prison."

"Do you mean that?"

"Yes," she said, and kissed him. "Can we go home now? I feel much better. Ever so much."

———

The phone rang one evening a week later, and when Morrison recognized Donatti's voice, he said, "Your boys have got it wrong. I haven't even been near a cigarette."

"We know that. We have a final matter to talk over. Can you stop by tomorrow afternoon?"

"Is it—"

"No, nothing serious. Bookkeeping really. By the way, congratulations on your promotion."

"How did you know about that?"

"We're keeping tabs," Donatti said noncommittally, and hung up.

———

When they entered the small room, Donatti said, "Don't look so nervous. No one's going to bite you. Step over here, please."

Morrison saw an ordinary bathroom scale. "Listen, I've gained a little weight, but—"

"Yes, seventy-three percent of our clients do. Step up, please."

Morrison did, and tipped the scales at one seventy-four.

"Okay, fine. You can step off. How tall are you, Mr. Morrison?"

"Five-eleven."

"Okay, let's see." He pulled a small card laminated in plastic from his breast pocket. "Well, that's not too bad. I'm going to write you a prescrip for some highly illegal diet pills. Use them sparingly and according to directions. And I'm going to set your maximum weight at . . . let's see . . ." He consulted the card again. "One eighty-two, how does that sound? And since this is December first, I'll expect you the first of every month for a weigh-in. No problem if you can't make it, as long as you call in advance."

"And what happens if I go over one eighty-two?"

Donatti smiled. "We'll send someone out to your house to cut off your wife's little finger," he said. "You can leave through this door, Mr. Morrison. Have a nice day."

———

Eight months later:

Morrison runs into the crony from the Larkin Studios at Dempsey's bar. Morrison is down to what Cindy proudly calls his fighting weight: one sixty-seven. He works out three times a week and looks as fit as whipcord. The crony from Larkin, by comparison, looks like something the cat dragged in.

Crony: Lord, how'd you ever stop? I'm locked into this damn habit tighter than Tillie. The crony stubs his cigarette out with real revulsion and drains his scotch.

Morrison looks at him speculatively and then takes a small white business card out of his wallet. He puts it on the bar between them. You know, he says, these guys changed my life.

———

Twelve months later:

Morrison receives a bill in the mail. The bill says:

QUITTERS, INC.
237 East 46th Street
New York, N.Y. 10017

1 Treatment	$2500.00
Counselor (Victor Donatti)	$2500.00
Electricity	$ .50
TOTAL (Please pay this amount)	$5000.50

Those sons of bitches! he explodes. They charged me for the electricity they used to . . . to . . .

Just pay it she says, and kisses him.

———

Twenty months later:

Quite by accident, Morrison and his wife meet the Jimmy McCanns at the Helen Hayes Theatre. Introductions are made all around. Jimmy looks as good, if not better than he did on that day in the airport terminal so long ago. Morrison has never met his wife. She is pretty in the radiant way plain girls sometimes have when they are very, very happy.

She offers her hand and Morrison shakes it. There is something odd about her grip, and halfway through the second act, he realizes what it was. The little finger on her right hand is missing.

I KNOW WHAT YOU NEED

"I know what you need."

Elizabeth looked up from her sociology text, startled, and saw a rather nondescript young man in a green fatigue jacket. For a moment she thought he looked familiar, as if she had known him before; the feeling was close to déjà vu. Then it was gone. He was about her height, skinny, and . . . twitchy. That was the word. He wasn't moving, but he seemed to be twitching inside his skin, just out of sight. His hair was black and unkempt. He wore thick horn-rimmed glasses that magnified his dark brown eyes, and the lenses looked dirty. No, she was quite sure she had never seen him before.

"You know," she said, "I doubt that."

"You need a strawberry double-dip cone. Right?"

She blinked at him, frankly startled. Somewhere in the back of her mind she *had* been thinking about breaking for an ice cream. She was studying for finals in one of the third-floor carrels of the Student Union, and there was still a woefully long way to go.

"Right?" he persisted, and smiled. It transformed his face from something over-intense and nearly ugly into something else that was oddly appealing. The word "cute" occurred to her, and that wasn't a good word to afflict a boy with, but this one was when he smiled. She smiled back before she could roadblock it behind her lips. This she didn't need, to have to waste time brushing off some weirdo who had decided to pick the worst time of the year to try to make an impression. She still had sixteen chapters of *Introduction to Sociology* to wade through.

"No thanks," she said.

"Come on, if you hit them any harder you'll give yourself a headache. You've been at it two hours without a break."

"How would you know that?"

"I've been watching you," he said promptly, but this time his gamin grin was lost on her. She already had a headache.

"Well, you can stop," she said, more sharply than she had intended. "I don't like people staring at me."

"I'm sorry." She felt a little sorry for him, the way she sometimes felt sorry for stray dogs. He seemed to float in the green fatigue jacket and . . . yes, he had on mismatched socks. One black, one brown. She felt herself getting ready to smile again and held it back.

"I've got these finals," she said gently.

"Sure," he said. "Okay."

She looked after him for a moment pensively. Then

she lowered her gaze to her book, but an afterimage of the encounter remained: *strawberry double-dip*.

When she got back to the dorm it was 11:15 P.M. and Alice was stretched out on her bed, listening to Neil Diamond and reading *The Story of O*.

"I didn't know they assigned that in Eh-17," Elizabeth said.

Alice sat up. "Broadening my horizons, darling. Spreading my intellectual wings. Raising my . . . Liz?"

"Hmmm?"

"Did you hear what I said?"

"No, sorry, I—"

"You look like somebody conked you one, kid."

"I met a guy tonight. Sort of a funny guy, at that."

"Oh? He must be something if he can separate the great Rogan from her beloved texts."

"His name is Edward Jackson Hamner, Junior, no less. Short. Skinny. Looks like he washed his hair last around Washington's birthday. Oh, and mismatched socks. One black, one brown."

"I thought you were more the fraternity type."

"It's nothing like that, Alice. I was studying at the Union on the third floor—the Think Tank—and he invited me down to the Grinder for an ice-cream cone. I told him no and he sort of slunk off. But once he started me thinking about ice cream, I couldn't stop. I'd just decided to give up and take a break and there he was, holding a big, drippy strawberry double-dip in each hand."

"I tremble to hear the denouement."

Elizabeth snorted. "Well, I couldn't really say no. So he sat down, and it turns out he had sociology with Professor Branner last year."

"Will wonders never cease, lawd a mercy. Goshen to Christmas—"

"Listen, this is really amazing. You know the way I've been sweating that course?"

"Yes. You talk about it in your sleep, practically."

"I've got a seventy-eight average. I've got to have an eighty to keep my scholarship, and that means I need at least an eighty-four on the final. Well, this Ed Hamner says Branner uses almost the same final every year. And Ed's eidetic."

"You mean he's got a whatzit . . . photographic memory?"

"Yes. Look at this." She opened her sociology book and took out three sheets of notebook paper covered with writing.

Alice took them. "This looks like multiple-choice stuff."

"It is. Ed says it's Branner's last year's final *word for word*."

Alice said flatly, "I don't believe it."

"But it covers all the material!"

"Still don't believe it." She handed the sheets back. "Just because this spook—"

"He isn't a spook. Don't call him that."

"Okay. This little *guy* hasn't got you bamboozled into just memorizing this and not studying at all, has he?"

"Of course not," she said uneasily.

"And even if this is like the exam, do you think it's exactly ethical?"

Anger surprised her and ran away with her tongue before she could hold it. "That's great for you, sure. Dean's List every semester and your folks paying your way. You aren't . . . Hey, I'm sorry. There was no call for that."

Alice shrugged and opened *O* again, her face carefully neutral. "No, you're right. Not my business. But why don't you study the book, too . . . just to be safe?"

"Of course I will."

But mostly she studied the exam notes provided by Edward Jackson Hamner, Jr.

———

When she came out of the lecture hall after the exam he was sitting in the lobby, floating in his green army fatigue coat. He smiled tentatively at her and stood up. "How'd it go?"

Impulsively, she kissed his cheek. She could not remember such a blessed feeling of relief. "I think I aced it."

"Really? That's great. Like a burger?"

"Love one," she said absently. Her mind was still on the exam. It was the one Ed had given her, almost word for word, and she had sailed through.

Over hamburgers, she asked him how his own finals were going.

"Don't have any. I'm in Honors, and you don't take them unless you want to. I was doing okay, so I didn't."

"Then why are you still here?"

"I had to see how you did, didn't I?"

"Ed, you didn't. That's sweet, but—" The naked look in his eyes troubled her. She had seen it before. She was a pretty girl.

"Yes," he said softly. "Yes, I did."

"Ed, I'm grateful. I think you saved my scholarship. I really do. But I have a boyfriend, you know."

"Serious?" he asked, with a poor attempt to speak lightly.

"Very," she said, matching his tone. "Almost engaged."

"Does he know he's lucky? Does he know how lucky?"

"I'm lucky, too," she said, thinking of Tony Lombard.

"Beth," he said suddenly.

"What?" she asked, startled.

"Nobody calls you that, do they?"

"Why . . . no. No, they don't."

"Not even this guy?"

"No—" Tony called her Liz. Sometimes Lizzie, which was even worse.

He leaned forward. "But Beth is what you like best, isn't it?"

She laughed to cover her confusion. "Whatever in the world—"

"Never mind." He grinned his gamin grin. "I'll call you Beth. That's better. Now eat your hamburger."

Then her junior year was over, and she was saying goodbye to Alice. They were a little stiff together, and Elizabeth was sorry. She supposed it was her own fault; she *had* crowed a little loudly about her sociology final when grades were posted. She had scored a ninety-seven—highest in the division.

Well, she told herself as she waited at the airport for her flight to be called, it wasn't any more unethical than the cramming she had been resigned to in that third-floor carrel. Cramming wasn't real studying at all; just rote memorization that faded away to nothing as soon as the exam was over.

She fingered the envelope that poked out of her purse. Notice of her scholarship-loan package for her senior year—two thousand dollars. She and Tony would be working together in Boothbay, Maine, this summer, and the money she would earn there would put her over the top. And thanks to Ed Hamner, it was going to be a beautiful summer. Clear sailing all the way.

But it was the most miserable summer of her life.

June was rainy, the gas shortage depressed the tourist trade, and her tips at the Boothbay Inn were mediocre. Even worse, Tony was pressing her on the subject of marriage. He could get a job on or near campus, he said, and with her Student Aid grant, she could get her degree in style. She was surprised to find that the idea scared rather than pleased her.

Something was *wrong*.

She didn't know what, but something was missing, out of whack, out of kilter. One night late in July she frightened herself by going on a hysterical crying jag in her apartment. The only good thing about it was that her roommate, a mousy little girl named Sandra Ackerman, was out on a date.

The nightmare came in early August. She was lying in the bottom of an open grave, unable to move. Rain fell from a white sky onto her upturned face. Then Tony was standing over her, wearing his yellow high-impact construction helmet.

"Marry me, Liz," he said, looking down at her expressionlessly. "Marry me or else."

She tried to speak, to agree; she would do anything if only he would take her out of this dreadful muddy hole. But she was paralyzed.

"All right," he said. "It's or else, then."

He went away. She struggled to break out of her paralysis and couldn't.

Then she heard the bulldozer.

A moment later she saw it, a high yellow monster, pushing a mound of wet earth in front of the blade. Tony's merciless face looked down from the open cab.

He was going to bury her alive.

Trapped in her motionless, voiceless body, she could only watch in dumb horror. Trickles of dirt began to run down the sides of the hole—

A familiar voice cried, "Go! Leave her now! *Go!*"

Tony stumbled down from the bulldozer and ran.

Huge relief swept her. She would have cried had she been able. And her savior appeared, standing at the foot of the open grave like a sexton. It was Ed Hamner, floating in his green fatigue jacket, his hair awry, his horn-rims slipped down to the small bulge at the end of his nose. He held his hand out to her.

"Get up," he said gently. "I know what you need. Get up, Beth."

And she could get up. She sobbed with relief. She tried to thank him; her words spilled out on top of each other. And Ed only smiled gently and nodded. She took his hand and looked down to see her footing. And when she looked up again, she was holding the paw of a huge, slavering timber wolf with red hurricane-lantern eyes and thick, spiked teeth open to bite.

She woke up sitting bolt upright in bed, her night-gown drenched with sweat. Her body was shaking uncontrollably. And even after a warm shower and a glass of milk, she could not reconcile herself to the dark. She slept with the light on.

A week later Tony was dead.

———

She opened the door in her robe, expecting to see Tony, but it was Danny Kilmer, one of the fellows he worked with. Danny was a fun guy; she and Tony had doubled with him and his girl a couple of times. But standing in the doorway of her second-floor apartment, Danny looked not only serious but ill.

"Danny?" she said. "What—"

"Liz," he said. "Liz, you've got to hold on to yourself. You've . . . *ah, God!*" He pounded the jamb of the door with one big-knuckled, dirty hand, and she saw he was crying.

"Danny, is it Tony? Is something—"

"Tony's dead," Danny said. "He was—" But he was talking to air. She had fainted.

———

The next week passed in a kind of dream. The story pieced itself together from the woefully brief newspaper account and from what Danny told her over a beer in the Harbor Inn.

They had been repairing drainage culverts on Route 16. Part of the road was torn up, and Tony was flagging traffic. A kid driving a red Fiat had been coming down the hill. Tony had flagged him, but the kid never even slowed. Tony had been standing next to a dump truck, and there was no place to jump back. The kid in the Fiat had sustained head lacerations and a broken arm; he was hysterical and also cold sober. The police found several holes in his brake lines, as if they had over-heated and then melted through. His driving record was A-1; he had simply been unable to stop. Her Tony had been a victim of that rarest of automobile mishaps: an honest accident.

Her shock and depression were increased by guilt. The fates had taken out of her hands the decision on what to do about Tony. And a sick, secret part of her was glad it was so. Because she hadn't wanted to marry Tony . . . not since the night of her dream.

———

She broke down the day before she went home.

She was sitting on a rock outcropping by herself, and after an hour or so the tears came. They surprised her with their fury. She cried until her stomach hurt and her head ached, and when the tears passed she felt not better but at least drained and empty.

And that was when Ed Hamner said, "Beth?"

She jerked around, her mouth filled with the copper taste of fear, half expecting to see the snarling wolf of her dream. But it was only Ed Hamner, looking sunburned and strangely defenseless without his fatigue jacket and blue jeans. He was wearing red shorts that stopped just ahead of his bony knees, a white T-shirt that billowed on his thin chest like a loose sail in the ocean breeze, and rubber thongs. He wasn't smiling and the fierce sun glitter on his glasses made it impossible to see his eyes.

"Ed?" she said tentatively, half convinced that this was some grief-induced hallucination. "Is that really—"

"Yes, it's me."

"How—"

"I've been working at the Lakewood Theater in

Skowhegan. I ran into your roommate . . . Alice, is that her name?"

"Yes."

"She told me what happened. I came right away. Poor Beth." He moved his head, only a degree or so, but the sun glare slid off his glasses and she saw nothing wolfish, nothing predatory, but only a calm, warm sympathy.

She began to weep again, and staggered a little with the unexpected force of it. Then he was holding her and then it was all right.

———

They had dinner at the Silent Woman in Waterville, which was twenty-five miles away; maybe exactly the distance she needed. They went in Ed's car, a new Corvette, and he drove well—neither showily nor fussily, as she guessed he might. She didn't want to talk and she didn't want to be cheered up. He seemed to know it, and played quiet music on the radio.

And he ordered without consulting her—seafood. She thought she wasn't hungry, but when the food came she fell to ravenously.

When she looked up again her plate was empty and she laughed nervously. Ed was smoking a cigarette and watching her.

"The grieving damsel ate a hearty meal," she said. "You must think I'm awful."

"No," he said. "You've been through a lot and you need to get your strength back. It's like being sick, isn't it?"

"Yes. Just like that."

He took her hand across the table, squeezed it briefly, then let it go. "But now it's recuperation time, Beth."

"Is it? Is it really?"

"Yes," he said. "So tell me. What are your plans?"

"I'm going home tomorrow. After that, I don't know."

"You're going back to school, aren't you?"

"I just don't know. After this, it seems so . . . so trivial. A lot of the purpose seems to have gone out of it. And all the fun."

"It'll come back. That's hard for you to believe now, but it's true. Try it for six weeks and see. You've got nothing better to do." The last seemed a question.

"That's true, I guess. But . . . Can I have a cigarette?"

"Sure. They're menthol, though. Sorry."

She took one. "How did you know I didn't like menthol cigarettes?"

He shrugged. "You just don't look like one of those, I guess."

She smiled. "You're funny, do you know that?"

He smiled neutrally.

"No, really. For you of all people to turn up . . . I thought I didn't want to see anyone. But I'm really glad it was you, Ed."

"Sometimes it's nice to be with someone you're not involved with."

"That's it, I guess." She paused. "Who are you, Ed, besides my fairy godfather? Who are you really?" It was suddenly important to her that she know.

He shrugged. "Nobody much. Just one of the sort of funny-looking guys you see creeping around campus with a load of books under one arm—"

"Ed, you're not funny-looking."

"Sure I am," he said, and smiled. "Never grew all the way out of my high-school acne, never got rushed by a big frat, never made any kind of splash in the social whirl. Just a dorm rat making grades, that's all. When the big corporations interview on campus next spring, I'll probably sign on with one of them and Ed Hamner will disappear forever."

"That would be a great shame," she said softly.

He smiled, and it was a very peculiar smile. Almost bitter.

"What about your folks?" she asked. "Where you live, what you like to do—"

"Another time," he said. "I want to get you back. You've got a long plane ride tomorrow, and a lot of hassles."

———

The evening left her relaxed for the first time since Tony's death, without that feeling that somewhere inside a mainspring was being wound and wound to the breaking point. She thought sleep would come easily, but it did not.

Little questions nagged.

Alice told me . . . poor Beth.

But Alice was summering in Kittery, eighty miles from Skowhegan. She must have been at Lakewood for a play.

The Corvette, this year's model. Expensive. A backstage job at Lakewood hadn't paid for that. Were his parents rich?

He had ordered just what she would have ordered herself. Maybe the only thing on the menu she would have eaten enough of to discover that she was hungry.

The menthol cigarettes, the way he had kissed her good night, exactly as she had wanted to be kissed. And—

You've got a long plane ride tomorrow.

He knew she was going home because she had told him. But how had he known she was going by plane? Or that it was a long ride?

It bothered her. It bothered her because she was halfway to being in love with Ed Hamner.

I know what you need.

Like the voice of a submarine captain tolling off fathoms, the words he had greeted her with followed her down to sleep.

He didn't come to the tiny Augusta airport to see her off, and waiting for the plane, she was surprised by her own disappointment. She was thinking about how quietly you could grow to depend on a person, almost like a junkie with a habit. The hype fools himself that he can take this stuff or leave it, when really—

"Elizabeth Rogan," the PA blared. "Please pick up the white courtesy phone."

She hurried to it. And Ed's voice said, "Beth?"

"Ed! It's good to hear you. I thought maybe . . ."

"That I'd meet you?" He laughed. "You don't need me for that. You're a big strong girl. Beautiful, too. You can handle this. Will I see you at school?"

"I . . . yes, I think so."

"Good." There was a moment of silence. Then he said, "Because I love you. I have from the first time I saw you."

Her tongue was locked. She couldn't speak. A thousand thoughts whirled through her mind.

He laughed again, gently. "No, don't say anything. Not now. I'll see you. There'll be time then. All the time in the world. Good trip, Beth. Goodbye."

And he was gone, leaving her with a white phone in her hand and her own chaotic thoughts and questions.

———

September.

Elizabeth picked up the old pattern of school and classes like a woman who has been interrupted at knitting. She was rooming with Alice again, of course; they had been roomies since freshman year, when they had been thrown together by the housing-department computer. They had always gotten along well, despite differing interests and personalities. Alice was the studious one, a chemistry major with a 3.6 average. Elizabeth was more social, less bookish, with a split major in education and math.

They still got on well, but a faint coolness seemed to have grown up between them over the summer. Elizabeth chalked it up to the difference of opinion over the sociology final, and didn't mention it.

The events of the summer began to seem dreamlike. In a funny way it sometimes seemed that Tony might have been a boy she had known in high school. It still hurt to think about him, and she avoided the subject with Alice, but the hurt was an old-bruise throb and not the bright pain of an open wound.

What hurt more was Ed Hamner's failure to call.

A week passed, then two, then it was October. She got a student directory from the Union and looked up his name. It was no help; after his name were only the words "Mill St." And Mill was a very long street indeed. And so she waited, and when she was called for dates—which was often—she turned them down. Alice raised her eyebrows but said nothing; she was buried alive in a six-week biochem project and spent most of her evenings at the library. Elizabeth noticed the long white envelopes that her roommate was receiving once or twice a week in the mail—since she was usually back from class first but thought nothing of them. The private detective agency was discreet; it did not print its return address on its envelopes.

When the intercom buzzed, Alice was studying. "You get it, Liz. Probably for you anyway."

Elizabeth went to the intercom. "Yes?"

"Gentleman door-caller, Liz."

Oh, Lord.

"Who is it?" she asked, annoyed, and ran through her tattered stack of excuses. Migraine headache. She hadn't used that one this week.

The desk girl said, amused, "His name is Edward Jackson Hamner. *Junior,* no less." Her voice lowered. "His socks don't match."

Elizabeth's hand flew to the collar of her robe. "Oh, God. Tell him I'll be right down. No, tell him it will be just a minute. No, a couple of minutes, okay?"

"Sure," the voice said dubiously. "Don't have a hemorrhage."

Elizabeth took a pair of slacks out of her closet. Took out a short denim skirt. Felt the curlers in her hair and groaned. Began to yank them out.

Alice watched all this calmly, without speaking, but she looked speculatively at the door for a long time after Elizabeth had left.

———

He looked just the same; he hadn't changed at all. He was wearing his green fatigue jacket, and it still looked at least two sizes too big. One of the bows of his horn-rimmed glasses had been mended with electrician's tape. His jeans looked new and stiff, miles from the soft and faded "in" look that Tony had achieved effortlessly. He was wearing one green sock, one brown sock.

And she knew she loved him.

"Why didn't you call before?" she asked, going to him.

He stuck his hands in the pockets of his jacket and grinned shyly. "I thought I'd give you some time to date around. Meet some guys. Figure out what you want."

"I think I know that."

"Good. Would you like to go to a movie?"

"Anything," she said. "Anything at all."

———

As the days passed it occurred to her that she had never met anyone, male or female, that seemed to understand her moods and needs so completely or so wordlessly. Their tastes coincided. While Tony had enjoyed violent movies of the *Godfather* type, Ed seemed more into comedy or nonviolent dramas. He took her to the circus one night when she was feeling low and they had a hilariously wonderful time. Study dates were real study dates, not just an excuse to grope on the third floor of the Union. He took her to dances and seemed especially good at the old ones, which she loved. They won a fifties Stroll trophy at a Homecoming Nostalgia Dance. More important, he seemed to understand when she wanted to be passionate. He didn't force her or hurry her; she never got the feeling that she had with some of the other boys she had gone out with—that there was an inner timetable for sex, beginning with a kiss good night on Date 1 and ending with a night in some friend's borrowed apartment on Date 10. The Mill Street apartment was Ed's exclusively, a third-floor walk-up. They went there often, and Elizabeth went without the feeling that she was walking into some minor-league Don Juan's passion pit. He didn't push. He honestly seemed to want what she wanted, when she wanted it. And things progressed.

———

When school reconvened following the semester break, Alice seemed strangely preoccupied. Several times that afternoon before Ed came to pick her up— they were going out to dinner—Elizabeth looked up to see her roommate frowning down at a large manila envelope on her desk. Once Elizabeth almost asked about it, then decided not to. Some new project probably.

———

It was snowing hard when Ed brought her back to the dorm.

"Tomorrow?" he asked. "My place?"

"Sure. I'll make some popcorn."

"Great," he said, and kissed her. "I love you, Beth."

"Love you, too."

"Would you like to stay over?" Ed asked evenly. "Tomorrow night?"

"All right, Ed." She looked into his eyes. "Whatever you want."

"Good," he said quietly. "Sleep well, kid."

"You, too."

She expected that Alice would be asleep and entered the room quietly, but Alice was up and sitting at her desk.

"Alice, are you okay?"

"I have to talk to you, Liz. About Ed."

"What about him?"

Alice said carefully, "I think that when I finish talking to you we're not going to be friends anymore. For me, that's giving up a lot. So I want you to listen carefully."

"Then maybe you better not say anything."

"I have to try."

Elizabeth felt her initial curiosity kindle into anger. "Have you been snooping around Ed?"

Alice only looked at her.

"Were you jealous of us?"

"No. If I'd been jealous of you and your dates, I would have moved out two years ago."

Elizabeth looked at her, perplexed. She knew what Alice said was the truth. And she suddenly felt afraid.

"Two things made me wonder about Ed Hamner," Alice said. "First, you wrote me about Tony's death and said how lucky it was that I'd seen Ed at the Lakewood Theater . . . how he came right over to Boothbay and really helped you out. But I never saw him, Liz. I was never near the Lakewood Theater last summer."

"But . . ."

"But how did he know Tony was dead? I have no idea. I only know he didn't get it from me. The other thing was that eidetic-memory business. My God, Liz, he can't even remember which socks he's got on!"

"That's a different thing altogether," Liz said stiffly. "It—"

"Ed Hamner was in Las Vegas last summer," Alice said softly. "He came back in mid-July and took a motel room in Pemaquid. That's just across the Boothbay Harbor town line. Almost as if he were waiting for you to need him."

"That's crazy! And how would you know Ed was in Las Vegas?"

"I ran into Shirley D'Antonio just before school started. She worked in the Pines Restaurant, which is just across from the playhouse. She said she never saw anybody who looked like Ed Hamner. So I've known he's been lying to you about several things. And so I went to my father and laid it out and he gave me the go-ahead."

"To do what?" Elizabeth asked, bewildered.

"To hire a private detective agency."

Elizabeth was on her feet. "No more, Alice. That's it." She would catch the bus into town, spend tonight at Ed's apartment. She had only been waiting for him to ask her, anyway.

"At least *know,*" Alice said. "Then make your own decision."

"I don't have to know anything except he's kind and good and—"

"Love is blind, huh?" Alice said, and smiled bitterly. "Well, maybe I happen to love you a little, Liz. Have you ever thought of that?"

Elizabeth turned and looked at her for a long moment. "If you do, you've got a funny way of showing it," she said. "Go on, then. Maybe you're right. Maybe I owe you that much. Go on."

"You knew him a long time ago," Alice said quietly.

"I . . . what?"

"P.S. 119, Bridgeport, Connecticut."

Elizabeth was struck dumb. She and her parents had lived in Bridgeport for six years, moving to their present home the year after she had finished the second grade. She *had* gone to P.S. 119, but—

"Alice, are you sure?"

"Do you remember him?"

"No, of course not!" But she *did* remember the feeling she'd had the first time she had seen Ed—the feeling of déjà vu.

"The pretty ones never remember the ugly ducklings, I guess. Maybe he had a crush on you. You were in the first grade with him, Liz. Maybe he sat in the back of the room and just . . . watched you. Or on the playground. Just a little nothing kid who already wore glasses and probably braces and you couldn't even remember him, but I'll bet he remembers you."

Elizabeth said, "What else?"

"The agency traced him from school fingerprints. After that it was just a matter of finding people and talking to them. The operative assigned to the case said he couldn't understand some of what he was getting. Neither do I. Some of it's scary."

"It better be," Elizabeth said grimly.

"Ed Hamner, Sr., was a compulsive gambler. He worked for a top-line advertising agency in New York and then moved to Bridgeport sort of on the run. The operative says that almost every big-money poker game and high-priced book in the city was holding his markers."

Elizabeth closed her eyes. "These people really saw you got a full measure of dirt for your dollar, didn't they?"

"Maybe. Anyway, Ed's father got in another jam in Bridgeport. It was gambling again, but this time he got mixed up with a big-time loan shark. He got a broken leg and a broken arm somehow. The operative says he doubts it was an accident."

"Anything else?" Elizabeth asked. "Child beating? Embezzlement?"

"He landed a job with a two-bit Los Angeles ad agency in 1961. That was a little too close to Las Vegas. He started to spend his weekends there, gambling heavily . . . and losing. Then he started taking Ed Junior with him. And he started to win."

"You're making all of this up. You must be."

Alice tapped the report in front of her. "It's all here, Liz. Some of it wouldn't stand up in court, but the operative says none of the people he talked with would have a reason to lie. Ed's father called Ed his 'good luck charm.' At first, nobody objected to the boy even though it was illegal for him to be in the casinos. His father was a prize fish. But then the father started sticking just to roulette, playing only odd-even and red-black. By the end of the year the boy was off-limits in every casino on the strip. And his father took up a new kind of gambling."

"What?"

"The stock market. When the Hamners moved to L.A. in the middle of 1961, they were living in a ninety-dollar-a-month cheese box and Mr. Hamner was driving a '52 Chevrolet. At the end of 1962, just sixteen months later, he had quit his job and they were living in their own home in San Jose. Mr. Hamner was driving a brand-new Thunderbird and Mrs. Hamner had a Volkswagen. You see, it's against the law for a small boy to be in the Nevada casinos, but no one could take the stock-market page away from him."

"Are you implying that Ed . . . that he could . . . Alice, you're crazy!"

"I'm not implying anything. Unless maybe just that he knew what his daddy needed."

I know what you need.

It was almost as if the words had been spoken into her ear, and she shuddered.

"Mrs. Hamner spent the next six years in and out of various mental institutions. Supposedly for nervous disorders, but the operative talked to an orderly who said she was pretty close to psychotic. She claimed her son was the devil's henchman. She stabbed him with a pair of scissors in 1964. Tried to kill him. She . . . Liz? Liz, what is it?"

"The scar," she muttered. "We went swimming at the University pool on an open night about a month ago. He's got a deep, dimpled scar on his shoulder . . . here." She put her hand just above her left breast. "He said . . ." A wave of nausea tried to climb up her throat and she had to wait for it to recede before she could go on. "He said he fell on a picket fence when he was a little boy."

"Shall I go on?"

"Finish, why not? What can it hurt now?"

"His mother was released from a very plush mental institution in the San Joaquin Valley in 1968. The three of them went on a vacation. They stopped at a picnic spot on Route 101. The boy was collecting firewood when she drove the car right over the edge of the dropoff above the ocean with both her and her husband in it. It might have been an attempt to run Ed down. By then he was nearly eighteen. His father left him a million-dollar stock portfolio. Ed came east a year and a half later and enrolled here. And that's the end."

"No more skeletons in the closet?"

"Liz, aren't there enough?"

She got up. "No wonder he never wants to mention his family. But you had to dig up the corpse, didn't you?"

"You're blind," Alice said. Elizabeth was putting on her coat. "I suppose you're going to him."

"Right."

"Because you love him."

"Right."

Alice crossed the room and grabbed her arm. "Will you get that sulky, petulant look off your face for a second and *think!* Ed Hamner is able to do things the rest of us only dream about. He got his father a stake at roulette and made him rich playing the stock market. He seems to be able to will winning. Maybe he's some kind of low-grade psychic. Maybe he's got precognition. I don't know. There are people who seem to have a dose of that. Liz, hasn't it ever occurred to you that he's forced you to love him?"

Liz turned to her slowly. "I've never heard anything so ridiculous in my life."

"Is it? He gave you that sociology test the same way he gave his father the right side of the roulette board! He was never enrolled in any sociology course! I checked. He did it because it was the only way he could make you take him seriously!"

"Stop it!" Liz cried. She clapped her hands over her ears.

"He knew the test, and he knew when Tony was killed, and he knew you were going home on a plane! He even knew just the right psychological moment to step back into your life last October."

Elizabeth pulled away from her and opened the door.

"Please," Alice said. "Please, Liz, listen. I don't know how he can do those things. I doubt if even *he* knows for sure. He might not mean to do you any harm, but he already is. He's made you love him by knowing every secret thing you want and need, and that's not love at all. That's rape."

Elizabeth slammed the door and ran down the stairs.

———

She caught the last bus of the evening into town. It was snowing more heavily than ever, and the bus lumbered through the drifts that had blown across the road like a crippled beetle. Elizabeth sat in the back, one of only six or seven passengers, a thousand thoughts in her mind.

Menthol cigarettes. The stock exchange. The way he had known her mother's nickname was Deedee. A little boy sitting at the back of a first-grade classroom, making sheep's eyes at a vivacious little girl too young to understand that—

I know what you need.

No. No. No. I do love him!

Did she? Or was she simply delighted at being with someone who always ordered the right thing, took her to the right movie, and did not want to go anywhere or do anything she didn't? Was he just a kind of psychic mirror, showing her only what she wanted to see? The presents he gave were always the right presents. When the weather had turned suddenly cold and she had been longing for a hair dryer, who gave her one? Ed Hamner, of course. Just happened to see one on sale in Day's, he had said. She, of course, had been delighted.

That's not love at all. That's rape.

The wind clawed at her face as she stepped out on the corner of Main and Mill, and she winced against it as the bus drew away with a smooth diesel growl. Its tail-lights twinkled briefly in the snowy night for a moment and were gone.

She had never felt so lonely in her life.

————————

He wasn't home.

She stood outside his door after five minutes of knocking, nonplussed. It occurred to her that she had no idea what Ed did or whom he saw when he wasn't with her. The subject had never come up.

Maybe he's raising the price of another hair dryer in a poker game.

With sudden decision she stood on her toes and felt along the top of the doorjamb for the spare key she knew he kept there. Her fingers stumbled over it and it fell to the hall floor with a clink.

She picked it up and used it in the lock.

The apartment looked different with Ed gone— artificial, like a stage set. It had often amused her that someone who cared so little about his personal appearance should have such a neat, picture-book domicile. Almost as if he had decorated it for her and not himself. But of course that was crazy. Wasn't it?

It occurred to her again, as if for the first time, how much she liked the chair she sat in when they studied or watched TV. It was just right, the way Baby Bear's chair had been for Goldilocks. Not too hard, not too soft. Just right. Like everything else she associated with Ed.

There were two doors opening off the living room. One went to the kitchenette, the other to his bedroom.

The wind whistled outside, making the old apartment building creak and settle.

In the bedroom, she stared at the brass bed. It looked neither too hard nor too soft, but just right. An insidious voice smirked: *It's almost too perfect, isn't it?*

She went to the bookcase and ran her eye aimlessly over the titles. One jumped at her eyes and she pulled it out: *Dance Crazes of the Fifties.* The book opened cleanly to a point some three-quarters through. A section titled "The Stroll" had been circled heavily in red grease pencil and in the margin the word "BETH" had been written in large, almost accusatory letters.

I ought to go now, she told herself. I can still save something. If he came back now I could never look him in the face again and Alice would win. Then she'd really get her money's worth.

But she couldn't stop, and knew it. Things had gone too far.

She went to the closet and turned the knob, but it didn't give. Locked.

On the off chance, she stood on tiptoe again and felt along the top of the door. And her fingers felt a key. She took it down and somewhere inside a voice said very clearly: *Don't do this.* She thought of Bluebeard's wife and what she had found when she opened the wrong door. But it was indeed too late; if she didn't proceed now she would always wonder. She opened the closet.

And had the strangest feeling that this was where the real Ed Hamner, Jr., had been hiding all the time.

The closet was a mess—a jumbled rickrack of clothes, books, an unstrung tennis racket, a pair of tattered tennis shoes, old prelims and reports tossed helter-skelter, a spilled pouch of Borkum Riff pipe tobacco. His green fatigue jacket had been flung in the far corner.

She picked up one of the books and blinked at the title. *The Golden Bough.* Another. *Ancient Rites, Modern Mysteries.* Another. *Haitian Voodoo.* And a last one, bound in old, cracked leather, the title almost rubbed off the binding by much handling, smelling vaguely like rotted fish: *Necronomicon.* She opened it at random, gasped, and flung it away, the obscenity still hanging before her eyes.

More to regain her composure than anything else, she reached for the green fatigue jacket, not admitting to herself that she meant to go through its pockets. But as she lifted it she saw something else. A small tin box . . .

Curiously, she picked it up and turned it over in her hands, hearing things rattle inside. It was the kind of box a young boy might choose to keep his treasures in. Stamped in raised letters on the tin bottom were the words "Bridgeport Candy Co." She opened it.

The doll was on top. The Elizabeth doll.

She looked at it and began to shudder.

The doll was dressed in a scrap of red nylon, part

of a scarf she had lost two or three months back. At a movie with Ed. The arms were pipe cleaners that had been draped in stuff that looked like blue moss. Graveyard moss, perhaps. There was hair on the doll's head, but that was wrong. It was fine white flax, taped to the doll's pink gum-eraser head. Her own hair was sandy blond and coarser than this. This was more the way her hair had been—

When she was a little girl.

She swallowed and there was a clicking in her throat. Hadn't they all been issued scissors in the first grade, tiny scissors with rounded blades, just right for a child's hand? Had that long-ago little boy crept up behind her, perhaps at nap time, and—

Elizabeth put the doll aside and looked in the box again. There was a blue poker chip with a strange six-sided pattern drawn on it in red ink. A tattered newspaper obituary—Mr. and Mrs. Edward Hamner. The two of them smiled meaninglessly out of the accompanying photo, and she saw that the same six-sided pattern had been drawn across their faces, this time in black ink, like a pall. Two more dolls, one male, one female. The similarity to the faces in the obituary photograph was hideous, unmistakable.

And something else.

She fumbled it out, and her fingers shook so badly she almost dropped it. A tiny sound escaped her.

It was a model car, the sort small boys buy in drugstores and hobby shops and then assemble with airplane glue. This one was a Fiat. It had been painted red. And a piece of what looked like one of Tony's shirts had been taped to the front.

She turned the model car upside down. Someone had hammered the underside to fragments.

"So you found it, you ungrateful bitch."

She screamed and dropped the car and the box. His foul treasures sprayed across the floor.

He was standing in the doorway, looking at her. She had never seen such a look of hate on a human face.

She said, "You killed Tony."

He grinned unpleasantly. "Do you think you could prove it?"

"It doesn't matter," she said, surprised at the steadiness of her own voice. "I know. And I never want to see you again. Ever. And if you do . . . anything . . . to anyone else, I'll know. And I'll fix you. Somehow."

His face twisted. "That's the thanks I get. I gave you everything you ever wanted. Things no other man could have. Admit it. I made you perfectly happy."

"You killed Tony!" She screamed it at him.

He took another step into the room. "Yes, and I did it for you. And what are you, Beth? You don't know what love is. I loved you from the first time I saw you, over seventeen years ago. Could Tony say that? It's never been hard for you. You're *pretty*. You never had to think about wanting or needing or about being lonely. You never had to find . . . other ways to get the things you had to have. There was always a Tony to give them to you. All you ever had to do was smile and say please." His voice rose a note. "*I* could never get what I wanted that way. Don't you think I tried? It didn't work with my father. He just wanted more and more. He never even kissed me good night or gave me a hug until I made him rich. And my mother was the same way. I gave her her marriage back, but was that enough for her? She hated me! She wouldn't come near me! She said I was unnatural! I gave her nice things but . . . Beth, don't do that! Don't . . . *dooon't*—"

She stepped on the Elizabeth doll and crushed it, turning her heel on it. Something inside her flared in agony, and then was gone. She wasn't afraid of him now. He was just a small, shrunken boy in a young man's body. And his socks didn't match.

"I don't think you can do anything to me now, Ed," she told him. "Not now. Am I wrong?"

He turned from her. "Go on," he said weakly. "Get out. But leave my box. At least do that."

"I'll leave the box. But not the things in it." She walked past him. His shoulders twitched, as if he might turn and try to grab her, but then they slumped.

As she reached the second-floor landing, he came to the top of the stairs and called shrilly after her: "Go on then! But you'll never be satisfied with any man after me! And when your looks go and men stop trying to give you anything you want, you'll wish for me! You'll think of what you threw away!"

She went down the stairs and out into the snow. Its coldness felt good against her face. It was a two-mile walk back to the campus, but she didn't care. She wanted the walk, wanted the cold. She wanted it to make her clean.

In a queer, twisted way she felt sorry for him—a little boy with a huge power crammed inside a dwarfed spirit. A little boy who tried to make humans behave like toy soldiers and then stamped on them in a fit of temper when they wouldn't or when they found out.

And what was she? Blessed with all the things he was not, through no fault of his or effort of her own? She remembered the way she had reacted to Alice, trying blindly and jealously to hold on to something that was easy rather than good, not caring, not caring.

When your looks go and men stop trying to give you anything you want, you'll wish for me! . . . I know what you need.

But was she so small that she actually needed so little?

Please, dear God, no.

On the bridge between the campus and town she paused and threw Ed Hamner's scraps of magic over the side, piece by piece. The red-painted model Fiat went last, falling end over end into the driven snow until it was lost from sight. Then she walked on.

CHILDREN OF THE CORN

Burt turned the radio on too loud and didn't turn it down because they were on the verge of another argument and he didn't want it to happen. He was desperate for it not to happen.

Vicky said something.

"What?" he shouted.

"Turn it down! Do you want to break my eardrums?"

He bit down hard on what might have come through his mouth and turned it down.

Vicky was fanning herself with her scarf even though the T-Bird was air-conditioned. "Where are we, anyway?"

"Nebraska."

She gave him a cold, neutral look. "Yes, Burt. I know we're in Nebraska, Burt. But where the hell *are* we?"

"You've got the road atlas. Look it up. Or can't you read?"

"Such wit. This is why we got off the turnpike. So we

could look at three hundred miles of corn. And enjoy the wit and wisdom of Burt Robeson."

He was gripping the steering wheel so hard his knuckles were white. He decided he was holding it that tightly because if he loosened up, why, one of those hands might just fly off and hit the ex–Prom Queen beside him right in the chops. We're saving our marriage, he told himself. Yes. We're doing it the same way us grunts went about saving villages in the war.

"Vicky," he said carefully. "I have driven fifteen hundred miles on turnpikes since we left Boston. I did all that driving myself because you refused to drive. Then—"

"I did not refuse!" Vicky said hotly. "Just because I get migraines when I drive for a long time—"

"Then when I asked you if you'd navigate for me on some of the secondary roads, you said sure, Burt. Those were your exact words. Sure, Burt. Then—"

"Sometimes I wonder how I ever wound up married to you."

"By saying two little words."

She stared at him for a moment, white-lipped, and then picked up the road atlas. She turned the pages savagely.

It *had* been a mistake leaving the turnpike, Burt thought morosely. It was a shame, too, because up until then they had been doing pretty well, treating each other almost like human beings. It had sometimes seemed that this trip to the coast, ostensibly to see Vicky's brother and his wife but actually a last-ditch attempt to patch up their own marriage, was going to work.

But since they left the pike, it had been bad again. How bad? Well, terrible, actually.

"We left the turnpike at Hamburg, right?"

"Right."

"There's nothing more until Gatlin," she said. "Twenty miles. Wide place in the road. Do you suppose we could stop there and get something to eat? Or does your almighty schedule say we have to go until two o'clock like we did yesterday?"

He took his eyes off the road to look at her. "I've about had it, Vicky. As far as I'm concerned, we can turn around right here and go home and see that lawyer you wanted to talk to. Because this isn't working at—"

She had faced forward again, her expression stonily set. It suddenly turned to surprise and fear. *"Burt look out you're going to—"*

He turned his attention back to the road just in time to see something vanish under the T-Bird's bumper. A moment later, while he was only beginning to switch from gas to brake, he felt something thump sickeningly under the front and then the back wheels. They were thrown forward as the car braked along the centerline, decelerating from fifty to zero along black skidmarks.

"A dog," he said. "Tell me it was a dog, Vicky."

Her face was a pallid, cottage-cheese color. "A boy. A little boy. He just ran out of the corn and . . . congratulations, tiger."

She fumbled the car door open, leaned out, threw up.

Burt sat straight behind the T-Bird's wheel, hands still gripping it loosely. He was aware of nothing for a long time but the rich, dark smell of fertilizer.

Then he saw that Vicky was gone and when he looked in the outside mirror he saw her stumbling clumsily back toward a heaped bundle that looked like a pile of rags. She was ordinarily a graceful woman but now her grace was gone, robbed.

It's manslaughter. That's what they call it. I took my eyes off the road.

He turned the ignition off and got out. The wind rustled softly through the growing man-high corn, making a weird sound like respiration. Vicky was standing over the bundle of rags now, and he could hear her sobbing.

He was halfway between the car and where she stood and something caught his eye on the left, a gaudy splash of red amid all the green, as bright as barn paint.

He stopped, looking directly into the corn. He found himself thinking (anything to untrack from those rags that were not rags) that it must have been a fantastically good growing season for corn. It grew close together, almost ready to bear. You could plunge into those neat, shaded rows and spend a day trying to find your way out again. But the neatness was broken here. Several tall cornstalks had been broken and leaned askew. And what was that further back in the shadows?

"Burt!" Vicky screamed at him. "Don't you want to come see? So you can tell all your poker buddies what you bagged in Nebraska? Don't you—" But the rest was lost in fresh sobs. Her shadow was puddled starkly around her feet. It was almost noon.

Shade closed over him as he entered the corn. The red barn paint was blood. There was a low, somnolent buzz as flies lit, tasted, and buzzed off again . . . maybe to tell others. There was more blood on the leaves further in. Surely it couldn't have splattered this far? And then he was standing over the object he had seen from the road. He picked it up.

The neatness of the rows was disturbed here. Several stalks were canted drunkenly, two of them had been broken clean off. The earth had been gouged. There was blood. The corn rustled. With a little shiver, he walked back to the road.

Vicky was having hysterics, screaming unintelligible words at him, crying, laughing. Who would have thought it could end in such a melodramatic way? He looked at her and saw he wasn't having an identity crisis or a difficult life transition or any of those trendy things. He hated her. He gave her a hard slap across the face.

She stopped short and put a hand against the reddening impression of his fingers. "You'll go to jail, Burt," she said solemnly.

"I don't think so," he said, and put the suitcase he had found in the corn at her feet.

"What—?"

"I don't know. I guess it belonged to him." He pointed to the sprawled, face-down body that lay in the road. No more than thirteen, from the look of him.

The suitcase was old. The brown leather was battered and scuffed. Two hanks of clothesline had been wrapped around it and tied in large, clownish grannies. Vicky bent to undo one of them, saw the blood greased into the knot, and withdrew.

Burt knelt and turned the body over gently.

"I don't want to look," Vicky said, staring down helplessly anyway. And when the staring, sightless face flopped up to regard them, she screamed again. The boy's face was dirty, his expression a grimace of terror. His throat had been cut.

Burt got up and put his arms around Vicky as she began to sway. "Don't faint," he said very quietly. "Do you hear me, Vicky? Don't faint."

He repeated it over and over and at last she began to recover and held him tight. They might have been dancing, there on the noon-struck road with the boy's corpse at their feet.

"Vicky?"

"What?" Muffled against his shirt.

"Go back to the car and put the keys in your pocket. Get the blanket out of the back seat, and my rifle. Bring them here."

"The rifle?"

"Someone cut his throat. Maybe whoever is watching us."

Her head jerked up and her wide eyes considered the corn. It marched away as far as the eye could see, undulating up and down small dips and rises of land.

"I imagine he's gone. But why take chances? Go on. Do it."

She walked stiltedly back to the car, her shadow following, a dark mascot who stuck close at this hour of the day. When she leaned into the back seat, Burt squatted beside the boy. White male, no distinguishing marks. Run over, yes, but the T-Bird hadn't cut the kid's throat. It had been cut raggedly and inefficiently—no army sergeant had shown the killer the finer points of hand-to-hand assassination—but the final effect had been deadly. He had either run or been pushed through the last thirty feet of corn, dead or mortally wounded. And Burt Robeson had run him down. If the boy had still been alive when the car hit him, his life had been cut short by thirty seconds at most.

Vicky tapped him on the shoulder and he jumped.

She was standing with the brown army blanket over her left arm, the cased pump shotgun in her right hand, her face averted. He took the blanket and spread it on the road. He rolled the body onto it. Vicky uttered a desperate little moan.

"You okay?" He looked up at her. "Vicky?"

"Okay," she said in a strangled voice.

He flipped the sides of the blanket over the body and scooped it up, hating the thick, dead weight of it. It tried to make a U in his arms and slither through his grasp. He clutched it tighter and they walked back to the T-Bird.

"Open the trunk," he grunted.

The trunk was full of travel stuff, suitcases and souvenirs. Vicky shifted most of it into the back seat and

Burt slipped the body into the made space and slammed the trunklid down. A sigh of relief escaped him.

Vicky was standing by the driver's side door, still holding the cased rifle.

"Just put it in the back and get in."

He looked at his watch and saw only fifteen minutes had passed. It seemed like hours.

"What about the suitcase?" she asked.

He trotted back down the road to where it stood on the white line, like the focal point in an Impressionist painting. He picked it up by its tattered handle and paused for a moment. He had a strong sensation of being watched. It was a feeling he had read about in books, mostly cheap fiction, and he had always doubted its reality. Now he didn't. It was as if there were people in the corn, maybe a lot of them, coldly estimating whether the woman could get the gun out of the case and use it before they could grab him, drag him into the shady rows, cut his throat—

Heart beating thickly, he ran back to the car, pulled the keys out of the trunk lock, and got in.

Vicky was crying again. Burt got them moving, and before a minute had passed, he could no longer pick out the spot where it had happened in the rearview mirror.

"What did you say the next town was?" he asked.

"Oh." She bent over the road atlas again. "Gatlin. We should be there in ten minutes."

"Does it look big enough to have a police station?"

"No. It's just a dot."

"Maybe there's a constable."

They drove in silence for a while. They passed a silo on the left. Nothing else but corn. Nothing passed them going the other way, not even a farm truck.

"Have we passed anything since we got off the turnpike, Vicky?"

She thought about it. "A car and a tractor. At that intersection."

"No, since we got on this road. Route 17."

"No. I don't think we have." Earlier this might have been the preface to some cutting remark. Now she only stared out of her half of the windshield at the unrolling road and the endless dotted line.

"Vicky? Could you open the suitcase?"

"Do you think it might matter?"

"Don't know. It might."

While she picked at the knots (her face was set in a peculiar way—expressionless but tight-mouthed—that Burt remembered his mother wearing when she pulled the innards out of the Sunday chicken), Burt turned on the radio again.

The pop station they had been listening to was almost obliterated in static and Burt switched, running the red marker slowly down the dial. Farm reports. Buck Owens. Tammy Wynette. All distant, nearly distorted into babble. Then, near the end of the dial, one single word blared out of the speaker, so loud and clear that the lips which uttered it might have been directly beneath the grille of the dashboard speaker.

"*ATONEMENT!*" this voice bellowed.

Burt made a surprised grunting sound. Vicky jumped.

"*ONLY BY THE BLOOD OF THE LAMB ARE WE SAVED!*" the voice roared, and Burt hurriedly turned the sound down. This station was close, all right. So close that . . . yes, there it was. Poking out of the corn at the horizon, a spidery red tripod against the blue. The radio tower.

"Atonement is the word, brothers 'n' sisters," the voice told them, dropping to a more conversational pitch. In the background, offmike, voices murmured amen. "There's some that thinks it's okay to get out in the world, as if you could work and walk in the world without being smirched by the world. Now is that what the word of God teaches us?"

Offmike but still loud: "No!"

"*HOLY JESUS!*" the evangelist shouted, and now the words came in a powerful, pumping cadence, almost as compelling as a driving rock-and-roll beat: "When they gonna know that way is death? When they gonna know that the wages of the world are paid on the other side? Huh? Huh? The Lord has said there's many mansions in His house. But there's no room for the fornicator. No room for the coveter. No room for the defiler of the corn. No room for the hommasexshul. No room—"

Vicky snapped it off. "That drivel makes me sick."

"What did he say?" Burt asked her. "What did he say about corn?"

"I didn't hear it." She was picking at the second clothesline knot.

"He said something about corn. I know he did."

"I got it!" Vicky said, and the suitcase fell open in her lap. They were passing a sign that said: GATLIN 5 MI. DRIVE CAREFULLY PROTECT OUR CHILDREN. The sign had been put up by the Elks. There were .22 bullet holes in it.

"Socks," Vicky said. "Two pairs of pants . . . a shirt . . . a belt . . . a string tie with a—" She held it up, showing him the peeling gilt neck clasp. "Who's that?"

Burt glanced at it. "Hopalong Cassidy, I think."

"Oh." She put it back. She was crying again.

After a moment, Burt said, "Did anything strike you funny about that radio sermon?"

"No. I heard enough of that stuff as a kid to last me forever. I told you about it."

"Didn't you think he sounded kind of young? That preacher?"

She uttered a mirthless laugh. "A teen-ager, maybe, so what? That's what's so monstrous about that whole trip. They like to get hold of them when their minds are still rubber. They know how to put all the emotional checks and balances in. You should have been at some of the tent meetings my mother and father dragged me to . . . some of the ones I was 'saved' at.

"Let's see. There was Baby Hortense, the Singing Marvel. She was eight. She'd come on and sing 'Leaning on the Everlasting Arms' while her daddy passed the plate, telling everybody to 'dig deep, now, let's not let this little child of God down.' Then there was Norman Staunton. He used to preach hellfire and brimstone in this Little Lord Fauntleroy suit with short pants. He was only seven."

She nodded at his look of unbelief.

"They weren't the only two, either. There were plenty of them on the circuit. They were good *draws*." She spat the word. "Ruby Stampnell. She was a ten-year-old faith healer. The Grace Sisters. They used to come out with little tin-foil haloes over their heads and—*oh!*"

"What is it?" He jerked around to look at her, and what she was holding in her hands. Vicky was staring at it raptly. Her slowly seining hands had snagged it on the bottom of the suitcase and had brought it up as she talked. Burt pulled over to take a better look. She gave it to him wordlessly.

It was a crucifix that had been made from twists of corn husk, once green, now dry. Attached to this by woven cornsilk was a dwarf corncob. Most of the kernels had been carefully removed, probably dug out one at a time with a pocketknife. Those kernels remaining formed a crude cruciform figure in yellowish bas-relief. Corn-kernel eyes, each slit longways to suggest pupils. Outstretched kernel arms, the legs together, terminating in a rough indication of bare feet. Above, four letters also raised from the bone-white cob: I N R I.

"That's a fantastic piece of workmanship," he said.

"It's hideous," she said in a flat, strained voice. "Throw it out."

"Vicky, the police might want to see it."

"Why?"

"Well, I don't know why. Maybe—"

"Throw it out. Will you please do that for me? I don't want it in the car."

"I'll put it in back. And as soon as we see the cops, we'll get rid of it one way or the other. I promise. Okay?"

"Oh, do whatever you want with it!" she shouted at him. "You will anyway!"

Troubled, he threw the thing in back, where it landed on a pile of clothes. Its corn-kernel eyes stared raptly at the T-Bird's dome light. He pulled out again, gravel splurting from beneath the tires.

"We'll give the body and everything that was in the suitcase to the cops," he promised. "Then we'll be shut of it."

Vicky didn't answer. She was looking at her hands.

A mile further on, the endless cornfields drew away from the road, showing farmhouses and outbuildings. In one yard they saw dirty chickens pecking listlessly at the soil. There were faded cola and chewing-tobacco ads on the roofs of barns. They passed a tall billboard that said: ONLY JESUS SAVES. They passed a café with a Conoco gas island, but Burt decided to go on into the center of town, if there was one. If not, they could come back to the café. It only occurred to him after they had passed it that the parking lot had been empty except for a dirty old pickup that had looked like it was sitting on two flat tires.

Vicky suddenly began to laugh, a high, giggling sound that struck Burt as being dangerously close to hysteria.

"What's so funny?"

"The signs," she said, gasping and hiccupping. "Haven't you been reading them? When they called this the Bible Belt, they sure weren't kidding. Oh Lordy, there's another bunch." Another burst of hysterical laughter escaped her, and she clapped both hands over her mouth.

Each sign had only one word. They were leaning on white-washed sticks that had been implanted in the sandy shoulder, long ago by the looks; the whitewash was flaked and faded. They were coming up at eighty-foot intervals and Burt read:

A . . . CLOUD . . . BY . . . DAY . . . A . . . PILLAR . . . OF . . . FIRE . . . BY . . . NIGHT

"They only forgot one thing," Vicky said, still giggling helplessly.

"What?" Burt asked, frowning.

"Burma Shave." She held a knuckled fist against her open mouth to keep in the laughter, but her semi-hysterical giggles flowed around it like effervescent ginger-ale bubbles.

"Vicky, are you all right?"

"I will be. Just as soon as we're a thousand miles away from here, in sunny sinful California with the Rockies between us and Nebraska."

Another group of signs came up and they read them silently.

TAKE . . . THIS . . . AND . . . EAT . . . SAITH . . . THE . . . LORD . . . GOD

Now why, Burt thought, should I immediately associate that indefinite pronoun with corn? Isn't that what they say when they give you communion? It had been so long since he had been to church that he really couldn't remember. He wouldn't be surprised if they used cornbread for holy wafer around these parts. He opened his mouth to tell Vicky that, and then thought better of it.

They breasted a gentle rise and there was Gatlin below them, all three blocks of it, looking like a set from a movie about the Depression.

"There'll be a constable," Burt said, and wondered why the sight of that hick one-timetable town dozing in the sun should have brought a lump of dread into his throat.

They passed a speed sign proclaiming that no more than thirty was now in order, and another sign, rust-flecked, which said: YOU ARE NOW ENTERING GATLIN, NICEST LITTLE TOWN IN NEBRASKA—OR ANYWHERE ELSE! POP. 5431.

Dusty elms stood on both sides of the road, most of them diseased. They passed the Gatlin Lumberyard and a 76 gas station, where the price signs swung slowly in a hot noon breeze: REG 35.9 HI-TEST 38.9, and another which said: HI TRUCKERS DIESEL FUEL AROUND BACK.

They crossed Elm Street, then Birch Street, and came up on the town square. The houses lining the streets were plain wood with screened porches. Angular and functional. The lawns were yellow and dispirited. Up ahead a mongrel dog walked slowly out into the middle of Maple Street, stood looking at them for a moment, then lay down in the road with its nose on its paws.

"Stop," Vicky said. "Stop right here."

Burt pulled obediently to the curb.

"Turn around. Let's take the body to Grand Island. That's not too far, is it? Let's do that."

"Vicky, what's wrong?"

"What do you mean, what's wrong?" she asked, her voice rising thinly. "This town is empty, Burt. There's nobody here but us. Can't you feel that?"

He had felt something, and still felt it. But—

"It just seems that way," he said. "But it sure is a one-hydrant town. Probably all up in the square, having a bake sale or a bingo game."

"There's no one here." She said the words with a queer, strained emphasis. "Didn't you see that 76 station back there?"

"Sure, by the lumberyard, so what?" His mind was elsewhere, listening to the dull buzz of a cicada burrowing into one of the nearby elms. He could smell corn, dusty roses, and fertilizer—of course. For the first time they were off the turnpike and in a town. A town in a state he had never been in before (although he had flown over it from time to time in United Airlines 747s) and somehow it felt all wrong but all right. Somewhere up ahead there would be a drugstore with a soda fountain, a movie house named the Bijou, a school named after JFK.

"Burt, the prices said thirty-five-nine for regular and thirty-eight-nine for high octane. Now how long has it been since anyone in this country paid those prices?"

"At least four years," he admitted. "But, Vicky—"

"We're right in town, Burt, and there's not a car! *Not one car!*"

"Grand Island is seventy miles away. It would look funny if we took him there."

"I don't care."

"Look, let's just drive up to the courthouse and—"

"No!"

There, damn it, there. Why our marriage is falling apart, in a nutshell. No I won't. No sir. And furthermore, I'll hold my breath till I turn blue if you don't let me have my way.

"Vicky," he said.

"I want to get out of here, Burt."

"Vicky, listen to me."

"Turn around. Let's go."

"Vicky, will you stop a minute?"

"I'll stop when we're driving the other way. Now let's go."

"We have a dead child in the trunk of our car!" he roared at her, and took a distinct pleasure at the way she flinched, the way her face crumbled. In a slightly lower voice he went on: "His throat was cut and he was shoved out into the road and I ran him over. Now I'm going to drive up to the courthouse or whatever they have here, and I'm going to report it. If you want to start walking back toward the pike, go to it. I'll pick you up. But don't you tell me to turn around and drive seventy miles to Grand Island like we had nothing in the trunk but a bag of garbage. He happens to be some mother's son, and

I'm going to report it before whoever killed him gets over the hills and far away."

"You bastard," she said, crying. "What am I doing with you?"

"I don't know," he said. "I don't know anymore. But the situation can be remedied, Vicky."

He pulled away from the curb. The dog lifted its head at the brief squeal of the tires and then lowered it to its paws again.

They drove the remaining block to the square. At the corner of Main and Pleasant, Main Street split in two. There actually was a town square, a grassy park with a bandstand in the middle. On the other end, where Main Street became one again, there were two official-looking buildings. Burt could make out the lettering on one: GATLIN MUNICIPAL CENTER.

"That's it," he said. Vicky said nothing.

Halfway up the square, Burt pulled over again. They were beside a lunchroom, the Gatlin Bar and Grill.

"Where are you going?" Vicky asked with alarm as he opened his door.

"To find out where everyone is. Sign in the window there says 'open.' "

"You're not going to leave me here alone."

"So come. Who's stopping you?"

She unlocked her door and stepped out as he crossed in front of the car. He saw how pale her face was and felt an instant of pity. Hopeless pity.

"Do you hear it?" she asked as he joined her.

"Hear what?"

"The nothing. No cars. No people. No tractors. Nothing."

And then, from a block over, they heard the high and joyous laughter of children.

"I hear kids," he said. "Don't you?"

She looked at him, troubled.

He opened the lunchroom door and stepped into dry, antiseptic heat. The floor was dusty. The sheen on the chrome was dull. The wooden blades of the ceiling fans stood still. Empty tables. Empty counter stools. But the mirror behind the counter had been shattered and there was something else . . . in a moment he had it. All the beer taps had been broken off. They lay along the counter like bizarre party favors.

Vicky's voice was gay and near to breaking. "Sure. Ask anybody. Pardon me, sir, but could you tell me—"

"Oh, shut up." But his voice was dull and without force. They were standing in a bar of dusty sunlight that fell through the lunchroom's big plate-glass window and again he had that feeling of being watched and he thought of the boy they had in their trunk, and of the high laughter of children. A phrase came to him for no reason, a legal-sounding phrase, and it began to repeat mystically in his mind: *Sight unseen. Sight unseen. Sight unseen.*

His eyes traveled over the age-yellowed cards thumbtacked up behind the counter: CHEESEBURG 35¢ WORLD'S BEST JOE 10¢ STRAWBERRY RHUBARB PIE 25¢ TODAY'S SPECIAL HAM & RED EYE GRAVY W/ MASHED POT 80¢.

How long since he had seen lunchroom prices like that?

Vicky had the answer. "Look at this," she said shrilly. She was pointing at the calendar on the wall. "They've been at that bean supper for twelve years, I guess." She uttered a grinding laugh.

He walked over. The picture showed two boys swimming in a pond while a cute little dog carried off their clothes. Below the picture was the legend: COMPLIMENTS OF GATLIN LUMBER & HARDWARE *You Breakum, We Fixum.* The month on view was August 1964.

"I don't understand," he faltered, "but I'm sure—"

"You're sure!" she cried hysterically. "Sure, you're sure! That's part of your trouble, Burt, you've spent your whole life being *sure!*"

He turned back to the door and she came after him.

"Where are you going?"

"To the Municipal Center."

"Burt, why do you have to be so stubborn? You know something's wrong here. Can't you just admit it?"

"I'm not being stubborn. I just want to get shut of what's in that trunk."

They stepped out onto the sidewalk, and Burt was struck afresh with the town's silence, and with the smell of fertilizer. Somehow you never thought of that smell when you buttered an ear and salted it and bit in. Compliments of sun, rain, all sorts of man-made phosphates, and a good healthy dose of cow shit. But somehow this smell was different from the one he had grown up with in rural upstate New York. You could say whatever you wanted to about organic fertilizer, but there was something almost fragrant about it when the spreader was laying it down in the fields. Not one of your great perfumes, God no, but when the late-afternoon spring breeze would pick up and waft it over the freshly turned fields, it *was* a smell with good associations. It meant winter was over for good. It meant that school doors were going to bang closed in six weeks or so and spill everyone out into summer. It was a smell tied irrevocably in his mind with other aromas that *were* perfume: timothy grass, clover, fresh earth, hollyhocks, dogwood.

But they must do something different out here, he thought. The smell was close but not the same. There was a sickish-sweet undertone. Almost a death smell. As a medical orderly in Vietnam, he had become well versed in that smell.

Vicky was sitting quietly in the car, holding the corn crucifix in her lap and staring at it in a rapt way Burt didn't like.

"Put that thing down," he said.

"No," she said without looking up. "You play your games and I'll play mine."

He put the car in gear and drove up to the corner. A dead stoplight hung overhead, swinging in a faint breeze. To the left was a neat white church. The grass was cut. Neatly kept flowers grew beside the flagged path up to the door. Burt pulled over.

"What are you doing?"

"I'm going to go in and take a look," Burt said. "It's

the only place in town that looks as if there isn't ten years' dust on it. And look at the sermon board."

She looked. Neatly pegged white letters under glass read: THE POWER AND GRACE OF HE WHO WALKS BEHIND THE ROWS. The date was July 24, 1976—the Sunday before.

"He Who Walks Behind the Rows," Burt said, turning off the ignition. "One of the nine thousand names of God only used in Nebraska, I guess. Coming?"

She didn't smile. "I'm not going in with you."

"Fine. Whatever you want."

"I haven't been in a church since I left home and I don't want to be in *this* church and I don't want to be in *this* town, Burt. I'm scared out of my mind, can't we just *go?*"

"I'll only be a minute."

"I've got my keys, Burt. If you're not back in five minutes, I'll just drive away and leave you here."

"Now just wait a minute, lady."

"That's what I'm going to do. Unless you want to assault me like a common mugger and take my keys. I suppose you could do that."

"But you don't think I will."

"No."

Her purse was on the seat between them. He snatched it up. She screamed and grabbed for the shoulder strap. He pulled it out of her reach. Not bothering to dig, he simply turned the bag upside down and let everything fall out. Her keyring glittered amid tissues, cosmetics, change, old shopping lists. She lunged for it but he beat her again and put the keys in his own pocket.

"You didn't have to do that," she said, crying. "Give them to me."

"No," he said, and gave her a hard, meaningless grin. "No way."

"Please, Burt! I'm scared!" She held her hand out, pleading now.

"You'd wait two minutes and decide that was long enough."

"I wouldn't—"

"And then you'd drive off laughing and saying to yourself, 'That'll teach Burt to cross me when I want something.' Hasn't that pretty much been your motto during our married life? That'll teach Burt to cross me?"

He got out of the car.

"Please, Burt!" she screamed, sliding across the seat. "Listen . . . I know . . . we'll drive out of town and call from a phone booth, okay? I've got all kinds of change. I just . . . we can . . . *don't leave me alone, Burt, don't leave me out here alone!"*

He slammed the door on her cry and then leaned against the side of the T-Bird for a moment, thumbs against his closed eyes. She was pounding on the driver's side window and calling his name. She was going to make a wonderful impression when he finally found someone in authority to take charge of the kid's body. Oh yes.

He turned and walked up the flagstone path to the

church doors. Two or three minutes, just a look-around, and he would be back out. Probably the door wasn't even unlocked.

But it pushed in easily on silent, well-oiled hinges (reverently oiled, he thought, and that seemed funny for no really good reason) and he stepped into a vestibule so cool it was almost chilly. It took his eyes a moment to adjust to the dimness.

The first thing he noticed was a pile of wooden letters in the far corner, dusty and jumbled indifferently together. He went to them, curious. They looked as old and forgotten as the calendar in the bar and grill, unlike the rest of the vestibule, which was dust-free and tidy. The letters were about two feet high, obviously part of a set. He spread them out on the carpet—there were eighteen of them—and shifted them around like anagrams. HURT BITE CRAG CHAP CS. Nope. CRAP TARGET CHIBS HUC. That wasn't much good either. Except for the CH in CHIBS. He quickly assembled the word CHURCH and was left looking at RAP TAGET CIBS. Foolish. He was squatting here playing idiot games with a bunch of letters while Vicky was going nuts out in the car. He started to get up, and then saw it. He formed BAPTIST, leaving RAG EC—and by changing two letters he had GRACE. GRACE BAPTIST CHURCH. The letters must have been out front. They had taken them down and had thrown them indifferently in the corner, and the church had been painted since then so that you couldn't even see where the letters had been.

Why?

It wasn't the Grace Baptist Church anymore, that was why. So what kind of church was it? For some reason that question caused a trickle of fear and he stood up quickly, dusting his fingers. So they had taken down a bunch of letters, so what? Maybe they had changed the place into Flip Wilson's Church of What's Happening Now.

But what had happened then?

He shook it off impatiently and went through the inner doors. Now he was standing at the back of the church itself, and as he looked toward the nave, he felt fear close around his heart and squeeze tightly. His breath drew in, loud in the pregnant silence of this place.

The space behind the pulpit was dominated by a gigantic portrait of Christ, and Burt thought: If nothing else in this town gave Vicky the screaming meemies, this would.

The Christ was grinning, vulpine. His eyes were wide and staring, reminding Burt uneasily of Lon Chaney in *The Phantom of the Opera*. In each of the wide black pupils someone (a sinner, presumably) was drowning in a lake of fire. But the oddest thing was that this Christ had green hair . . . hair which on closer examination revealed itself to be a twining mass of early-summer corn. The picture was crudely done but effective. It looked like a comic-strip mural done by a gifted child— an Old Testament Christ, or a pagan Christ that might slaughter his sheep for sacrifice instead of leading them.

At the foot of the left-hand rank of pews was a pipe organ, and Burt could not at first tell what was wrong with it. He walked down the left-hand aisle and saw with slowly dawning horror that the keys had been ripped up, the stops had been pulled out . . . and the pipes themselves filled with dry cornhusks. Over the organ was a carefully lettered plaque which read: MAKE NO MUSIC EXCEPT WITH HUMAN TONGUE SAITH THE LORD GOD.

Vicky was right. Something was terribly wrong here. He debated going back to Vicky without exploring any further, just getting into the car and leaving town as quickly as possible, never mind the Municipal Building. But it grated on him. Tell the truth, he thought. You want to give her Ban 5000 a workout before going back and admitting she was right to start with.

He would go back out in a minute or so.

He walked toward the pulpit, thinking: People must go through Gatlin all the time. There must be people in the neighboring towns who have friends and relatives here. The Nebraska SP must cruise through from time to time. And what about the power company? The stoplight had been dead. Surely they'd know if the power had been off for twelve long years. Conclusion: What seemed to have happened in Gatlin was impossible.

Still, he had the creeps.

He climbed the four carpeted steps to the pulpit and looked out over the deserted pews, glimmering in the half-shadows. He seemed to feel the weight of those eldritch and decidedly unchristian eyes boring into his back.

There was a large Bible on the lectern, opened to the thirty-eighth chapter of Job. Burt glanced down at it and read: "Then the Lord answered Job out of the whirl-wind, and said, Who is this that darkeneth counsel by words without knowledge? . . . Where wast thou when I laid the foundations of the earth? declare, if thou hast understanding." The lord. He Who Walks Behind the Rows. Declare if thou hast understanding. And please pass the corn.

He fluttered the pages of the Bible, and they made a dry whispering sound in the quiet—the sound that ghosts might make if there really were such things. And in a place like this you could almost believe it. Sections of the Bible had been chopped out. Mostly from the New Testament, he saw. Someone had decided to take on the job of amending Good King James with a pair of scissors.

But the Old Testament was intact.

He was about to leave the pulpit when he saw another book on a lower shelf and took it out, thinking it might be a church record of weddings and confirmations and burials.

He grimaced at the words stamped on the cover, done inexpertly in gold leaf: THUS LET THE INIQUITOUS BE CUT DOWN SO THAT THE GROUND MAY BE FERTILE AGAIN SAITH THE LORD GOD OF HOSTS.

There seemed to be one train of thought around here, and Burt didn't care much for the track it seemed to ride on.

He opened the book to the first wide, lined sheet. A child had done the lettering, he saw immediately. In places an ink eraser had been carefully used, and while there were no misspellings, the letters were large and childishly made, drawn rather than written. The first column read:

Amos Deigan (Richard), b. Sept. 4, 1945   Sept. 4, 1964
Isaac Renfrew (William), b. Sept. 19, 1945   Sept. 19, 1964
Zepeniah Kirk (George), b. Oct. 14, 1945   Oct. 14, 1964
Mary Wells (Roberta), b. Nov. 12, 1945   Nov. 12, 1964
Yemen Hollis (Edward), b. Jan. 5, 1946   Jan. 5, 1965

Frowning, Burt continued to turn through the pages. Three-quarters of the way through, the double columns ended abruptly:

Rachel Stigman (Donna), b. June 21, 1957   June 21, 1976
Moses Richardson (Henry), b. July 29, 1957
Malachi Boardman (Craig), b. August 15, 1957

The last entry in the book was for Ruth Clawson (Sandra), b. April 30, 1961. Burt looked at the shelf where he had found this book and came up with two more. The first had the same INIQUITOUS BE CUT DOWN logo, and it continued the same record, the single column tracing birth dates and names. In early September of 1964 he found Job Gilman (Clayton), b. September 6, and the next entry was Eve Tobin, b. June 16, 1965. No second name in parentheses.

The third book was blank.

Standing behind the pulpit, Burt thought about it.

Something had happened in 1964. Something to do with religion, and corn . . . and children.

Dear God we beg thy blessing on the crop. For Jesus' sake, amen.

And the knife raised high to sacrifice the lamb—but had it been a lamb? Perhaps a religious mania had swept them. Alone, all alone, cut off from the outside world by hundreds of square miles of the rustling secret corn. Alone under seventy million acres of blue sky. Alone under the watchful eye of God, now a strange green God, a God of corn, grown old and strange and hungry. He Who Walks Behind the Rows.

Burt felt a chill creep into his flesh.

Vicky, let me tell you a story. It's about Amos Deigan, who was born Richard Deigan on September 4, 1945. He took the name Amos in 1964, fine Old Testament name, Amos, one of the minor prophets. Well, Vicky, what happened—don't laugh—is that Dick Deigan and his friends—Billy Renfrew, George Kirk, Roberta Wells, and Eddie Hollis among others—they got religion and they killed off their parents. All of them. Isn't that a scream? Shot them in their beds, knifed them in their bathtubs, poisoned their suppers, hung them, or disemboweled them, for all I know.

Why? The corn. Maybe it was dying. Maybe they got the idea somehow that it was dying because there was too much sinning. Not enough sacrifice. They would have done it in the corn, in the rows.

And somehow, Vicky, I'm quite sure of this, somehow they decided that nineteen was as old as any of them could live. Richard "Amos" Deigan, the hero of our little story, had his nineteenth birthday on September 4, 1964—the date in the book. I think maybe they killed him. Sacrificed him in the corn. Isn't that a silly story?

But let's look at Rachel Stigman, who was Donna Stigman until 1964. She turned nineteen on June 21, just about a month ago. Moses Richardson was born on July 29—just three days from today he'll be nineteen. Any idea what's going to happen to ole Mose on the twenty-ninth?

I can guess.

Burt licked his lips, which felt dry.

One other thing, Vicky. Look at this. We have Job Gilman (Clayton) born on September 6, 1964. No other births until June 16, 1965. A gap of ten months. Know what I think? They killed all the parents, even the pregnant ones, that's what I think. And one of *them* got pregnant in October of 1964 and gave birth to Eve. Some sixteen- or seventeen-year-old girl. *Eve. The first woman.*

He thumbed back through the book feverishly and found the Eve Tobin entry. Below it: "Adam Greenlaw, b. July 11, 1965."

They'd be just eleven now, he thought, and his flesh began to crawl. And maybe they're out there. Someplace.

But how could such a thing be kept secret? How could it go on?

How unless the God in question approved?

"Oh Jesus," Burt said into the silence, and that was when the T-Bird's horn began to blare into the afternoon, one long continuous blast.

Burt jumped from the pulpit and ran down the center aisle. He threw open the outer vestibule door, letting in hot sunshine, dazzling. Vicky was bolt upright behind the steering wheel, both hands plastered on the horn ring, her head swiveling wildly. From all around the children were coming. Some of them were laughing gaily. They held knives, hatchets, pipes, rocks, hammers. One girl, maybe eight, with beautiful long blond hair, held a jackhandle. Rural weapons. Not a gun among them. Burt felt a wild urge to scream out: *Which of you is Adam and Eve? Who are the mothers? Who are the daughters? Fathers? Sons?*

Declare, if thou hast understanding.

They came from the side streets, from the town green, through the gate in the chain-link fence around the school playground a block further west. Some of them glanced indifferently at Burt, standing frozen on the church steps, and some nudged each other and pointed and smiled . . . the sweet smiles of children.

The girls were dressed in long brown wool and faded sunbonnets. The boys, like Quaker parsons, were all in black and wore round-crowned flat-brimmed hats. They streamed across the town square toward the car, across lawns, a few came across the front yard of what had been the Grace Baptist Church until 1964. One or two of them almost close enough to touch.

"The shotgun!" Burt yelled. "Vicky, get the shot-gun!"

But she was frozen in her panic, he could see that from the steps. He doubted if she could even hear him through the closed windows.

They converged on the Thunderbird. The axes and hatchets and chunks of pipe began to rise and fall. My God, am I seeing this? he thought frozenly. An arrow of chrome fell off the side of the car. The hood ornament went flying. Knives scrawled spirals through the side-walls of the tires and the car settled. The horn blared on and on. The windshield and side windows went opaque and cracked under the onslaught . . . and then the safety glass sprayed inward and he could see again. Vicky was crouched back, only one hand on the horn ring now, the other thrown up to protect her face. Eager young hands reached in, fumbling for the lock/unlock button. She beat them away wildly. The horn became intermittent and then stopped altogether.

The beaten and dented driver's side door was hauled open. They were trying to drag her out but her hands were wrapped around the steering wheel. Then one of them leaned in, knife in hand, and—

His paralysis broke and he plunged down the steps, almost falling, and ran down the flagstone walk, toward them. One of them, a boy of about sixteen with long red hair spilling out from beneath his hat, turned toward him, almost casually, and something flicked through the air. Burt's left arm jerked backward, and for a moment he had the absurd thought that he had been punched at long distance. Then the pain came, so sharp and sudden that the world went gray.

He examined his arm with a stupid sort of wonder. A buck and a half Pensy jackknife was growing out of it like a strange tumor. The sleeve of his J. C. Penney sport shirt was turning red. He looked at it for what seemed like forever, trying to understand how he could have grown a jackknife . . . was it possible?

When he looked up, the boy with the red hair was almost on top of him. He was grinning, confident.

"Hey, you bastard," Burt said. His voice was creaking, shocked.

"Remand your soul to God, for you will stand before His throne momentarily," the boy with the red hair said, and clawed for Burt's eyes.

Burt stepped back, pulled the Pensy out of his arm, and stuck it into the red-haired boy's throat. The gush of blood was immediate, gigantic. Burt was splashed with it. The red-haired boy began to gobble and walk in a large circle. He clawed at the knife, trying to pull it free, and was unable. Burt watched him, jaw hanging agape. None of this was happening. It was a dream. The red-haired boy gobbled and walked. Now his sound was the only one in the hot early afternoon. The others watched, stunned.

This part of it wasn't in the script, Burt thought numbly. Vicky and I, we were in the script. And the boy in the corn, who was trying to run away. But not one of their own. He stared at them savagely, wanting to scream, *How do you like it?*

The red-haired boy gave one last weak gobble, and sank to his knees. He stared up at Burt for a moment, and then his hands dropped away from the haft of the knife, and he fell forward.

A soft sighing sound from the children gathered around the Thunderbird. They stared at Burt. Burt stared back at them, fascinated . . . and that was when he noticed that Vicky was gone.

"Where is she?" he asked. "Where did you take her?"

One of the boys raised a blood-streaked hunting knife toward his throat and made a sawing motion there. He grinned. That was the only answer.

From somewhere in back, an older boy's voice, soft: "Get him."

The boys began to walk toward him. Burt backed up. They began to walk faster. Burt backed up faster. The shotgun, the goddamned shotgun! Out of reach. The sun cut their shadows darkly on the green church lawn . . . and then he was on the sidewalk. He turned and ran.

"*Kill him!*" someone roared, and they came after him.

He ran, but not quite blindly. He skirted the Municipal Building—no help there, they would corner him like a rat—and ran on up Main Street, which opened out and became the highway again two blocks further up. He and Vicky would have been on that road now and away, if he had only listened.

His loafers slapped against the sidewalk. Ahead of him he could see a few more business buildings, includ-

ing the Gatlin Ice Cream Shoppe and—sure enough—
the Bijou Theater. The dust-clotted marquee letters
read NOW HOWING L MITED EN AGEMEN ELI A TH TAYLOR
CLEOPA RA. Beyond the next cross street was a gas station that marked the edge of town. And beyond that the
corn, closing back in to the sides of the road. A green
tide of corn.

Burt ran. He was already out of breath and the knife
wound in his upper arm was beginning to hurt. And he
was leaving a trail of blood. As he ran he yanked his
handkerchief from his back pocket and stuck it inside
his shirt.

He ran. His loafers pounded the cracked cement of
the sidewalk, his breath rasped in his throat with more
and more heat. His arm began to throb in earnest. Some
mordant part of his brain tried to ask if he thought he
could run all the way to the next town, if he could run
twenty miles of two-lane blacktop.

He ran. Behind him he could hear them, fifteen years
younger and faster than he was, gaining. Their feet
slapped on the pavement. They whooped and shouted
back and forth to each other. They're having more fun
than a five-alarm fire, Burt thought disjointedly. They'll
talk about it for years.

Burt ran.

He ran past the gas station marking the edge of town.
His breath gasped and roared in his chest. The sidewalk
ran out under his feet. And now there was only one
thing to do, only one chance to beat them and escape
with his life. The houses were gone, the town was gone.

The corn had surged in a soft green wave back to the edges of the road. The green, swordlike leaves rustled softly. It would be deep in there, deep and cool, shady in the rows of man-high corn.

He ran past a sign that said: YOU ARE NOW LEAVING GATLIN, NICEST LITTLE TOWN IN NEBRASKA—OR ANY-WHERE ELSE! DROP IN ANYTIME!

I'll be sure to do that, Burt thought dimly.

He ran past the sign like a sprinter closing on the tape and then swerved left, crossing the road, and kicked his loafers away. Then he was in the corn and it closed behind him and over him like the waves of a green sea, taking him in. Hiding him. He felt a sudden and wholly unexpected relief sweep him, and at the same moment he got his second wind. His lungs, which had been shal-lowing up, seemed to unlock and give him more breath.

He ran straight down the first row he had entered, head ducked, his broad shoulders swiping the leaves and making them tremble. Twenty yards in he turned right, parallel to the road again, and ran on, keeping low so they wouldn't see his dark head of hair bobbing amid the yellow corn tassels. He doubled back toward the road for a few moments, crossed more rows, and then put his back to the road and hopped randomly from row to row, always delving deeper and deeper into the corn.

At last, he collapsed onto his knees and put his fore-head against the ground. He could only hear his own taxed breathing, and the thought that played over and over in his mind was: *Thank God I gave up smoking, thank God I gave up smoking, thank God—*

Then he could hear them, yelling back and forth to each other, in some cases bumping into each other ("Hey, this is my row!"), and the sound heartened him. They were well away to his left and they sounded very poorly organized.

He took his handkerchief out of his shirt, folded it, and stuck it back in after looking at the wound. The bleeding seemed to have stopped in spite of the workout he had given it.

He rested a moment longer, and was suddenly aware that he felt *good,* physically better than he had in years . . . excepting the throb of his arm. He felt well exercised, and suddenly grappling with a clearcut (no matter how insane) problem after two years of trying to cope with the incubotic gremlins that were sucking his marriage dry.

It wasn't right that he should feel this way, he told himself. He was in deadly peril of his life, and his wife had been carried off. She might be dead now. He tried to summon up Vicky's face and dispel some of the odd good feeling by doing so, but her face wouldn't come. What came was the red-haired boy with the knife in his throat.

He became aware of the corn fragrance in his nose now, all around him. The wind through the tops of the plants made a sound like voices. Soothing. Whatever had been done in the name of this corn, it was now his protector.

But they were getting closer.

Running hunched over, he hurried up the row he was

in, crossed over, doubled back, and crossed over more rows. He tried to keep the voices always on his left, but as the afternoon progressed, that became harder and harder to do. The voices had grown faint, and often the rustling sound of the corn obscured them altogether. He would run, listen, run again. The earth was hard-packed, and his stockinged feet left little or no trace.

When he stopped much later the sun was hanging over the fields to his right, red and inflamed, and when he looked at his watch he saw that it was quarter past seven. The sun had stained the corntops a reddish gold, but here the shadows were dark and deep. He cocked his head, listening. With the coming of sunset the wind had died entirely and the corn stood still, exhaling its aroma of growth into the warm air. If they were still in the corn they were either far away or just hunkered down and listening. But Burt didn't think a bunch of kids, even crazy ones, could be quiet for that long. He suspected they had done the most kidlike thing, regardless of the consequences for them: they had given up and gone home.

He turned toward the setting sun, which had sunk between the raftered clouds on the horizon, and began to walk. If he cut on a diagonal through the rows, always keeping the setting sun ahead of him, he would be bound to strike Route 17 sooner or later.

The ache in his arm had settled into a dull throb that was nearly pleasant, and the good feeling was still with him. He decided that as long as he was here, he would let the good feeling exist in him without guilt. The guilt would return when he had to face the authorities and account for what had happened in Gatlin. But that could wait.

He pressed through the corn, thinking he had never felt so keenly aware. Fifteen minutes later the sun was only a hemisphere poking over the horizon and he stopped again, his new awareness clicking into a pattern he didn't like. It was vaguely . . . well, vaguely frightening.

He cocked his head. The corn was rustling.

Burt had been aware of that for some time, but he had just put it together with something else. The wind was still. How could that be?

He looked around warily, half expecting to see the smiling boys in their Quaker coats creeping out of the corn, their knives clutched in their hands. Nothing of the sort. There was still that rustling noise. Off to the left.

He began to walk in that direction, not having to bull through the corn anymore. The row was taking him in the direction he wanted to go, naturally. The row ended up ahead. Ended? No, emptied out into some sort of clearing. The rustling was there.

He stopped, suddenly afraid.

The scent of the corn was strong enough to be cloying. The rows held on to the sun's heat and he became aware that he was plastered with sweat and chaff and thin spider strands of cornsilk. The bugs ought to be crawling all over him . . . but they weren't.

He stood still, staring toward that place where the

corn opened out onto what looked like a large circle of bare earth.

There were no minges or mosquitoes in here, no blackflies or chiggers—what he and Vicky had called "drive-in bugs" when they had been courting, he thought with sudden and unexpectedly sad nostalgia. And he hadn't seen a single crow. How was that for weird, a cornpatch with no crows?

In the last of the daylight he swept his eyes closely over the row of corn to his left. And saw that every leaf and stalk was perfect, which was just not possible. No yellow blight. No tattered leaves, no caterpillar eggs, no burrows, no—

His eyes widened.

My God, there aren't any weeds!

Not a single one. Every foot and a half the corn plants rose from the earth. There was no witchgrass, jimson, pikeweed, whore's hair, or poke salad. Nothing.

Burt stared up, eyes wide. The light in the west was fading. The raftered clouds had drawn back together. Below them the golden light had faded to pink and ocher. It would be dark soon enough.

It was time to go down to the clearing in the corn and see what was there—hadn't that been the plan all along? All the time he had thought he was cutting back to the highway, hadn't he been being led to this place?

Dread in his belly, he went on down to the row and stood at the edge of the clearing. There was enough light left for him to see what was here. He couldn't scream. There didn't seem to be enough air left in his lungs. He tottered in on legs like slats of splintery wood. His eyes bulged from his sweaty face.

"Vicky," he whispered. "Oh, Vicky, my God—"

She had been mounted on a crossbar like a hideous trophy, her arms held at the wrists and her legs at the ankles with twists of common barbed wire, seventy cents a yard at any hardware store in Nebraska. Her eyes had been ripped out. The sockets were filled with the moonflax of cornsilk. Her jaws were wrenched open in a silent scream, her mouth filled with cornhusks.

On her left was a skeleton in a moldering surplice. The nude jawbone grinned. The eye sockets seemed to stare at Burt jocularly, as if the onetime minister of the Grace Baptist Church was saying: *It's not so bad, being sacrificed by pagan devil-children in the corn is not so bad, having your eyes ripped out of your skull according to the Laws of Moses is not so bad—*

To the left of the skeleton in the surplice was a second skeleton, this one dressed in a rotting blue uniform. A hat hung over the skull, shading the eyes, and on the peak of the cap was a greenish-tinged badge reading POLICE CHIEF.

That was when Burt heard it coming: not the children but something much larger, moving through the corn and toward the clearing. Not the children, no. The children wouldn't venture into the corn at night. This was the holy place, the place of He Who Walks Behind the Rows.

Jerkily Burt turned to flee. The row he had entered the clearing by was gone. Closed up. All the rows had closed up. It was coming closer now and he could hear it, pushing through the corn. He could hear it breathing. An ecstasy of superstitious terror seized him. It was coming. The corn on the far side of the clearing had suddenly darkened, as if a gigantic shadow had blotted it out.

Coming.

He Who Walks Behind the Rows.

It began to come into the clearing. Burt saw something huge, bulking up to the sky . . . something green with terrible red eyes the size of footballs.

Something that smelled like dried cornhusks years in some dark barn.

He began to scream. But he did not scream long.

Some time later, a bloated orange harvest moon came up.

———

The children of the corn stood in the clearing at midday, looking at the two crucified skeletons and the two bodies . . . the bodies were not skeletons yet, but they would be. In time. And here, in the heartland of Nebraska, in the corn, there was nothing but time.

"Behold, a dream came to me in the night, and the Lord did shew all this to me."

They all turned to look at Isaac with dread and wonder, even Malachi. Isaac was only nine, but he had been the Seer since the corn had taken David a year ago. David had been nineteen and he had walked into the corn on his birthday, just as dusk had come drifting down the summer rows.

Now, small face grave under his round-crowned hat, Isaac continued:

"And in my dream the Lord was a shadow that walked behind the rows, and he spoke to me in the words he used to our older brothers years ago. He is much displeased with this sacrifice."

They made a sighing, sobbing noise and looked at the surrounding walls of green.

"And the Lord did say: Have I not given you a place of killing, that you might make sacrifice there? And have I not shewn you favor? But this man has made a blasphemy within me, and I have completed this sacrifice myself. Like the Blue Man and the false minister who escaped many years ago."

"The Blue Man . . . the false minister," they whispered, and looked at each other uneasily.

"So now is the Age of Favor lowered from nineteen plantings and harvestings to eighteen," Isaac went on relentlessly. "Yet be fruitful and multiply as the corn multiplies, that my favor may be shewn you, and be upon you."

Isaac ceased.

The eyes turned to Malachi and Joseph, the only two among this party who were eighteen. There were others back in town, perhaps twenty in all.

They waited to hear what Malachi would say, Malachi who had led the hunt for Japheth, who evermore would be known as Ahaz, cursed of God. Malachi had cut the throat of Ahaz and had thrown his body out of the corn so the foul body would not pollute it or blight it.

"I obey the word of God," Malachi whispered.

The corn seemed to sigh its approval.

In the weeks to come the girls would make many corncob crucifixes to ward off further evil.

And that night all of those now above the Age of Favor walked silently into the corn and went to the clearing, to gain the continued favor of He Who Walks Behind the Rows.

"Goodbye, Malachi," Ruth called. She waved disconsolately. Her belly was big with Malachi's child and tears coursed silently down her cheeks. Malachi did not turn. His back was straight. The corn swallowed him.

Ruth turned away, still crying. She had conceived a secret hatred for the corn and sometimes dreamed of walking into it with a torch in each hand when dry September came and the stalks were dead and explosively combustile. But she also feared it. Out there, in the night, something walked, and it saw everything . . . even the secrets kept in human hearts.

Dusk deepened into night. Around Gatlin the corn rustled and whispered secretly. It was well pleased.

THE LAST RUNG ON THE LADDER

I got Katrina's letter yesterday, less than a week after my father and I got back from Los Angeles. It was addressed to Wilmington, Delaware, and I'd moved twice since then. People move around so much now, and it's funny how those crossed-off addresses and change-of-address stickers can look like accusations. Her letter was rumpled and smudged, one of the corners dog-eared from handling. I read what was in it and the next thing I knew I was standing in the living room with the phone in my hand, getting ready to call Dad. I put the phone down with something like horror. He was an old man, and he'd had two heart attacks. Was I going to call him and tell about Katrina's letter so soon after we'd been in L.A.? To do that might very well have killed him.

So I didn't call. And I had no one I could tell . . . a thing like that letter, it's too personal to tell anyone except a wife or a very close friend. I haven't made many close friends in the last few years, and my wife Helen and I divorced in 1971. What we exchange now are Christmas cards. How are you? How's the job? Have a happy New Year.

I've been awake all night with it, with Katrina's letter. She could have put it on a postcard. There was only a single sentence below the "Dear Larry." But a sentence can mean enough. It can do enough.

I remembered my dad on the plane, his face seeming old and wasted in the harsh sunlight at 18,000 feet as we went west from New York. We had just passed over Omaha, according to the pilot, and Dad said, "It's a lot further away than it looks, Larry." There was a heavy sadness in his voice that made me uncomfortable because I couldn't understand it. I understood it better after getting Katrina's letter.

We grew up eighty miles west of Omaha in a town called Hemingford Home—my dad, my mom, my sister Katrina, and me. I was two years older than Katrina, whom everyone called Kitty. She was a beautiful child and a beautiful woman—even at eight, the year of the incident in the barn, you could see that her cornsilk hair was never going to darken and that those eyes would always be a dark, Scandinavian blue. A look in those eyes and a man would be gone.

I guess you'd say we grew up hicks. My dad had three hundred acres of flat, rich land, and he grew feed corn and raised cattle. Everybody just called it "the home place." In those days all the roads were dirt except Interstate 80 and Nebraska Route 96, and a trip to town was something you waited three days for.

Nowadays I'm one of the best independent corporation lawyers in America, so they tell me—and I'd have to admit for the sake of honesty that I think they're right. A president of a large company once introduced me to his board of directors as his hired gun. I wear expensive suits and my shoeleather is the best. I've got three assistants on full-time pay, and I can call in another dozen if I need them. But in those days I walked up a dirt road to a one-room school with books tied in a belt over my shoulder, and Katrina walked with me. Sometimes, in the spring, we went barefoot. That was in the days before you couldn't get served in a diner or shop in a market unless you were wearing shoes.

Later on, my mother died—Katrina and I were in high school up at Columbia City then—and two years after that my dad lost the place and went to work selling tractors. It was the end of the family, although that didn't seem so bad then. Dad got along in his work, bought himself a dealership, and got tapped for a management position about nine years ago. I got a football scholarship to the University of Nebraska and managed to learn something besides how to run the ball out of a slot-right formation.

And Katrina? But it's her I want to tell you about.

It happened, the barn thing, one Saturday in early November. To tell you the truth I can't pin down the actual year, but Ike was still President. Mom was at a bake fair in Columbia City, and Dad had gone over to our nearest neighbor's (and that was seven miles away) to help the man fix a hayrake. There was supposed to be a hired man on the place, but he had never showed up that day, and my dad fired him not a month later.

Dad left me a list of chores to do (and there were some for Kitty, too) and told us not to get to playing until they were all done. But that wasn't long. It was November, and by that time of year the make-or-break time had gone past. We'd made it again that year. We wouldn't always.

I remember that day very clearly. The sky was overcast and while it wasn't cold, you could feel it *wanting* to be cold, wanting to get down to the business of frost and freeze, snow and sleet. The fields were stripped. The animals were sluggish and morose. There seemed to be funny little drafts in the house that had never been there before.

On a day like that, the only really nice place to be was the barn. It was warm, filled with a pleasant mixed aroma of hay and fur and dung, and with the mysterious chuckling, cooing sounds of the barnswallows high up in the third loft. If you cricked your neck up, you could see the white November light coming through the chinks in the roof and try to spell your name. It was a game that really only seemed agreeable on overcast autumn days.

There was a ladder nailed to a crossbeam high up in the third loft, a ladder that went straight down to the main barn floor. We were forbidden to climb on it because it was old and shaky. Dad had promised Mom a thousand times that he would pull it down and put up a stronger one, but something else always seemed to come up when there was time . . . helping a neighbor with his hayrake, for instance. And the hired man was just not working out.

If you climbed up that rickety ladder—there were exactly forty-three rungs, Kitty and I had counted them enough to know—you ended up on a beam that was seventy feet above the straw-littered barn floor. And then if you edged out along the beam about twelve feet, your knees jittering, your ankle joints creaking, your mouth dry and tasting like a used fuse, you stood over the haymow. And then you could jump off the beam and fall seventy feet straight down, with a horrible hilarious dying swoop, into a huge soft bed of lush hay. It has a sweet smell, hay does, and you'd come to rest in that smell of reborn summer with your stomach left behind you way up there in the middle of the air, and you'd feel . . . well, like Lazarus must have felt. You had taken the fall and lived to tell the tale.

It was a forbidden sport, all right. If we had been caught, my mother would have shrieked blue murder and my father would have laid on the strap, even at our advanced ages. Because of the ladder, and because if you happened to lose your balance and topple from the beam before you had edged out over the loose fathoms of hay, you would fall to utter destruction on the hard planking of the barn floor.

But the temptation was just too great. When the cats are away . . . well, you know how that one goes.

That day started like all the others, a delicious feeling of dread mixed with anticipation. We stood at the foot of the ladder, looking at each other. Kitty's color was high, her eyes darker and more sparkling than ever.

"Dare you," I said.

Promptly from Kitty: "Dares go first."

Promptly from me: "Girls go before boys."

"Not if it's dangerous," she said, casting her eyes down demurely, as if everybody didn't know she was the second-biggest tomboy in Hemingford. But that was how she was about it. She would go, but she wouldn't go first.

"Okay," I said. "Here I go."

I was ten that year, and thin as Scratch-the-demon, about ninety pounds. Kitty was eight, and twenty pounds lighter. The ladder had always held us before, we thought it would always hold us again, which is a philosophy that gets men and nations in trouble time after time.

I could feel it that day, beginning to shimmy around a little bit in the dusty barn air as I climbed higher and higher. As always, about halfway up, I entertained a vision of what would happen to me if it suddenly let go and gave up the ghost. But I kept going until I was able to clap my hands around the beam and boost myself up and look down.

Kitty's face, turned up to watch me, was a small white oval. In her faded checked shirt and blue denims, she looked like a doll. Above me still higher, in the dusty reaches of the eaves, the swallows cooed mellowly.

Again, by rote:

"Hi, down there!" I called, my voice floating down to her on motes of chaff.

"Hi, up there!"

I stood up. Swayed back and forth a little. As always, there seemed suddenly to be strange currents in the air that had not existed down below. I could hear my own heartbeat as I began to inch along with my arms held out for balance. Once, a swallow had swooped close by my head during this part of the adventure, and in drawing back I had almost lost my balance. I lived in fear of the same thing happening again.

But not this time. At last I stood above the safety of the hay. Now looking down was not so much frightening as sensual. There was a moment of anticipation. Then I stepped off into space, holding my nose for effect, and as it always did, the sudden grip of gravity, yanking me down brutally, making me plummet, made me feel like yelling: *Oh, I'm sorry, I made a mistake, let me back up!*

Then I hit the hay, shot into it like a projectile, its sweet and dusty smell billowing up around me, still going down, as if into heavy water, coming slowly to rest buried in the stuff. As always, I could feel a sneeze building up in my nose. And hear a frightened field mouse or two fleeing for a more serene section of the haymow. And feel, in that curious way, that I had been reborn. I remember Kitty telling me once that after diving into the hay she felt fresh and new, like a baby. I shrugged it off at the time—sort of knowing what she meant, sort of not knowing—but since I got her letter I think about that, too.

I climbed out of the hay, sort of swimming through it, until I could climb out onto the barn floor. I had hay down my pants and down the back of my shirt. It was on my sneakers and sticking to my elbows. Hayseeds in my hair? You bet.

She was halfway up the ladder by then, her gold pigtails bouncing against her shoulderblades, climbing through a dusty shaft of light. On other days that light might have been as bright as her hair, but on this day her pigtails had no competition—they were easily the most colorful thing up there.

I remember thinking that I didn't like the way the ladder was swaying back and forth. It seemed like it had never been so loosey-goosey.

Then she was on the beam, high above me—now I was the small one, my face was the small white upturned oval as her voice floated down on errant chaff stirred up by my leap:

"Hi, down there!"

"Hi, up there!"

She edged along the beam, and my heart loosened a little in my chest when I judged she was over the safety of the hay. It always did, although she was always more graceful than I was . . . and more athletic, if that doesn't sound like too strange a thing to say about your kid sister.

She stood, poising on the toes of her old low-topped Keds, hands out in front of her. And then she swanned. Talk about things you can't forget, things you can't describe. Well, I can describe it . . . in a way. But not in a way that will make you understand how beautiful that was, how perfect, one of the few things in my life that seem utterly real, utterly true. No, I can't tell you like that. I don't have the skill with either my pen or my tongue.

For a moment she seemed to hang in the air, as if borne up by one of those mysterious updrafts that only existed in the third loft, a bright swallow with golden plumage such as Nebraska has never seen since. She was Kitty, my sister, her arms swept behind her and her back arched, and how I loved her for that beat of time!

Then she came down and plowed into the hay and out of sight. An explosion of chaff and giggles rose out of the hole she made. I'd forgotten about how rickety the ladder had looked with her on it, and by the time she was out, I was halfway up again.

I tried to swan myself, but the fear grabbed me the way it always did, and my swan turned into a cannon-ball. I think I never believed the hay was there the way Kitty believed it.

How long did the game go on? Hard to tell. But I looked up some ten or twelve dives later and saw the light had changed. Our mom and dad were due back and we were all covered with chaff . . . as good as a signed confession. We agreed on one more turn each.

Going up first, I felt the ladder moving beneath me and I could hear—very faintly—the whining rasp of old nails loosening up in the wood. And for the first time I was really, actively scared. I think if I'd been closer to the bottom I would have gone down and that would have been the end of it, but the beam was closer and seemed safer. Three rungs from the top the whine of pulling nails grew louder and I was suddenly cold with terror, with the certainty that I had pushed it too far.

Then I had the splintery beam in my hands, taking my weight off the ladder, and there was a cold, unpleasant sweat matting the twigs of hay to my forehead. The fun of the game was gone.

I hurried out over the hay and dropped off. Even the pleasurable part of the drop was gone. Coming down, I imagined how I'd feel if that was solid barn planking coming up to meet me instead of the yielding give of the hay.

I came out to the middle of the barn to see Kitty hurrying up the ladder. I called: "Hey, come down! It's not safe!"

"It'll hold me!" she called back confidently. "I'm lighter than you!"

"Kitty—"

But that never got finished. Because that was when the ladder let go.

It went with a rotted, splintering crack. I cried out and Kitty screamed. She was about where I had been when I'd become convinced I'd pressed my luck too far.

The rung she was standing on gave way, and then both sides of the ladder split. For a moment the ladder below her, which had broken entirely free, looked like a ponderous insect—a praying mantis or a ladderbug—which had just decided to walk off.

Then it toppled, hitting the barn floor with a flat clap

that raised dust and caused the cows to moo worriedly. One of them kicked at its stall door.

Kitty uttered a high, piercing scream.

"Larry! Larry! Help me!"

I knew what had to be done, I saw right away. I was terribly afraid, but not quite scared out of my wits. She was better than sixty feet above me, her blue-jeaned legs kicking wildly at the blank air, then barnswallows cooing above her. I was scared, all right. And you know, I still can't watch a circus aerial act, not even on TV. It makes my stomach feel weak.

But I knew what had to be done.

"Kitty!" I bawled up at her. "Just hold still! *Hold still!*"

She obeyed me instantly. Her legs stopped kicking and she hung straight down, her small hands clutching the last rung on the ragged end of the ladder like an acrobat whose trapeze has stopped.

I ran to the haymow, clutched up a double handful of the stuff, ran back, and dropped it. I went back again. And again. And again.

I really don't remember it after that, except the hay got up my nose and I started sneezing and couldn't stop. I ran back and forth, building a haystack where the foot of the ladder had been. It was a very small haystack. Looking at it, then looking at her hanging so far above it, you might have thought of one of those cartoons where the guy jumps three hundred feet into a water glass.

Back and forth. Back and forth.

"Larry, I can't hold on much longer!" Her voice was high and despairing.

"Kitty, you've got to! You've got to hold on!"

Back and forth. Hay down my shirt. Back and forth. The haystack was as high as my chin now, but the hay-mow we had been diving into was twenty-five feet deep. I thought that if she only broke her legs it would be getting off cheap. And I knew if she missed the hay altogether, she would be killed. Back and forth.

"Larry! The rung! It's letting go!"

I could hear the steady, rasping cry of the rung pulling free under her weight. Her legs began to kick again in panic, but if she was thrashing like that, she would surely miss the hay.

"No!" I yelled. "No! Stop that! Just let go! Let go, Kitty!" Because it was too late for me to get any more hay. Too late for anything except blind hope.

She let go and dropped the second I told her to. She came straight down like a knife. It seemed to me that she dropped forever, her gold pigtails standing straight up from her head, her eyes shut, her face as pale as china. She didn't scream. Her hands were locked in front of her lips, as if she was praying.

And she struck the hay right in the center. She went down out of sight in it—hay flew up all around as if a shell had struck—and I heard the thump of her body hitting the boards. The sound, a loud thud, sent a deadly chill into me. It had been too loud, much too loud. But I had to see.

Starting to cry, I pounced on the haystack and pulled

it apart, flinging the straw behind me in great handfuls. A blue-jeaned leg came to light, then a plaid shirt . . . and then Kitty's face. It was deadly pale and her eyes were shut. She was dead, I knew it as I looked at her. The world went gray for me, November gray. The only things in it with any color were her pigtails, bright gold.

And then the deep blue of her irises as she opened her eyes.

"Kitty?" My voice was hoarse, husky, unbelieving. My throat was coated with haychaff. "Kitty?"

"Larry?" she asked, bewildered. "Am I alive?"

I picked her out of the hay and hugged her and she put her arms around my neck and hugged me back.

"You're alive," I said. "You're alive, you're alive."

———

She had broken her left ankle and that was all. When Dr. Pedersen, the GP from Columbia City, came out to the barn with my father and me, he looked up into the shadows for a long time. The last rung on the ladder still hung there, aslant, from one nail.

He looked, as I said, for a long time. "A miracle," he said to my father, and then kicked disdainfully at the hay I'd put down. He went out to his dusty DeSoto and drove away.

My father's hand came down on my shoulder. "We're going to the woodshed, Larry," he said in a very calm voice. "I believe you know what's going to happen there."

"Yes, sir," I whispered.

"Every time I whack you, Larry, I want you to thank God your sister is still alive."

"Yes, sir."

Then we went. He whacked me plenty of times, so many times I ate standing up for a week and with a cushion on my chair for two weeks after that. And every time he whacked me with his big red callused hand, I thanked God.

In a loud, loud voice. By the last two or three whacks, I was pretty sure He was hearing me.

———

They let me in to see her just before bedtime. There was a catbird outside her window, I remember that. Her foot, all wrapped up, was propped on a board.

She looked at me so long and so lovingly that I was uncomfortable. Then she said, "Hay. You put down hay."

"Course I did," I blurted. "What else would I do? Once the ladder broke there was no way to get up there."

"I didn't know what you were doing," she said.

"You must have! I was right under you, for cripe's sake!"

"I didn't dare look down," she said. "I was too scared. I had my eyes shut the whole time."

I stared at her, thunderstruck.

"You didn't know? Didn't know what I was doing?"

She shook her head.

"And when I told you to let go you . . . you just *did it?*"

She nodded.

"Kitty, how could you do that?"

She looked at me with those deep blue eyes. "I knew you must have been doing something to fix it," she said. "You're my big brother. I knew you'd take care of me."

"Oh, Kitty, you don't know how close it was."

I had put my hands over my face. She sat up and took them away. She kissed my cheek. "No," she said. "But I knew you were down there. Gee, am I sleepy. I'll see you tomorrow, Larry. I'm going to have a cast, Dr. Pedersen says."

She had the cast on for a little less than a month, and all her classmates signed it—she even got me to sign it. And when it came off, that was the end of the barn incident. My father replaced the ladder up to the third loft with a new strong one, but I never climbed up to the beam and jumped off into the haymow again. So far as I know, Kitty didn't either.

It was the end, but somehow not the end. Somehow it never ended until nine days ago, when Kitty jumped from the top story of an insurance building in Los Angeles. I have the clipping from the L.A. *Times* in my wallet. I guess I'll always carry it, not in the good way you carry snapshots of people you want to remember or theater tickets from a really good show or part of the program from a World Series game. I carry that clipping the way you carry something heavy, because carrying it is your work. The headline reads: *CALL GIRL SWAN-DIVES TO HER DEATH*.

We grew up. That's all I know, other than facts that don't mean anything. She was going to go to business college in Omaha, but in the summer after she graduated from high school, she won a beauty contest and married one of the judges. It sounds like a dirty joke, doesn't it? My Kitty.

While I was in law school she got divorced and wrote me a long letter, ten pages or more, telling me how it had been, how messy it had been, how it might have been better if she could have had a child. She asked me if I could come. But losing a week in law school is like losing a term in liberal-arts undergraduate. Those guys are greyhounds. If you lose sight of the little mechanical rabbit, it's gone forever.

She moved to L.A. and got married again. When that one broke up I was out of law school. There was another letter, a shorter one, more bitter. She was never going to get stuck on *that* merry-go-round, she told me. It was a fix job. The only way you could catch the brass ring was to tumble off the horse and crack your skull. If that was what the price of a free ride was, who wanted it? PS, Can you come, Larry? It's been a while.

I wrote back and told her I'd love to come, but I couldn't. I had landed a job in a high-pressure firm, low guy on the totem pole, all the work and none of the credit. If I was going to make it up to the next step, it would have to be that year. That was *my* long letter, and it was all about my career.

I answered all of her letters. But I could never really believe that it was really Kitty who was writing them, you know, no more than I could really believe that the hay was really there . . . until it broke my fall at the bottom of the drop and saved my life. I couldn't believe that my sister and the beaten woman who signed "Kitty" in a circle at the bottom of her letters were really the same person. My sister was a girl with pigtails, still without breasts.

She was the one who stopped writing. I'd get Christmas cards, birthday cards, and my wife would reciprocate. Then we got divorced and I moved and just forgot. The next Christmas and the birthday after, the cards came through the forwarding address. The first one. And I kept thinking: Gee, I've got to write Kitty and tell her that I've moved. But I never did.

———

But as I've told you, those are facts that don't mean anything. The only things that matter are that we grew up and she swanned from that insurance building, and that Kitty was the one who always believed the hay would be there. Kitty was the one who had said, "I knew you must be doing something to fix it." Those things matter. And Kitty's letter.

People move around so much now, and it's funny how those crossed-off addresses and change-of-address stickers can look like accusations. She'd printed her return address in the upper left corner of the envelope, the place she'd been staying at until she jumped. A very nice apartment building on Van Nuys. Dad and I went there to pick up her things. The landlady was nice. She had liked Kitty.

The letter was postmarked two weeks before she died. It would have gotten to me a long time before, if not for the forwarding addresses. She must have gotten tired of waiting.

> *Dear Larry,*
>
> *I've been thinking about it a lot lately . . . and what I've decided is that it would have been better for me if that last rung had broken before you could put the hay down.*
>
> > *Your,*
> > *Kitty*

Yes, I guess she must have gotten tired of waiting. I'd rather believe that than think of her deciding I must have forgotten. I wouldn't want her to think that, because that one sentence was maybe the only thing that would have brought me on the run.

But not even that is the reason sleep comes so hard now. When I close my eyes and start to drift off, I see her coming down from the third loft, her eyes wide and dark blue, her body arched, her arms swept up behind her.

She was the one who always knew the hay would be there.

THE MAN WHO LOVED FLOWERS

On an early evening in May of 1963, a young man with his hand in his pocket walked briskly up New York's Third Avenue. The air was soft and beautiful, the sky was darkening by slow degrees from blue to the calm and lovely violet of dusk. There are people who love the city, and this was one of the nights that made them love it. Everyone standing in the doorways of the delicatessens and dry-cleaning shops and restaurants seemed to be smiling. An old lady pushing two bags of groceries in an old baby pram grinned at the young man and hailed him: "Hey, beautiful!" The young man gave her a half-smile and raised his hand in a wave.

She passed on her way, thinking: *He's in love.*

He had that look about him. He was dressed in a light gray suit, the narrow tie pulled down a little, his top collar button undone. His hair was dark and cut short. His complexion was fair, his eyes a light blue. Not an extraordinary face, but on this soft spring evening, on this avenue, in May of 1963, he *was* beautiful, and the old woman found herself thinking with a moment's sweet nostalgia that in spring anyone can be beautiful . . . if they're hurrying to meet the one of their dreams for dinner and maybe dancing after. Spring is the only season when nostalgia never seems to turn bitter, and she went on her way glad that she had spoken to him and glad he had returned the compliment by raising his hand in half-salute.

The young man crossed Sixty-third Street, walking with a bounce in his step and that same half-smile on his lips. Partway up the block, an old man stood beside a chipped green handcart filled with flowers—the predominant color was yellow; a yellow fever of jonquils and late crocuses. The old man also had carnations and a few hothouse tea roses, mostly yellow and white. He was eating a pretzel and listening to a bulky transistor radio that was sitting kitty-corner on his handcart.

The radio poured out bad news that no one listened to: a hammer murderer was still on the loose; JFK had declared that the situation in a little Asian country called Vietnam ("Vitenum" the guy reading the news called it) would bear watching; an unidentified woman had been pulled from the East River; a grand jury had failed to indict a crime overlord in the current city administration's war on heroin; the Russians had exploded a nuclear device. None of it seemed real, none of it seemed to matter. The air was soft and sweet. Two men with beer bellies stood outside a bakery, pitching nickels and ribbing each other. Spring trembled on the edge of summer, and in the city, summer is the season of dreams.

The young man passed the flower stand and the sound of the bad news faded. He hesitated, looked over his shoulder, and thought it over. He reached into his coat pocket and touched the something in there again. For a moment his face seemed puzzled, lonely, almost haunted, and then, as his hand left the pocket, it regained its former expression of eager expectation.

He turned back to the flower stand, smiling. He would bring her some flowers, that would please her. He loved to see her eyes light up with surprise and joy when he brought her a surprise—little things, because he was far from rich. A box of candy. A bracelet. Once only a bag of Valencia oranges, because he knew they were Norma's favorite.

"My young friend," the flower vendor said, as the man in the gray suit came back, running his eyes over the stock in the handcart. The vendor was maybe sixty-eight, wearing a torn gray knitted sweater and a soft cap in spite of the warmth of the evening. His face was a map of wrinkles, his eyes were deep in pouches, and a cigarette jittered between his fingers. But he also remembered how it was to be young in the spring— young and so much in love that you practically zoomed everywhere. The vendor's face was normally sour, but now he smiled a little, just as the old woman pushing the groceries had, because this guy was such an obvious case. He brushed pretzel crumbs from the front of his baggy sweater and thought: If this kid were sick, they'd have him in intensive care right now.

"How much are your flowers?" the young man asked.

"I'll make you up a nice bouquet for a dollar. Those tea roses, they're hothouse. Cost a little more, seventy cents apiece. I sell you half a dozen for three dollars and fifty cents."

"Expensive," the young man said.

"Nothing good comes cheap, my young friend. Didn't your mother ever teach you that?"

The young man grinned. "She might have mentioned it at that."

"Sure. Sure she did. I give you half a dozen, two red, two yellow, two white. Can't do no better than that, can I? Put in some baby's breath—they love that—and fill it out with some fern. Nice. Or you can have the bouquet for a dollar."

"They?" the young man asked, still smiling.

"My young friend," the flower vendor said, flicking his cigarette butt into the gutter and returning the smile, "no one buys flowers for themselves in May. It's like a national law, you understand what I mean?"

The young man thought of Norma, her happy, surprised eyes and her gentle smile, and he ducked his head a little. "I guess I do at that," he said.

"Sure you do. What do you say?"

"Well, what do *you* think?"

"I'm gonna tell you what I think. Hey! Advice is still free, isn't it?"

The young man smiled and said, "I guess it's the only thing left that is."

"You're damn tooting it is," the flower vendor said. "Okay, my young friend. If the flowers are for your mother, you get her the bouquet. A few jonquils, a few crocuses, some lily of the valley. She don't spoil it by saying, 'Oh Junior I love them how much did they cost oh that's too much don't you know enough not to throw your money around?' "

The young man threw his head back and laughed.

The vendor said, "But if it's your girl, that's a different thing, my son, and you know it. You bring her the tea roses and she don't turn into an accountant, you take my meaning? Hey! She's gonna throw her arms around your neck—"

"I'll take the tea roses," the young man said, and this time it was the flower vendor's turn to laugh. The two men pitching nickels glanced over, smiling.

"Hey, kid!" one of them called. "You wanna buy a weddin' ring cheap? I'll sell you mine . . . I don't want it no more."

The young man grinned and blushed to the roots of his dark hair.

The flower vendor picked out six tea roses, snipped the stems a little, spritzed them with water, and wrapped them in a large conical spill.

"Tonight's weather looks just the way you'd want it," the radio said. "Fair and mild, temps in the mid to upper sixties, perfect for a little rooftop stargazing, if you're the romantic type. Enjoy, Greater New York, enjoy!"

The flower vendor Scotch-taped the seam of the paper spill and advised the young man to tell his lady that a little sugar added to the water she put them in would preserve them longer.

"I'll tell her," the young man said. He held out a five-dollar bill. "Thank you."

"Just doing the job, my young friend," the vendor said, giving him a dollar and two quarters. His smile grew a bit sad. "Give her a kiss for me."

On the radio, the Four Seasons began singing "Sherry." The young man pocketed his change and went on up the street, eyes wide and alert and eager, looking not so much around him at the life ebbing and flowing up and down Third Avenue as inward and ahead, anticipating. But certain things did impinge: a mother pulling a baby in a wagon, the baby's face comically smeared with ice cream; a little girl jumping rope and singsonging out her rhyme: "Betty and Henry up in a tree, K-I-S-S-I-N-G! First comes love, then comes marriage, here comes Henry with a baby carriage!" Two women stood outside a washateria, smoking and comparing pregnancies. A group of men were looking in a hardware-store window at a gigantic color TV with a four-figure price tag—a baseball game was on, and all the players' faces looked green. The playing field was a vague strawberry color, and the New York Mets were leading the Phillies by a score of six to one in the top of the ninth.

He walked on, carrying the flowers, unaware that the two women outside the washateria had stopped talking for a moment and had watched him wistfully as he walked by with his paper of tea roses; their days of receiving flowers were long over. He was unaware of a young traffic cop who stopped the cars at the intersection of Third and Sixty-ninth with a blast on his whistle to let him cross; the cop was engaged himself and recognized the dreamy expression on the young man's face from his own shaving mirror, where he had often seen it lately. He was unaware of the two teen-aged girls who passed him going the other way and then clutched themselves and giggled.

At Seventy-third Street he stopped and turned right. This street was a little darker, lined with brownstones and walk-down restaurants with Italian names. Three blocks down, a stickball game was going on in the fading light. The young man did not go that far; half a block down he turned into a narrow lane.

Now the stars were out, gleaming softly, and the lane was dark and shadowy, lined with vague shapes of garbage cans. The young man was alone now—no, not quite. A wavering yowl rose in the purple gloom, and the young man frowned. It was some tomcat's love song, and there was nothing pretty about *that*.

He walked more slowly, and glanced at his watch. It was quarter of eight and Norma should be just—

Then he saw her, coming toward him from the courtyard, wearing dark blue slacks and a sailor blouse that made his heart ache. It was always a surprise seeing her for the first time, it was always a sweet shock—she looked so *young*.

Now his smile shone out—*radiated* out, and he walked faster.

"Norma!" he said.

She looked up and smiled . . . but as they drew together, the smile faded.

His own smile trembled a little, and he felt a moment's disquiet. Her face over the sailor blouse suddenly seemed blurred. It was getting dark now . . . could he have been mistaken? Surely not. It *was* Norma.

"I brought you flowers," he said in a happy relief, and handed the paper spill to her.

She looked at them for a moment, smiled—and handed them back.

"Thank you, but you're mistaken," she said. "My name is—"

"Norma," he whispered, and pulled the short-handled hammer out of his coat pocket where it had been all along. "They're for you, Norma . . . it was always for you . . . all for you."

She backed away, her face a round white blur, her mouth an opening black O of terror, and she wasn't Norma, Norma was dead, she had been dead for ten years, and it didn't matter because she was going to scream and he swung the hammer to stop the scream, to kill the scream, and as he swung the hammer the spill of flowers fell out of his hand, the spill spilled and broke open, spilling red, white, and yellow tea roses beside the dented trash cans where cats made alien love in the dark, screaming in love, screaming, screaming.

He swung the hammer and she didn't scream, but she might scream because she wasn't Norma, none of them were Norma, and he swung the hammer, swung the hammer, swung the hammer. She wasn't Norma and so he swung the hammer, as he had done five other times.

Some unknown time later he slipped the hammer

back into his inner coat pocket and backed away from the dark shadow sprawled on the cobblestones, away from the litter of tea roses by the garbage cans. He turned and left the narrow lane. It was full dark now. The stickball players had gone in. If there were bloodstains on his suit, they wouldn't show, not in the dark, not in the soft late spring dark, and her name had not been Norma but he knew what his name was. It was . . . was . . .

Love.

His name was love, and he walked these dark streets because Norma was waiting for him. And he would find her. Someday soon.

He began to smile. A bounce came into his step as he walked on down Seventy-third Street. A middle-aged married couple sitting on the steps of their building watched him go by, head cocked, eyes far away, a half-smile on his lips. When he had passed by the woman said, "How come *you* never look that way anymore?"

"Huh?"

"Nothing," she said, but she watched the young man in the gray suit disappear into the gloom of the encroaching night and thought that if there was anything more beautiful than springtime, it was young love.

ONE FOR THE ROAD

It was quarter past ten and Herb Tooklander was thinking of closing for the night when the man in the fancy overcoat and the white, staring face burst into Tookey's Bar, which lies in the northern part of Falmouth. It was the tenth of January, just about the time most folks are learning to live comfortably with all the New Year's resolutions they broke, and there was one hell of a northeaster blowing outside. Six inches had come down before dark and it had been going hard and heavy since then. Twice we had seen Billy Larribee go by high in the cab of the town plow, and the second time Tookey ran him out a beer—an act of pure charity my mother would have called it, and my God knows she put down enough of Tookey's beer in her time. Billy told him they were keeping ahead of it on the main road, but the side ones were closed and apt to stay that way until next morning. The radio in Portland was forecasting another foot and a forty-mile-an-hour wind to pile up the drifts.

There was just Tookey and me in the bar, listening to the wind howl around the eaves and watching it dance the fire around on the hearth. "Have one for the road, Booth," Tookey says, "I'm gonna shut her down."

He poured me one and himself one and that's when the door cracked open and this stranger staggered in, snow up to his shoulders and in his hair, like he had rolled around in confectioner's sugar. The wind billowed a sand-fine sheet of snow in after him.

"Close the door!" Tookey roars at him. "Was you born in a barn?"

I've never seen a man who looked that scared. He was like a horse that's spent an afternoon eating fire nettles. His eyes rolled toward Tookey and he said, "My wife—my daughter—" and he collapsed on the floor in a dead faint.

"Holy Joe," Tookey says. "Close the door, Booth, would you?"

I went and shut it, and pushing it against the wind was something of a chore. Tookey was down on one knee holding the fellow's head up and patting his cheeks. I got over to him and saw right off that it was nasty. His face was fiery red, but there were gray blotches here and there, and when you've lived through winters in Maine since the time Woodrow Wilson was President, as I have, you know those gray blotches mean frostbite.

"Fainted," Tookey said. "Get the brandy off the back-bar, will you?"

I got it and came back. Tookey had opened the fellow's coat. He had come around a little; his eyes were half open and he was muttering something too low to catch.

"Pour a capful," Tookey says.

"Just a cap?" I asks him.

"That stuff's dynamite," Tookey says. "No sense overloading his carb."

I poured out a capful and looked at Tookey. He nodded. "Straight down the hatch."

I poured it down. It was a remarkable thing to watch. The man trembled all over and began to cough. His face got redder. His eyelids, which had been at half-mast, flew up like window shades. I was a bit alarmed, but Tookey only sat him up like a big baby and clapped him on the back.

The man started to retch, and Tookey clapped him again.

"Hold on to it," he says, "that brandy comes dear."

The man coughed some more, but it was diminishing now. I got my first good look at him. City fellow, all right, and from somewhere south of Boston, at a guess. He was wearing kid gloves, expensive but thin. There were probably some more of those grayish-white patches on his hands, and he would be lucky not to lose a finger or two. His coat was fancy, all right; a three-hundred-dollar job if ever I'd seen one. He was wearing tiny little boots that hardly came up over his ankles, and I began to wonder about his toes.

"Better," he said.

"All right," Tookey said. "Can you come over to the fire?"

"My wife and my daughter," he said. "They're out there . . . in the storm."

"From the way you came in, I didn't figure they were at home watching the TV," Tookey said. "You can tell us by the fire as easy as here on the floor. Hook on, Booth."

He got to his feet, but a little groan came out of him and his mouth twisted down in pain. I wondered about his toes again, and I wondered why God felt he had to make fools from New York City who would try driving around in southern Maine at the height of a northeast blizzard. And I wondered if his wife and his little girl were dressed any warmer than him.

We hiked him across to the fireplace and got him sat down in a rocker that used to be Missus Tookey's favorite until she passed on in '74. It was Missus Tookey that was responsible for most of the place, which had been written up in *Down East* and the *Sunday Telegram* and even once in the Sunday supplement of the Boston *Globe*. It's really more of a public house than a bar, with its big wooden floor, pegged together rather than nailed, the maple bar, the old barn-raftered ceiling, and the monstrous big fieldstone hearth. Missus Tookey started to get some ideas in her head after the *Down East* article came out, wanted to start calling the place Tookey's Inn or Tookey's Rest, and I admit it has sort of a Colonial ring to it, but I prefer plain old Tookey's Bar. It's one thing to get uppish in the summer, when the state's full of tourists, another thing altogether in the winter, when you and your neighbors have to trade together. And there had been plenty of winter nights, like this one, that Tookey and I had spent all alone together, drinking scotch and water or just a few beers. My own Victoria passed on in '73, and Tookey's was a place to go where there were enough voices to mute the steady ticking of the deathwatch beetle—even if there was just Tookey and me, it was enough. I wouldn't have felt the same about it if the place had been Tookey's Rest. It's crazy but it's true.

We got this fellow in front of the fire and he got the shakes harder than ever. He hugged onto his knees and his teeth clattered together and a few drops of clear mucus spilled off the end of his nose. I think he was starting to realize that another fifteen minutes out there might have been enough to kill him. It's not the snow, it's the wind-chill factor. It steals your heat.

"Where did you go off the road?" Tookey asked him.

"S-six miles s-s-south of h-here," he said.

Tookey and I stared at each other, and all of a sudden I felt cold. Cold all over.

"You sure?" Tookey demanded. "You came six miles through the snow?"

He nodded. "I checked the odometer when we came through t-town. I was following directions . . . going to see my wife's s-sister . . . in Cumberland . . . never been there before . . . we're from New Jersey . . ."

New Jersey. If there's anyone more purely foolish than a New Yorker it's a fellow from New Jersey.

"Six miles, you're sure?" Tookey demanded.

"Pretty sure, yeah. I found the turnoff but it was drifted in . . . it was . . ."

Tookey grabbed him. In the shifting glow of the fire his face looked pale and strained, older than his sixty-six years by ten. "You made a right turn?"

"Right turn, yeah. My wife—"

"Did you see a sign?"

"Sign?" He looked up at Tookey blankly and wiped the end of his nose. "Of course I did. It was on my instructions. Take Jointner Avenue through Jerusalem's Lot to the 295 entrance ramp." He looked from Tookey to me and back to Tookey again. Outside, the wind whistled and howled and moaned through the eaves. "Wasn't that right, mister?"

"The Lot," Tookey said, almost too soft to hear. "Oh my God."

"What's wrong?" the man said. His voice was rising. "Wasn't that right? I mean, the road looked drifted in, but I thought . . . if there's a town there, the plows will be out and . . . and then I . . ."

He just sort of tailed off.

"Booth," Tookey said to me, low. "Get on the phone. Call the sheriff."

"Sure," this fool from New Jersey says, "that's right. What's wrong with you guys, anyway? You look like you saw a ghost."

Tookey said, "No ghosts in the Lot, mister. Did you tell them to stay in the car?"

"Sure I did," he said, sounding injured. "I'm not crazy."

Well, you couldn't have proved it by me.

"What's your name?" I asked him. "For the sheriff."

"Lumley," he says. "Gerard Lumley."

He started in with Tookey again, and I went across to the telephone. I picked it up and heard nothing but dead silence. I hit the cutoff buttons a couple of times. Still nothing.

I came back. Tookey had poured Gerard Lumley another tot of brandy, and this one was going down him a lot smoother.

"Was he out?" Tookey asked.

"Phone's dead."

"Hot damn," Tookey says, and we look at each other. Outside the wind gusted up, throwing snow against the windows.

Lumley looked from Tookey to me and back again.

"Well, haven't either of you got a car?" he asked. The anxiety was back in his voice. "They've got to run the engine to run the heater. I only had about a quarter of a tank of gas, and it took me an hour and a half to . . . Look, will you *answer* me?" He stood up and grabbed Tookey's shirt.

"Mister," Tookey says, "I think your hand just ran away from your brains, there."

Lumley looked at his hand, at Tookey, then dropped it. "Maine," he hissed. He made it sound like a dirty word about somebody's mother. "All right," he said. "Where's the nearest gas station? They must have a tow truck—"

"Nearest gas station is in Falmouth Center," I said. "That's three miles down the road from here."

"Thanks," he said, a bit sarcastic, and headed for the door, buttoning his coat.

"Won't be open, though," I added.

He turned back slowly and looked at us.

"What are you talking about, old man?"

"He's trying to tell you that the station in the Center belongs to Billy Larribee and Billy's out driving the plow, you damn fool," Tookey says patiently. "Now why don't you come back here and sit down, before you bust a gut?"

He came back, looking dazed and frightened. "Are you telling me you can't . . . that there isn't . . . ?"

"I ain't telling you nothing," Tookey says. "You're doing all the telling, and if you stopped for a minute, we could think this over."

"What's this town, Jerusalem's Lot?" he asked. "Why was the road drifted in? And no lights on anywhere?"

I said, "Jerusalem's Lot burned out two years back."

"And they never rebuilt?" He looked like he didn't believe it.

"It appears that way," I said, and looked at Tookey. "What are we going to do about this?"

"Can't leave them out there," he said.

I got closer to him. Lumley had wandered away to look out the window into the snowy night.

"What if they've been got at?" I asked.

"That may be," he said. "But we don't know it for sure. I've got my Bible on the shelf. You still wear your Pope's medal?"

I pulled the crucifix out of my shirt and showed him. I was born and raised Congregational, but most folks

who live around the Lot wear something—crucifix,
St. Christopher's medal, rosary, something. Because
two years ago, in the span of one dark October month,
the Lot went bad. Sometimes, late at night, when there
were just a few regulars drawn up around Tookey's fire,
people would talk it over. Talk around it is more like
the truth. You see, people in the Lot started to disappear. First a few, then a few more, then a whole slew.
The schools closed. The town stood empty for most of
a year. Oh, a few people moved in—mostly damn fools
from out of state like this fine specimen here—drawn
by the low property values, I suppose. But they didn't
last. A lot of them moved out a month or two after they'd
moved in. The others . . . well, they disappeared. Then
the town burned flat. It was at the end of a long dry fall.
They figure it started up by the Marsten House on the
hill that overlooked Jointner Avenue, but no one knows
how it started, not to this day. It burned out of control
for three days. After that, for a time, things were better.
And then they started again.

I only heard the word "vampires" mentioned once.
A crazy pulp truck driver named Richie Messina from
over Freeport way was in Tookey's that night, pretty
well liquored up. "Jesus Christ," this stampeder roars,
standing up about nine feet tall in his wool pants and
his plaid shirt and his leather-topped boots. "Are you
all so damn afraid to say it out? Vampires! That's what
you're all thinking, ain't it? Jesus-jumped-up-Christ in
a chariot-driven sidecar! Just like a bunch of kids scared
of the movies! You know what there is down there in

'Salem's Lot? Want me to tell you? Want me to tell you?"

"Do tell, Richie," Tookey says. It had got real quiet in the bar. You could hear the fire popping, and outside the soft drift of November rain coming down in the dark. "You got the floor."

"What you got over there is your basic wild dog pack," Richie Messina tells us. "That's what you got. That and a lot of old women who love a good spook story. Why, for eighty bucks I'd go up there and spend the night in what's left of that haunted house you're all so worried about. Well, what about it? Anyone want to put it up?"

But nobody would. Richie was a loudmouth and a mean drunk and no one was going to shed any tears at his wake, but none of us were willing to see him go into 'Salem's Lot after dark.

"Be screwed to the bunch of you," Richie says. "I got my four-ten in the trunk of my Chevy, and that'll stop anything in Falmouth, Cumberland, *or* Jerusalem's Lot. And that's where I'm goin'."

He slammed out of the bar and no one said a word for a while. Then Lamont Henry says, real quiet, "That's the last time anyone's gonna see Richie Messina. Holy God." And Lamont, raised to be a Methodist from his mother's knee, crossed himself.

"He'll sober off and change his mind," Tookey said, but he sounded uneasy. "He'll be back by closin' time, makin' out it was all a joke."

But Lamont had the right of that one, because no one

ever saw Richie again. His wife told the state cops she thought he'd gone to Florida to beat a collection agency, but you could see the truth of the thing in her eyes— sick, scared eyes. Not long after, she moved away to Rhode Island. Maybe she thought Richie was going to come after her some dark night. And I'm not the man to say he might not have done.

Now Tookey was looking at me and I was looking at Tookey as I stuffed my crucifix back into my shirt. I never felt so old or so scared in my life.

Tookey said again, "We can't just leave them out there, Booth."

"Yeah. I know."

We looked at each other for a moment longer, and then he reached out and gripped my shoulder. "You're a good man, Booth." That was enough to buck me up some. It seems like when you pass seventy, people start forgetting that you are a man, or that you ever were.

Tookey walked over to Lumley and said, "I've got a four-wheel-drive Scout. I'll get it out."

"For God's sake, man, why didn't you say so before?" He had whirled around from the window and was staring angrily at Tookey. "Why'd you have to spend ten minutes beating around the bush?"

Tookey said, very softly, "Mister, you shut your jaw. And if you get urge to open it, you remember who made that turn onto an unplowed road in the middle of a god-damned blizzard."

He started to say something, and then shut his mouth. Thick color had risen up in his cheeks. Tookey went out to get his Scout out of the garage. I felt around under the bar for his chrome flask and filled it full of brandy. Figured we might need it before this night was over.

Maine blizzard—ever been out in one?

The snow comes flying so thick and fine that it looks like sand and sounds like that, beating on the sides of your car or pickup. You don't want to use your high beams because they reflect off the snow and you can't see ten feet in front of you. With the low beams on, you can see maybe fifteen feet. But I can live with the snow. It's the wind I don't like, when it picks up and begins to howl, driving the snow into a hundred weird flying shapes and sounding like all the hate and pain and fear in the world. There's death in the throat of a snowstorm wind, white death—and maybe something beyond death. That's no sound to hear when you're tucked up all cozy in your own bed with the shutters bolted and the doors locked. It's that much worse if you're driving. And we were driving smack into 'Salem's Lot.

"Hurry up a little, can't you?" Lumley asked.

I said, "For a man who came in half frozen, you're in one hell of a hurry to end up walking again."

He gave me a resentful, baffled look and didn't say anything else. We were moving up the highway at a steady twenty-five miles an hour. It was hard to believe that Billy Larribee had just plowed this stretch an hour ago; another two inches had covered it, and it was drifting in. The strongest gusts of wind rocked the Scout on her springs. The headlights showed a swirling white nothing up ahead of us. We hadn't met a single car.

About ten minutes later Lumley gasps: "Hey! What's that?"

He was pointing out my side of the car; I'd been looking dead ahead. I turned, but was a shade too late. I thought I could see some sort of slumped form fading back from the car, back into the snow, but that could have been imagination.

"What was it? A deer?" I asked.

"I guess so," he says, sounding shaky. "But its eyes—they looked red." He looked at me. "Is that how a deer's eyes look at night?" He sounded almost as if he were pleading.

"They can look like anything," I says, thinking that might be true, but I've seen a lot of deer at night from a lot of cars, and never saw any set of eyes reflect back red.

Tookey didn't say anything.

About fifteen minutes later, we came to a place where the snowbank on the right of the road wasn't so high because the plows are supposed to raise their blades a little when they go through an intersection.

"This looks like where we turned," Lumley said, not sounding too sure about it. "I don't see the sign—"

"This is it," Tookey answered. He didn't sound like himself at all. "You can just see the top of the signpost."

"Oh. Sure." Lumley sounded relieved. "Listen, Mr. Tooklander, I'm sorry about being so short back there. I was cold and worried and calling myself two hundred kinds of fool. And I want to thank you both—"

"Don't thank Booth and me until we've got them in

this car," Tookey said. He put the Scout in four-wheel drive and slammed his way through the snowbank and onto Jointner Avenue, which goes through the Lot and out to 295. Snow flew up from the mudguards. The rear end tried to break a little bit, but Tookey's been driving through snow since Hector was a pup. He jockeyed it a bit, talked to it, and on we went. The headlights picked out the bare indication of other tire tracks from time to time, the ones made by Lumley's car, and then they would disappear again. Lumley was leaning forward, looking for his car. And all at once Tookey said, "Mr. Lumley."

"What?" He looked around at Tookey.

"People around these parts are kind of superstitious about 'Salem's Lot," Tookey says, sounding easy enough—but I could see the deep lines of strain around his mouth, and the way his eyes kept moving from side to side. "If your people are in the car, why, that's fine. We'll pack them up, go back to my place, and tomorrow, when the storm's over, Billy will be glad to yank your car out of the snowbank. But if they're not in the car—"

"Not in the car?" Lumley broke in sharply. "Why wouldn't they be in the car?"

"If they're not in the car," Tookey goes on, not answering, "we're going to turn around and drive back to Falmouth Center and whistle for the sheriff. Makes no sense to go wallowing around at night in a snow-storm anyway, does it?"

"They'll be in the car. Where else would they be?"

I said, "One other thing, Mr. Lumley. If we should

see anybody, we're not going to talk to them. Not even if they talk to us. You understand that?"

Very slow, Lumley says, "Just what are these superstitions?"

Before I could say anything—God alone knows what I would have said—Tookey broke in. "We're there."

We were coming up on the back end of a big Mercedes. The whole hood of the thing was buried in a snowdrift, and another drift had socked in the whole left side of the car. But the taillights were on and we could see exhaust drifting out of the tailpipe.

"They didn't run out of gas, anyway," Lumley said.

Tookey pulled up and pulled on the Scout's emergency brake. "You remember what Booth told you, Lumley."

"Sure, sure." But he wasn't thinking of anything but his wife and daughter. I don't see how anybody could blame him, either.

"Ready, Booth?" Tookey asked me. His eyes held on mine, grim and gray in the dashboard lights.

"I guess I am," I said.

We all got out and the wind grabbed us, throwing snow in our faces. Lumley was first, bending into the wind, his fancy topcoat billowing out behind him like a sail. He cast two shadows, one from Tookey's headlights, the other from his own taillights. I was behind him, and Tookey was a step behind me. When I got to the trunk of the Mercedes, Tookey grabbed me.

"Let him go," he said.

"Janey! Francie!" Lumley yelled. "Everything okay?"

He pulled open the driver's-side door and leaned in. "Everything—"

He froze to a dead stop. The wind ripped the heavy door right out of his hand and pushed it all the way open.

"Holy God, Booth," Tookey said, just below the scream of the wind. "I think it's happened again."

Lumley turned back toward us. His face was scared and bewildered, his eyes wide. All of a sudden he lunged toward us through the snow, slipping and almost falling. He brushed me away like I was nothing and grabbed Tookey.

"How did you know?" he roared. "Where are they? What the hell is going on here?"

Tookey broke his grip and shoved past him. He and I looked into the Mercedes together. Warm as toast it was, but it wasn't going to be for much longer. The little amber low-fuel light was glowing. The big car was empty. There was a child's Barbie doll on the passenger's floormat. And a child's ski parka was crumpled over the seatback.

Tookey put his hands over his face . . . and then he was gone. Lumley had grabbed him and shoved him right back into the snowbank. His face was pale and wild. His mouth was working as if he had chewed down on some bitter stuff he couldn't yet unpucker enough to spit out. He reached in and grabbed the parka.

"Francie's coat?" he kind of whispered. And then loud, bellowing: *"Francie's coat!"* He turned around, holding it in front of him by the little fur-trimmed hood.

He looked at me, blank and unbelieving. "She can't be out without her coat on, Mr. Booth. Why . . . why . . . she'll freeze to death."

"Mr. Lumley—"

He blundered past me, still holding the parka, shouting: *"Francie! Janey! Where are you? Where are youuu?"*

I gave Tookey my hand and pulled him onto his feet. "Are you all—"

"Never mind me," he says. "We've got to get hold of him, Booth."

We went after him as fast as we could, which wasn't very fast with the snow hip-deep in some places. But then he stopped and we caught up to him.

"Mr. Lumley—" Tookey started, laying a hand on his shoulder.

"This way," Lumley said. "This is the way they went. Look!"

We looked down. We were in a kind of dip here, and most of the wind went right over our heads. And you could see two sets of tracks, one large and one small, just filling up with snow. If we had been five minutes later, they would have been gone.

He started to walk away, his head down, and Tookey grabbed him back. "No! No, Lumley!"

Lumley turned his wild face up to Tookey's and made a fist. He drew it back . . . but something in Tookey's face made him falter. He looked from Tookey to me and then back again.

"She'll freeze," he said, as if we were a couple of stupid kids. "Don't you get it? She doesn't have her jacket on and she's only seven years old—"

"They could be anywhere," Tookey said. "You can't follow those tracks. They'll be gone in the next drift."

"What do you suggest?" Lumley yells, his voice high and hysterical. "If we go back to get the police, she'll freeze to death! Francie *and* my wife!"

"They may be frozen already," Tookey said. His eyes caught Lumley's. "Frozen, or something worse."

"What do you mean?" Lumley whispered. "Get it straight, goddamn it! Tell me!"

"Mr. Lumley," Tookey says, "there's something in the Lot—"

But I was the one who came out with it finally, said the word I never expected to say. "Vampires, Mr. Lumley. Jerusalem's Lot is full of vampires. I expect that's hard for you to swallow—"

He was staring at me as if I'd gone green. "Loonies," he whispers. "You're a couple of loonies." Then he turned away, cupped his hands around his mouth, and bellowed, "*FRANCIE! JANEY!*" He started floundering off again. The snow was up to the hem of his fancy coat.

I looked at Tookey. "What do we do now?"

"Follow him," Tookey says. His hair was plastered with snow, and he *did* look a little bit loony. "I can't just leave him out here, Booth. Can you?"

"No," I says. "Guess not."

So we started to wade through the snow after Lumley as best we could. But he kept getting further and further ahead. He had his youth to spend, you see. He was breaking the trail, going through that snow like a bull. My arthritis began to bother me something terrible, and I started to look down at my legs, telling myself: A little further, just a little further, keep goin', damn it, keep goin' . . .

I piled right into Tookey, who was standing spread-legged in a drift. His head was hanging and both of his hands were pressed to his chest.

"Tookey," I says, "you okay?"

"I'm all right," he said, taking his hands away. "We'll stick with him, Booth, and when he fags out he'll see reason."

We topped a rise and there was Lumley at the bottom, looking desperately for more tracks. Poor man, there wasn't a chance he was going to find them. The wind blew straight across down there where he was, and any tracks would have been rubbed out three minutes after they was made, let alone a couple of hours.

He raised his head and screamed into the night: "*FRANCIE! JANEY! FOR GOD'S SAKE!*" And you could hear the desperation in his voice, the terror, and pity him for it. The only answer he got was the freight-train wail of the wind. It almost seemed to be laughin' at him, saying: *I took them Mister New Jersey with your fancy car and camel's-hair topcoat. I took them and I rubbed out their tracks and by morning I'll have them just as neat and frozen as two strawberries in a deep-freeze . . .*

"Lumley!" Tookey bawled over the wind. "Listen,

you never mind vampires or boogies or nothing like that, but you mind this! You're just making it worse for them! We got to get the—"

And then there *was* an answer, a voice coming out of the dark like little tinkling silver bells, and my heart turned cold as ice in a cistern.

"Jerry . . . Jerry, is that you?"

Lumley wheeled at the sound. And then *she* came, drifting out of the dark shadows of a little copse of trees like a ghost. She was a city woman, all right, and right then she seemed like the most beautiful woman I had ever seen. I felt like I wanted to go to her and tell her how glad I was she was safe after all. She was wearing a heavy green pullover sort of thing, a poncho, I believe they're called. It floated all around her, and her dark hair streamed out in the wild wind like water in a December creek, just before the winter freeze stills it and locks it in.

Maybe I did take a step toward her, because I felt Tookey's hand on my shoulder, rough and warm. And still—how can I say it?—I *yearned* after her, so dark and beautiful with that green poncho floating around her neck and shoulders, as exotic and strange as to make you think of some beautiful woman from a Walter de la Mare poem.

"Janey!" Lumley cried. *"Janey!"* He began to struggle through the snow toward her, his arms outstretched.

"No!" Tookey cried. *"No, Lumley!"*

He never even looked . . . but she did. She looked up at us and grinned. And when she did, I felt my longing, my yearning turn to horror as cold as the grave, as white and silent as bones in a shroud. Even from the rise we could see the sullen red glare in those eyes. They were less human than a wolf's eyes. And when she grinned you could see how long her teeth had become. She wasn't human anymore. She was a dead thing somehow come back to life in this black howling storm.

Tookey made the sign of the cross at her. She flinched back . . . and then grinned at us again. We were too far away, and maybe too scared.

"Stop it!" I whispered. "Can't we stop it?"

"Too late, Booth!" Tookey says grimly.

Lumley had reached her. He looked like a ghost himself, coated in snow like he was. He reached for her . . . and then he began to scream. I'll hear that sound in my dreams, that man screaming like a child in a nightmare. He tried to back away from her, but her arms, long and bare and as white as the snow, snaked out and pulled him to her. I could see her cock her head and then thrust it forward—

"Booth!" Tookey said hoarsely. "We've got to get out of here!"

And so we ran. Ran like rats, I suppose some would say, but those who would weren't there that night. We fled back down along our own backtrail, falling down, getting up again, slipping and sliding. I kept looking back over my shoulder to see if that woman was coming after us, grinning that grin and watching us with those red eyes.

We got back to the Scout and Tookey doubled over,

holding his chest. "Tookey!" I said, badly scared. "What—"

"Ticker," he said. "Been bad for five years or more. Get me around in the shotgun seat, Booth, and then get us the hell out of here."

I hooked an arm under his coat and dragged him around and somehow boosted him up and in. He leaned his head back and shut his eyes. His skin was waxy-looking and yellow.

I went back around the hood of the truck at a trot, and I damned near ran into the little girl. She was just standing there beside the driver's-side door, her hair in pigtails, wearing nothing but a little bit of a yellow dress.

"Mister," she said in a high, clear voice, as sweet as morning mist, "won't you help me find my mother? She's gone and I'm so cold—"

"Honey," I said, "honey, you better get in the truck. Your mother's—"

I broke off, and if there was ever a time in my life I was close to swooning, that was the moment. She was standing there, you see, but she was standing *on top of* the snow and there were no tracks, not in any direction.

She looked up at me then, Lumley's daughter Francie. She was no more than seven years old, and she was going to be seven for an eternity of nights. Her little face was a ghastly corpse white, her eyes a red and silver that you could fall into. And below her jaw I could see two small punctures like pinpricks, their edges horribly mangled.

She held out her arms at me and smiled. "Pick me up,

mister," she said softly. "I want to give you a kiss. Then you can take me to my mommy."

I didn't want to, but there was nothing I could do. I was leaning forward, my arms outstretched. I could see her mouth opening, I could see the little fangs inside the pink ring of her lips. Something slipped down her chin, bright and silvery, and with a dim, distant, faraway horror, I realized she was drooling.

Her small hands clasped themselves around my neck and I was thinking: Well, maybe it won't be so bad, not so bad, maybe it won't be so awful after a while—when something black flew out of the Scout and struck her on the chest. There was a puff of strange-smelling smoke, a flashing glow that was gone an instant later, and then she was backing away, hissing. Her face was twisted into a vulpine mask of rage, hate, and pain. She turned sideways and then . . . and then she was gone. One moment she was there, and the next there was a twisting knot of snow that looked a little bit like a human shape. Then the wind tattered it away across the fields.

"Booth!" Tookey whispered. "Be quick, now!"

And I was. But not so quick that I didn't have time to pick up what he had thrown at that little girl from hell. His mother's Douay Bible.

———

That was some time ago. I'm a sight older now, and I was no chicken then. Herb Tooklander passed on two years ago. He went peaceful, in the night. The bar is still there, some man and his wife from Waterville bought it, nice people, and they've kept it pretty much the same. But I don't go by much. It's different somehow with Tookey gone.

Things in the Lot go on pretty much as they always have. The sheriff found that fellow Lumley's car the next day, out of gas, the battery dead. Neither Tookey nor I said anything about it. What would have been the point? And every now and then a hitchhiker or a camper will disappear around there someplace, up on Schoolyard Hill or out near the Harmony Hill cemetery. They'll turn up the fellow's packsack or a paperback book all swollen and bleached out by the rain or snow, or some such. But never the people.

I still have bad dreams about that stormy night we went out there. Not about the woman so much as the little girl, and the way she smiled when she held her arms up so I could pick her up. So she could give me a kiss. But I'm an old man and the time comes soon when dreams are done.

You may have an occasion to be traveling in southern Maine yourself one of these days. Pretty part of the countryside. You may even stop by Tookey's Bar for a drink. Nice place. They kept the name just the same. So have your drink, and then my advice to you is to keep right on moving north. Whatever you do, don't go up that road to Jerusalem's Lot.

Especially not after dark.

There's a little girl somewhere out there. And I think she's still waiting for her good-night kiss.

THE WOMAN IN THE ROOM

The question is: Can he do it?

He doesn't know. He knows that she chews them sometimes, her face wrinkling at the awful orange taste, and a sound comes from her mouth like splintering popsicle sticks. But these are different pills . . . gelatin capsules. The box says DARVON COMPLEX on the outside. He found them in her medicine cabinet and turned them over in his hands, thinking. Something the doctor gave her before she had to go back to the hospital. Something for the ticking nights. The medicine cabinet is full of remedies, neatly lined up like a voodoo doctor's cures. Gris-gris of the Western world. FLEET SUPPOSITORIES. He has never used a suppository in his life and the thought of putting a waxy something in his rectum to soften by body heat makes him feel ill. There is no dignity in putting things up your ass. PHILLIPS MILK OF MAGNESIA. ANACIN ARTHRITIS PAIN FORMULA. PEPTO-BISMOL. More. He can trace the course of her illness through the medicines.

But these pills are different. They are like regular
Darvon only in that they are gray gelatin capsules. But
they are bigger, what his dead father used to call hoss-
cock pills. The box says Asp. 350 gr, Darvon 100 gr, and
could she chew them even if he was to give them to her?
Would she? The house is still running; the refrigerator
runs and shuts off, the furnace kicks in and out, every
now and then the cuckoo bird pokes grumpily out of the
clock to announce an hour or a half. He supposes that
after she dies it will fall to Kevin and him to break up
housekeeping. She's gone, all right. The whole house
says so. She

———

is in the Central Maine Hospital, in Lewiston. Room
312. She went when the pain got so bad she could no
longer go out to the kitchen and make her own coffee.
At times, when he visited, she cried without knowing it.

The elevator creaks going up, and he finds himself
examining the blue elevator certificate. The certificate
makes it clear that the elevator is safe, creaks or no
creaks. She has been here for nearly three weeks now
and today they gave her an operation called a "cortotomy." He is not sure if that is how it's spelled, but that
is how it sounds. The doctor has told her that the "cortotomy" involves sticking a needle into her neck and then
into her brain. The doctor has told her that this is like
sticking a pin into an orange and spearing a seed. When
the needle has poked into her pain center, a radio signal

will be sent down to the tip of the needle and the pain center will be blown out. Like unplugging a TV. Then the cancer in her belly will stop being such a nuisance.

The thought of this operation makes him even more uneasy than the thought of suppositories melting warmly in his anus. It makes him think of a book by Michael Crichton called *The Terminal Man,* which deals with putting wires in people's heads. According to Crichton, this can be a very bad scene. You better believe it.

The elevator door opens on the third floor and he steps out. This is the old wing of the hospital, and it smells like the sweet-smelling sawdust they sprinkle over puke at a county fair. He has left the pills in the glove compartment of his car. He has not had anything to drink before this visit.

The walls up here are two-tone: brown on the bottom and white on top. He thinks that the only two-tone combination in the whole world that might be more depressing than brown and white would be pink and black. Hospital corridors like giant Good 'n' Plentys. The thought makes him smile and feel nauseated at the same time.

Two corridors meet in a T in front of the elevator, and there is a drinking fountain where he always stops to put things off a little. There are pieces of hospital equipment here and there, like strange playground toys. A litter with chrome sides and rubber wheels, the sort of thing they use to wheel you up to the "OR" when they are ready to give you your "cortotomy." There is a large circular object whose function is unknown to him.

It looks like the wheels you sometimes see in squirrel cages. There is a rolling IV tray with two bottles hung from it, like a Salvador Dali dream of tits. Down one of the two corridors is the nurses' station, and laughter fueled by coffee drifts out to him.

He gets his drink and then saunters down toward her room. He is scared of what he may find and hopes she will be sleeping. If she is, he will not wake her up.

Above the door of every room there is a small square light. When a patient pushes his call button this light goes on, glowing red. Up and down the hall patients are walking slowly, wearing cheap hospital robes over their hospital underwear. The robes have blue and white pinstripes and round collars. The hospital underwear is called a "johnny." The "johnnies" look all right on the women but decidedly strange on the men because they are like knee-length dresses or slips. The men always seem to wear brown imitation-leather slippers on their feet. The women favor knitted slippers with balls of yarn on them. His mother has a pair of these and calls them "mules."

The patients remind him of a horror movie called *The Night of the Living Dead*. They all walk slowly, as if someone had unscrewed the tops of their organs like mayonnaise jars and liquids were sloshing around inside. Some of them use canes. Their slow gait as they promenade up and down the halls is frightening but also dignified. It is the walk of people who are going nowhere slowly, the walk of college students in caps and gowns filing into a convocation hall.

Ectoplasmic music drifts everywhere from transistor radios. Voices babble. He can hear Black Oak Arkansas singing "Jim Dandy" ("Go Jim Dandy, go Jim Dandy!" a falsetto voice screams merrily at the slow hall walkers). He can hear a talk-show host discussing Nixon in tones that have been dipped in acid like smoking quills. He can hear a polka with French lyrics—Lewiston is still a French-speaking town and they love their jigs and reels almost as much as they love to cut each other in the bars on lower Lisbon Street.

He pauses outside his mother's room and

———

for a while there he was freaked enough to come drunk. It made him ashamed to be drunk in front of his mother even though she was too doped and full of Elavil to know. Elavil is a tranquilizer they give to cancer patients so it won't bother them so much that they're dying.

The way he worked it was to buy two six-packs of Black Label beer at Sonny's Market in the afternoon. He would sit with the kids and watch their afternoon programs on TV. Three beers with "Sesame Street," two beers during "Mister Rogers," one beer during "Electric Company." Then one with supper.

He took the other five beers in the car. It was a twenty-two-mile drive from Raymond to Lewiston, via Routes 302 and 202, and it was possible to be pretty well in the bag by the time he got to the hospital, with one or two beers left over. He would bring things for his mother and leave them in the car so there would be an excuse to go back and get them and also drink another half beer and keep the high going.

It also gave him an excuse to piss outdoors, and somehow that was the best of the whole miserable business. He always parked in the side lot, which was rutted, frozen November dirt, and the cold night air assured full bladder contraction. Pissing in one of the hospital bathrooms was too much like an apotheosis of the whole hospital experience: the nurses' call button beside the hopper, the chrome handle bolted at a 45-degree angle, the bottle of pink disinfectant over the sink. Bad news. You better believe it.

The urge to drink going home was nil. So leftover beers collected in the icebox at home and when there were six of them, he would

———

never have come if he had known it was going to be this bad. The first thought that crosses his mind is *She's no orange* and the second thought is *She's really dying quick now,* as if she had a train to catch out there in nullity. She is straining in the bed, not moving except for her eyes, but straining inside her body, something is moving in there. Her neck has been smeared orange with stuff that looks like Mercurochrome, and there is a bandage below her left ear where some humming doctor put the radio needle in and blew out 60 percent of her motor controls along with the pain center. Her eyes follow him like the eyes of a paint-by-the-numbers Jesus.

—I don't think you better see me tonight, Johnny. I'm not so good. Maybe I'll be better tomorrow.

—What is it?

—It itches. I itch all over. Are my legs together?

He can't see if her legs are together. They are just a raised V under the ribbed hospital sheet. It's very hot in the room. No one is in the other bed right now. He thinks: Roommates come and roommates go, but my mom stays on forever. Christ!

—They're together, Mom.

—Move them down, can you, Johnny? Then you better go. I've never been in a fix like this before. I can't move anything. My nose itches. Isn't that a pitiful way to be, with your nose itching and not able to scratch it?

He scratches her nose and then takes hold of her calves through the sheet and pulls them down. He can put one hand around both calves with no trouble at all, although his hands are not particularly large. She groans. Tears are running down her cheeks to her ears.

—Momma?

—Can you move my legs down?

—I just did.

—Oh. That's all right, then. I think I'm crying. I don't mean to cry in front of you. I wish I was out of this. I'd do anything to be out of this.

—Would you like a smoke?

—Could you get me a drink of water first, Johnny? I'm as dry as an old chip.

—Sure.

He takes her glass with a flexible straw in it out and around the corner to the drinking fountain. A fat man with an elastic bandage on one leg is sailing slowly down the corridor. He isn't wearing one of the pinstriped robes and is holding his "johnny" closed behind him.

He fills the glass from the fountain and goes back to Room 312 with it. She has stopped crying. Her lips grip the straw in a way that reminds him of camels he has seen in travelogues. Her face is scrawny. His most vivid memory of her in the life he lived as her son is of a time when he was twelve. He and his brother Kevin and this woman had moved to Maine so that she could take care of her parents. Her mother was old and bedridden. High blood pressure had made his grandmother senile, and, to add insult to injury, had struck her blind. Happy eighty-sixth birthday. Here's one to grow on. And she lay in a bed all day long, blind and senile, wearing large diapers and rubber pants, unable to remember what breakfast had been but able to recite all the Presidents right up to Ike. And so the three generations of them had lived together in that house where he had so recently found the pills (although both grandparents are now long since dead) and at twelve he had been lipping off about something at the breakfast table, he doesn't remember what, but something, and his mother had been washing out her mother's pissy diapers and then running them through the wringer of her ancient washing machine, and she had turned around and laid into him with one of them, and the first snap of the wet, heavy diaper had upset his bowl of Special K and sent it spinning wildly across the table like a large blue tiddlywink, and the second blow had stropped his back, not hurting but stunning the smart talk out of his mouth and the woman now lying shrunken in this bed in this room had whopped him again and again, saying: You keep your big mouth *shut,* theres nothing big about you right now but your *mouth* and so you keep it shut until the rest of you grows the same *size,* and each italicized word was accompanied by a strop of his grandmother's wet diaper—*WHACKO!*—and any other smart things he might have had to say just evaporated. There was not a chance in the world for smart talk. He had discovered on that day and for all time that there is nothing in the world so perfect to set a twelve-year-old's impression of his place in the scheme of things into proper perspective as being beaten across the back with a wet grandmother-diaper. It had taken four years after that day to relearn the art of smarting off.

She chokes on the water a little and it frightens him even though he has been thinking about giving her pills. He asks her again if she would like a cigarette and she says:

—If it's not any trouble. Then you better go. Maybe I'll be better tomorrow.

He shakes a Kool out of one of the packages scattered on the table by her bed and lights it. He holds it between the first and second fingers of his right hand, and she puffs it, her lips stretching to grasp the filter. Her inhale is weak. The smoke drifts from her lips.

—I had to live sixty years so my son could hold my cigarettes for me.

—I don't mind.

She puffs again and holds the filter against her lips so long that he glances away from it to her eyes and sees they are closed.

—Mom?

The eyes open a little, vaguely.

—Johnny?

—Right.

—How long have you been here?

—Not long. I think I better go. Let you sleep.

—Hnnnnn.

He snuffs the cigarette in her ashtray and slinks from the room, thinking: I want to talk to that doctor. Goddamn it, I want to talk to the doctor who did that.

Getting into the elevator he thinks that the word "doctor" becomes a synonym for "man" after a certain degree of proficiency in the trade has been reached, as if it was an expected, provisioned thing that doctors must be cruel and thus attain a special degree of humanity. But

———

"I don't think she can really go on much longer," he tells his brother later that night. His brother lives in Andover, seventy miles west. He only gets to the hospital once or twice a week.

"But is her pain better?" Kev asks.

"She says she itches." He has the pills in his sweater pocket. His wife is safely asleep. He takes them out, stolen loot from his mother's empty house, where they all once lived with the grandparents. He turns the box over and over in his hand as he talks, like a rabbit's foot.

"Well then, she's better." For Kev everything is always better, as if life moved toward some sublime vertex. It is a view the younger brother does not share.

"She's paralyzed."

"Does it matter at this point?"

"Of course it *matters!*" he bursts out, thinking of her legs under the white ribbed sheet.

"John, she's dying."

"She's not dead yet." This in fact is what horrifies him. The conversation will go around in circles from here, the profits accruing to the telephone company, but this is the nub. Not dead yet. Just lying in that room with a hospital tag on her wrist, listening to phantom radios up and down the hall. And

————

she's going to have to come to grips with time, the doctor says. He is a big man with a red, sandy beard. He stands maybe six foot four, and his shoulders are heroic. The doctor led him tactfully out into the hall when she began to nod off.

The doctor continues:

—You see, some motor impairment is almost unavoidable in an operation like the "cortotomy." Your mother has some movement in the left hand now. She may reasonably expect to recover her right hand in two to four weeks.

—Will she walk?

The doctor looks at the drilled-cork ceiling of the corridor judiciously. His beard crawls all the way down to the collar of his plaid shirt, and for some ridiculous reason Johnny thinks of Algernon Swinburne; why, he could not say. This man is the opposite of poor Swinburne in every way.

—I should say not. She's lost too much ground.

—She's going to be bedridden for the rest of her life?

—I think that's a fair assumption, yes.

He begins to feel some admiration for this man who he hoped would be safely hateful. Disgust follows the feeling; must he accord admiration for the simple truth?

—How long can she live like that?

—It's hard to say. (That's more like it.) The tumor is blocking one of her kidneys now. The other one is operating fine. When the tumor blocks it, she'll go to sleep.

—A uremic coma?

—Yes, the doctor says, but a little more cautiously. "Uremia" is a techno-pathological term, usually the property of doctors and medical examiners alone. But Johnny knows it because his grandmother died of the same thing, although there was no cancer involved. Her kidneys simply packed it in and she died floating in internal piss up to her rib cage. She died in bed, at home, at dinnertime. Johnny was the one who first suspected she was truly dead this time, and not just sleeping in the comatose, open-mouthed way that old people have. Two small tears had squeezed out of her eyes. Her old tooth-less mouth was drawn in, reminding him of a tomato that has been hollowed out, perhaps to hold egg salad, and then left forgotten on the kitchen shelf for a stretch of days. He held a round cosmetic mirror to her mouth for a minute, and when the glass did not fog and hide the image of her tomato mouth, he called for his mother. All of that had seemed as right as this did wrong.

—She says she still has pain. And that she itches.

The doctor taps his head solemnly, like Victor DeGroot in the old psychiatrist cartoons.

—She *imagines* the pain. But it is nonetheless real. Real to her. That is why time is so important. Your mother can no longer count time in terms of seconds and minutes and hours. She must restructure those units into days and weeks and months.

He realizes what this burly man with the beard is say-ing, and it boggles him. A bell dings softly. He cannot talk more to this man. He is a technical man. He talks smoothly of time, as though he has gripped the concept as easily as a fishing rod. Perhaps he has.

—Can you do anything more for her?

—Very little.

But his manner is serene, as if this were right. He is, after all, "not offering false hope."

—Can it be worse than a coma?

—Of course it *can*. We can't chart these things with any real degree of accuracy. It's like having a shark loose in your body. She may bloat.

—Bloat?

—Her abdomen may swell and then go down and then swell again. But why dwell on such things now? I believe we can safely say

———————

that they would do the job, but suppose they don't? Or suppose they catch me? I don't want to go to court on a mercy-killing charge. Not even if I can beat it. I have no causes to grind. He thinks of newspaper headlines screaming MATRICIDE and grimaces.

Sitting in the parking lot, he turns the box over and over in his hands. DARVON COMPLEX. The question still is: *Can he do it?* Should he? She has said: *I wish I were out of this. I'd do anything to be out of this.* Kevin is talking of fixing her a room at his house so she won't die in the hospital. The hospital wants her out. They gave her some new pills and she went on a raving bummer. That was four days after the "cortotomy." They'd like her someplace else because no one has perfected a really foolproof "cancerectomy" yet. And at this point if they got it all out of her she'd be left with nothing but her legs and her head.

He has been thinking of how time must be for her, like something that has gotten out of control, like a sewing basket full of threaded spools spilled all over the floor for a big mean tomcat to play with. The days in Room 312. The night in Room 312. They have run a string from the call button and tied it to her left index finger because she can no longer move her hand far enough to press the button if she thinks she needs the bedpan.

It doesn't matter too much anyway because she can't feel the pressure down there; her midsection might as well be a sawdust pile. She moves her bowels in the bed and pees in the bed and only knows when she smells it. She is down to ninety-five pounds from one-fifty and her body's muscles are so unstrung that it's only a loose bag tied to her brain like a child's sack puppet. Would it be any different at Kev's? Can he do murder? He knows it is murder. The worst kind, matricide, as if he were a sentient fetus in an early Ray Bradbury horror story, determined to turn the tables and abort the animal that has given it life. Perhaps it is his fault anyway. He is the only child to have been nurtured inside her, a change-of-life baby. His brother was adopted when another smiling doctor told her she would never have any children of her own. And of course, the cancer now in her began in the womb like a second child, his own darker twin. His life and her death began in the same place. Should he not do what the other is doing already, so slowly and clumsily?

He has been giving her aspirin on the sly for the pain she *imagines* she has. She has them in a Sucrets box in her hospital-table drawer, along with her get-well cards and her reading glasses that no longer work. They have taken away her dentures because they are afraid she might pull them down her throat and choke on them, so now she simply sucks the aspirin until her tongue is slightly white.

Surely he could give her the pills; three or four would be enough. Fourteen hundred grains of aspirin and four hundred grains of Darvon administered to a woman whose body weight has dropped 33 percent over five months.

No one knows he has the pills, not Kevin, not his wife. He thinks that maybe they've put someone else in Room 312's other bed and he won't have to worry about it. He can cop out safely. He wonders if that wouldn't be best, really. If there is another woman in the room, his options will be gone and he can regard the fact as a nod from Providence. He thinks

———

—You're looking better tonight.

—Am I?

—Sure. How do you feel?

—Oh, not so good. Not so good tonight.

—Let's see you move your right hand.

She raises it off the counterpane. It floats splay-fingered in front of her eyes for a moment, then drops. Thump. He smiles and she smiles back. He asks her,

—Did you see the doctor today?

—Yes, he came in. He's good to come every day. Will you give me a little water, John?

He gives her some water from the flexible straw.

—You're good to come as often as you do, John. You're a good son.

She's crying again. The other bed is empty, accusingly so. Every now and then one of the blue and white pinstriped bathrobes sails by them up the hall. The door stands open halfway. He takes the water gently away from her, thinking idiotically: Is this glass half empty or half full?

—How's your left hand?

—Oh, pretty good.

—Let's see.

She raises it. It has always been her smart hand, and perhaps that is why it has recovered as well as it has from the devastating effects of the "cortotomy." She clenches it. Flexes it. Snaps the fingers weakly. Then it falls back to the counterpane. Thump. She complains,

—But there's no feeling in it.

—Let me see something.

He goes to her wardrobe, opens it, and reaches behind the coat she came to the hospital in to get at her purse. She keeps it in here because she is paranoid about robbers; she has heard that some of the orderlies are rip-off artists who will lift anything they can get their hands on. She has heard from one of her roommates who has since gone home that a woman in the new wing lost five hundred dollars which she kept in her shoe. His mother is paranoid about a great many things lately, and has once told him a man sometimes hides under her bed in the late-at-night. Part of it is the combination of drugs they are trying on her. They make the bennies he occasionally dropped in college look like Excedrin. You can have your pick from the locked drug cabinet at the end of the corridor just past the nurses' station: ups and downs, highs and bummers. Death, maybe, merciful death like a sweet black blanket. The wonders of modern science.

He takes the purse back to her bed and opens it.

—Can you take something out of here?

—Oh, Johnny, I don't know . . .

He says persuasively:

—Try it. For me.

The left hand rises from the counterpane like a crippled helicopter. It cruises. Dives. Comes out of the purse with a single wrinkled Kleenex. He applauds:

—Good! Good!

But she turns her face away.

—Last year I was able to pull two full dish trucks with these hands.

If there's to be a time, it's now. It is very hot in the room but the sweat on his forehead is cold. He thinks: If she doesn't ask for aspirin, I won't. Not tonight. And he knows if it isn't tonight it's never. Okay.

Her eyes flick to the half-open door slyly.

—Can you sneak me a couple of my pills, Johnny?

It is how she always asks. She is not supposed to have any pills outside of her regular medication because she has lost so much body weight and she has built up what his druggie friends of his college days would have called "a heavy thing." The body's immunity stretches to within a fingernail's breadth of lethal dosage. One more pill and you're over the edge. They say it is what happened to Marilyn Monroe.

—I brought some pills from home.

—Did you?

—They're good for pain.

He holds the box out to her. She can only read very close. She frowns over the large print and then says,

—I had some of that Darvon stuff before. It didn't help me.

—This is stronger.

Her eyes rise from the box to his own. Idly she says,

—Is it?

He can only smile foolishly. He cannot speak. It is like the first time he got laid, it happened in the back of some friend's car and when he came home his mother asked him if he had a good time and he could only smile this same foolish smile.

—Can I chew them?

—I don't know. You could try one.

—All right. Don't let them see.

He opens the box and pries the plastic lid off the bottle. He pulls the cotton out of the neck. Could she do all that with the crippled helicopter of her left hand? Would they believe it? He doesn't know. Maybe they don't either. Maybe they wouldn't even care.

He shakes six of the pills into his hand. He watches her watching him. It is many too many, even she must know that. If she says anything about it, he will put them all back and offer her a single Arthritis Pain Formula.

A nurse glides by outside and his hand twitches, clicking the gray capsules together, but the nurse doesn't look in to see how the "cortotomy kid" is doing.

His mother doesn't say anything, only looks at the pills like they were perfectly ordinary pills (if there is such a thing). But on the other hand, she has never liked ceremony; she would not crack a bottle of champagne on her own boat.

—Here you go,

he says in a perfectly natural voice, and pops the first one into her mouth.

She gums it reflectively until the gelatin dissolves, and then she winces.

—Taste bad? I won't . . .

—No, not too bad.

He gives her another. And another. She chews them with that same reflective look. He gives her a fourth. She smiles at him and he sees with horror that her tongue is yellow. Maybe if he hits her in the belly she will bring them up. But he can't. He could never hit his mother.

—Will you see if my legs are together?

—Just take these first.

He gives her a fifth. And a sixth. Then he sees if her legs are together. They are. She says,

—I think I'll sleep a little now.

—All right. I'm going to get a drink.

—You've always been a good son, Johnny.

He puts the bottle in the box and tucks the box into her purse, leaving the plastic top on the sheet beside her. He leaves the open purse beside her and thinks: *She asked for her purse. I brought it to her and opened it just before I left. She said she could get what she wanted out of it. She said she'd get the nurse to put it back in the wardrobe.*

He goes out and gets his drink. There is a mirror over the fountain, and he runs out his tongue and looks at it.

When he goes back into the room, she is sleeping with her hands pressed together. The veins in them are big, rambling. He gives her a kiss and her eyes roll behind their lids, but do not open.

Yes.

He feels no different, either good or bad.

He starts out of the room and thinks of something else. He goes back to her side, takes the bottle out of the box, and rubs it all over his shirt. Then he presses the limp fingertips of her sleeping left hand on the bottle. Then he puts it back and goes out of the room quickly, without looking back.

He goes home and waits for the phone to ring and wishes he had given her another kiss. While he waits, he watches TV and drinks a lot of water.

CARRIE

Carrie White may have been unfashionable and unpopular, but she had a gift. Carrie could make things move by concentrating on them. A candle would fall. A door would lock. This was her power and her sin. Then, an act of kindness, as spontaneous as the vicious taunts of her classmates, offered Carrie a chance to be normal and go to her senior prom. But another act—of ferocious cruelty—turned her gift into a weapon of horror and destruction that her classmates would never forget.

Fiction/Horror

'SALEM'S LOT

Ben Mears has returned to Jerusalem's Lot in hopes that exploring the history of the Marsten House, an old mansion long the subject of rumor, will help him cast out his devils and provide inspiration for his new book. But when two boys venture into the woods, and only one returns alive, Mears realizes that something sinister is at work—his hometown is under siege from dark forces beyond his imagination. And only he, with a small group of allies, can hope to contain the evil growing in this small New England town.

Fiction/Horror

THE SHINING

Jack Torrance's new job at the Overlook Hotel is the perfect chance for a fresh start. As the off-season care-taker at the old atmospheric hotel, he'll have plenty of time to spend reconnecting with his family and working on his writing. But as the harsh winter weather sets in, the idyllic location feels ever more remote . . . and more sinister. And the only one to notice the strange and terrible forces gathering around the Overlook is Danny Torrance, a uniquely gifted five-year-old.

Fiction/Horror

THE STAND

When a man escapes from a biological testing facility, he sets in motion a deadly domino effect, spreading a mutated strain of the flu that will wipe out ninety-nine percent of humanity within a few weeks. The survivors who remain are scared, bewildered, and in need of a leader. Two emerge—Mother Abagail, the benevolent 108-year-old woman who urges them to build a community in Boulder, Colorado; and Randall Flagg, the nefarious "Dark Man," who delights in chaos and violence.

Fiction/Horror

ANCHOR BOOKS
Available wherever books are sold.
www.anchorbooks.com